CORY'S
FEAST

Other Books by Sallie Bingham

After Such Knowledge (Novel), Houghton-Miffin

The Touching Hand (Novella and Short Stories), Houghton-Miffin
"There is no doubt about it—Sallie Bingham can hold her own with many of the best stylists writing in America today." *The Chicago Tribune*

The Way It Is Now (Short Stories), Viking Press
"The people of whom Bingham writes in these 15 stories come alive through her penetrating characterizations." *Booklist*

Passion and Prejudice, A Family Memoir, Alfred A. Knopf
"Sallie Bingham's lively account of her life has the feel of a novel." *The New Yorker*
"A feisty figure with an eye for hypocrisy, Bingham creates images of the world of the Binghams with a kind of iron grace." *The New York Times Book Review*

Upstate (Novel), Permanent Press

Small Victories (Novel), Zoland Books
"An absorbing novel." *The New York Times Book Review*

Matron of Honor (Novel), Zoland Books
"This powerful narrative is her best yet." *Publishers Weekly*

Straight Man (Novel), Zoland Books

Trangressions (Short Stories), Sarabande Press
"These are marvelous stories of experience and have the ripeness of wry, hard-won wisdom." *Phillip Lopate*

CORY'S FEAST

Sallie Bingham

SUNSTONE
PRESS

SANTA FE

The events, people, and incidents in this story are the sole product
of the author's imagination. The story is fictional and any resemblance
to individuals living or dead is purely coincidental.

Sunstone books may be purchased for educational, business, or sales promotional
use. For information please write: Special Markets Department, Sunstone Press,
P.O. Box 2321, Santa Fe, New Mexico 87504-2321.

Library of Congress Cataloging-in-Publication Data:

Bingham, Sallie.
    Cory's feast / by Sallie Bingham.
        p. cm.
    ISBN 0-86534-479-5 (hardcover : alk. paper)
    ISBN 0-86534-502-3 (softcover : alk. paper)
    1. Middle aged women—Fiction. 2. Moving, Household—Fiction.
3. Self-realization—Fiction. 4. Taos (N.M.)—Fiction. I. Title.

PS3552.I5C67 2005
813'.54—dc22

                                    2005016900

WWW.SUNSTONEPRESS.COM
SUNSTONE PRESS / POST OFFICE BOX 2321 / SANTA FE, NM 87504-2321 /USA
(505) 988-4418 / *ORDERS ONLY* (800) 243-5644 / FAX (505) 988-102

In memory of Mabel Dodge Luhan
and the house she built in Taos, New Mexico.

1

Horny, desperate and gullible—the human condition, Cory thinks as she drives out of Taos, right hand on the jeep's steering wheel, left jammed between her thighs. The road is full of five o'clock traffic, mostly pick-ups bleary with mud from the unpaved roads; snow is banked along the sidewalk where a few tourists hop, hesitate. Most of them are at the ski basin, sporting brilliant clothes, falling down into the deep powder like birds into their nests.

The traffic light changes and Cory drives the jeep through, past the Cafe Tazza where Leonard Gross is playing his guitar behind steamed windows, past Primrose's little white house, the farolitos from Christmas still up on the wall. Cory is aiming for Morada Road, must dart through the on-coming traffic to make her turn. Horns blare, she skirts a collision, and her jeep's rear tire mounts the sidewalk. Cory laughs, bumps down.

At the crossroads she looks up and sees the black flank of the sacred mountain and, to the east, a new moon—a slipper moon, her mother would have called it. Martin has warned her that this particular new moon will precipitate radical change. Now she's seen it, big as life and twice as natural, as her sister Adeline would say. Apple, that was.

Cory drives into the field in front of Mabel's house.

When spring comes, Cory plans to plant alfalfa, then buy a few horses, sturdy western ponies the guests can manage, recreating the field as it looked fifty years ago when Mabel described it in her second book. Then the field was her husband Tony's; he'd pastured his horses there, lending one to D.H. Lawrence for his ranch further up the mountain, where Lawrence is buried now under a monument that looks like a car-wash.

For now, for the rest of the winter, the field is a make-shift parking lot for the shabby but atmospheric bed and breakfast Mabel's house has become since Cory bought it.

She slides the jeep in between a van from Colorado with three pairs of skis on top and a dark sedan with New Mexico plates, hardly speckled with mud: the nice young family, and the couple from Albuquerque. Shoshona will have registered them and shown them their rooms.

The couple is to have Spud's Room, Cory remembers. They may not like it, it's dark, shares a bath, and the bed has a valley in the middle. But the nice young family should be pleased with Mabel's room and Tony's which adjoins it—the best rooms in the house, looking out toward the pueblo and the mountain.

Cory sleeps at the top of the house in an unheated porch Mabel used for her naked sunbaths, much to D.H.'s consternation. He painted the windows, for privacy; peacocks and plumed serpents have survived. Cory sees them now, from the parking lot, patrolling the windows as they have for almost sixty years.

Getting out of the jeep, she reaches for the Smith and Wesson .357 she's carried since the murder. She pushes the heavy cropped muzzle into her leather holster, snaps the strap over it. Practicing at the dump outside of town, she's mastered the kick but still can't get the pistol out of its holster fast enough to suit her.

Taking a bag of groceries in each arm, she heads for the house.

On the steps, she smiles at the warning sign about falling, posted courtesy of Lawyer Tuttle who worries about liability. Cory has already had her day in court; she knows now how to buy off trouble which is one good use, she thinks, for money. The woman from Montana who fell on the steps was soothed out of her rage in a different way, Cory on her knees applying ice to the badly swollen ankle.

She's learned, since coming into her late maturity and buying Mabel's house, that there's a cure for every illness, a solution for every problem, except the ones that are too important to be solved: life, death, things like that. Long patience and sleeplessness—she rarely gets more than four hours a night— bring answers, cures and solutions winged with blue feathers like the birds that bicker on the fence behind the house, barricading N.A. land.

"Indian, Indian, Indian," she chanted in the old days, the fighter days—her first days in Taos—into the face of the West Coast academic who'd dared to challenge her usage, but she's learned since then to get by with an ironic pair of initials, the closest she'll come to being correct: N.A.

Yet her house, because of Tony, Mabel's lover and husband, belongs in spirit if not in fact to the pueblo behind it. The land was Tony's, sliced off from the tribal pie. Sixty years ago that had been possible; Mabel's St. Louis money and Tony's access to her generous heart made it a good bargain. At Christmas, Cory has heard, he'd bring a load of pueblo kids in Mabel's big car to her tree hung with presents; the rest of the year, hidden channels carried Mabel's money onto the reservation.

Now, thirty years after their deaths—Mabel buried in the untidy little graveyard up the hill, Tony separately, at the pueblo—Cory can't hire anyone who isn't N.A. Not that she wants to; the women from the pueblo treat the old house like a grandmother, clean and massage her, keep her warm, and everyone—transient skiers, Cory's protégés, unlabeled guests—benefits.

She crosses the acequia, part of an old system of irrigating ditches which will run with snow water in a month. Mabel had tea on this bridge, a practice Cory wants to re-introduce with warm weather, although she's not sure her guests can measure up to Mabel's. Still, there's a Quimper teapot in the pantry and a dozen mostly uncracked porcelain cups; she'll set Conchita to slicing cucumbers paper-thin for sandwiches and brewing up pots of Orange Pekoe.

The strangers Cory imagines strolling up from their cars after a hard day of sight-seeing (the pueblo, the five museums, the recreated fort) will have parasols and long dusters, slim volumes of poetry and little notebooks for recording their observations.

All this of course is imaginary, but after a year of owning and running Mabel's house, Cory knows everything can be made better with the use of the imagination, added like the local green chili: not too much, or the burn will destroy appetite, not too little, or reality will remain dead-bland.

Mabel's house is ahead of her now, looming up, a homely, molten lump of adobe. Mabel and Tony added rooms to the original cube year by year to accommodate the ever-increasing flow of guests. Mabel hoped to teach those eastern sophisticates something about the West, Cory remembers, its earlier, more authentic civilization. She tried, and even succeeded, in introducing the brightest minds of her era to an image of vastness: the New Mexico sky, the mountains. Finally, though, there was disillusionment: drunkenness, law suits, even a shooting.

Cory thanks Mabel aloud for providing her with a model of sorts for her on-going efforts to instruct her guests; their methods are the same although the subject matter, after half a century, is considerably different. Most Anglos have learned to respect or at least fear the N.A.

culture they've come so close to destroying, the culture Mabel proselytized. Another education is needed now, of the heart, not the busy-busy mind. Cory's vocation, she believes, is to provide that education, often to the surprise of her guests.

She walks under the portal where Manuel keeps the wood pile—logs are free to guests for the kiva fireplaces in their bedrooms, Cory insists on that—and pushes open the carved wooden door that always sticks on the rubber mat laid down for the skiers. Their huge plastic boots clump through the narrow halls and up and down the even narrower stairs. Still, they bring essential income, and they are often more open to enlightenment than Cory expected.

Afternoon light is flowing steadily out of the living room that Mabel christened the Big Room. Adeline's poinsettia is faded; Christmas cards still flock along the wooden mantel.

Manuel is down on his knees, coaxing the fire, and Cory admires his blue-black hair, neatly edged, swinging across his shoulder. Tomorrow—New Years Day—he'll dance the deer dance at the pueblo.

"I'm glad you're going to work for me," Cory said to him in the spring, under the blossoming peach tree in the courtyard, and he looked at her without answering. They both know the stories, going back a century, of eastern ladies coming West to claim Indians as the solution to their problems with the men of their own tribes: Protestants, Roman Catholics, atheists, Jews, what does it matter? All seem at both ends of the twentieth century impotent, spiritually bankrupt. Replacing them is not so easy now, the pattern if not destroyed is at least discredited, and all the handsome N.A.s Cory knows look at her speculatively, wondering what she expects. As Manuel looked, before she explained to him: she only wants his labor, not his appreciation.

They do not exist to satisfy me, I do not exist to satisfy them, Cory thinks, her New Year's mantra, replacing useless resolutions, and notices Manuel's thighs in his tight jeans. Perhaps maturity is all about giving up, but she's not prepared to accept that. Maturity may just as well be about holding on.

She goes into the office, where Mabel's three books and postcards of the house and the pueblo line a glass-fronted cabinet behind Shoshona's desk. The actor who owned the house for a while after Mabel's death displayed his collection of pipes there—not the peaceful kind; this was the same man who went at Mabel's big bed with a chain saw, determined to take it with him when he left. Tony's great nephew— Ur-Tony, Cory called him once—dissuaded him.

Shoshona is sitting at the desk, talking on the telephone. Cory admires her turquoise earrings, dangling against pink-stained cheeks. Shoshona hangs up, apologizing,

"Don't. I can wait, it's good for me." Cory won't play the mistress. "Did that couple from Albuquerque get here? I thought I saw a car that looked likely, no mud at all"—it's all throughway to Albuquerque, a city one hundred miles to the south where the streets are paved, a city with an airport where Apple will have just landed.

Shoshona nods. "I put them in Spud's room—they didn't like it."

"They'll get used to it," Cory says. "After Conchita's burritos for breakfast, they'll be talking about local color. Who else is here?"

"The couple with the little girl, they're in Mabel's and Tony's. Those two men from Texas haven't come yet."

"A long drive." Cory hesitates. "Have you heard from my sister?"

Conchita glances at her. Cory knows they are all wondering about the only relative she ever mentions. "She hasn't called."

"She's driving up from the airport, she won't be here for a while"—and tries to imagine Adeline, little Apple, planted behind the wheel of a rented car, maps, credit cards, the whole panoply of modern life spread beside her. "I hope she gets here before dark; it's clear now, but I can tell from the smell of the air it's coming on to snow." Her southern background still shows, she knows, in certain expressions.

Conchita smiles. "You said you're not going to worry about roads this winter."

"I never worry about anything," Cory says. It is nearly true.

"Where do you want me to put her?"

Cory has given this some thought. "In the kiva room. It's quiet, at that end of the house."

"Cold, though."

"She can light a fire"—also rather difficult to imagine.

Conchita goes on, "Those two from Texas called. They made a fuss about the bed they want, firm mattress, a queen."

"Just out of the closet and wanting respect."

Conchita nods. There's little prejudice in Taos against what the newspapers have taken to calling alternate lifestyles; the tribes had ways of incorporating berdarches, winktes—healers. Cory thinks of herself as an emblem of a certain alternate lifestyle: aging into herself at last, financially and emotionally independent, aching.

At this point the taste of life, she thinks, is as sweet as it is sour, like the little plums she gathered along the fence line in August, too pretty to be edible, she'd thought, till Manuel slit a plum with his nail and showing her the soft yellow inside. She ate one off his nail as though she'd never heard of knives.

She goes up to the sun porch at the top of the house to change into the red-velvet broomstick skirt and matching overblouse she bought to go with her turquoise. She straps the Smith and Wesson in its holster to her concha belt. The pink custom-made cowboy boots she ordered for Christmas slide on smoothly, and as she clicks over to the mirror she admires once again the way boots add length to her stride.

She admires herself in the mirror. East coast sophisticates make fun of Anglo women gotten up in native attire, but she knows what makes her guests look up when she enters the dining room.

She brushes out her long pale hair and braids it, tying the end of the plait with a dark-red satin ribbon from her extensive collection; she keeps it in a ribbon box just like the one Mabel had, growing up in St. Louis.

As she ties the bow, one of D.H.'s peacocks, flaunting red and blue stripes on the window, cocks a staring eye.

Conchita taps with a broom on the ceiling; Cory's sun porch is over the dining room. Now it is time to clip on the big turquoise earrings—genuine pawn—and light the tall taper and the cedar smudge. Cory blows the smudge out, and its sharp smell fills her room. She'll find it there later, a comforting presence, when she comes up to sleep.

As she starts down the narrow stairs, the updraft flaps the candle flame and sends the long stream of smoke from the smudge skittering. Cory breathes the sharp frank smell of the cedar, raw as the late-winter cold, as she tramps down the last steps directly into the dining room. All heads turn as Conchita douses the electric lights.

"Good evening," Cory says, raising her candle, "and welcome. You are all enrolled, though you don't know it yet, in my School for the Numb, the As-If School that teaches manners as a prelude to feeling."

They laugh.

Across the dining room, a woman in a wide coat stands in the doorway. Drawn by the laughter, the woman steps into the dining room and looks around half-dazed.

There she is, my sister, standing at the head of her own table— not a position I've ever seen her in—dressed like a Red Indian, as Frankie would say (Frankie was used to being called colored and worse, so she never learned the right way to identify other people). Cory's wearing some kind of silver belt with a holster tied to it—I see that right away, and a pistol in the holster, too. So has she gone mad, or what?

I stand there rooted in the doorway, I don't know which way to turn. And every face at that table—there is a small group of them, sitting there, over the remains of some kind of dinner—turns to me like a sunflower. So I'm the sun now, I think; confused, that's the best I can do. I don't feel sunny.

She doesn't recognize me. I'm sure of that. Of course it's been ten years, and I've changed, but then, so has she, and still I would know Cory anywhere. Even in that heathen outfit. Even faded, now, in spite of her intensity. Even giving out some kind of advice—I heard the tail end of it—to strangers at her own table.

So I make the first move.

"I'm here," I say, and she comes striding down the length of the room and puts her arms around me.

Cory. My sister. Her long thin arms around my neck.

"I'm about to cry," I say, into the side of her head.

"Cry," she says.

"Not in front of all these people."

"They don't matter."

"Your guests!" And I'm composed, suddenly, thinking of what Mother would say. "Your guests, Cory! You have to think of them"— one of the best reasons for having guests, I've always thought, so you'll have a good excuse to ignore family.

She turns then—she has hold of my wrist—and begins to introduce me all around, but I'm dazed, again, I don't catch a single name. Then she brings me around to the head of the table and a young woman, an Indian, brings me a chair.

"We're about to have dessert," Cory says. "Will you have some?"

Now I have my dignity gathered around me. I remember that she has never once thanked me. "Is it Indian pudding?"

She is not amused. No one at the table is amused. I am the heathen now.

"Brownies," she says, "and ice cream"—something we had on Sundays, as children.

"No, thank you," I say. "Please go on with your lesson." I want her to know I know I've interrupted something.

She turns to these people, these strangers, who I think must now be the substance of her life.

"Welcome to the school of As If," she says. "You're all enrolled, although you don't know it."

That brings a laugh.

The Indian girl is passing the Brownies and they smell rich and I wish I hadn't said no.

"What in the world—?" a nice-looking middle-aged woman asks, biting into her Brownie.

"It's a school for the numb," my sister says, and I realize I've wandered in on the beginning of her performance.

I think my presence is making her a little awkward; her voice sounds strained, and I remember the way her voice would always change when I came into the room.

Am I an audience for you, Cory? Still? Am I the outsider, the critic?

But of course there is no room to wedge that in. Cory is explaining her philosophy.

"We all know the world is in bad shape," she begins, and now her voice is leveling off, weighted with authority. "We talk about it all the time—crime, broken families, schools systems failing, the government out of step."

A man says, "It seems like maybe we don't need them at all."

Cory says, "We still have troops stationed all over the world." Then she continues quickly before the fair-haired man on the other side of the table can begin to disagree, which he clearly wants to do. "I believe the public sector can only be reformed if each one of us changes her own life."

I note the pronoun.

"Like Public Radio, that program, isn't that what he always says?" the woman who spoke up first asks her husband.

"Something like that." Her husband is concentrating on Cory, and I think it's her bosom, conspicuous in her pleated lawn shirt, or else it's the pistol but gleaming in her holster.

"Other people are realizing the dilemma," Cory says, nodding at the woman who has mentioned Public Radio. "But most of them haven't an idea in the world what to do about it. The numbness. None of this would happen—the Sudan, rape, capital punishment—if we weren't all to one degree or another numb."

"I don't know about that," an older man who's been silent until now puts in; he looks irritable, like an old bird perched on the edge of his chair. "I feel plenty."

Cory is prepared for this. I begin to think she may be prepared for anything.

"Let me ask you one question," she says to the old bird. "Do you watch the news?"

"Every night."

"And when they show what's happening in the Sudan, for example, do you cry?"

He feels the trap shutting. "They don't show that."

"But have you cried?"

He shakes his head, offended. It is none of her business. But Cory has made her point.

She goes on, "There's no way to start feeling on command when you haven't felt anything for years—"

"I feel for my family," the woman who listens to Public Radio says. "I wake up in the night, listening for the baby."

"That doesn't count," Cory says, a tad too quickly. "We all feel for our families, they're extensions of ourselves."

But do you, Cory? I want to ask. It has never been apparent that she does.

"What I'm talking about is the gift of empathy, the only gift that has a chance of changing the disastrous course of history. If you could feel for a tree the way you feel for your baby," she says, addressing the woman who loves her family, "you wouldn't allow that tree to be cut down. If you could feel for a stream the way you feel for your husband, you wouldn't allow it to be polluted. We all claim to care—" she is squelching the bird man who is waving his raised hand—"but do we really feel anything? We know, intellectually, what we're supposed to care about, but that doesn't mean anything on the emotional level."

"Touchy-feely. Wasn't that what the sixties was all about?" the woman who loves her family asks. Cory doesn't deign to answer.

"So what do you suggest?" the bird man asks. "I mean, even if what you say is true, what can be done about it?"

"I suggest pretending," Cory says, and suddenly I am back in Mother's dining room on a day shortly before my wedding.

"If you pretend to care, if you mouth the words, the feeling usually comes, in time," my sister says.

"But that's what we're already doing," a younger man who has been silent until now objects. "We're all pretending to care. Nobody talks about anything except the sorry state of the world."

"You're right—people are always saying this or that is terrible. But I don't hear anyone saying, It breaks my heart, or, I cried last night over that."

"I see," the young man says, leaning toward Cory across the table. "You mean we should all start taking it personally."

"Exactly," Cory says. "What could be more personal than the destruction of our world?"

"But sitting around crying isn't going to make anything change." the bird man says bitterly.

"Pain after a while usually forces a change in behavior," Cory says. "The first step's always the hardest—expressing the pain, I mean, before you actually feel it."

"Isn't that hypocritical?" the family woman asks, and I remember Cory in Mother's dining room asking the same thing.

"It sounds like a lesson in manners," I say.

Cory looks at me as though she's forgotten I'm in the room. "You could call it that. Naming feelings."

"Naming feelings that don't exist," the bird man says.

"That don't exist yet," Cory corrects him. "Let me give you an example." She turns to me, and I feel the hot wave of her attention.

She takes my arm in a firm grip as though I am about to run away, and in fact I would like, immediately, to do that—back to the rented car, down the long dark road between the mountains, into the airport, back to my home.

"Sister," she breathes at me, and I smell her musky perfume, "I've missed you so terribly my heart has felt as though it's about to break. And here you are, for the first time in so long."

Somehow she has produced tears. They are shimmering on her cheeks.

I stare at her, frowning.

She holds out her other arm and beckons as though to draw me into an embrace, but I stand firm on my own two feet. We've had our embrace already.

"There's been anger between us," she says, and her urgency is fixing everyone's attention on each word. "There's been a world of hurt. But you've come, anyway, you've taken this risk; and now I want to tell you how sorry I am—see, I'm crying, my heart is opening to you, Sister."

"You never called me that in your life," I hiss.

"Yes, anger, pure venom, let it all come out."

"What is this, therapy?"

"No, it's asking for forgiveness, Apple," she says, calling me by my baby name.

I am bending back at the waist, trying to get away from her, but she is strong—Cory has always been strong—and I can't escape her.

"How many years has it been?" the woman asks.

"Ten years," Cory says, still pulling.

"It's closer to eleven," I mutter, and then something is bending, something is breaking, and I feel myself being reeled in like a reluctant fish.

Over Cory's shoulder, I see the face of the parrot man, staring, fascinated, offended, and I feel the butt of Cory's pistol dig into my side.

"That's enough, Cory," I whisper into her ear; her hair is braided like Pocahontas and pomaded with something herbal, and I hate the smell of it.

"I'm so sorry, Little Sister," she sobs, and now the table of strangers is discomfited, I can feel them shifting in their seats, glancing at each other; and the Indian girl hurries in from the kitchen.

"Sorry for what?" I ask in my normal voice, pulling back.

The Indian girl must be used to this. She hands Cory a tissue.

Cory blows her nose thoroughly, and I can feel the people at the table behind me start to relax.

"I'm sorry for everything," she says with a simplicity I have to accept, especially when I see her mascara is running.

"Wipe under your eyes," I tell her conspiratorially, and remember the last time she gave me that kind of advice.

She does so, amenable as a child, amenable as the child she never was, and I wonder how much of this is for the company, how much of this is to prove a point, and my irritation and incredulity begin to mount again.

"Do you accept my apology?" she asks, wiping under her eyes and looking at the black streaks on the tissue.

"We'll talk about it later," I mutter, "not in front of all these strangers—"

"Guests, not strangers." And she is in charge again, turning to the table. "Did any of this make sense to you?" she graciously asks.

"Well, I guess you're glad to see your sister," the family woman says. Her husband, in great discomfort, is trying to rise, but she pulls him down firmly. "I have a sister, too, and we haven't spoken since I don't know when."

"Your sister is crazy," her husband says with asperity.

"Maybe I'm crazy too, have you ever considered that?" The words are out of my mouth before I'm aware of them.

"Not crazy, Apple," Cory says, "never crazy. Just willing to let other people run your life."

"I need to go to the room," the husband tells his wife urgently.

"Don't worry." Cory is smooth now. "I've said all I have to say about my philosophy. Does anyone want to contribute something of their own?"

"Share, don't you call it?" I snarl.

She smiles at me. "I'm not part of the program, Apple—not that program, or any other."

"Well, good," the woman says, getting up at last with her husband. "I always thought that was a kind of cult."

"It's done my nephew some good, apparently," Cory says, and I wonder from what sector of the heavens she's drawn that information. Anything that will serve your purpose, Cory.

She turns, sharply, as though she's heard me. "You told me that yourself, Apple, you said they were trying to help him."

"That was so long ago I don't even remember it," I say lamely, adding, under my breath, "Don't bring that up now."

"There are no secrets here," Cory says, in a ringing tone.

The Indian girl is beginning to clear the table.

"I guess you're a prophetess," the bird man says as he gets up. "A Cassandra."

For the first time, an unplanned feeling shadows my sister's smooth face. "Not a Cassandra," she says, and I hear something like a note of pleading in her voice. "Not crying from the walls of Troy. Not yet, at least. Maybe never."

But the bird man has made his point. He smiles at her.

As the group files out of the dining room, Cory turns slightly toward the door that leads to the kitchen, and I become aware of someone standing there, in the shadow.

"Who's there, Cory?" I ask, and this time I don't whisper, although the man, whose face I can't see, is only a few feet away. "Don't you want to introduce us?"

I say that out of pure devilment, because she has used me to teach her guests a lesson, but I am shocked to see how quickly she turns away.

There are secrets here, I think, of course there are secrets, there are secrets everywhere, they are what hold up the walls—and then I follow my sister's swirling red velvet skirt out of the dining room.

2

The two sisters are packed into the jeep next morning before eight o'clock, and Cory is thinking that with any luck they will make it to the pueblo in time to find a parking space in the plaza. It is New Year's Day, there will be a crowd at the dances.

For a while there is silence, and Cory is grateful for that.

Then Apple asks, "Why do you wear that pistol all the time?" She has said nothing since breakfast, not even commenting on her sister's rousing talk, over the burritos, on the usefulness of pretending.

"I need it," Cory says. When Apple presses her for more, she admits, "There's been some trouble here."

"What kind of trouble?"

"A murder."

Apple seems oddly satisfied, as though her worst fears have been realized. After a moment, she says, softly, "You hurt me last night, Cory."

"I'm sorry to hear it." Cory's tone is brisk; she is negotiating a line of traffic, turning onto the main road.

"Those tears—they weren't real."

"How do you know?" Cory's laughter almost silences her sister.

"I can tell real from false," Apple says finally, with dignity. "Those tears of yours were for show."

"To teach the lesson of forgiveness, maybe," Cory concedes.

"Forgiveness!" Apple gasps.

"It works both ways, Sister."

"And another thing—you never called me Sister before, not even when we were children."

"I want my guests to be clear about our relation."

"How can it be clear?" Apple asks. "It's not clear to me."

Cory sighs. "A lot of water over the dam. Or is it under the bridge?"

"Always joking," Apple says.

"I hoped you'd be absorbed into the household, act like another guest."

"Why should I act like a guest?"

"Because that's the best way to act."

"They don't really matter. A crowd of strangers. . . "

After a moment, Cory says, "You remember that passage from Matthew about the wedding guests?"

"No."

"Mother read it aloud to us. The king plans a wedding for his son—"

"You're no king, Cory," Apple says succinctly.

"—And then he decides that the people who've been invited— his friends, and his son's friends, I suppose—are not worthy of the feast he's planned, so he sends out his servants—"

"into the byways." Apple is remembering now. "She used to read us Bible lessons before bedtime."

". . . to bring in anyone they find."

"Blood is thicker," Apple murmurs.

"Blood doesn't listen."

"And these people do?"

Cory passes a slow car, pulls back into the clogged lane. A few inches of snow have turned the little town back into what it once must have been, she thinks, blunted, squat, nothing taller than two stories; the adobe windowsills are thick with it, the trees are outlined in white. She wishes she was alone in the car, alone with her recreation of what Taos was, or might have been, before she and all the others came to spoil it, but Apple is insisting on an answer.

"I don't know whether they listen or not, but at least they have to sit there," Cory says. "Nobody's gotten up and left the table yet. The seed is sown, maybe on barren ground, maybe on rocks, who knows? But it's sown, that's all I can do."

"Matthew doesn't explain why the wedding guests had to be replaced," Apple muses. "The parables are always like that, aren't they?"

"They weren't worthy," Cory says.

A thicker quiet settles.

"I don't want to talk about that now," she says hastily.

"I've come all this way to talk," Apple says ominously. "I won't be put off forever."

"Just for today, just so we can concentrate on the dances." Before Apple can answer, Cory begins to explain the role the dancers play in the pueblo's sacred life, the community thriving still or at least continuing on its way because of these seasonal observances; no electricity, even now—she's heard the elders drove the electric company trucks off with guns—no television, just the simple old ways that no longer exist anywhere else. "You need to see this," she tells Apple.

"You don't know what I need," Apple says. It is a statement of fact, and Cory accepts it in silence. "You've never even thanked me."

"Thanked you for what?" She glances at her sister, sitting in the corner; she looks like a little hedgehog.

"Everything Billy and I did for you—Billy, mainly—during the sale. You'd never be able to live the way you do—"

"It's not that expensive!"

". . . if Billy hadn't protected your interests as a minority stockholder."

"I thought he was protecting his interests. Everybody was in the same boat."

"You don't know the whole story."

Indian ponies line the fence; beyond, the broad fields of the pueblo stretch up to the sacred mountain. Cory wants to look at the mountain, to recreate the silence of the rest of her life, but she knows she has been cornered.

"I don't know the whole story," Cory says, "and I'm not sure I want to. It's ten years ago, Apple!"

"You need to understand, so you can thank Billy," Apple says, and Cory hears something new in her voice, something solid and flat.

Apple will not be turned aside this time, she will not be bribed with candy or a new doll or a special on television; she is herself, at last, this prickly hedgehog sister Cory has hardly thought about in a decade, except when the exasperating poinsettia arrives, or the printed Christmas card, and then she thinks, resignedly, Oh that's just little Apple, taking over from Mother: keeping up the appearances.

Later she watches Adeline leaning against the low adobe wall that surrounds the pueblo church. Her sister's thick dark coat and knitted hat mark her an outsider. Most of the visiting Anglos wear some version of N.A. attire—blanket-like jackets in Rio Grande colors, fancy boots, shawls. We want to be accepted and we show it, Cory thinks, particularly in a certain deferential stance, shoulders hunched, knees slightly bent, feet planted close together to take up as little of their space as possible. Boots are everywhere—Cory has on her flamingo-pink ones—but Adeline in spite of Cory's offer of an extra pair is wearing her big lined nylon bear paws (as Conchita called them), still muddy from her last tramp on the farm thirteen hundred miles due east.

Adeline is studying the north and south pueblo buildings that back up the plaza, adobe mounds with terraces, windows and turquoise-blue doors. Cory tells her that many of the people who used to live there are now scattered in trailer parks with televisions and running water, but they have returned for the dances. They stand ranked on terraces and stoops, wrapped in blankets.

She wants her sister to see the significance of this. And Apple seems to understand. "We have no ceremonies," she says.

In the middle of the plaza, drying racks cast striped shadows, and the icy stream, source of the pueblo's drinking water, flows under a bridge that connects the two buildings. Down a narrow alley, the kiva stands isolated, crowned by the prongs of the ladder that goes down into its center, a hole in the ground from which the world began, according to the traditions, Cory tells Apple. The kiva is forbidden territory.

Far away over the cottonwoods, the sacred mountain juts, blue in the shadowless light from the early morning sun.

Cory darts across the plaza to speak to Luisa, who's taken up her position on the stoop of her grandmother's house. Cory is hoping Luisa will invite the two sisters inside for fry bread and strong coffee, but the young woman seems distracted. By the time Cory turns to look for her sister, the plaza is separating them. Adeline is planted against a wall, motionless as the N.A. women, Cory thinks, wrapped in her untranslatable thoughts.

Crossing the plaza, Cory stops or is stopped to speak to various acquaintances. Lawyer Tuttle wants her attention badly. "We need to talk, I've found someone to do the job," he says, his face shaded by the brim of his cowboy hat so Cory only sees the flash of his blue eyes.

"You sure this one can do it?"

He shakes his head, summoning discretion. "Come to my office tomorrow. Ten o'clock? I think you'll be pleased. And don't pack that pistol."

Cory nods, indicating only that she has heard him.

Moving along through the crowd, she sees Leonard Gross and stops to ask him how the concert went. He says the cafe was wall-to-wall, they sold more lattés than ever before. Enough money was raised to pay for the next step in the discovery process, although no one was told exactly what their donations were to be used for; the sign Leonard propped against the donations cup only said, FUND TO SAVE OUR FORESTS, and now he calls it, "The purpose we agreed on." Taos is a tiny town and they can't be too careful.

Primrose is next. She reaches for Cory's hand. "I haven't seen you since Christmas—"

"Just a week ago." They shared champagne and a walk around the town, lit with bonfires and farolitos.

"Bring your sister over tomorrow, we'll have tea."

Cory nods. Adeline will be reassured by Primrose's cozy little house. Primrose is a lady, her southern accent fastened on like a small but priceless heirloom brooch.

"We need your professional services, as well," Cory says.

"Your sister wants that?"

"She doesn't know enough to want it," Cory says, laughing.

It's harder to deal with Andrew, who's come down from his mountain fastness for the dances. His blue eyes are bleak. He's nearly out of food and doesn't know where the next meal will come from. Cory admires his prophet's head, the fine white hair and beard, but refuses to invite him to supper; they've agreed that she won't help him anymore since she feels he's too fine a man to become a dependant. (Whether he agrees with her or not she doesn't want to know.) She turns away, thinking, Love, abandonment—is there really any difference?

By now she's close to the church. Its squat twin towers with the white-railed balcony between them stand out against the blue sky. Before she can get to the wall and Adeline, however, Martin the astrologer catches her elbow: "Did you listen to what I told you about the new moon?"

"Yes, but I don't know what I can do."

"Nothing, of course, Cory, except be prepared." He rubs his hands together and she notices, again, the long fingers she's watched so many times, tapping the faces of Tarot cards or gesturing toward a perception.

"Do I have to be prepared for anything?" She smiles at him affectionately. They were lovers for a few months until they were pulled in different directions, he by his seer's fatalism, she by her ever-recurring hope.

"Yes. I see your sister's here. That's part of it."

She squeezes his hand and passes on, wondering if Adeline could tolerate his company; he smells of patchouli and beyond that of something unapproachable, cool.

Passing along, she nods at her couple from Albuquerque, dropping her hand on the head of their little blond daughter. The girl glances up at her, her wire-rimmed glasses enlarging her pale eyes. "Hello hello," she says in a gurgling undertone—a strange creature; Cory saw her hopping around in her undershirt in the hall before breakfast, her little slit naked and innocent. But she interrupted ceaselessly during the breakfast talk until Cory has to ask her mother to take her out of the room.

Now her two Texan guests are talking to Adeline, and Cory sees her sister's tired face over their broad, matched shoulder. She would do anything to relieve Apple's tiredness, accumulated now for so many years, and knows at the same time that there is nothing she can do but offer her the sky, the mountain behind the pueblo, the sound of drums just now beginning—exactly what Mabel offered her guests, who were often no more prepared to accept.

Reaching her, Cory nods at the Texans and says, "Let's get closer to the dancers," taking her sister's hand. It flutters like a trapped bird. Cory holds firmly, sensibly, she's in charge. If it was the house they shared, growing up, Apple, the governing little sister, would be leading, but now in this strangeness, in the thin air that hardly has enough oxygen to sustain her, Apple is willing to be led. They skirt the crowd and although uninvited join Luisa on her grandmother's stoop.

Cory introduces her sister but the drums have started and Luisa doesn't hear.

Far away, at the other end of the bridge that leads to the south building, the shadow of a wooly head with twin horns is cast on an adobe wall. The invisible drum, slow, insistent, follows the motion of the horns, advancing toward the plaza. The shadow is joined by another, blurs, disappears.

Apple is plucking at Cory's jacket. "They don't want us here," she mutters, glancing at Luisa who has turned away, wrapped in her blanket, eyes fixed on the entrance to the kiva.

"They just don't make nice. Why should they? Remember what we did to them—"

"WE didn't do anything," Apple interrupts. "Why do they resent us? Remember Frankie—"

"Frankie never had a culture to defend."

"Wait a minute—what about spirituals?"

"Frankie never sang spirituals. She didn't believe in civil rights, either. Maybe there's a connection."

Apple sighs; Cory knows her humor irritates her.

The first dancers have appeared at the opening between two adobe walls.

A herd of deer comes first, following the four drummers, their sleek antlered heads bobbing, their forelegs supplied by sticks; they've learned the way the deer walk, a few steps forward, a few to the side, a hesitation with a bent knee. At their ankles, clusters of cowry shells— ("Where did they come from?" Apple asks, and Cory answers, "Trade with Mexico")—brush and shiver. The sound is faint, a rattling, a scratching—("Like that old magnolia against our bedroom window, in the winter when its leaves were brittle," Apple reminds Cory, who doesn't need reminding.) The dancers wear aprons of painted deerskin, wrapped and tied with long hairy tails that brush the backs of their thighs. Their chests are bare, muscled, swarthy, heavy with flesh.

The crowd around Cory and Apple stirs, bending its united attention on these dancers who must not be noticed individually, picked out, spoken to, waved at: they are parts of the whole, their individuality lost, Cory tells Apple, who says, still translating, "Like water ballet when we were girls, that star we made floating on our backs with our toes together," and Luisa, overhearing, suppresses a smile.

"Water ballet had no spiritual component that I'm aware of," Cory says, wanting Luisa to understand that she recognizes her sister's limitations.

"Who's to say?" Apple remarks with a sharpness that surprises Cory, who remembers her sister in her tight little bright-blue bathing suit, meekly tilting her chin up as she lay on the surface of the water, pointing her toes: a spiritual component in that? And the modest crowd of dutiful mothers applauding . . .

The buffalo dancers are entering the plaza now, passing so close Cory knows Apple is tempted to reach out and touch a great bushy weaving head, but she does not have to restrain Apple's hand—she's catching on. The stench of partly-tanned hides reaches them and Apple holds her nose.

Luisa twitches her blanket. She still has not spoken one word and Cory wonders if she will ever again be asked inside for fry bread and strong coffee, will ever again glance cautiously at Luisa's father, Tony's uncle, sometime cacique of the pueblo, who spends most of his time now sitting in the corner of Luisa's room, his chief's blanket over his humped shoulders, meditating, praying.

The dancers begin to mime the hunt that was never theirs, Cory explains to Apple; the buffalo were plains animals, the pueblo people copied the dance from their neighbors to the east. Perhaps that is why the buffalo loom large and graceless in the scalding light while the deer, which are native, plunge and pause, following some natural surging and relapse of energy.

"The hunters," Cory explains as dancers armed with bows and arrows, insubstantial, toy-like, enter the arena, and then the chase is on: one animal is singled out, there's a scuffle, harsh cries, and the deer is carried off, limp on the shoulder of his killer.

"Do any of them get away?" Apple asks, awed, and Cory explains that there's a quota system, at least in theory; only enough animals are killed to feed the people, the rest are released into the wild. Symbols follow practice, in the dance.

"But when is enough enough?" Apple asks in her literal way, and Cory glances at Luisa, hoping to catch her eye, but Luisa has turned aside to say something to her father.

The old man is there beside her on the stoop, his blanket drawn over his head so his face is nearly invisible, a humped shape, ancient, although Cory knows he led the dance only a year ago.

She does the unthinkable, reaches across Luisa to greet him. He resembles his uncle in every detail, and Cory remembers the rumor that all of the first Tony's so-called nephews and nieces were really his sons and daughters. He had the run of the pueblo for a decade in the twenties, recognized as a medicine man, a strange and holy one.

The old man barely acknowledges her.

They turn up, she thinks, even now, in gas stations or roadside vegetable stand, these men who don't need us—nice Anglo ladies looking for something a little different.

But not this different, she thinks; this is beyond what anyone, even I, could imagine—the weight of this man's presence, the length of his distance, stranger and more compelling than his flat, untranslatable eyes. Strangeness breeds attraction, then repels, she thinks with a detachment that is not available to her, back at Mabel's.

That's what Mabel Dodge Luhan saw half a century ago, Cory thinks, after she was released from her Manhattan penthouse and her Venetian palazzo: that energy, status, purpose—that's what she longed for and took, after which the first Tony was no longer as welcome in the pueblo, was cast out, in fact, from the circle of elders—although Mabel's money in the end bought him a measure of respect.

A few minutes later, the old man reaches across Luisa to take Cory's hand with an abrupt gesture that unsettles her and startles Apple, standing nearby. He gestures with his chin toward the kiva, then starts off. Cory stumbles after him.

☞ ☞ ☞

I cannot stand to see my sister treated as she is here, Apple thinks, shrinking back against the adobe wall which, she realizes, is pancake-warm from its soaking in the noonday sun. These people have no idea who she is.

But who is she? the mocking voice she's heard since childhood asks.

Your sister, yes. Your sister who has never had what you and your family call a normal life; instead, a divorce, long since, in bitter secrecy, no children (and there's a mystery), no career or job or profession for all her brilliance, living hand-to-mouth in some hole in Manhattan until the sale, after which she could afford to go west and try to establish herself.

But is this establishing herself? Apple wonders, appalled by the buff-colored dirt under her feet, the matching adobe wall, the window with its crusted turquoise-blue sill, the half open door that has let her eye into a dark interior where she knows she is not supposed to look—and now these weird dancers, these stinking skins, and the woman who won't give her the time of day—and Cory is being dragged around the barricades in front of the kiva by the old man, as though she belongs to him.

The drummers are passing so close that Apple's attention is caught and held. She tries to imagine what her husband Billy Long or their son Little Billy would say if they were present: the skeptical distance they'd maintain, the complaints about not being able to use a camera, the wrist-watch consulted so that the lunch reservation at the one decent restaurant in town is not missed.

But both Billys are far away, will probably never see these strange rites, although Apple has dreamed that her husband, after a while, will come to find her. (This is one purpose, she knows, of her leaving home.) But he would not tolerate this situation; Billy has less and less patience as the years roll rapidly by with anything unexplained. She wonders if he will ever tolerate her description of the water ballet, which is one of her strongest memories: smell of chlorine, feel of her wet hair swinging down from her shoulders—and is this what has blotted out memories that are supposed to be so much more important, first love, first sex, the birth of their son?

"Who decides what matters, anyway?" Apple asks suddenly, and the woman beside her, the silent one, turns black eyes on Apple as though she's never seen her before. So I exist at last, Apple thinks, leaning back against the warm wall, and wonders why it has taken so many years to ask the only question that matters.

The other questions she has never dared ask her sister are measured out now to the beat of the drums, the shuffle of moccasined feet in the red clay dust: Why did you never thank me for the sale that has made this new life possible? Where have you been, dearest sister, the last ten years of my life?

In this dance there are no questions asked or answered, she realizes; the women wrapped in their blankets watching their dancing men have nothing to say, nothing to ask, whereas Apple realizes that she is nothing but questions, a ball of them—twisted odd bits of string saved over the years.

She wonders why she imagines—still—that Cory has all the answers.

I don't imagine it, she thinks with the stoicism that has carried her straight through so many disappointments. I know. Yes. I know.

She remembers Cory as big sister, unimaginably distant, refusing in spite of their mother's cajoling and threats to take responsibility for little Apple, to help her wash and iron her dolls' clothes—that had been one hell of a scene—to take her on walks when their mother wanted both girls out of the way (and for what secret purpose in their mother's exposed life? Apple wonders, for the first time), to supervise Apple's finicky appetite when their parents went out for the evening, to put her to bed with a pat, a prayer, a bedtime story. Cory refused from the outset to play that role. Instead, Apple was left to lead.

The south was never the right place for Cory, Apple realizes, and wonders if it is right for her, or if she has only accepted what seemed to be her fate.

But why my fate, and not my sister's? she asks herself. I married the right man and stayed married, raised my son. The loss of Little Billy is not really my fault but the result of living in disjointed times; his addiction if I must call it that (and she resists the label) is part of modern life, has little do to with his fundamental personality, which could still be put to so many other purposes.

The same relentless drive, after all, propelled his father to chairmanship of the board and eventual possession and sale of the company's assets—the drive that propelled Little Billy into those dives under the Indiana bridge, those lost holes in the old warehouse district where junkies and ex-cons bullied blues out of broken pianos and the smell of whiskey never faded even during the day, then to the projects where Little Billy with his father's bravado bought and used and sold at a profit whatever substance was available at the time: was not this only another version of the entrepreneur's pluck that had carried his father from stock-boy to head of the firm?

Apple knows she is compromising something essential when she thinks of her beloved lost son in this way, knows it is more acceptable to blame her loss on Little Billy's wife, Maureen Grauman with her nasal Hoosier accent, her German family crouching like big toads in their overheated kitchen. Little Billy even claims to like Mother Grauman's (as he actually calls her) greasy wiener schnitzel.

But she knows her son was gone long before that.

Apple is appalled by this realization, wants to push it away, back into oblivion (which Billy's counselors used to call denial, and how she resisted their interpretations, flaming as so rarely into anger). Now she blames her clear-sightedness on this terrible alien light, not strained through wispy mares-tail clouds as at home or blocked by low-lying banks of cumulus but searing down from the sky itself, not just from the tiny sun.

She blames her unwelcome vision, too, on those animal dancers, the disturbing beat of those drums. Little Billy uses magic now to cure himself—all those exhortations, prayers, slogans, chants, words and gestures that came with the Program, the litany of self-revelation, lacking even the grace of these strange dancers. The result is a hammered-flat replica, she thinks, a tin version of her son.

She does not want to think of that—that he is altered, almost beyond her recognition.

The last deer are passing out of the plaza now and Cory is coming back, followed too closely by the Indian Apple saw in the kitchen. He seems to be stepping on her heels.

"What happened?" Apple asks under her breath as Cory steps up onto the stoop.

"He took me to the kiva. It's not allowed." Cory frowns. "Tony came and got me."

"You were a fool to go with that old man."

Cory glances at her. "It was a priceless opportunity. Women are never allowed in there. I wanted to see the hole in the middle of the floor where we all come from."

"But of course we don't," Apple says.

"Who's to say?" Cory smiles at her. "I never knew where I came from."

"You've never had a baby," Apple says before she realizes it.

"I'll tell you right now—" and Cory turns with a roguish smile—"I've never been sure where babies came from, either."

Apple looks away. He knows something, she realizes, meeting Tony's dark eyes, and she remembers the retablo behind the alter in the pueblo church at the other end of the plaza: the virgin in her familiar blue mantle, framed with cornstalks. Here the familiar and the exotic are mixed without comment, as Cory and this Tony are mixed, blended into a grainy new relation Apple has never expected, and she remembers, again, their courtly father murmuring when their mother complained about the Negroes' unrealistic demands for equal rights, "Tout comprendre c'est tout pardoner."

But I do not understand everything, Apple thinks, humbly, or even anything. I do not understand how these people come to be here:

an ancient tribe, come down from the mountains on the other side of the Rio Grande, she remembers Cory saying, and before that, possibly from Mongolia or Mexico, who knows, their swarthy good looks are not what Adeline thinks of as American. But how did they come to survive, even thrive, owning their own territory, making their own laws?

As she is savoring her ignorance, a man who has been standing near her unnoticed, wrapped in a hairy blanket, an Indian—one of them—suddenly kisses her.

Apple is already straining back from his hand on her shoulder even as she feels the flick of his tongue in the corner of her mouth.

Germs! She thinks.

She sees his mouth, the dark thin lips open, something liquid and vividly pink inside. She can't remember in her blaze of indignation that her mouth ever had such a use, not for words, not for eating—a purely sexual use, as insultingly obvious as one of Georgia O'Keefe's lilies, no wonder people were shocked, nothing so private should be revealed in coarse-grained petals and pulsing pistols. All this is flooding her mind as the man, smiling, turns away.

Apple runs the back of her hand across her mouth.

Then she hears Cory laughing.

She turns to stare at her. If she could not prevent the attack— and Apple realizes she still thinks Cory can prevent anything—at least she can take it seriously.

"You used to wipe off kisses like that when you were five years old," Cory says. Tony and Luisa are smiling, too.

"Why didn't you do something?" Apple asks fiercely.

"What's to do?" Cory asks, still smiling. "Don't tell me you've never been kissed by a stranger."

Apple wants to claim she's been kissed by many strangers but never by an Indian smelling sour of beer in a hairy blanket. However she knows she cannot say this untruth into the faces of Luisa and Tony who are still smiling tolerantly.

"Drunk," she says harshly to Cory. She doesn't want to take on the other two, probably this is some ritual they understand and accept, part of the feast day—to humiliate a foreign woman—but she, Apple, will never accept it, the kisses she wants are the ones Billy gives her when he leaves for the office, a light pressure on her cheek, priceless token of respect.

She is still hot with rage and embarrassment—an over-reaction, she begins to see, but that does nothing to cool her—when Cory pulls her inside the doorway and she finds herself, willy-nilly, in the camp of the enemy (as she thinks of it now, as she insists on thinking of it): Luisa's grandmother's bare dark room on the first floor of the pueblo.

A fire is burning in a curved corner fireplace and the wooden table is loaded with condiment bottles, paper cups and plates, soda and beer—like a picnic from the fifties, Apple thinks, before we all began to eat right and refrain from using paper and plastic.

She feels herself shoved into a chair—she thinks it is Cory who does the shoving—and her hand forms itself around a paper cup of something sweet. She takes a taste to calm her nerves but she is still raging, all that energy now turned against people who use non-recyclable paper cups.

Tony has settled himself into what must be his usual chair, the only comfortable one, by the fire, and Apple sees her sister go over and crouch beside him. He doesn't even offer her the stool but props his feet on it.

Apple doesn't know any more whether she is more angered for her own sake or for her sister's. She doesn't care and refuses to take responsibility. If Cory places her in impossible situations and exposes her to violation, Cory will have to bear the consequences.

"I believe we're about to find out who killed Roy," Cory is telling Tony. "We have leads. The police still say they have no suspects, and now they're trying to rig a drug charge."

Luisa is stirring a pot on the stove with unnecessary vigor, Apple thinks, then wonders if she doesn't want to hear the conversation—or rather the lecture—by the fire.

"They're saying he O.D.'d on methadone," Cory is explaining, still crouching by that man's chair like a supplicant in a church. "You and I know Roy was never—"

"I don't know," Tony says, reaching out to poke the fire.

"You knew him!" Cory insists, her voice rising. "Even if you disagreed with what he was trying to do—"

"We got to log those forests," Tony says. "Only thing we got left, if the government won't let us build the casino."

"Never mind the casino," Cory says. "That's not the point now. Roy didn't deserve to be murdered—"

"Killed himself, it sounds like," Luisa puts in from the stove.

"His wife says he never was that depressed, even when things were going badly. He was planning to go to Washington to see those Interior Department people," Cory says.

"I never did know him," Luisa puts in, "except to see him come by now and then bothering Tony—" and she turns with a pot of something steaming hot and spicy which she begins to ladle onto paper plates.

"Sure, he wanted Tony's help when he was governor," Cory says. "There was a time you could have swung the whole pueblo—"

"That time's gone," Tony says, and he begins to spoon the hot dark stew into his mouth. "They don't want to hear me talk about money, joining the modern world."

Cory says, "Roy was trying to save every tree you wanted to cut down."

"We need to cut," Tony says, chewing. "People matter more than owls."

"It's also erosion."

Tony wipes his mouth. "You see anything here today matters more than that?"

"Yes," Cory says, and falls silent. Apple knows she means the dancing and the kiva, even that preposterous story of the hole in the floor.

Tony says, "We got to keep all that going. We got to find a way. Everybody young's leaving here for jobs. Most of them never come back."

Luisa dishes stew onto another plate and hands it to Apple, but her eyes are on Cory. "How come you care so much what happened to Roy?" Luisa asks.

"I'm a friend of his wife's," Cory says, "and besides, I care about justice"—sitting back on her heels. But she is smiling slightly, and Apple realizes her sister is not insulted by Luisa's question, she accepts it as she accepts her place at the feet of the man who is refusing to do anything to help her.

She swallows a spoonful of the stew, so strong it burns the roof of her mouth and for a moment destroys her ability to taste. "What is all this about, Cory?" she asks as soon as her taste buds recover, and feels Luisa's eyes on her, appraising.

"We're trying to find out who murdered a good man," Cory says, getting up and coming to the table for her plateful. "He was trying to stop the corruption—vote-buying, padded expense accounts—at the pueblo's logging company up the mountain. They're clear-cutting old growth, trying to get around the spotted-owl law. It was a can of worms and it cost Roy his life."

"We got to log," Tony says firmly. "State governor vetoed the casino, we ain't got nothing else."

Luisa says, "Casino nothing but drinking, drugs, all kinds of bad acting."

Tony says, "Pojoaque's going to build, ten thousand square feet, I hear, two hundred and thirty machines, open night and day."

"Pojoaque's close to the highway, don't care about the old ways," Luisa says. "This ain't Pojoaque."

Apple hardly hears her. She has intercepted a glance between her sister and Tony, and she knows something she would never have suspected.

Tony says quietly, "We're sovereign here, we make our own laws, your governor got no right to tell us what to do about the casino or anything else."

Cory nods. She doesn't even argue as she crouches on the floor by Tony's knee.

Suddenly Luisa leans across the table and asks Apple, "You ready to wake up now?" and laughs, widely, revealing empty gums. To Apple's horror, everyone, even Cory, joins in, and she has nothing to say, nothing to offer but a pained, polite smile because she doesn't know what Luisa is asking and suspects she never will.

Then Luisa is hurrying them out of the house. The drums are starting again. The other Anglos are still hanging around the plaza, stamping their feet to keep warm, eating whatever snacks they've thought to bring, drinking out of thermoses.

Then the strange horned creatures are emerging from the kiva, and Apple thinks she can't bear to listen to those drums, to hear that rhythm that doesn't connect to any of the rhythms she's ever heard, blues, jazz, pop, even the wild wailing music Little Billy listened to when he was still safe, living at home.

She puts her hand on Cory's arm, about to tell her that they must leave, but at the same time she hears a scuffling noise overhead and looks to the rooftop.

Five men striped black and white and wearing long-horned masks are cavorting on Luisa's roof.

One mimes taking out his penis to urinate on the crowd below and people scream and run out of the way. The other four laugh and shout, stamping their feet, hectoring the crowd in their language, leaning down, their masks leering. They seem to be particularly interested in the young girls, whom they gesture to obscenely.

"The clowns," Cory says, patting Apple's hand.

"Clowns?" Apple gasps, remembering mild ridiculous men running around in big shoes.

"They bring in a necessary element of anarchy," Cory says.

"What are they going to do?"

"Make jokes, maybe tease a few people—" but the black-and-white striped men are leaping down off the roof now, and Apple presses against her sister.

The biggest of the men snatches the little blond girl from the arms of the couple that's visiting Cory. The mother screams and reaches for her daughter, who is being bourn away; Apple doesn't hear the girl cry out. The father darts after the clowns.

"Don't be afraid," Cory tells her sister, and Apple, ashamed, pulls herself away and tries to wipe her face free of expression.

Now the clowns are streaming through the crowd, their leader holding the girl up like a trophy, and again Apple strains to hear the child's screams.

The father, flying along behind, can't keep up—Cory has never seen men move so quickly—and by the time the clowns reach the bank of the stream, he has dropped behind, winded.

"What are they going to do to her? I knew we shouldn't have brought her," the mother whimpers.

"It's all right, just a joke," Cory tells her.

Apple can't see the clowns over the shoulders and heads of the crowd—everyone has turned, like cows, to see what's happening at the stream—but she hears a cry, a small, faint cry, and then the sound of ice shattering.

"No!" the girl's mother cries, starting forward, and then more swiftly than Apple would have thought possible, the clowns are surging back, the leader holding the dripping child.

The biggest clown drops the girl into her mother's arms.

Apple catches the stench of half-cured hides, and a few drops of icy water sprinkle her face.

The Anglos nearby begin to commiserate, but Apple has seen what she knows Cory has seen: the girl is lying quietly, dripping wet, in her frightened mother's arms.

3

Smoke from Conchita's breakfast burritos hangs in the hallway as Apple hurries to the dining room next morning. In spite of herself, she remembers the way it began with little Billy—sights, sounds, but particularly smells, the harsh dislocated smell of marijuana, the heavy sourness of Bourbon, finally the acrid distillation of crack. Change is always smells, is always danger.

Cory is sitting at the head of the long table. On either side, the parents of the little blond girl lean forward, frowning.

Cory is saying, "Clowns, mudheads, koshares, part of an old tradition."

"She could have caught her death, that stream had ice on it," the mother says. She is pale, small, so fragile-appearing Apple can not imagine her making a fuss.

The father, bluff and determined in his ersatz hunting jacket, adds, "I'm going up there this morning, lodge a protest."

"Oh, please," Cory says, and Apple, unobserved in the doorway, thinks how rarely she's heard her sister plead. "It's a ritual, a way of honoring the ridiculous and unexpected—"

"We didn't come here for that," the father says.

"But no harm was done. Your daughter isn't actually hurt, is she?" Cory asks.

"She was up half the night." He purses his lips, aims blue eyes in Apple's direction, soliciting an ally.

"Yes, indeed she was," Apple says, coming to the table. "Dancing and singing and jumping on the bed. I hardly got any sleep. If you're staying another night, I'll have to ask for a different room. Hyperactive," she mutters to Cory, just loud enough for the parents to hear. It has the desired effect; they sit back.

"Where is she now?" Cory asks. "Did she already eat?"

"Wouldn't touch a thing," the mother says ominously.

"Too excited, I expect. This has been a vacation she won't forget," Apple says, and at the same time, the sprite, the topic of perpetual concern, comes dancing down the steps from the kitchen, a slice of bread in each hand.

"Come here, Ann, I want to feel your forehead," the mother says, but the child is used to commands she doesn't have to obey. She frisks off toward the Big Room, gnawing alternately on one slice, then the other.

"Nothing wrong with her," Apple says, and takes her plate to the kitchen for a burrito.

Conchita smiles at her—already, Apple realizes, she's a familiar of the household—and asks if she'd prefer cold cereal, but Apple is forcing herself to try harsh unfamiliar tastes and she takes two burritos with green chile.

In the dining room, the couple is nowhere to be seen.

"I wish I could educate them beforehand about what to expect at the dances. I'd print up a brochure, but they wouldn't read it," Cory says, stirring her coffee. "Were you really up all night?"

"Of course not, I sleep like a horse. But I did hear the little girl laughing early this morning. Laughing like a fiend."

"'Hid in a cloud.'" Blake—another of the memories they share: their father stretched out in a lounge chair, reading startling stanzas from a small book with a faded red-leather cover.

"She's just what you would expect, with those parents. Are they really leaving because of what happened?"

Cory nods. "They didn't demand a refund, though. They want to take the child back to her pediatrician."

"Too much attention. They'll learn, in time. Having children late is a big mistake, if you ask me," Apple goes on. Cory has taken a list out of her pocket. "I was so young when I had Little Billy, I couldn't hope to do anything right, I just went with my instincts when I could find them."

"How is the boy?" Cory asks vaguely, studying her list, which Apple, craning, sees is not a list at all but a long poem.

"He's not a boy, Cory, he's almost twenty-three. He's . . ." She stops, waiting for some sign of interest from her sister, but Cory continues to study the poem. "What have you got there?" Apple asks finally.

"'By the shores of Gitchikumee, by the shining big sea waters.' I copied it out of an old anthology at the library, as a sort of penance. Don't you remember learning it, in school?"

"Penance?"

"'Stood the wigwam of Noclomus, daughter of the moon, Noclomus.' How many other children learned it, shaping their attitudes toward Native Americans—"

"I thought you called them Indians, on principle," Apple interrupts, trying to get a hold on the conversation.

"I call them N.A.'s when I'm reading Longfellow, for a corrective. I expect that couple knows 'By the shores.'"

"Too young. As I'm too young. We weren't memorizing anything by the time I got to school. You've forgotten, Cory."

Cory recites, "Indian-Giver, Indian Pipe, Indian red, Indian sign, Indian tobacco, Indian summer, Indian wrestle . . . Not to mention all those teams."

"What's wrong with that?" Apple asks, wanting to argue against the political in all its forms when it obscures—as with Cory it always does, always has—the personal.

"Whore, cunt, nympho, twat, bitch," Cory says meditatively, stirring her coffee. "Nothing wrong with those either, purely descriptive. Have you ever wondered why when men hate somebody they call him a son of a bitch? Why 'fuck' is a favorite curse?"

"Cory, I need to ask you something—"

"Or take nigger, darky, jungle bunny—"

"Please, Cory!"

At last her sister looks at her. "I'm here to make these connections, Apple. My reason for living. Forgive me. What did you want?"

"Penance? Did you say penance, a while back?"

Cory smiles. "You think you're the only one saddled with guilt?"

Apple leans forward and says evenly, "I don't regret anything, Cory."

"Well, I do."

"What?"

"Choices," Cory says, retreating into vagueness. Conchita, as though on call, comes in with questions about the morning's errands.

I'll find out, in time, Apple promises herself; but she doesn't believe Cory, suspects some plan to escape, easily, from blame. Always smart to take the offensive, Apple thinks, claim regrets before they can be forced on you. "I heard that child laughing," she mutters, disconnected. "How terrified I would have been at that age, to be dunked in an icy stream."

Cory says, "Did it remind you of Little Billy? I know you've been worried about him."

But Apple is not thinking about Little Billy; she feels a space in her heart opening where that preoccupation usually lodges. She shakes her head slowly. "You don't care about your nephew," she says, and nearly chokes on a forkful of green chile. "You never have." She wipes her streaming eyes with her sister's napkin, which Cory offers, sympathetically.

"I'm sorry I've been so out of touch," Cory says, but Apple refuses to accept this mechanical apology. She wants the real thing, or nothing.

"When are we going to be able to talk?" she asks.

The two men from Texas come into the room, hesitating on the doorstep as though they sense a barrier.

"Later," Cory tells her sister as she turns with her professional smile to welcome her guests.

Conchita comes in with fresh coffee, and as Apple leaves (silently, resentfully, she can't help it, the possibility of really talking is so precious, so rare), Cory is encouraging the larger of the two men to go skiing up in the mountains where there's been a fresh fall of snow, and Apple knows if she knows nothing else that Cory is at the same time thinking about Apple's statement—"You don't care,"—which must eventually be accepted in silence or repudiated out loud.

In any event, I'll find something out, Apple thinks, and wants to leap in the air like a youngster, click her heels, but instead she goes back to her dark silent room and sits on the bed, looking out the window at what she knows now are inaccessible lands, belonging to the pueblo. In the far distance she sees a low square hulk with a tower.

They can keep their millions of acres, their sacred mountain, their dances, their strange rites. All that matters is talking to Cory, really talking, laying it all out, Apple thinks.

But something else matters, too, she knows, even as she pushes the thought away: Cory must admit the importance of their exchange, laying aside for once and for all her presumption that only the affairs of the world are worth consideration; and Apple remembers Tony, the failed leader, by the fire in the room in the pueblo, and the look he and Cory exchanged, and wonders, Is he a cause? Was he a cause?

That look had nothing political about it as Apple defines political: remote, abstract, possibly or probably fraudulent. No. That look was pure man-woman, she thinks, desire capped but never forgotten, and realizes she did not think of Tony as a man until then, he was Indian before that, or N.A.—is there really any difference? Desire identified him, made him at least partly familiar.

How do you make love to a cause, she wonders.

But then, how do you make love to a stranger (and Cory's men are all strangers, as far as Apple is concerned, she's gathered scraps, fragments, over the years, too much and at the same time too little), and Apple remembers Billy's arms around her in the big comfortable bed on the farm. Differences they might never have ironed out with words were accepted there: the losses of time.

Resignation makes her furious at herself, and she kicks the leg of the wooden bureau someone (and she knows it might even have been Lawrence) decorated long ago with orange birds.

⬤⸺⸪⬤⸺⸪⬤⸺⸪

A little later that morning, Cory gets in the jeep and drives to town.

She is thinking of her chickens-all-in-a-row (for the moment) as she searches for a parking place on the plaza. Christmas tree lights still dangle from the wires and muddy pick-ups and busted sedans lounge at the curbs. She thinks with satisfaction that the two men from Texas are launched on the mountain to ski, and the parents and their child are loading the car for the drive home. A series of miniature crises has been averted; only Apple's mention of Cory's carelessness (for what is lack of love but carelessness?) hangs in the air, unresolved.

Later, for that.

She waits for an irritated-looking woman in a pick-up to pull out of a slot, then slides the jeep in, fender to the curb. Out of the car, she stops briefly to look at the mountain, snared in electric lines, looming blue above this chaos: the mountain that caused the pueblo to exist, a mile north, then caused the town. For without that to worship—the mountain, and its hidden lake—the people coming down from the mountains to the west would have moved further south; and without the pueblo, the town, even if it had existed, would have no name, no magic, no continuing appeal.

Cory knows the exact terms of her deal with the mountain: I am here, do with me what you will.

What the mountain wills, this morning, is another session with Lawyer Tuttle.

She climbs the dark stairs lined with a faded fresco of Indians dancing—how has anything authentic survived these endless copies?—and looks through the pebbled-glass of the law-office door at Miss Stew, Tuttle's all-purpose receptionist and (Cory's suspects) part-time lover. Mrs. Tuttle is away a lot on environmental business, fighting for the spotted owl against the B.L.M.'s contention that Indians don't like owls.

Mrs. Tuttle is not an Indian but one of their advocates, like Roy Cross, a Navajo the Pueblo never accepted, especially after he began to fight their logging company.

Lawyer Tutle, now shaking Cory's hand, doesn't claim to be anyone's advocate. "I'm just another exploiter," he likes to confess when he's had a couple of beers.

"How can I call you Cory when you won't call me by my first

name?" he asks after she has addressed him in her usual way. "Here we've known each other how long—"

"A year, almost to the day, since I first got here—" driving the jeep, loaded with plunder, in from the highway that led back, it seemed then to Cory, only to the old place in the south.

"And you still insist on such formality." The lawyer is a small man, distinct, the sum of his details; he makes Cory smile with his predictable solemnity, but there's a twist of silver in his character—stubbornness, integrity—that makes him valuable. She has a hunch they would do almost anything for each other.

"Tell me your news," she says, taking the cracked leather armchair he indicates.

Lawyer Tuttle closes the door, and Cory imagines Miss Stew casting a baleful eye just before the click.

"I see you've brought that thing," Tuttle says, settling behind his overloaded desk. "I asked you not to."

Cory pats her holster. "I take it everywhere now."

"You haven't actually received any threats, have you?" he asks with the avidity Cory associates with professional side-liners.

"I don't need threats to know what the situation is. How does your wife manage, going around the state at all hours alone? People are claiming she's the only one in living memory who's actually seen a spotted owl, or says she has. That's dangerous."

"I gave her one of those little purse deals for Christmas. It's registered," he adds.

"So is mine. I'm sorry it's so large." She leers and crinkles her eyes but he won't play, already absorbed in papers he is spreading on top of the piles on the desk.

"The F.B.I. still refuses to get involved," he tells her.

"I don't believe that shabby old character—what's his name?—in Albuquerque could help us much anyway."

"I was hoping for somebody big time, from the east."

"The Feds don't want to get into this. Too much local opposition."

"Just one man against the pueblo—"

"You think that's not a powerful force?"

"I do think it's a powerful force—or was," Cory says after a moment.

He sighs, glances out the window; Christmas stars and bells from the line that crosses the plaza are rocking and glittering there. "So we're on our own."

"Even the newspaper has quit asking questions about Roy's death."

He nods. "I tried to interest Ferguson—"

"As soon as he realized who we're up against . . . not just the pueblo."

"Yes." He looks at her, trying to calculate, Cory thinks, how compliant she is. Her chair is tilted back, her cowboy boots are snubbed under the bottom edge of his desk; she is not being meek. Perhaps, she thinks, she no longer remembers how to play that game.

She enjoys Lawrence Tuttle, always has, but she also knows he is equal to the task at hand. He understands the connections between the pueblo logging company and the powers-that-be, for example Peso Montoya, the town's distinctly unsavory mayor, and his band of supporters, all big-time contractors who need lumber to build the vast new mansions going up on the edge of town.

"Why did you ask me to come in?" Cory asks after a long pause.

"I've found the right person—a private investigator," Tuttle says quickly, pulling his rabbit out of the hat. "Someone very familiar with Taos."

"Who?"

"Andrew Price."

"I know him," she says, laughing. "He may be down and out but he's no private investigator." Then she feels a stab of disloyalty: this is the job Andrew has been needing, it will buy pinon for his stove and food for his rickety table.

"He's very bright, he's lived here forever, he's discreet, and he knows all the players," Lawyer Tuttle insists, and Cory remembers that he and Andrew were drinking buddies in the bad old days before A.A.

"Fine with me," she says, enjoying the prospect of discussing the elements of this drama with Andrew. He will fit them into his dark view of reality, and for once, his interpretation will be valid.

Ms. Stew taps hesitantly on the door and announces an urgent telephone call. Irritation passes across the lawyer's smoothly-planed face. "I told you no calls."

"It's the widow," she mutters with a sideways glance at Cory.

"Ah." He reaches for the desk phone. Ms. Stew retreats with a backward glance at Cory's boots.

"I'm sorry to hear that," Lawyer Tuttle is saying into the phone. "When was the call?"

Cory can hear Roy's widow Nancy's voice grating inside the receiver.

Tuttle hangs up, shaking his head. "She had another call last night."

"The usual?"

"They're threatening the boy again. They know everything about him, she says, what time he leaves for school—"

"She can change that."

"They'll catch on to a new routine soon enough. She wants us to lay off."

"No." Cory tips her chair forward, the front legs striking the floor.

"Cory, it's her son, maybe you can't understand—"

"Don't pull that with me." She leans toward him, elbows on knees. "We have to make her see something bigger's at stake here—the whole old-growth forest—"

"Bigger than her boy?"

"Look, Tuttle, I hired you to do this job, not teach me sensitivity. You're not interested, I'll go elsewhere." She stands up, pushing her thumbs into her belt; the holster settles softly into her left hip.

His eyes go there instantly. "Hold on a minute—"

"Either with me or against me, Tuttle. There ain't no two ways."

"I'm with you, Cory, always have been, I just think we have to proceed with care."

"Care!" She tosses the word off. "Where was care when Roy was driving his van over the Raton pass two months ago? Was there anyone there—you, me, his wife, his son? Who was there when they forced his van off the road—"

"We don't know that, Cory, that's pure supposition—"

"You saw the skid marks."

"It was icy that night."

"Hush, Tuttle, and listen to me. Skid marks or no, something happened to Roy, something the police have already decided was a drug overdose. It's as important to find out what it was and who did it as it is to protect innocent life—"

"That's where you and I disagree, Cory—"

"—because how can there be innocent life or even the possibility of innocent life when a man who was simply trying to save the trees gets murdered for it?"

"We don't know what happened, of course, but with the power of the construction industry here—"

"This cowardly threat," she allows herself to say, blooming into rage. "Against a child! And you say we should let that hamstring us—"

"I'm not saying anything, Cory."

She is looming over him; he leans back in his chair. She sees this shrinking and steps back down onto her boot heels, subsides into her smaller self. "I'm sorry, I get carried away."

He shuffles papers. "So we agree to hire Andrew-"

"What are you going to pay him?"

When he tells her what he claims is the going rate, Cory insists, "That's not anywhere near enough. You're asking this man to put his life on the line for a pittance." She does not tell Tuttle that Andrew is living hand-to-mouth; it's irrelevant, and a confidence besides.

They decide on a slightly larger sum, and Cory spoons cash out of her back pocket. She and Tuttle usually deal in cash, it makes things easier. Sometimes she refers to herself as the bag lady, but she's in no joking mood now. "I'm going out to see Nancy," she says. The decision comes with the words.

As she turns toward the door, Lawyer Tuttle says, "I know I can't persuade you, but that poor woman, surely . . ." As she leaves, she hears him pick up the telephone; he will warn Nancy, which is just as well.

Now she must drive ten miles northwest, out of town, onto the mesa. Cory is grateful for the excuse. Since starting the B & B at Mabel's, she doesn't get outside of town often enough, and the blue mesa with its mountain was what drew her to Taos in the very beginning.

Nancy, who is an R.N. at the hospital in town, built the first tire-house on the mesa when she married Roy. The tire-house, Cory sees as she approaches, has nearly vanished into the landscape. There isn't a tree to cast a shadow this bright winter day, and yet the house seems to live in its own shadow. She imagines all habitations built on the mesa, even those as ecologically correct as the tire-house, live in a perpetual self-made shadow, a penance for intruding on the landscape.

Chosa skeletons celled like long brains rap against the jeep as she steps out.

The panels over the windows of the tire-house face East to catch the morning sun for solar purposes, and she remembers Nancy complaining during the unusually dark early months of the winter that she hadn't been able to run the washing machine. Those were the ordinary sacrifices Roy demanded of the people who cared about him; at the time, Cory thought Nancy's complaint was trivial. Now she remembers Nancy had a child's clothes to wash, and wonders for the first time if Apple's (and now Tuttle's) accusation carries weight: perhaps she can't feel for other people because of her solitariness. She cares more for the spotted owl or old-growth timber.

Something else to think about later.

She knocks on Nancy's turquoise-blue door.

A dream-catcher hovering inside the window is stirred as Nancy looks out. Cory sees the terror on her thin white face.

"What do you want?" she asks, opening the door.

Cory doesn't wait to be invited in. She steps smoothly through, and Nancy backs away. "I hear they've been trying to frighten you."

Nancy stiffens. They face each other. "I don't frighten easy. I see you're packing a pistol."

"We have to be careful," Cory concedes. "But we can't give in to blackmail."

"Sit down."

Cory is glad Nancy's once too-nice manners have worn away. They sit down knee-to-knee in a pair of rough wooden chairs she recognizes as Roy's handiwork. "Where's your son?"

"I made him go to school, he didn't want to, but we can't give in to pressure," Nancy says, to Cory's surprise.

"That's right, I'm glad you understand. But Tuttle says you want us to back off."

Nancy looks at her, pale eyes hardly defined in her fair flat face. Cory thinks she must have been very pretty once, a fragile girl

Roy picked up on one of his peregrinations east, on his way to testify in front of some yawning committee. "If you can take it, I can," Nancy says, and Cory realizes that she knows.

"I have bad days, too." she says.

"They've called you?"

"No—they don't know I'm involved, yet. But Tuttle's had several threats."

"He doesn't have a child."

"How old, now?"

"Seven—second grade. He was doing so well 'til Roy . . ." She reaches a hand to her face, as though to squeeze it shut. A tear slides down the side of her nose. "Excuse me." She feels in her pocket for something, doesn't find it. Cory steps to the sink and pulls off a piece of paper towel.

"Here."

"Thanks." Nancy wipes her face, then blows her nose noisily. "I should hate you," she says.

"I wasn't the only one, Nancy."

The woman shakes her head. "I have to hand it to Roy, even now. The women were always all over him, like flies."

"And I was one of the flies. That's all. He always came back to you."

"Yes." She glances around the house, which is full of Roy's hand-made furniture and his framed photographs of the desert. She has pride of place, Cory thinks, and sighs a little, relieved and saddened. "So what did the person on the phone say?"

"Just recited every step of little Roy's day. They know his bus driver, his friends' names and addresses, his teachers."

"They didn't say what they plan to do?"

"They didn't need to." Nancy wraps one hand with the other, and Cory wonders what her hands get up to when unrestrained: breaking things? Strangling? She feels the woman's strength, a tough wire inside all that paleness. Roy knew the kind of wife he needed for the life he planned.

"They're just trying to scare you," Cory says, a little impatient now that she senses Nancy's strength. "What can I do to help?" she makes herself ask, knowing that if she can create a sense of partnership they will be able to proceed.

"Nothing."

Cory looks at her, surprised. "So you'll allow us to go on?"

"It's not up to me."

Cory would like to agree that it's not up to Nancy or anyone else: in death Roy has been released to the world he tried to defend, his personal ties are annihilated. She remembers the phrase that defined her attempt, two years ago when she gave up the old way: ERADICATE YOUR PERSONAL LIFE. That comes from a discredited prophet, but a good phrase anyway, one to meditate on when she has a chance.

"I can't go forward with this if you're opposed," she says, taking a risk.

Nancy touches the edge of a table, as though to remind herself of the setting: the small room brightened by the big south-facing windows, the blooming geraniums on the low sill, the fireplace stained from the winter's smoky piñon. Roy's furniture is uncouth, off-balance, yet oddly attractive, like inferior inhabitants of a second-class zoo. Cory has a sense suddenly of Nancy's life among these things, these endless reminders. She will need to move into town before she can forget, Cory thinks, before she can release Roy.

"I'm not going to give you permission," Nancy says. "I don't want to be responsible for what might happen."

"I'm not asking for permission—just don't oppose us. It's important, for Roy," Cory says. "So he didn't die in vain."

"He died, that's all that matters."

"But he died for something," Cory insists, then wonders how many death beds Nancy as nurse has attended. Her perspective must have been altered by that—the ordinariness of death, even the death of a beloved. "He died because he believed in something," Cory says, trying one last time.

"Yes." They lock eyes, and Cory feels for the first time the possibility of a real agreement.

"So you'll let us go on?"

Nancy sighs, and Cory imagines all she will regret later, as the afternoon shadows fall and she waits for her boy to come home, as she puts him to bed and prepares to leave for the night shift—how impossibly difficult it will all seem, then, how she will long for an easier way.

"The police tried to tell me he was an addict. Roy never would have done that," Nancy says.

"I know."

"First they told me there was blood in the van, then they said there wasn't. And why were his shoes off? It was bitter cold that night. And why did no one see the van all those weeks they claim it was parked up there at the pass? It's hunting season, and besides, a lot of our friends were out looking—"

"A put-up job, you and I know that. He was leaving in what, two days, for Washington?"

"To testify." She nods.

"His work needs to be carried on." Cory lets that sink in for a minute. "Your son will be proud of his father when he understands what he died for. That's worth something, isn't it?" The question is a risk; she looks away from Nancy, dreading her answer.

"Yes," Nancy says.

"For Roy."

"For Roy—"

They kiss, at the door.

Nancy watches from the window as Cory climbs into the jeep, locking both doors—a new precaution—and slips the pistol out of its holster to lay it on the seat beside her.

She waves at Nancy as she starts the engine, then takes the dirt track to the East which will merge with the paved road into town. She bounces over the ruts, enjoying the sensation; it would be fun, she thinks, to career off into the canyon to the left (she's pretty sure the jeep could manage it). Perhaps in the spring, when there's no chance of ice in the gullies—

The crack is such an unfamiliar sound she's not sure what she's heard. Then she sees the pin-hole in the windshield, six inches above her head.

Bastards, she thinks, mashing the brakes, reaching for her pistol, but when she finally has it cocked she sees nothing but sky and mesa and hears only a chosa skeleton tapping at the jeep's window.

I'll call the police as soon as I get to town, she thinks, turning onto the paved road, the gunshot hole a tiny winking star above her head, then remembers that the police are not on her side anymore, will probably never be on her side—and thinks, out of context and season, of the old black woman, Frankie, disoriented at the end of her life, repeating, "Call the police . . . Call the police."

Not then, Cory thinks. Not for her. Not now. Not for me.

☞ *4*

*T*o get into Primrose's spirit-calling chamber, the sisters must walk through her closet, which Apple says she feels is an intrusion. Cory tells her this is the way Primrose set it up, and not for lack of space.

"She wants us to feel her presence first through her clothes," she explains as they part wafting draperies and push through.

Primrose appears at the other end of the closet as the sisters emerge, sitting in an old arm chair with her tools around her—the sacred pipe with its long feathers, the bowl for ashes, the semiprecious stones and crystals she's accepted, Cory knows, in lieu of payment. In her long robe, her feet tucked under her, Primrose seems a Buddha-like rounded creature although Cory knows she is long and thin.

"Come in and make yourselves comfortable," she says. She's been smudging, and Cory sees Apple sniff, confusing the sharp smell of cedar with something more familiar and illegal.

"It's O.K., just cedar," Cory tells her.

Primrose chats and smiles, telling Apple, who needs to hear this, about her childhood in Atlanta, her years in a girls' school in the mountains of Virginia, an early, perfectly acceptable marriage, and eventual flight.

All of it seems of a piece, the edges neatly tucked under and stitched with Primrose's southern accent. She lets down at one point and calls Apple "Honey" but this is going too far; a short silence ensues.

"So you have questions." Primrose turns to Cory. "Different from last time?"

Cory is not interested in references to the last time. That was just after Roy's death, when she had been distraught in the usual way, unable to accept his loss.

"Yes, different. I want you to ask Mabel some things." Primrose nods confidently. They have been calling up Mabel off and on for months now, and usually she cooperates.

"Doesn't she mind being disturbed?" Apple, always polite, asks, and Cory remembers the way their mother used to invoke the little privacies so essential to her: the closed bedroom door, the nap in the middle of the day.

"I think Mabel likes being disturbed," Cory says.

"She's still very much involved in Taos," Primrose explains to Apple. "As in life, so in death."

"I've been reading her book about moving here, it's almost like the story of a love affair," Apple says. "But isn't she tired of it after all this time? She died in, what, 1963?"

Primrose explains, "Her love of this world has not yet been transformed. She'll need to be released, eventually; our questions are holding her back."

"I still need her," Cory says firmly. Mabel when she ran the big house was at her guests' beck and call. There is no reason to suppose death altered her availability. At least, not yet.

"I don't want to be part of keeping her here forever," Primrose insists, smoothing her peach-colored robe over her knees; the sun, strained through spangled muslin curtains, is casting stars into her dark, coiled hair.

"I want to release her too, when the time comes," Cory says.

Primrose is mollified. "We should plan something. For Easter, maybe—Mabel loved Easter, she made little frilled baskets of dyed eggs for the pueblo kids, who'd never seen anything like that. What do you want to ask her now?"

"The roof's leaking over Spud's room and we can't find the hole."

Primrose starts to smile, then thinks better of it—she's never been one, Cory knows, to scorn the practical—spreads her hands on her knees, tips up her chin, and stares at a corner of the ceiling. A distinct silence falls, different in its weight. Cory hears Apple, alarmed, draw a breath. After a minute, Primrose's dark eyes slip back in her head and her lips purse and tremble. Cory reaches for Apple's chilly hand.

Primrose speaks in a husky whisper. "Under the last viga on the north side."

"That's what I thought all along, but I didn't want Manuel to begin tearing the ceiling apart before making sure." Cory has learned the hard way that the house can only be fixed or changed with Mabel's cooperation: six months ago she tried to install a new bathtub upstairs, without consulting Primrose first, and the ceiling fell. "I appreciate your help, Mabel," she says, and Primrose ducks her head, receiving the thanks for her patron. "Now please tell us whether we'll find Roy's murderer."

Primrose's face moves slightly under the mask of her concentration. She knew Roy, and has certainly heard the rumors.

This time her trance is longer and ends with a convulsive shudder.

She speaks at last in the hoarse whispery voice Cory knows or has learned to believe is Mabel's. No one remembers what Mabel's voice sounded like, although Cory thinks she has recognized its inflections in Mabel's books.

"Very dangerous, proceed with caution," Primrose says. "The District Attorney is the problem."

Cory is surprised. Mabel is seldom this explicit. "He got off the case because of a conflict of interest," she explains to Apple. "The DA's brother owns an interest in the logging company Roy was protesting."

"How in the world would Mabel know . . ." A glance from Cory silences her.

Primrose's next words are muffled. "Nothing happening there."

"But the files were passed along to the Attorney General, Tuttle checked," Cory protests.

"Nothing happening," Primrose repeats, with a vexed frown. "His wife's sister."

Cory sighs. "I heard she was involved in the logging company—receptionist, isn't she? And with jobs this scarce . . ."

"Is everybody connected here?" Apple asks.

"Just about. Taos is a small town, and the ruling Democratic party's always been hostage to local interests," Cory explains, then turns to Primrose. "Ask Mabel if we'll eventually find out who murdered Roy."

"Much spiritual risk as well as financial," the hoarse voice proclaims. Primrose has accessed Mabel's public persona, she is booming as though to a roomful of attentive guests. "Beware!"

"I know this is going to cost," Cory says patiently. "I've got the money. But what is the spiritual risk?"

"Your hands are not clean," the disembodied voice booms, and Cory smiles, reminded suddenly of the Wizard of Oz behind his curtain. She glances at Apple, but she is transfixed, mouth open, staring at Primrose.

"You mean because I was involved with Roy," Cory says.

"His wife has to decide, his wife has to want to go on," Primrose says, her own voice breaking through the scrim. "Not for you to make this decision."

"I know that," Cory says, "I saw her yesterday. She didn't tell me to stop. How will it end—does Mabel know?"

"The end is unclear," Primrose says with another convulsive start, and opens her eyes.

"I want to ask something," Apple says.

"What?" Cory is surprised.

"I want to ask Primrose," Apple says, with a trace of her old stubbornness.

Primrose is exhausted; her eyelids flutter. But she sinks gradually back into a trance as though she is disappearing slowly under the surface of clear water.

"How can I get my son back?" Apple asks.

Primrose is silent for a long time. "Too late," she says, finally, opening her eyes to stare at Apple.

"Too late?"

"He's a grown man, Apple," Cory reminds her gently.

"But I want my son!" her voice, stripped of its usual veneer, is thin and sharp. "I want to have a relationship with him again—talk to him on the telephone, see him without that girl."

"His wife, Apple," Cory says.

"You don't know—you don't understand!" Apple turns on her, tears brimming in her eyes.

"Maybe I don't," Cory says reluctantly. "I think they all have to grow up."

"Oh, stop it! You don't understand—you never have understood."

Cory tries to pat her sister's arm, but Apple pulls away, wiping her tears on the back of her hand.

"I have another client waiting," Primrose says, pushing a basket toward Cory. "I don't like to cut this off, but. . ."

Cory thumbs a wad of bills out of her back pocket, peels off two twenties and drops them in the basket. She always overpays, it's the best possible use for her money. She likes to think of the proceeds from the sale of the hardware company going to various practitioners of magic.

"Can you get something more specific out of her, later?" she asks. Mabel sometimes hovers after having been called up.

"I'll try." Primrose reaches for the basket and tucks it out of sight. "She's been keeping herself to herself, lately, a good deal of interior work still to do. She wasn't completed, you know, at the end. Major issues with all those husbands, and her son."

"When we're through, I'm going to get her reburied up at the pueblo, next to her Tony," Cory says. "That ought to resolve some things."

Primrose looks dubious. "The pueblo's changed a lot since Tony and Mabel fell in love.   I know people at the pueblo who may be able to help."

Primrose nods. "Well, I hope so, for Mabel's sake. If she can identify herself, finally, as Tony's wife, she may be ready to let go of the rest."

Apple, still angry, asks, "How in the world does Mabel know who we are?"

"She knows Cory. She says she chose her to run the Big House. She certainly was there when we did the exorcism."

"We had to get rid of some bad karma from that actor who owned the house for a while," Cory explains to her sister. "Primrose did a ritual."

"I'm good at ending things," Primrose says. She stands up.

The sisters walk out through the closet, parting the softly-swaying clothes. Cory plans to ask Primrose up to Mabel's at Easter, to invent a ritual. By then, surely, it will be time to move on; either Roy's murder will have been solved, or she will have to find a way to resign herself to never knowing.

As they walk down the garden path between rows of sagging farolitos (Primrose won't take them down till the spring solstice, it's something about the good vibes they bring to her garden), Apple says, "Did you see the window curtain move when she first called Mabel?"

"No."

"It moved, and there wasn't a breath of air." Apple draws a breath. "How long have you been doing this?"

"Since I decided to buy the Big House. I knew I'd need some help with Mabel. Women like that aren't easily ended."

"I think it's hateful she's not buried with Tony."

"The pueblo didn't want her." Cory has reached the jeep and is about to unlock the driver's door. Then she sees a word painted in large white letters on the windshield.

"What's that?" Apple asks, catching a glimpse.

Cory walks to the front of the Jeep to get a better look. The letters have dripped white paint down on the hood; they are so large she's not sure she'll be able to see through them to drive home.

Apple has followed her. "Who would do that?" she asks. "Who would have the gall . . ." Her voice peters out. A couple of tourists strolls toward them.

Cory studies the windshield. It has become, she thinks, the map of her life: first the little star-shaped bullet hole, now these swaggering letters.

"Come on, Cory," Apple pleads. The couple is staring as they pass.

"It's only a word, Apple," Cory says as she gets into the Jeep, but she does not expect her sister to accept this. The word has a sharper edge than the little bullet-hole, which Apple has not even noticed.

"It's not true, is it, Cory?" Apple asks in a low, troubled voice as Cory backs the Jeep away from the curb. "I know you've always had problems with men, but—"

Cory laughs. After a moment Apple laughs too, a little uncomfortably, leaning forward as her sister leans forward to see the road through the four large, dripping white letters.

"I'm not a dyke, Apple," Cory says. "I'm a lot of things, but I'm not that—" and hears, for the first time, a note of desperation in her voice.

So they have gotten to me, at last, she thinks, with painted letters on my windshield, the paint still wet.

⇥·⇥·⇥·

Back at Mabel's, Apple goes at once to her room. Walking under the long portal that shelters all the ground-floor windows, she stops to look at a tile painting of the Virgin of Guadalupe, but even the Virgin's slippers set on a new moon fail to reassure her.

A Roman Catholic goddess, she thinks, much closer to the pagan than the diminished figure she's used to in the Episcopalian church at home. In fact, the Virgin hardly figures at all there except as receptacle for the Son.

She slips into the semi-darkness of her room with a sigh of relief.

Sitting on her bed, Apple realizes that she does not want to talk to Cory about anything that has happened. The time for talking has passed.

"Speak now, or forever hold your peace," the minister said at Apple's wedding. And Cory spoke.

What exactly she said, Apple has never been able to remember. It was something about Billy—Apple's groom, her young about-to-be husband: that he didn't love Apple.

How to forgive that? How, even, to remember it clearly?

For years, Apple thought Cory did that to get attention—their mother's tart explanation. Cory was just being Cory, making a scene, splitting out of her pretty matron-of-honor dress so Frankie had to come running down the aisle to sew her up.

But Cory can't always get away with everything. Apple remembers how furious she was with her sister at the time of the sale—another thorn, deeply buried.

Again she accepted their mother's brutal comment: Cory wanted to rule the roost, she couldn't bear for Billy to make the decisions, and so she had to ask all kinds of unnecessary questions about the valuation of the stock and the qualifications of the purchaser, questions Billy of course had addressed long before but which were not meant to be public knowledge. Certain information had to be confidential, revealed only to the actual players, and Cory, minority stockholder who'd never taken the slightest interest in the business, was not a player at all.

Apple remembers that when she left home—and how long ago that seems now, although only two days have passed—she thought there was a question she needed to ask her sister. Now there seems to be a whole thorn-field of them. And words may never work.

Cory is too strange, too unpredictable. Why, Apple wonders, was her sister so calm about that terrible word, splashed on her Jeep?

Of course it would explain so many things. People pushed to the sexual fringe tend to be radicals.

Apple remembers that Cory spent nearly all her time when she was thirteen or fourteen with that girl—what was her name? The doctor's daughter, her long hair as slinky as snakes (little Apple thought that at the time, watching the two girls from a window), her loud laughter and her lips that were already bright with lipstick.

Their mother put an end to the friendship, forbidding overnight visits, after Apple one Sunday morning found the two girls together in Cory's bed. They were asleep, heads on one pillow, long hair, brown and gold, meshed together. The sight made Apple feel so strange she ran right off to tell their mother. Just girls being girls, their mother said with pinched lips, but she called the other mother, and that was the end of the overnights.

Perhaps that's when it all started, Apple thinks. Cory's deviance.

Good Lord, she thinks, it really would explain everything, and tries to resist the satisfaction of that conclusion.

Not even wanting children, for instance. Aborting that one, all those years ago. Never remarrying after her divorce. Cory would chew her own foot off if she was caught in a trap.

Snuggling into herself, Apple remembers her first months with Little Billy (when he was Little Billy, her own baby), remembers sitting in a rocking chair in the warm spring sun, nursing him, dozing, rocking, dozing—the happiest time of her life.

Cory missed all that.

And for what? This peculiar house filled with strangers, and the company of her own will?

Then Apple remembers that her sister missed, as well, the agony of losing a beloved child; but that is nothing, she thinks, compared to the delight of having owned him for a while.

Apple will never use those words, of course, to Cory or Billy or anyone else. You are not supposed to own anyone, even a being who has lived in your womb and come out through your vagina with unspeakable suffering.

No: everyone is free, as Cory is free—free even to rip out an unborn child, as Cory did all those years ago, the child whose birth and raising might have made her fully human; and Apple resolves, at last, to ask her sister about the abortion which must have ended her pregnancy after Apple's nearly-derailed wedding.

Little Billy still belongs to me in some way, she thinks, which is probably why I never see him, and Big Billy belongs to me, too, because of the time we've spent together and my many sacrifices and the access he has to my body.

Cory has nothing and nobody.

Even this big house is only hers on loan, she has to go to that seer or whatever she is to get permission for everything from Mabel, and what if one day Mabel decides Cory won't do anymore as owner? Well, then, Cory will be out on her rear-end, no son or husband or lover even to take her in.

To have no one inside her means having no one outside her, Apple thinks.

Cory did look at that Tony, that strange man, in a certain way, but what does that mean?

Cory is alone as she has always been alone, and the reason for it is becoming clear.

All the causes in the world can't make up for loneliness, for emptiness, Apple knows.

She also knows this line of thinking is unworthy of her but she clutches it as once, she remembers, she clutched a cheap tube of hideous magenta lipstick their mother was trying to take away.

It's an explanation, after all these years, all these thorns, a usable explanation, and she intends to hug it to her at least until Cory persuades her she's wrong.

⌁ *5*

*S*tepping out into the chill dusk under the portal, Apple sees the lantern-shaped light burning over the door to what Cory (or was it Mabel?) calls the Big Room and wraps herself protectively in her sweater.

Stooping to a pile of firewood, she hears a strange treble cry and wonders if it's coyotes on the desolate land in back of the house.

Uneasy, she gathers up a few logs; they fit awkwardly into her arms. She will have bits of bark on her sweater, her pretty pale-pink sweater embroidered with morning glories, which Billy gave her for her birthday.

Packing it, Apple imagined her sister asking where it came from, imagined telling her it was a present from Billy, ordered from New York, the right size, the right color: proof that Billy whom Cory had not yet even asked after functions smoothly as husband, present-giver, lover.

Back in her dim room, Apple gets down on her knees in front of the rounded corner fireplace—she's a little creaky, getting down, she plans to start an exercise program—,and props her armload of logs as

Cory has instructed her upright against the back of the fireplace.

She lights some paper, sticks it under the logs, and sits back on her heels to watch, remembering their father poking furiously at fires that seemed always to go out just when guests were expected, sending up thin expiring spirals of smoke.

The fire smolders, a few brief flames emerging from the paper, then dies down, and Apple adds another log.

Feeding the fire reminds her of the pony she had as a girl. At first when she offered him a pinch of grain, he would snag her palm with the edges of his teeth. During the ten years she rode him (before Billy took the pony in hand, then replaced him with Corabelle, her hunter), Apple taught the pony to take a pinch of oats delicately from her hand. It was an accomplishment, and suddenly Apple wants to tell Cory about it: I trained that pony out of his meanness, by the time Billy took him over he was eating out of my hand.

Finally, her patience pays off; the fire catches. She watches it for a while, then goes to the dismal little bathroom, nothing more than a closet, really, to wash her hands before dinner.

Who will be here, she wonders; it's the first time in years she hasn't known. When Billy takes her out to the club, or John Henry's, their really fine steak house (although now no one is eating red meat, J.H. has to serve a lot of chicken) or to Chez Maude, their first-class French cafe, Apple knows most of the people at the neighboring tables, and the ones she doesn't recognize, Billy does. When they invite guests for dinner, there's never a new face, unless someone has a houseguest; and of course when they eat alone . . .

She dismisses the brief memory of the little table where they eat together, always something special, poached breast of chicken with asparagus, for example, or lemon sole you can hardly tell was frozen, with a spinach salad. No desserts, neither of them can afford the calories anymore, and she remembers seeing Conchita rolling out pie dough that morning.

How does pie dough relate to strange faces, new faces? Perhaps, Apple thinks, it's like the chili, sweet tastes, strong tastes, all leading in unlikely directions.

Ten minutes later she has dressed, made up her face—and the fire is out. There is nothing more depressing, she thinks, than a clutch of half-burned logs. She decides to give it up and join the other guests.

She walks into the Big Room where the new couple from Albuquerque is sitting by Manuel's hot evening blaze. (How does he do it, Apple wonders, and decides to ask him.)

The couple is paging through magazines. Apple guesses they've been locked together in the car all day, sight-seeing, and may be relieved to encounter a stranger.

"Where did you go today?" she asks.

"We wanted to walk," the husband explains—and he is a husband, Apple thinks, a neatly-turned-out middle-aged man, certainly a lawyer or a businessman, with well-tended hair and nails and a firm, managed body, "but the sidewalks here are so narrow."

"All ice, I'm surprised they don't have law suits," his wife, a larger, more untidy person with red hair flying around her face puts in.

"And the cars throw up water—Muriel was drenched," the husband says indignantly. "So we got the car and drove everywhere." He hasn't yet surmounted the chagrin of changing plans.

"You were probably looking forward to the fresh mountain air," Apple says sympathetically, and the wife admits that she was before the husband has time to respond.

"It's beautiful here, though, isn't it?" Apple asks.

They both nod, but the wife adds, "They don't seem very friendly—the natives, I mean."

"You've been to the pueblo?"

"Yes, and Ron's camera was knocked out of his hand!"

"I didn't see the sign saying you can't take pictures," he admits, "but they could have told me."

Apple says, "They've had photographs turn up in National Geographic and a description of their dances even found its way into some comic book. They're sensitive."

"They sure are," the man says.

Cory has come in the front door. She is on her way up to her desolate sun porch (as Apple thinks of it; she hasn't actually been invited to visit), and she hears the last few words of the conversation. "They have reason to be sensitive," she says and continues on up the narrow stairs.

"All that money the government hands out—and now they're getting casinos, nuclear waste, logging," Ron complains.

"Not here," Apple says, and wonders at her defensiveness. What is the pueblo to her? Only a locus of strangeness where she watched dances and recognized another of her sister's secrets. "This is a very conservative pueblo, they won't hear of endangering their traditions."

The husband has nothing more to say, but the wife is less easily turned off. Apple guesses that she champions her husband's opinions. She believes in him; and Apple remembers her own voice ringing out, justifying Billy's decisions about the terms of the sale, until finally one late evening he asked her to stop: "I can fight my own battles."

But can he? Will he? She imagines him now eating a dismal dinner alone at the table in the window; she froze six casseroles before she left. She decides to telephone him after supper.

As they walk into the dining room, the two men from Texas emerge from their room. They introduce themselves all around.

"They take our money," the wife is continuing her critique of the pueblo. "They don't have any trouble with that. My feeling is if they take our money, they ought to treat us decently."

"With manners, you mean," Apple says, and remembers Cory's

lecture. What does she call it? Instruction for the numb? The school of as-if? Whatever it's called, it has something to do with manners, their usefulness.

"Exactly," the wife says.

"We're in the minority here," Apple reminds her kindly; after all she can't be blamed for not understanding.

One of the Texas pair laughs. "An unfamiliar feeling for you people," he says, glancing at Apple, who has taken what seems already to be her assigned seat at the foot of the long table.

"You're right, we white people are not accustomed to being less than all-powerful," she says, looking at him curiously, separating him from his partner, which she must always do in order to see the individual more clearly than the bond. "It takes some getting used to."

"Not for us," the Texan says, glancing at his partner, and Apple wonders why in all these years she's never called Billy that. Perhaps partnership only develops as an alliance against a hostile world.

"How so?" Ron asks, and Apple knows he is interested in making a stir.

"We just went through the business of trying to get married," the smaller man says, not willing, Apple guesses, to be consigned to what might be construed as embarrassed silence. "The Bishop of Dallas, no less, turned us down."

"Not in his church, he said—as though it belongs to him," the taller man explains, and Apple knows they've orchestrated this, taking parts, determined (and this is a kind of courage she's seldom witnessed) to make their situation clear, no matter what company they find themselves in.

No one asks to hear more. Conchita is passing bowls of soup, deep red, with a single green leaf of basil in the middle. Apple knows the soup will be fiery-hot. She picks up a large spoon.

"We wrote a perfectly tasteful ceremony," the smaller man

continues as spoons begin to clack inside bowls. "Our mothers were coming. No one was going to be offended—but the Bishop refused."

"Well, after all, a lot of people do just live together," Apple murmurs.

"We felt excluded. It nearly broke our hearts," the taller man says, and she stares at him, wondering by what act of will he has brought himself to make this revelation. His partner reaches out and takes his hand.

"How do you know when your heart is broken?" she asks, to her own surprise.

"It just happened," he says, and she doesn't know if he means the confession or the heartbreak that prompted it.

"I want to know something," she says, leaning toward them down the length of the table, and hears silence deepening in the peculiar way it does in Cory's house, as though it gains density from suppressed feelings.

Both men stare at her.

"Are you in love? The way we are in love?" she asks, then gasps at her own temerity.

"Who's we?" Ron asks.

"The majority," Apple says with a confidence she doesn't feel. "Heterosexuals. That sounds like some kind of zoo animal, doesn't it, something with zigzag stripes."

"A zebra," Muriel suggests, smiling.

They all laugh, and the moment passes. Apple doesn't dare to repeat her question.

"Truth is pain," Cory said once, years ago, and Apple knows it's so and welcomes the pain, or at least the possibility of pain, as when she was younger and riding Corabelle she welcomed the possibility of a fall. She lost that willingness after Little Billy's birth, after she gave up riding.

"I can accept your lifestyle better than I can what's happened to our son," Muriel says after a while to the two men. Conchita, removing the soup plates, glances at her sharply. "Our son's an alcoholic," Muriel goes on, turning her stemmed glass between her finger and thumb. "Has been for years. We've tried everything."

"All the detox places, psychiatrists, twelve-step," the husband says. And then he looks at Apple. "I don't know what more we can do."

"How old is he?" Apple asks.

"Seventeen. Our only one."

"I lost mine that way, too," she says. "Also my only one."

"What happened?' Muriel asks.

"He started taking everything he could lay his hands on when he was fourteen years old," Apple says, and realizes that the words come easily now, she has repeated them so often in so many settings they no longer cause her shame or grief. "We tried everything too, but none of it worked—all those forced cures. Then, after we gave up, he got married and joined AA."

"Thank God," Muriel breathes. "I only wish—"

"No, you don't. The marriage ate him alive, and so did AA. There's nothing left of the son I knew."

"But surely . . ."

"No. It's a cure, all right, but the way I look at it, the cure is worse than the disease. He won't come near us anymore and when we do manage to see him, either the girl is with him—his wife—or he just wants to talk Program. He thinks his father and I should go to one of those support groups, tell total strangers all kinds of things."

"We tried that, too," Ron says. "I hated it."

"I thought it did some good," his wife demurs. "Still, I can't help feeling that anything that would get our Ronny to stop drinking—"

"Not anything," Apple says. "Not another addiction that makes you lose him all over again."

"But all mothers lose their sons," the smaller of the two Texans says. "My mother always blamed it on Donald here, but it would have happened anyway. We all have to separate, eventually, in order to become who we are."

"I know that's what everyone says, but I feel differently about it. In the old days families used to stay together." Apple notices that Donald is calmly eating his chicken mole. "My husband likes to eat, too," she says, surprising herself. "I've always kind of admired the way he can eat in the middle of anything."

No one knows what to say. Soon they are all cutting up their chicken and commenting on the strange chocolate sauce.

Apple eats too, mechanically. She remembers it all, too clearly. When young Billy started to go off the tracks, his father separated himself from her lectures, her sobs, her sleeplessness: for his own survival, he said. He'd long ago separated himself from the boy himself.

Apple feels as though her heart is breaking again. "My husband won't deal with our son," she tells her new friends.

"Why should he deal with him?" Cory asks in her priestess voice, throaty, too assured, as though she is drawing on years of experience flavored with whiskey and cigarette smoke.

She is standing in the doorway; Conchita must have knocked with her broom on the kitchen ceiling. Cory is wearing turquoise-blue, this evening, Apple notices, it looks like velvet, shirred at the hips, flaring below the knee, and a blouse with a low-cut neck. Heavy silver petals strung on a black cord hang around her neck. And of course underneath it all her bright-pink boots.

What does it matter what she's wearing, Apple thinks. What if Cory came in naked, the long body Apple hasn't seen in a quarter of a century displayed like one of those silver petals?

Yes, naked, she thinks. That would be more appropriate.

"He should deal with him because Billy's his son," she says, and knows her voice sounds flat, the words chosen years ago.

"But if he wasn't his son," Cory says in her smoky voice (and where did her southern accent go, Apple wonders, and imagines it flying off like a butterfly), "he wouldn't have any obligation to interfere."

"That's true," Apple says, troubled. She feels her sister is trying to wedge her into a corner.

Cory sits down, spreads a napkin across her lap and accepts a slice of Conchita's cherry pie. "So does love mean an obligation to meddle?"

"I guess he wants his son to be healthy," Muriel says hesitantly. Clearly she thinks this may be a family argument with hidden rules.

"Meddling doesn't work," the smaller of the Texas couple says, taking a bite of his pie. "They tried it for years on me, psychiatrists, personality tests, mood-altering drugs to cure me of what they call my depression." He glances with a smile at Donald, who has refused dessert and pushed back his chair. "They think love is depression. I agree it can be depressing."

Cory says, "If we acted toward the people we love as though we accept them unconditionally, perhaps in the end we would."

Apple's been hearing that term a lot lately—unconditional love—and for some reason it always sets her off, reminding her of her earliest days with Little Billy, before he learned to purse his mouth against her nipple or bruise it with his gums. "I don't think unconditional love exists," she says with asperity, resenting the fact that Cory has launched so smoothly into her evening's lesson. How long will it be before the guests catch on, refuse, rebel? Grown-ups don't want to be taught, Apple longs to tell Cory. "We can't love people that way because we're all sinners," Muriel says softly.

"Sinners?" Her husband laughs, wiping his mouth.

"That could be," Donald says thoughtfully. "I mean, if we're flawed from the start—"

"Babies? Little babies?" Apple cries indignantly.

"The sins of the fathers," Cory says from her end of the table. "I've always taken that literally: aggression, dominance. Not the sins of the mothers: depression, passivity."

"What's that got to do with Little Billy taking drugs, drinking, going off and getting married without letting us know?" Apple asks, and feels as though she's slit her wrist and is bleeding all over the table cloth.

"Maybe he's meant to be a drug fiend, as our parents used to call it," Cory says with a glint. "How do we know?"

"My God, Cory!" Apple gasps.

"Our son nearly died!" Muriel protests.

Now the room is full of their voices. Only Cory is silent, smiling, sipping her coffee. Apple realizes this is just what she wants—the necessary wall that keeps stranger from stranger ripped down, appropriate restraints canceled. Some day there'll be blows at this table, she thinks, some day Cory will be sorry she started it.

She reminds herself that Cory always started scenes, stirring up the most peaceful settings—Sunday lunch in summer, tea on a winter afternoon.

What is love? she asked once.

What does sex have to do with love?

Why do women have children?

Why do some grown-ups stay married?

Their parents tried to put her off with laughter, or silence, or suggestions that this (the country club dining room or the old Earlbach Hotel lobby, packed with people they knew) was really not the time or the place . . .

"This is not the time or the place," Apple tells her sister.

"We have to begin to tell the truth, no matter what the situation," the little Texan says.

Apple gets up from the table and carries her dessert plate into the kitchen, ignoring Cory's hand-painted sign, GUESTS BE GUESTS. She is cursing all of them, silently, but especially Cory, who never reveals anything while she fishes painful confessions out of the others, even strangers.

But she won't get at me, Apple thinks, thanking Conchita for the pie and refusing coffee. She won't split me open.

Then she sees the silent man from the pueblo, Luisa's brother, that Tony, sitting by the stove. Apple knows with a fresh surge of irritation that he's waiting for her sister.

⟜≡⟜ ⟜≡⟜ ⟜≡⟜

Sometimes I do regret, or resent, Cory thought an hour earlier, fastening the silver petals around her neck.

Or at least I came close to regretting, or resenting, closer than I want; those are two emotions I've tried to scour out of my life.

But to have to listen to that man—my guest, after all! So new-come from L.A. he hasn't a notion of what life is like here—speaking of the Indians with undisguised scorn!

Or fear, perhaps. But either way—totally unacceptable (a phrase she recognizes as her mother's.)

She glanced away from the mirror and caught the eye of her benefactress, Mabel Dodge Luhan, gazing blandly from the photograph hanging over her bed.

"Your house is full of guests tonight, just the way it always was," Cory told Mabel. "How do I look?" She turned, twirled her skirt, flirted up an edge of petticoat, then buckled on her concha belt and slipped in the pistol.

Looking at the photograph, she imagined she caught a gleam of approbation.

She slid her shawl over her shoulders, its ends covering her pistol. "Not your kind of guests, though," she told the photograph. "Not artists and philosophers and writers—important people. I take whoever comes."

She wondered whether Mabel really believed she personally selected each of her guests, drawing them to her from the East Coast, from Europe, the way she believed she drew D.H. Lawrence, even against his will.

"Maybe you did have special powers. You certainly believed in them," Cory said.

Mabel is labeled and made familiar by the symbols in her portraits: Navajo jewelry worn like Tiffany pearls. Hard to believe D.H. forced her into Mother-Hubbards, briefly, had her scrubbing her floor, but Mabel was in love with him, that explains everything. She recovered, in the end.

Power is power, Cory thought, it has no camouflage, even for a woman who still wants to be loved.

Power, the great aphrodisiac when it belongs to men, strands us in an emotional desert.

One, or the other.

Not in my case, she thought, with more confidence than she felt.

Mabel, my great queen, transformer of her world, was all for love, Cory thought, going carefully down the narrow stairs, her boots clicking on the painted runner. She was also all for power, refused to acknowledge a contradiction. That's why she won't leave us, Cory thought, she hasn't given up the world, its pleasures and triumphs.

A few minutes later, she crosses the office and hears the uneven surge of conversation in the dining room.

Now she hears her sister, complaining.

Apple hasn't liked her life for years, yet shows no signs of changing it or getting out. There are rewards Apple won't acknowledge which must have to do, Cory thinks, with Billy's solid middle-aged body. It's more than the security, though. Since the sale, Apple has plenty of money of her own; she doesn't need to compromise the way she did all those years when she needed to be supported.

Cory stops, stands staring at the glass-fronted case where Mabel's books are stacked.

She's always believed her little sister was doing what was expected when she married, especially since it was before the new word on women came to the south. Billy Long was the expected-unexpected man; there are always potent justifications, Cory thinks, for apparently unconventional choices. And Billy was only unconventional because he hadn't quite yet gotten there.

Crossing the Big Room, Cory remembers she couldn't bring herself to witness Apple's pregnancy, or the birth of that scruffy little boy she remembers as though he was still seven years old, runny nose, noisy demands and all.

She sees Apple clinging to Billy's arm at that ridiculous wedding. Perhaps Apple used both Billys for security—the security that comes from accepting and acting upon the dictates (which Cory calls possibilities, only) of biology.

Is this unwelcome revelation Mabel's doing—Mabel, who had one son, and called it quits, incorporating him into her life, willy-nilly?

Mabel has a way of forcing things, and her timing is always perfect, Cory thinks.

Cory wishes she hadn't looked at her portrait, asking for approval. There's always a price, and she's paying it now, in the coin of doubt.

I can't afford doubt, she thinks, not now. Things are too precarious.

Quickly she decides to lay all these questions aside; she'll never be able to deal with a tableful of would-be students (especially since they don't know they're would-be students) if she gets lost in a thicket of uncertainties.

She steps into the dining room, forgetting to make an entrance of it when she hears Apple saying piteously, "My husband won't deal with our son."

"Why should he?" Cory asks, fired with the energy which is also Mabel's unexpected gift.

Apple looks around, startled. "Because he's his son," she says automatically.

Cory delivers a statement about the connection between love and meddling; she knows her tone is harsh, and she sees the impact on her sister's face.

Apple is not ready for this. Cory sits down, spreads her napkin, accepts a slice of Conchita's cherry pie.

When does compassion come in, she wonders, when do I decide to cut her some slack? She condemns herself to silence until her pie is eaten.

Eventually she allows herself to make a statement she prizes, about unconditional love, even though she knows that to Apple it can only be theory—painful theory; no woman wants to believe in the existence of what she's never had.

Then Cory returns to her silence—a penance, a practical discipline—while the table erupts with the words Apple, she imagines, never wants to speak or hear: love, sin, babies.

She fingers the silver petals on the black cord around her neck and imagines Mabel retreating into a similar silence at the head of her table. Most is learned, Mabel knows—and she taught Cory this, in the dead of sleepless nights—from silence.

They are teaching each other now, at her table, lessons Cory had planned to impart herself. Perhaps it works better this way, they will remember longer, she thinks.

Unconditional love.

Sin.

Let them make the connection.

Apple stands up suddenly and stalks to the kitchen with her dessert plate, although there's a rule that guests don't go there, it's Conchita's domain.

She comes back in a minute, looking pacified, and Cory stands up to signal that the meal is over. The guests leave, still disputing, and go to take up positions by the fire in the Big Room.

Cory wonders how long it will last, this brief flare-up, this unusual preoccupation with the truth.

As Apple passes her, head up, Cory realizes her sister is prepared for any revelation now.

I never expected it, Cory thinks. But then, I have no faith.

Faith is not practical, Cory has told Mabel, nothing is accomplished through faith. It has become their sticking point, battered at during Cory's sleepless nights until she thinks she'll never sleep again until the question of faith is resolved.

She turns back toward the kitchen, thinking she will rest awhile in Conchita's silence before venturing into the Big Room, the lions' den of her arguing guests.

Apple glances at her, then sets her mouth and proceeds on her course. Disappointed again, Cory thinks, and refuses to feel the sting. Apple must find a Mabel, a mother, Cory won't serve, for that.

Conchita is stacking the dishwasher. She argued for it when Cory, believing in the virtues of simplicity, wanted to keep the double chrome sinks that served Mabel's household. The hotel-sized dishwasher with its three racks is Conchita's prize, and she stacks it with jaunty disregard, putting in everything, even the wooden-handled knives.

Cory has ceased disputing with her. Knives are replaceable, while Conchita's satisfaction is hard won and not likely to last.

"Good pie," she says.

"They ate it all." Conchita shows her the pie pan. "Didn't even leave a slice for Tony—"

And now Cory sees him, sitting by the fire.

She's still caught in their silence of the day before, and so she's surprised to see him; usually that kind of silence keeps them apart for weeks.

"Did you walk over?" she asks. He looks cold, huddled in his old fake-leather jacket, rubbing his hands.

"Manuel gave me a ride." The two men are friends of a sort, although Manuel was born outside the pueblo and is for that reason divided by an invisible line from Tony, son and grandson of governors.

Conchita makes herself busy cleaning up the kitchen. She is used to being a silent partner to their conversations, Cory thinks, as indeed are many other people. Tony and Cory exist within sight and hearing of the town and the pueblo, as in any village in the south, she thinks, exactly the setting she tried to escape.

It is only a problem when Cory insists it is. For Tony, she knows, this is life as it has always been, the individual functioning as a visible part of the whole, and she remembers the discredited prophet's axiom, ELIMINATE YOUR PERSONAL LIFE.

She comes closer to Tony, and as she does, she steps inside the circle that surrounds him, which creates not so much an impression on the senses as a change in the laws of gravity.

Close to Tony, Cory feels that her feet are flying off the ground. He sits as though planted for life in the chair beside the fire; his weight unseats her, his steadiness makes her light.

He looks up. His face is sown with observations and reactions she can't quite make out. He has, as usual, nothing to say.

"I have to see to my guests. You'll be here awhile?"

He nods.

Cory leaves the kitchen.

Once, she took Tony into the Big Room and gave him the armchair by the fire where he sat quietly while her guests talked around him, over him and finally through him. She did not repeat the experiment. "They don't bother me," he told her later, but they bothered her, she hated their disrespect, their ignorance. Now, she's not sure how she would feel—and then she remembers Apple. Apple didn't like Tony, at the dances.

So it cuts both ways, she thinks, striding through the dining room, it's not just Apple who wants approval. A bitter pill.

She knows, and doesn't want to remember, the parallel Apple, given a chance, would draw—Apple who has often accused her sister of placing principles before people.

You wanted to work your will on Tony, Apple would say (although Cory doesn't think she uses that vocabulary), just the way you wanted to work your will on Billy and me during the sale. Except you couldn't, then. That's what you call principle, I guess—and these are words Apple has actually used.

That's why we're still avoiding each other, Cory thinks, because of these unnamed disagreements. We're still speaking to each other only inside our heads. Perhaps if Apple knew I nearly lost Tony a month ago, because I thought I had him, she'd forgive me sooner for my other acts of will. Perhaps.

(And how Tony rejected her, pushing her away in bed—and she had bought a new black satin nightgown especially to please him— is still almost too sore a memory to touch. He's come back to me, she thinks, but on his own terms, the terms of no possession, of an absolute and horrifying freedom.)

Cory sits down with her guests by the dying fire in the Big

Room, but they have already learned everything the evening can offer—
and exactly what that is, Cory no longer knows—and before long they
begin to yawn, wanting the privacy of their bedrooms where they can
discuss the evening in peace and quiet.

The couple from Texas goes first, and Cory hears their voices
in their room on the other side of the office; how companionable they
sound. Then the Albuquerque duo—and Cory realizes, now, they are
far more L.A. than Duke City—go off sourly, having lost in their own
minds a battle for definition. Cory imagines the husband describing
his wife in the same sure terms he's tried to use for the pueblo: a
dependant. A ward. In his wife's case, no one will dispute him.

Apple is left, sitting on the stool, hugging her arms.

"I'm afraid you didn't enjoy the evening," Cory, as hostess, says.

"Oh, can that, Cory." Apple's voice has an edge that's new. "It
was fine. I'm just getting tired of us never talking, you never having
time."

Now Cory feels panic. Apple, little Apple, is trying to pin her
down. "Tomorrow we'll go off somewhere alone together."

"Not the pueblo," Apple says, with her unfamiliar fierceness.
"Not that crazy seer, or whatever she is, and not any of your other local
characters. The two of us, alone. I came for that."

"All right," Cory agrees, although she feels cornered and is
already imagining a way out.

"And now I'm going to call my husband," Apple says, getting
up. "Where's the phone?"

"There's only one, in the office."

Apple sighs as though this is the last indignity and clumps off.
Cory knows she doesn't want to be overheard.

For a second, she thinks this is the reason she jumps up and
heads for the kitchen—to give Apple some privacy for her phone call.

6

*T*ony does not say, "Take it off," but Cory expects to hear him say it and begins her argument: "Yesterday somebody shot through my windshield."

She hopes to get his attention, maybe even arouse his fears, but Tony stays on his knees by her fireplace, arranging sticks.

Once, she tried to dissuade him from making her fire, thinking it was servile, but he said, "I do it," and she was silenced.

"I would have reported it to the police but of course they're not on our side," she says.

Still, nothing.

Cory knows she should have learned by now to tolerate his silence. She often quotes to herself passages from Mabel's book about her Tony, a monument to silence, but the respect implied in those passages doesn't come easily. Mabel was after love, too, and got it in the end, but still she is buried alone in the cemetery up the hill.

Sitting on the edge of the bed, Cory takes off her bright pink boots. As they fall to the floor, she wiggles her bare feet in the chilly air, admiring her magenta toenails. A preoccupation with politics, she thinks, doesn't preclude vanity; she has a pedicure once a week, also a facial and hair-do. Even Apple couldn't be more vain—although Apple, Cory realizes, doesn't hide it. Sometimes after the hairdresser, Cory takes a comb and rats her long fair hair.

"Why you want to know what happened to Roy?" Tony turns at last from the fire, which he has lit.

"I need to know the truth. Are you afraid for me?"

"No," Tony says.

"I loved Roy," Cory says, touching her pistol, tucked into her belt.

"Won't bring him back."

"Of course not. This must run in your family. I'm sure your great-uncle was always trying to stop Mabel from doing something she set her heart on."

"He not try to stop that woman," Tony says, still planted by the fire.

Cory lets the tone of that remark pass. "Who's to say? Mabel never did." She unties the black cord of her necklace and the silver petals slide off into her lap. Her bare neck and shoulders flash out. She wore the necklace partly for Tony's sake, but he never acknowledges such gestures; his eyes stay fixed on her eyes as though nothing else exists in the chill room where they are at last—and how rare it is— alone.

Then she unbuttons the front of her blue velvet blouse. "Tuttle's hiring a private investigator: Andrew, he's starting tomorrow."

"You going to pay him?"

With an impatient gesture, she shrugs off the blouse and begins to unbutton her creamy silk chemise, her fingers lingering on the tiny covered buttons. "Of course. Who else?"

Tony's eyes remain fixed on her eyes. Cory slips the chemise down to her waist and stands up to unfasten her skirt, pulling it out from under the concha belt. Then she unfastens the belt and lays it with the pistol on the table beside the bed.

"Not the job for Andrew," Tony observes, turning to poke the fire which is dying down.

"He needs the money, and he knows everyone in Taos, or they know him." She lets the skirt slide down to her bare feet and steps out of it.

Tony turns slowly. "How come you don't wear underpants?"

"I don't like them." She stands before him in the uneven firelight.

"So many letters," he says, looking at the pile on the table by the bed.

"Spotted owls, old-growth timber—they bring in a lot of mail."

"Nice color," he says later, touching the purple ribbon she's untied from her braid.

"Are we repeating something?" she asks.

"Repeating?" The word is strange on his lips.

"Your great-uncle liked Mabel's purple ribbon—that's in one of her books."

"So—?"

"I want this to be new . . . new as it feels to me." Her words have no meaning, for him; she knows that even before she speaks, yet must speak, again and again. Tony turns off the light.

Then he puts his right hand on her hip. She is on her side, facing him, and her hip juts up into the darkness. His hand presses her hip down. Then he moves his hand across her belly. "Why never any baby?"

"I had one, a long time ago."

His hand moves over the crest of her pubic hair, rests there, flattening it. She waits for him to ask another question, but he is not curious; she realizes that a baby is not especially surprising or even interesting. The weight of her great secret lifts.

She shifts herself closer to him, fitting her breasts into his chest. He curves his arm over her, clasping her, motionless, his chin resting on top of her head. She pushes her feet between his ankles.

Downstairs in the office, Apple is still talking on the telephone. Her voice, bouncing into its highest register, penetrates the adobe walls, the heavy carved door. "My sister!" she's exclaiming. Cory twists restlessly onto her other side and presses her back against Tony's chest.

He touches his lips to the crown of her head, and she imagines a soft spot still pulsing there—the fontanel. She remembers putting her finger to that soft, pulsing spot on her baby boy's head just before they took him away.

"My soft spot, it's never closed," she says.

He chuckles.

His hand finds the cleft between her buttocks. She shifts herself, bringing up her knees. He slides two fingers between her buttocks, then brings his fingers up to his mouth; she hears him sucking. Then he slides his two wet fingers into her crack.

Later she begins to moan. He puts his other hand over her mouth. She presses her lips, then her teeth into his meaty palm.

He is pushing heavily, softly, far too slowly. She draws her knees up further, arches her back, bangs back against him. "No," he says, clasping her hips with his knees, slowing, stopping her.

She lies still, clamped between his knees. After a long time, he begins to move again inside her.

Apple's laughter flies up the stairs.

He stops. She arches her back and tries to pump him, but he's too heavy, she can't move him, he's pinning her to the mattress.

"I can't breathe . . ." Her chest feels collapsed under his weight. She struggles, tries to flail her way out, and her free hand touches the cool steel muzzle of the pistol on the table beside the bed.

She grasps it. "I want to come."

"Shouting and screaming, that's not coming," he says.

Now she is crying. "Don't tell me what I can't do." Her fingers tighten on the pistol.

"Not me, telling you," he says. "You telling you."

"Fuck me hard, I'll come."

"No." He is moving so slowly she can hardly feel him. Still she dreads that he will stop.

"I can't come if you don't push harder." She inches the pistol closer, on the flannel sheet.

"No," he says. She thinks it is his only word.

"Then come, and let me do myself." She hears his no even before he says it. "Say yes to me, Tony."

"That what you need?"

She doesn't know anymore.

"Yes," he says and moves once more, coming so gently and quietly she doesn't know it's happened till he rests his head on her shoulder. "Now, you."

"I can't once you're finished. I need hardness"—and remembers soreness, even blood, with other men—the necessary pain. As she says it, he reaches across the sheet and begins to unfold her fingers, one by one, from the pistol.

"I show you," he says, pushing the pistol out of her reach. Then he flips her expertly onto her back. His tongue begins to moisten a path between her breasts, across her belly.

"No." She clutches his head.

With two hands he moves her thighs apart. She tries to press them back together, but she is not strong enough.

His tongue traces the left lip of her vulva, begins to descend toward the tip of her clitoris. Her hands patter on his head.

His tongue touches the tip of her clitoris and she screams. He waits, his hands still parting her thighs.

Her hand scrambles across the sheet but the pistol is out of reach now.

Still he waits.

She sobs, curses him, pulls his hair with both hands. She sobs until she's exhausted. And finally she is quiet, her numb body subsiding, small muscles trembling in the insides of her thighs.

She is so quiet she hears her own breath, slowly inflating her crushed lungs.

They ache, quivering from spent sobs. She feels a fear, too big to be contained by her clenched jaws.

Then she tips her head back, opens her mouth and breathes.

◦═◦═◦═◦

"I miss you," Apple says.

It's midnight on the other side of the country. Billy, asleep when she called, knocked the telephone off the bedside table as he lunged in the dark to answer it.

"Miss you, too," he says thickly. She wonders how much he had to drink with his dinner.

"Which casserole did you defrost?"

"Ate out. Sorry." He's coming to, taking his part in the conversation.

Apple asks him where he ate, doesn't bother to listen to the answer. She wants to ask him if he ate alone but knows that would not be acceptable. They preserve the illusion of freedom by never asking such questions.

"Sounds good," she says, although she no longer knows what she's commenting on. She wonders if he hears her vagueness, if that will disturb him.

"What's it like up there?" She can tell from the changed timbre of his voice that he's sat up in bed, plumped a pillow behind his shoulders and turned on the light, preparing for a long talk.

"The house is sort of run-down but the setting is beautiful." She knows this is inadequate. "I wish you were here," she says, and wonders if she does.

"Wish I was there, too. Lots of work here, though—" and he tells her in detail about various scrambles at the Bootstrap Foundation, which they set up together after the sale. "You know how it is. Everybody expects something. Today old Matthew Horton came in, wouldn't even look at our guidelines, insisted we have to do something to help him save his farm."

"We get into real estate, we're finished," Apple says briskly.

"I have no intention. But it's hard to turn down old friends who don't understand our mission."

"Do we?"

After a moment, Billy laughs. "Come on, Apple. You wrote the mission statement yourself: 'To help those who help themselves.'"

"I'm not sure any of it matters anymore."

"You've been out there too long. Come on home."

"I can't, Billy. We haven't even talked yet."

"How's the weather?" Billy asks, after a silence.

"It's cold, but the sun is warm in the middle of the day, I don't even need my coat."

"Terrible here, another ice storm—" She doesn't hear the details although she gathers the electricity was off for several hours. She wonders if the freezer has defrosted, if all her little casseroles are sitting in puddles of water.

"So what have you been doing?" he asks.

She knows he's being patient; it can't be clear yet why she woke him up in the middle of the night. "We went to some dances, at the pueblo."

"Dances?"

"Yes. They dance there."

He wants to know more but she is resistant, giving him only a bare description. "I can't explain," she says abruptly.

"You're in a strange mood."

"Cory won't talk to me. I haven't spent five minutes alone with her."

"Well, that's Cory," he says. Then he asks, with a lilt in his voice she recognizes, how Cory is.

"She's dressing Navajo now, you never saw such turquoise." Her disloyalty stings; she stares at one of Mabel's books in the glass-fronted case.

"Must be something! Only what you'd expect though, given Cory."

"She looks beautiful," Apple says, surprising herself.

"She got a boyfriend?"

Apple opens her mouth, then closes it. "I don't think Cory needs a boyfriend anymore." She gives the term an ironic twist.

Billy laughs conspiratorially. "She must be hiding him. Cory has to have a man."

Apple realizes she will never mention Tony. He's no boyfriend—of that she's sure. Instead she asks, so easily she feels she's cutting through butter with a silver knife, "What went on between you and my sister, anyway?"

She realizes it's been years since she surprised him.

"I don't want to talk about that on the phone," Billy says at last.

"Well, when I get back, then" she says boldly, then asks, out of the blue, "Do you have anything on?"

"Apple, what kind of talk is this, the middle of the night. . . . No," he says, finally.

"You always wear pajamas when I'm home."

"Well, I went to bed kind of late—" (and drunk, she thinks). "I just didn't feel like bothering." Then he says, "I always make an effort when you're around, Apple."

"After twenty-five years, you must be tired of making an effort," she says, and sees in her mind's eye the quarter-sized bald spot in the middle of Billy's thick dark hair.

"I know you expect things," he says stiffly.

"I expect you to get old, at some point. And to quit making efforts."

"I'm doing that, fast enough." He is gruff, alarmed by the direction of this too-late talk. "I think maybe we should say goodnight."

"I guess we don't know how to talk on the telephone; we're almost never separated, are we," she says.

"Only spent what is it three nights apart . . ."

"When I was in the hospital having Little Billy. You hear from him?"

"No."

She wonders why she asked; there is never anything to hear. Sometimes she calls little Billy's number just to listen to his voice on the recording. "I haven't heard from him in weeks. That girl—"

"Woman, please. His wife. "

"Yes, indeed."

"She'll keep him on track. She's the masterful kind."

"Like me?"

She hears him laughing.

Softly, she hangs up, then imagines the miles of wires that have carried their two voices across mountains and plains, across big rivers and small ones, into the thicket of maples next to their house, where in summer she always sees fireflies.

Then she hears a cry.

All right, Cory, she thinks, enjoy yourself. You've earned it. She can't imagine anything more complicated than Cory's life in Mabel's house, with all those guests.

Another cry.

The Indian's up there, she knows. Cory didn't even wait.

Apple wishes now she'd complained to Billy about that—Cory's sheer lack of consideration.

Darkness presses against the small window behind the desk, darkness and cold, and she feels that the house is porous as a sieve.

As she starts down the long narrow hall to her room, she feels Cory's two cries following her, small dark-colored birds. They settle on her shoulders. "What do you want?" she asks them as she walks on steadily toward her room. "Are you hungry? Do you want me to feed you—" and then wonders if she is losing her mind.

At her door, the birds fly off, and she waits to hear something more from Cory's room far away at the other end of the house.

Hearing nothing, she focuses her eyes on the grain in the wooden door, then the curves of the design: another peacock, long snaky neck turned, tail feathers raised in a fan—maybe some more of Lawrence's work, although she thinks he was only a painter. A painter, and some kind of pornographer—she read one of his novels, a long time ago, locked in her bathroom—and Cory has mentioned paintings too terrible to be displayed in public that are locked up somewhere.

Then she remembers the other peacock, red and green, that Lawrence painted on Cory's window. She sees those stripes falling across her sister's body, marking it, as she lies with the Indian on her bed.

7

Sitting on a bench in the middle of an enormous crowd, Apple leans over and tries to push down the big plastic prong on the heel of her ski boot. Her arm trembles with the effort.

Cory squats beside her sister and presses the prong down easily.

"The way you used to pull up the zippers on my galoshes," Apple says.

"All I remember is refusing to zip up your snowsuit."

"But you did help me sometimes," Apple insists, her voice quavering. Since the night before, tears fill her eyes at unexpected moments—when the radio in the Jeep played "Jerusalem, My Happy Home" on the way up the mountain, when Cory brought her a paper cup of terrible coffee through the crowd at the ski-rental counter.

"That doesn't look like one of our old snowsuits," she says, admiring Cory's sleek purple nylon one-piece.

"We didn't have gold zippers," Cory says. "Come on," and she strides ahead through the crowd. Apple stands up to follow her.

She staggers. Her feet are encased in concrete; she can't bend her ankles, and the soles of her boots feel like iron plates.

"Wait," she gasps; Cory is already going out the door, parting a wave of people bristling with equipment.

Cory hears, turns back, and Apple catches her smile as though it's a diamond tossed through the air.

"Trouble?" Cory asks, then briskly shoves her hand under her sister's elbow, propelling her through the crowd.

Earlier, they stacked Apple's scarred black rented skis and Cory's long sleek purple ones in a rack, already so full of equipment Apple doesn't understand how they will ever find theirs. Then she notices that Cory has stuck a bright-red mitten (its mate is gone, she explains) on the tip of one pole.

Now Cory finds her skis and angles them down on the packed snow.

Apple is trying to avoid a large woman who is careening past, skis over her shoulder, eyes fixed on a distant destination.

Cory is already affixed to her skis. Apple reaches for her pair with a heady sense of despair. "How in the world do I put these on?"

"Lay them down flat and stamp on them," Cory says.

Apple puts the skis down on the snow, avoiding a child who comes tripping and stumbling along, and places her right foot on the metal mid-section that reminds her of the plate on an old-fashioned sander.

"Stamp," Cory says.

Apple tries to force life into the concrete boot in the form of a stamp, but her energy fails.

"Harder," Cory says.

Apple tries again and feels a mysterious click. When she raises her right boot, she realizes it's bonded to the ski. The feeling reminds her of getting her head caught in a sweater when she was four or five; Cory was trying to drag the sweater off.

"Do you remember—"

"Other foot now," Cory says. "We'll talk on the lift."

Apple's left foot goes in on the first stamp, and now, she realizes, she's permanently separated from her usual method of locomotion.

She stares around. People are dividing into currents around her, one headed toward a sort of gate and a wildly-swinging pair of chairs—she looks hastily away—the other toward an entrance to something she can't see.

"Follow me," Cory says, turning away in her flashing suit, "and do exactly what I tell you."

Cory slides rapidly along. Apple shuffles after her, trying to anticipate the abrupt changes in direction of people surging past. She realizes she's become an obstacle, moving too slowly for the general pace.

She's sweating, and her hands in Cory's big black gauntlets are trembling from her death-grip on her poles. "Wait," she gasps as Cory disappears into an eddy of thrusting skiers, and Cory, magically, looks back and smiles.

"We're almost there," she says. "We'll try the baby hill, first—"

"The baby hill is all I'll ever want."

Cory laughs. "Wait and see. Get in this line—" And suddenly Apple is behind a clot of steadily moving people, and realizes there is no escape.

A metal apparatus she can't see is clanging up ahead. She stares at her sister as though instructions will appear on Cory's face. But Cory has pulled on a pair of large, pink-lensed goggles, and Apple can't see her eyes.

Suddenly they are at the front of the line, standing side by side, and Cory sees a man snatching at a pair of metal chairs which is whirling away in front of them.

"Sit down fast when I tell you," Cory says, and then the man is beckoning to them and Cory has hooked one hand under Apple's elbow.

They plunge forward and the man, whom Cory addresses as an old friend, seizes the linked chairs that come flying in behind them, slowing them slightly. Cory shouts, "Sit!" and Apple bends her knees and sticks out the behind Billy used to call her best feature.

The left-hand chair catches her with a substantial blow; she sits, and the tip of one ski pole strikes firmly into the snow.

"Let it go!" Cory hollers but Apple, her dander up, hangs on. She thinks she'll be torn from the chair and thrown down on the snow, but her ski tip pulls loose and she sits back, triumphant, giving her sister her first smile of the day.

"I did it!"

"You sure did. And it's not easy," Cory says. "More people get injured on the lift than on the mountain."

At that word, Apple looks up for the first time and sees the mountain, gleaming under a sheathing of new snow, set with prickling evergreens. Their branches are hung with creamy festoons, and on the snow under the lift—which is rushing them through the air now, at a height of at least a hundred feet, Apple thinks—she sees the paw-marks of small animals who must have crossed during the peaceful night. "Remember when I used to always be a rabbit?"

Hidden by her goggles, Cory laughs. "I think sometimes you're still a rabbit."

"And you were the fox—"

"Chasing you around the house. I always caught you in the end, too."

"Well, you were a lot older."

"Five years. I was an outside girl, you were an inside girl."

"That's why you caught me," Apple says, and remembers the smell of the underside of the living room sofa where she used to lie pressed flat. When Cory's face appeared beneath the edge of the cretonne skirt, Apple never knew whether to laugh or cry. "I didn't know if you were rescuing me, or what," she says.

"I only tried to rescue you once," Cory says, and Apple knows exactly when she means.

"Shouldn't we talk about that?"

"Not right now," Cory says.

Now the chairs are swaying up to the summit of a long hill, and Cory warns her to prepare to get off.

Apple sits forward as directed and holds her poles up as though they display a banner. She begins to wonder, wildly, what slogan would be printed on such a banner: PRIDE COMETH BEFORE A FALL? THERE'S NO FOOL LIKE AN OLD FOOL? At forty-six, Apple's not quite old enough to claim that privilege—and then the chair suddenly dives out from under her, depositing her in a heap on the snow.

"Get up," Cory says, leaning down to help her, and then there's a shout and two more skiers, sliding from the lift, land on top of Apple. She is confused by metallic surfaces and the strange smell of someone's hair.

"Get up!" Cory exhorts from the other side of the pile, and Apple feels tugged at each extremity.

When she finally gets up, she's facing two people sitting in the halted chairs as though waiting to be served their first course. Two others are sprawled in the snow.

Cory is laughing.

"This is too tough," Apple pants and then, true to her training, turns to apologize to the people who fell on her. Then she nods and smiles hopefully at the couple in the stalled chairs. "I can't do this, Cory," she mutters.

"You have to." Her sister's hand is once more firmly tucked under her elbow, and Apple feels herself propelled forward on her sliding skis.

A blinding slope faces her. Figures she can't identify are flashing down, cutting from side to side as though, she thinks, their skis are knifing slices from an infernal cake.

She hears a distant voice as Cory begins to instruct her. The words sink in on a level below conscious reasoning, and she nods and begins to move.

At first she is only shuffling forward and then gravity catches her and she is sliding down the face of the slope.

She hears Cory shout behind her, but she knows nothing now except the sound of her skis sliding faster across the packed snow. A face flashes by her, then she passes someone lying crumpled, and she is picking up speed.

She hears Cory shouting instructions but they are nothing to her now because she is flying, and instinct warns her to crouch low and tuck her elbows close to her sides.

The wind in her face is sharp and raw and her skis sing over the snow.

At the bottom of the slope, she sees people shuffling out of her way or plodding along, oblivious, and she shoots through them, crouching low, and falls in a heap at the feet of a man drinking a cup of coffee.

He grabs her arm to drag her up, but she makes herself heavy as she used to when Cory was trying to haul her somewhere and lies peacefully on her back, looking up at the blue sky.

Cory skids to a stop beside her, casting a fountain of snow into her face. "Are you all right?"

"Right as rain," Apple says, studying her sister's face upside down. The goggles, she thinks, make Cory look like a praying mantis; she is rubbing her mittens together as the mantis used to do in their mother's garden.

"Get UP," Cory says, and reaches down for Apple's arm, but then she loses her balance and tumbles beside her sister and for a moment they both lie on their backs and stare up at the sky.

"You've got to make turns, you can't just go straight down," Cory says, close to Apple's ear, and Apple wants to dispute that but can't find the words.

"I like speed," she says and it is not an apology but a reclaiming. "I've been moving so slowly these last years," she goes on to no one in particular; Cory has scrambled up. "I forgot how much I like to fly."

"I'm going to put you in ski school, they'll teach you how to turn," Cory says ominously, and Apple remembers table manners, dancing lessons. "You're a menace on the mountain, you'll hit somebody," Cory goes on, and then she chuckles low in her throat and adds, "I didn't think you had it in you anymore, Apple."

She lets Cory haul her up and drag her along toward a knot of people who are wearing sky-blue uniforms, she lets Cory introduce her, produce a credit card, make all the arrangements, but really she is not there, she is up at the top of the slope when her skis began to slide and she knows she will not learn to slow down, now or ever, she knows the time for turns has passed.

A few minutes later she is standing at the top of the baby slope, watching the neat arabesque the instructor is carving in the snow.

He stops halfway down the slope and gestures at her to come, and Apple leans forward slightly and hears the packed surface begin to slide under her skis.

She is picking up speed and the wind is stinging her face, and just as she is about to crouch down and head for the bottom, she hears the instructor shout and leans slightly, shifting her weight, and one ski begins to carve a slow and graceful turn.

The other follows.

She is now heading in a completely unexpected direction, straight toward the festooned pine trees, but another shout alerts her to the possibilities and she feels herself shift and the ski she thought was going straight for a tree begins to turn slowly, carving its graceful turn.

She is heading now in the opposite direction, across the slope, and she sees the sun flashing on untrodden snow under the lift and catches sight of someone up on the chair, looking down. It is Cory in her purple suit, and she calls as Apple turns on her downhill ski and begins to carve her way across to the other side. The instructor is waiting for her, and when she stops at his feet—not knowing how, really, the skis seem to stop of their own accord—he tells her that her turns are not bad at all and she sees his reddish-blond moustache lifted by his kind and encouraging words and realizes with a burst of joy that here is a man who is trying to teach her something.

She listens as she listened when the obstetrician was guiding her through Little Billy's birth, as she listened to her father on his deathbed, passing on all he could remember of his life, as she listened to the cardiologist who told her their mother was dying—literally of a broken heart, she realizes now: all authorities she recognized as though by instinct. All men.

But this man, this instructor, is teaching her about speed in the guise of how to control it, and she knows no one, not even Billy, has ever taught her about speed.

They all wanted to teach her to slow down, and she learned that lesson well, until even the possibility of speed passed out of her life just when Little Billy was learning to drive, and she railed at him about obeying the speed limits and wished it was still possible to have a governor put on his car.

At the end of the hour, the instructor releases her to ski down the baby slope on her own, and she curves and swoops as gracefully as a swallow, she thinks, picking up some of the speed that intoxicated her on her first run.

At the bottom, she sees her sister, watching attentively in the midst of the mob, and raises her arm to wave. It is the first time since childhood she has learned something quickly, and she feels the instructor's kindness and her own competence like fresh blood running through her veins.

"I'm learning!" she calls to Cory. "Did you see me making my turns?" And in her excitement, she loses her balance and plunges head-first into the snow at Cory's feet.

⊶⊷⊶⊷⊶⊷

Of course Little Sister's fallen in love with her first ski instructor, it's only what I or anyone else would expect, given the situation she's lived in for so many years: Cory thinks this over and over to pacify herself as Apple babbles all the way down the mountain.

Cory has put on an old Leonard Cohen tape, and now she wonders if Apple notices: "For he has touched your perfect body with his mind."

That, it appears, is what Apple wants with all the intensity of a starved twelve-year-old, and Cory, suppressing a smile, guesses that her sister either believes her body is perfect or else—and this is really startling—that it doesn't matter: the stretch marks on her stomach, the sag of her breasts. Leonard Cohen, Cory suspects, would have something to say on that subject, something sweet and sharp about the foolishness and inevitability of middle-aged love.

"He was so darned kind to me," Apple is babbling, and she looks like a heap of indiscretion, Cory thinks indulgently, her hair pasted with sweat to her reddened forehead, her ski jacket open, her legs sprawled at odd angles, hands moving restlessly across her thighs. "I just don't understand why he was so darned kind to me."

"He's paid to be kind," Cory says, and then regrets her remark, knowing that kindness is never bought. "I'm glad you had such a good time," she adds quickly. "I thought for a minute there you weren't going to be willing to learn."

"I always learn when someone is kind to me," Apple says, and Cory wonders if there's an implied criticism here, something Apple has never before dared to voice.

"Wasn't I kind?" she asks, and realizes for the first time that she doesn't know what answer to expect. They are moving out of familiar territory.

"No, you weren't kind, you were a boss and a bully," Apple says quietly, and Cory knows the time is coming when much will be revealed.

"I made us a reservation at ALL OUR RELATIONS, I think you should soak in the hot tub, have a massage, otherwise you won't be able to walk tomorrow," Cory tells her, quickly changing the subject.

"What in the world is ALL OUR RELATIONS?"

"A spa. The best. You'll like it—" but Cory isn't so sure; this experience may lie even further outside of Apple's experience than flying down the mountain.

"Just tell me what to do when we get there," Apple says, and Cory forgives her for her remark about bossing and bullying.

They are silent, listening to the tape, until Cory pulls into the parking lot. In front of them, a set of low rounded buildings marks the hillside; a trail between totem-like piles of white stones leads to the entrance. Cory explains to Apple. "Navajo sweat lodges—I think it's a brilliant idea."

"What happens in there?" Apple asks.

"Just about anything you want."

Apple glances at her, but Cory realizes she is no longer afraid and feels a little ashamed of trying to intimidate her.

A cloud of cedar-smelling smoke billows out as they open the front door, designed to look like a tent flap. The front desk is presided over by a tall man with flowing white hair; Apple looks at him hungrily, and Cory wonders with a flash of dismay what kind of treat her sister is seeking.

They are handed towels, locker keys and kimonos in what Cory knows are intended to be Navajo blanket colors—red, black, blue— and dispatched to the locker room.

"Everything?" Apple asks as they stand in front of their lockers in the smoothly paneled, warm room.

"Everything," Cory tells her briskly, and remembers how frightened Apple used to be of their annual physical, how she pleaded to be allowed to keep on her white cotton underpants.

Cory turns her back and takes off her many layers; she wants to grant Apple the privacy she believes she needs.

Leading the way to the showers, Cory remembers Apple pattering along behind her in bunny slippers on the way to the evening bath, never protesting even though Cory sometimes handled her roughly and allowed shampoo to get in her eyes.

The shower is a single large cube with four outlets. Finding her sister by her side, Cory glances at her surreptitiously. Apple has aged into a rounder, more solid version of the little girl Cory remembers; short stout legs, curving belly shelving over the dark wedge of pubic hair, breasts tipped down by their big dark nipples (Cory remembers them small, new, pink as coral), thick muscular shoulders suspending arms that swing capable broad hands. Cory thinks her sister is a measure of all the responsibilities she's undertaken, then wonders what Apple sees in her body, what she's noticing.

"How do I look?" she asks. "Not bad for fifty-one?"

Apple considers her for a moment too long, then says, judiciously, "You're awfully thin."

"But I'm strong," Cory says, making a muscle, and Apple touches it.

"Not bad," Apple says, but then she flings up her right arm

and makes a muscle that moves like an independent creature under her skin.

"Where'd you get that?" Cory asks, feeling it gingerly.

"Gardening. I haven't completely given up," Apple says dryly.

Cory is suddenly dismayed by how little she knows.

"Have you started menopause?" she asks, as though to gain an advantage.

"Not really. My periods are a little shorter, that's all."

"You will, in the next year. It all happened to me between forty-six and forty-seven."

"What happened?" Apple asks, drying herself. "And don't make up a horror story, Cory."

"Me—!" But then she remembers. "You mean when I tried to tell you the so-called facts of life?"

"You just about put me off sex permanently." Apple leads the way into the changing room, where they put on their kimonos.

"Well, somebody had to tell you what to expect. Mother wasn't going to."

"She gave me a book," Apple says. "'The Stork Didn't Bring You.' I liked it better than what you told me."

"I wanted you to be careful."

"So tell me about menopause," Apple says.

"It's not bad. Some night sweats, hot flashes and then it's over. The whole mess, I mean."

"Mess—?" Apple looks at her.

"All those horrible birth-control devices, and the blood. You know what I mean."

"It isn't as bad as all that," Apple says quietly. "I mean, when you consider the alternative."

"The alternative is a lot more freedom, and a lot more energy, and I don't even take hormones," Cory says quickly.

"Dr. Stodgell has already told me I'll need to start taking them. He gave me a lot of very good reasons. You know Mother died of a heart attack."

"Let's go for our massage," Cory says wearily.

They walk back to the main building and wait in front of a fire, burning in a circle of stones in the middle of the floor. Apple looks at the people who stand warming themselves, anonymous in their blanket-colored wraps; in their near-nakedness, they seem child-like, passive and good-tempered. From time to time, a fully-clothed person arrives to escort one or two away.

"It's like the entrance to heaven," Apple whispers. "Maybe they'll keep us here forever."

"Dream on, they'll get us out exactly on schedule," Cory says.

Finally a slender young man comes calling their names ("St. Peter himself," Apple observes softly. "Only where are his keys?") and they follow him down a long sloping path, through bare trees, and out into the glittering sunlight.

St. Peter produces a key and unlocks a door. Cory ushers her sister in. She locks the door behind them while Cory admires the pool, oval, surrounded by carefully stacked stones and a fence made of silvery redwood. Steam rises from the surface of the water until Cory turns a switch and jets begin to bubble and spray.

Apple drops her kimono and jumps in, ducking her head and coming up smiling like the little girl Cory remembers, who began each day so hopefully.

Cory gets in more slowly. The warm water penetrates her skin, relaxes her bones; she leans back, floats, looks up at the sky, which is beginning to lose its extraordinary blueness. For a few minutes, she floats, her ears full of water, wondering if they really need to talk.

Then she hears Apple beginning. Her words are vibrations in the water. Cory looks at her sister, realizing for the first time how beautiful Apple is, round and sleek, rolling in the warm water as comfortably as a seal.

"So why did you try to ruin my wedding?" Apple asks.

"I didn't think you should marry Billy Long."

"That wasn't up to you." Apple paddles away, turning to look back at her sister.

"I know. Or at least I know that now. Twenty-one years ago—"

"Twenty-four—"

"—I thought I was responsible for you, I thought I could save you from a disaster."

"It hasn't been a disaster," Apple says, setting her back against a water jet; bubbles foam around her, and she points her toes, admiring, Cory can tell, her tangerine-colored toenail polish.

"If it hasn't been a disaster," Cory asks, "what has it been?"

"A marriage," Apple says.

"What's that?"

"You don't know, do you?"

"I managed to avoid it, except for that one slip, years ago."

Apple doesn't laugh. "There's a lot you don't know, Cory."

"Do I need to apologize? After all this time—"

"Yes," Apple says.

Cory draws a breath. She wants to lie back on the water, give herself to its warmth and motion. But Apple is waiting, and Cory feels the implacable tug of an old habit: she must answer her sister, she can't leave her empty, waiting. "All right," she says. "I apologize."

"I accept your apology," Apple says after a moment that seems, to Cory, agonizingly long.

"Is that what's kept you away all these years?" Cory asks. Apple doesn't say anything, and Cory adds, "I thought it was the sale."

"The sale was part of it," Apple says succinctly.

"You were mad at me about that, too, but I still think I was right."

Apple turns away, pressing her breasts against the water jet, and Cory admires her white shoulders. "Maybe you were right, in the end—" Cory paddles closer, to hear—"but you sure as hell made a lot of trouble for us."

"Who's us?" Cory asks, looking at Apple's curls (how she always envied them), catching bubbles from the swirling water.

"Billy and me, mainly, but also Mother and Father."

"I only wanted my fair share. The way you were all jiggling numbers, recalling stock, I had to protect myself."

"You didn't trust us," Apple says. "You didn't even trust me."

"You were protecting your interests, and Billy's. I wasn't a priority," Cory says, and tastes her old bitterness.

"We tried to be fair. You never had anything to do with the business, you couldn't possibly understand the complexities."

"Who said? Billy?"

"As CEO, Billy certainly understood the way the company worked better than anyone; Father knew that when he put him in charge."

"Common sense is all that's required," Cory says. "You always treated his job like some kind of mystical calling. I knew as much about the business as he did, just through osmosis."

Apple looks at her sister over her wet shoulder. "Billy gave his life to the company. That counts for something. You never even bothered to come to board meetings."

"I didn't see the point of being a rubber stamp."

"It was an obligation and an honor," Apple says. "When Father put us on the board, he expected us to attend regularly, learn something about the source of our income."

"But the one time I tried to ask why my dividends were never raised, you treated me like a pariah."

"You refused to understand why profits had to be ploughed back into the company. You never have understood loyalty, Cory, you're always out for yourself."

Cory calms herself, considering this. "You're right," she says, after a while. "I never have understood loyalty, and I'm always out for myself." She likes the feel of those dreaded words, as though by repeating them she's accepted their weight and authority.

"I call that selfish," Apple says. "There were a lot of other people involved."

"Sure, but if I hadn't insisted on knowing what was going on, you would have screwed me, you and Billy."

Apple turns. "Why do you hate him?"

"Because he separated you from me."

"He did no such thing—"

"All your loyalty went to him, Apple."

"That's marriage," Apple says, sliding onto her back to float, and Cory knows she is filling her ears with water, she doesn't want to hear anymore, at least not now.

They spend the rest of their hour in silence, paddling in the warm water, getting out on the edge to cool—Cory admires Apple's flushed skin, she looks like a ripe peach. Then they dip back into the water, float, stare at the sky. Cory knows this is only the first of many conversations and she tries not to dread what will come.

Silence has kept us apart all these years, she thinks, and remembers how she missed her sister, year after year, until the ache turned into a profound numbness.

Silence is what we were taught, she thinks, remembering their parents' white bed and how unwilling their mother always was to lie down in the middle of the day, disturbing the symmetry of the unwrinkled blanket cover.

A bell rings, alerting them to the fact that their time in the tub is over, and Cory gets out first—she has a feeling Apple may never come—and puts on her kimono. "We have a massage next," she says enticingly, and Apple clambers out and pulls her kimono on over her damp pink body.

St. Peter arrives smiling to lead them up to a room at the top of the biggest hogan, a long room with windows that look out on the mountain. Tall screens divide the room into sections, and Cory sees her sister look around uneasily. Other people are already lying prone on tables, half-covered by sheets.

They are led to two of the tables, and then St. Peter bows himself away and two men appear, dressed in white linen, like secular saints, Cory thinks, their attributes vials of oil. Dim drumming begins in the background.

A look of consternation passes across her sister's candid face.

"Men give the best massages, they have stronger hands," Cory says reassuringly, and notices that Apple after a moment of hesitation drops her kimono without a quiver.

Then they are both lying naked on the tables, face down, and the two white-clad men are advancing, preparing to lay on their hands.

As soon as she is touched, Cory drops away into vivid images. This touch is neither a caress nor a warning, it does not prepare the way for anything except the next touch, and then the angel is leaning on her spine, and she can feel his hands listening.

The core of my body must vibrate with messages, Cory thinks. Here is an interpreter who can't be put off with mere words. She sinks deeper into her visions as he begins to knead her knotted shoulders, and then she hears Apple groan.

That's not like her, Cory thinks, coming briefly and unwillingly to the surface. I've never heard Apple do anything but whine, sob, squeal—not a limited spectrum, but one that contains no shade darker than blue. At the dark end of the spectrum, she knows, her sister must match her groan for groan, in ecstasy as in misery. Apple's groans come from deep in her belly, they are as powerful as the last sounds wrenched from the dying.

Cory remembers their mother, narrow as a stick on her deathbed, her rattling breath the last sign of vitality, remembers how she died finally in choked silence, her chest too narrow to hold a sound, crushing her struggling heart.

Now she wishes for her sister's silence so she can sink back into the rose-petal heap of visions that succors her during dark nights when she knows she will always be alone. Pride is the first petal, and then the fanciful imagining of fresh starts, new directions: all the initiatives that are buried by love.

Finally Apple is quiet. The drumming has taken over along with the silent hands.

Soon the past begins to present Cory with precious flashing fragments: Apple's face at the alter when she heard Cory's protest— and Cory feels the flush of that triumph and wonders if the angel is feeling warmth under his hands.

Then she remembers Little Billy's face, a fat, preposterous boy-infant who never let Apple out of his sight, pawing at the buttons on her blouse, frowning over her shoulder at his intruding aunt;

And then their father, at the end, asking for a tape-recorder so he could whisper his memories into it. Later they found the tape had been erased and assumed he had, in a last spasm of discretion, destroyed everything they'd wanted to know. Apple had cried, burrowing into her sister's arms, Billy being absent on some errand.

Added to these signs and symbols is the dim flat kiss Roy gave me, Cory thinks, the last time I saw him, when against my own grain I pleaded with him to be careful. He'd already been warned. The kiss, colorless as glass, showed that he was already gone; and, more vividly, Tony's shoulder that morning, the solid feel of what she couldn't see, before he shoved himself out of her bed and pushed his feet into his boots; and in a rush after that, stained-glass-colored fragments of all the men she's loved, their names forgotten, their essential identities preserved in a glance, a touch, a certain tone, a bit of chest hair, a penis crooked like the neck of a summer squash, nipples dark as old coins, bellies and backs beginning to show the effects of labor, of the pull of gravity.

In their cries, I always hear that call, she thinks, the first and last summons, denied all day, until in the dark of the night in a strange woman's bed (and I know I've always been that to them, strange, a stranger), the essential cry flies out, indiscreet, indiscriminate, flashing jade-green and blood-red in a dark room.

Would Apple, faithful Apple, ever understand?

She feels her sister watching her and opens her eyes. Apple, on her back now under the masseuse's hands, has turned her head and is studying Cory.

"What is it?" Cory asks softly.

"Did you have that baby? Frankie said you were pregnant at my wedding," Apple says, without any hesitation.

"Yes," Cory says, as quickly.

"What happened to him?"

"I gave him away," Cory tells her, the familiar dryness slipping over her voice. "Put him up for adoption. I only saw him once, the day he was born."

"Oh, God," Apple groans, and Cory wonders why now under the hands of these silent healers the question and its answer have sprung.

"We'll talk later," Cory promises as Apple closes her eyes—is she close to tears? Cory wonders, amazed.

The silence between them now is a new silence, informed by what they have begun to say.

"Did you enjoy the massage?" Cory asks Apple later as they are making their way down to the locker room.

"I didn't know men could do that," Apple says soberly.

As they dress, they listen to the voices of the other women in the locker room. Women dressing and undressing together lose all discretion, Cory thinks.

"I like women," Apple admits softly, "sometimes I think I like them better than men. Not THAT way," she adds quickly.

"I don't like them THAT way, either," Cory says.

"You don't have to lie to me, Cory."

"My God—my life has been nothing but men," Cory says, and wishes it didn't sound like a boast. "When I think of all the time and energy—"

"People here apparently don't think that," Apple says, turning away to put on her jacket.

"And you want to believe them, you have some reason—"

"The truth, Cory. That's all. I remember the crush you had on that girl when you were twelve."

After a moment, Cory says, "You told on me, didn't you?"

"I was scared. I thought something bad was going to happen to you. I never saw anything like that before."

"Like what?"

They are facing each other, and the other women have fallen silent.

"The two of you in bed, that Sunday morning. Your hair on the pillow."

Cory laughs. "Is that all, Little Apple? Is that really what frightened you?"

"I shouldn't have told Mother. She broke up your friendship, didn't she?"

"Yes," Cory says, shortly.

"I have to take responsibility for that."

"It would have ended, sooner or later. Laura was already getting ashamed. Do you believe me, now?" she asks. "Or do you think Tony's just . . ."

"Entertainment? No, I don't think that. I don't know what to think about that man"—and Cory knows Apple has tried hard not to say, that Indian.

"It's complicated," Cory says, aware now of the other women's intent silence. "Let's get out of here, Apple." She straps on her concho belt and pushes in her .357.

"That's really outrageous, wearing that gun everywhere," Apple says indulgently, and Cory smiles. "I mean, it's not as though your life is in danger—"

Cory doesn't say anything.

Apple stares at her sister. "Oh no, Cory," she says. "No. Not when we've just found each other."

Cory turns away.

8

*T*he telephone rings before light. Reaching for it, Cory sees the stars, shining down through the skylight Tony put in for her, between the ceiling vigas.

"Who—?" she asks.

"They left me something," Nancy says. Her voice is brittle. "About an hour ago."

"What?"

"A dead dog. On the doorstep. I just barely got it out of the way before my boy saw it."

"They're trying to frighten us, Nancy. The old story."

"I am frightened," Nancy says. "I want you to stop. Now."

Silence lengthens between them. Cory reaches for a sweater, and Tony, beside her, stirs.

"I don't want to stop, Nancy. I want to find out who killed Roy."

"What difference does it make? It won't bring him back."

"But justice—"

Nancy slams down the phone.

As Cory lies down, Tony reaches for her. He holds her in his arms for a moment before saying, "Stop now. It's what she wants. You got to respect her wishes."

Cory doesn't answer.

"Why do you want me to stop?" she asks, after a while. When he doesn't answer, she goes on, "You never wanted me to start."

"Trouble," he says.

"There's no way to avoid trouble in this life," she says, remembering Frankie: Nobody knows the trouble I've seen. Nobody knows but Jesus.

"Not your trouble."

"Maybe it is, Tony." Then she lies in his arms for a few more minutes, waiting, knowing that there is something more to be said. When nothing comes, she feels the edge of something very sharp, fear, suspicion, carving its way into her preoccupation.

"Why do you want me to stop?" she asks, again.

But Tony is already out of bed, pulling on his boots.

At breakfast, lecturing the five guests on the value of opening doors for people and tipping hats to women, Cory manages to avoid telling her sister that Nancy has said, Lay off.

After the table has been cleared, she takes Apple through the gate to the field behind Mabel's to wait for Andrew. Cory's pistol, as usual, is pushed into her concho belt.

"You ever take it off?" Apple asks, sitting down on the bleached, stiff grass.

"Only at night," Cory says, throwing herself down, then leaning back on her elbows to look up at the startling blue sky.

"Why?" Apple asks cautiously.

Cory considers. "I like the feel," she confesses. "I always wanted a gun, even when we were little—I saw a boy in a movie, or on television,

I can't remember which, dressed in chaps with a tin toy pistol in his belt, and I wanted that."

"I hate to think what that means," Apple says, laughing.

Cory is serious. "I don't want to be a man, Apple, if that's what you mean. Especially now that menopause has ended most of the drawbacks of being a woman."

"But you still want . . ." Apple can't finish.

"Oh yes, Little Sister, I do. This is what I call Pure Wanting."

"What?"

"When the biological urge is removed. That's something I'd like to tell my guests."

"Don't," Apple advises. "You've already got them up in arms with this manners stuff. That woman at breakfast looked like she wanted to break your neck."

Cory holds up her finger. Andrew has appeared at the gate, and they watch him make his way slowly toward them along the path.

"He looks like an Old Testament prophet," Apple says, and indeed he does, Cory agrees, with his long snow-white hair, washed that morning, she expects, in a bucket of cold water, with a gourd dipper for rinsing.

Andrew leans forward with each step so that he seems to slope toward them; he's dissatisfied with the setting, Cory guesses, feels it lacks the solemnity required for an important transaction of information.

He arrives.

"This is my sister, Adeline Long," Cory says, and with his habitual worn gallantry, Andrew leans down to shake Apple's hand.

"Here visiting?" He's learned to ask the expected questions, Cory knows, but his training in the ways of a world he abhors has not reached the point of teaching him to listen.

Before Apple can answer, Andrew's blue eyes are raking the field, which stretches north toward the pueblo and its mountain, south to the morada. He says, sotto voce, to Cory, "I'm not sure this place is secure."

"Better than Mabel's house, with all those people going in and out."

"They couldn't get away fast enough after breakfast," Apple tells him. "Cory's lecturing on Courting the Lady was more than a bunch of skiers from Oklahoma could be expected to tolerate."

"Those rules of hers," Andrew agrees with a smile.

"Hush, Apple," Cory says, then watches Apple turning before her eyes into a stubborn girl, a determined bride.

"These are Cory's rules: explicit verbal invitations for overnights," Apple begins as though reading a long boring list. "A call for a call, she says, a letter for a letter—nothing in excess. No money or favors to lovers or would-be lovers—"

"I never said that last thing."

"The rest is all the same as it was when we were growing up. Mother's rules, or yours—I don't see the difference."

"Mother aimed to control. I want to aid and abet the expression of love."

"Oh, come on, Cory!"

"She's broken her own rules more than once," Andrew mutters with a glance at Cory, who is still leaning back on her elbows in the grass.

"You've changed the definition a little," Apple admits. "Good manners mean consideration. Honesty somehow goes along with kindness."

"A contradiction in terms," Andrew notes.

"And love, as the result of faithfully practicing the rules," Apple concludes. "You should have seen their faces, they couldn't stuff down Conchita's burritos fast enough."

"And the greatest of these is love,'" Cory says.

"The Great Commandment." Apple smiles. "I remember it from Sunday School. You never went to Sunday School, Cory—I remember you kicking up such a fuss. How'd you learn the commandments?"

"I learned," Cory says briefly.

"Those skiers staying with you should ask for a rate reduction," Apple says. "They didn't come to Taos to find out what you believe about sex, or manners. To my mind they're not even connected."

"They're the same thing."

"Can we get back to the matter at hand?" Andrew asks, looking at the sisters, and Cory knows he sees their similarities and is surprised; he's always thought of Cory as one-of-a-kind.

She laughs at his bewilderment. "We're not really the same, don't worry, Andrew," she says.

"Don't be so sure," Apple says.

But Andrew is taking his mission too seriously to be amused. He looks across the field at the dark rectangle of the morada. "Are you sure we won't be overheard?"

"There's nobody around here this time of year, we're safe till Holy Week," she tells him. "Sit down."

He sits down cross-legged and rests his hands, palm up, on his knees. But still he doesn't begin to speak, and after a while Cory understands and reassures him, "Apple is in on all this—"

"I'm not, really," Apple interrupts. "You haven't told me anything," she reminds Cory.

"There's nothing to tell, yet. Roy Cross was found dead in his van up at the pass two months ago, and the Attorney-General won't do anything about it."

"That's about the long and the short of it," Andrew says.

"Have you found something new?" As she asks, Cory smiles at him, remembering something she's sure he's tucked away, too: a morning on his narrow cot in the shack at Mora, where she went to taste and test his sympathy.

"Nothing much, at this point, it's going to take a long time, everybody's afraid to talk," he says. "The old system is alive and well here. The *patrons* control everything with threats and bribes—local elections, housing permits, road contracts, the schools, anything that's potentially a source of money or power," he explains to Apple, taking a small pad out of his pocket and beginning to leaf through microscopic notes which, Cory knows, are written in a Sanskrit-like lingo he's developed himself. Sometimes he forgets the key and is in despair. "They're connected to the Mafia, we all know that, but they've got everybody in Taos intimidated. You can be knocked in the head and thrown in an arroyo, the police are not going to ask embarrassing questions, they're all buddies, it goes on and on."

"*Patrons?*" Apple asks, carefully copying his pronunciation.

"Spanish for overseers—people unofficially in charge. It's an ancient system, came here with the conquistadores," Andrew says.

"You must have found out something, you've got a lot of notes there," Cory says. "Didn't you talk to anybody at all?" she asks sternly when he doesn't reply, knowing he will respond to maternal firmness.

"Of course," he says, wounded. "I don't waste your money, Cory."

"I wasn't implying that." She pats his knee, sees Apple notice, and guesses that her sister has drawn her own conclusions—the correct ones—about Cory's past connection with Andrew. "Who did talk?"

"Nancy," he says, proud as a child presenting a wildflower, and Cory refrains from mentioning that she's already plumbed that source. "She told me Roy never used any kind of drug, not even pot, and the newest is the police are claiming they found traces of pot as well as methadone in his system."

"Any chance of seeing the autopsy?"

Andrew shakes his head. "It'll take a subpoena, and by then they'll have found some way to loose it."

"Talk to Tuttle."

"Too soon. We don't have a case yet, Cory," he says somberly. "I'm not sure we ever will. I haven't found a single witness."

"What about that doctor friend of Roy's? He drove over the pass the day before the police say they found the van. He never saw it."

"He won't talk, says he has children, apparently there've been threats."

"Did you find those hunters who went back and forth over the pass that week? They never saw his van, either."

"Left town, apparently," Andrew says.

Cory is exasperated. Reality seems to be dropping away from her project like leaves from a dying tree. "Did you get the police photos of the van, at least?"

"They won't release them. My contact—" He offers this hopefully, a bright trinket, "told me the photos show blood on the back seat and an outside door handle, but he's already told me he won't testify, he'd lose his job, probably his life—"

"He'll get protection, at the trial."

"From who?"

"Is it really this bad here?" Apple asks.

"A terrible tight little town," Andrew calls it, and Cory remembers all the local candidates he's backed, walking the streets in his worn-out boots, pasting up posters, ringing doorbells, speaking to people chewing dinner about issues they want to ignore; and all the protests he's participated in, sometimes the only person marching up and down in front of the chain grocery store with a home-made sign, warning customers against some new horror—hormones in the milk, pesticides in the lettuce. Whatever has gone wrong in the world ends up in Andrew's net.

"So where do we go from here?" Cory asks wearily, wondering whether she is the only one now who cares what happened to the small-town, small-time activist, Roy Cross.

"I'm going to talk to Nancy again, if she'll let me; she's scared, too, because of the boy. I don't want her to back out, she's about all we have," Andrew says, and again Cory out of a profound sense of compassion that goes along with a profound irritation refrains from saying she knows everything there is to know about Nancy.

"Keep your peepers open," she says, and Andrew, dismissed, lopes off across the field toward the old station wagon, down at the rear, crusted with stickers, which is as familiar in Taos as the mail truck— a harbinger of change, somewhere far down the road, disappearing in a cloud of fumes from a defective exhaust.

Apple is excited. "What's this all about, Cory?"

"I told you."

"Tell me more."

Cory sighs. "Two months ago, Roy Cross, a principled guy, a "Greeny," as they call them here, was getting ready to go to Washington to testify against the timber company—owned by the pueblo, that's the irony. They're getting ready to clear-cut the mountain. He was found dead in his van, parked up at the pass, and there was an autopsy but it was never released, and no suspects, and no trial, and now the police are saying he died of an overdose of methadone."

"His poor wife. His poor child."

"His poor community. We need him," Cory says with some asperity.

"A husband, a father . . ." Apple is shaking her head. "I wonder did he have the right to put his life in danger?"

"Quit, Apple. He had an obligation, I'd call it a sacred obligation, to those trees, just as great as his obligation to his family."

"Well, the trees are still there."

"For the time being, but the hearing didn't get off the ground for lack of witnesses, and they'll be clear-cutting in another month. Those old-growth pine are part of sacred pueblo tradition; Roy felt they kept the people on the right path. Others disagreed. They say food and education are more important, and they don't have another source of revenue, especially with tourism down."

This doesn't interest Apple. "How's his wife going to survive, without him?"

"She works. She's OK."

"I thought Andrew said there were threats."

"Oh, threats . . ."

Apple looks shocked. "Like what they painted on your Jeep."

"That was nothing. We all get used to that, here—" Cory touches her pistol.

"I know you're tough, but that poor woman—doesn't she need to be afraid?"

"If we start being afraid, we're finished." Cory is glad Apple hasn't noticed the bullet hole in the jeep's windshield.

"She has a son," Apple says.

"Hostage to the future, you mean."

"Yes." Apple nods. "A woman with a child can't expose herself to danger."

"I have," Cory says rashly.

There is a silence. Cory stares at her sister. Apple returns her straight look.

"What happened to your baby?" Apple asks finally.

"I don't know, and I don't want to know."

"Oh, Cory." Apple slides her arm around her sister's waist and Cory thinks, This is what I've wanted since Mother died, this touch, this understanding, this comfort. "How have you stood it, all these years?" Apple asks.

Cory says proudly, "You're the first human being I've told."

"If I'd had to give up Little Billy . . ."

Cory musters herself. "It wasn't like that, Apple. I didn't want a child, I never have."

Apple pulls away. "I just don't see how that's possible."

"Well, it's always been possible, for me."

In the silence, Apple pulls a sprig off the chamisa; its sharp medicinal smell fills the air.

"I refuse to be a martyr to anyone's preconceptions," Cory says tartly, but she is aching; the feel of her sister's arm around her waist has been replaced by the cold touch of the air. Apple, she thinks, Apple— listen to the words I'm not saying.

But Apple is not a mind reader and as they sit in the prolonging silence, Cory remembers that she has not been willing to run the risk of telling the truth. Her account is nothing but an account, everything of importance has been left out. She draws a deep breath and says, "That's one of two secrets I've been meaning to share."

"Share?"

"The approved word for confidences nobody wants."

Apple ignores Cory's lightness. "What else do you want to tell me?"

Suddenly Cory is frightened, and as always fear pushes her further along the path; she can never turn back once she's recognized her own timidity. "It's about Billy," she says, and catches a glimpse of her motivation, so old now it has a faded familiar quality like a pillowcase washed too many times.

"What about Billy?" Apple's hand, mechanically picking the chamisa, quickens.

"It was years ago, Apple, it can't matter now."

Apple says, "If it can't matter now, there's no point in telling me." She gets up, brushing off her skirt, and starts back toward Mabel's before Cory can think of a reply.

Has she understood? Did she know, all along?

But if Apple knew all along, Cory thinks, then the wind has really gone out of my sails, there's nothing more for me to tell—and realizes for the first time how important it is to have something new to impart, some secret bit of information her sister will not be able to resist, a bright trinket for her magpie's nest. Now she remembers dancing along the terrace wall at Apple's wedding reception, dancing with her secret, which was her pregnancy but also her willfulness, her determination to survive, to flourish—and poor old Aunt Polly shouted at her to come down, to behave, with the tent full of wedding guests only a few feet away, and her dress, which Frankie had sewed up at the wedding, bursting open again.

She hurries after Apple, already halfway across the field on her determined retreat to Mabel's—for what? Cory wonders. What is her sister's purpose in life, other than simply to go blindly on?

Coming up behind her, she recognizes the stubborn line of her sister's neck and shoulders, and says, with as much fervor as she can summon, "Apple, we need to tell each other the truth—that's been the trouble, all these years."

"The truth?" Apple asks over her shoulder, still walking rapidly toward the refuge—other people—Mabel's will provide.

"Never talking, never seeing each other, never even writing— you sent me a Christmas card last year with "Mr. and Mrs. William Long" printed on it; this year it was a poinsettia."

"I came all this way to see you," Apple reminds her. "I practically invited myself."

Cory follows her through the gate. They stop in the lee of Mabel's house, and its stout shadow falls over them. "You came. But I still don't know why."

"I need you, Cory," Apple says in a stifled voice, and she wraps both arms around her sister so suddenly Cory nearly loses her balance.

"Billy—?"

"Not the way you think." Apple burrows her face into her sister's shoulder. "Time's wasting us like some tropical disease—"

"Tell me."

"Not yet."

"When?"

"Why do you want to know?" Apple is staring at her sister, and Cory feels ashamed.

"I don't want to know anything you don't want to tell me," she mumbles.

"Sorry." The single word is harsh.

"But why did you come here if you don't want to resolve any of this?" Cory asks, harsh in her turn.

"I wanted to see what's happened to you. We hear all kinds of rumors at home." They are back on familiar territory now, and as they walk into the house, Apple amuses Cory with a recital of gossip picked up here and there in the small town no one is ever allowed to escape.

They all come back in the end, Cory knows, the wildest reprobate buried under a neat stone in the family plot. Death and money will claim me, too, she thinks, and makes a mental note to transfer her investments to New Mexico, no matter what the accountant says, and to buy one of those pigeon-holes in the Episcopal church she noticed on Christmas Eve because they were five inches from her elbow: neatly-labeled drawers filled with the ashes of people who died here as strangers.

⊂══⊃⊷ ⊂══⊃⊷ ⊂══⊃⊷

I didn't want to do this, Apple thinks, jostled forward onto the neck of the Indian pony as it breaks into a wild shuffle. I told Cory I didn't want to. I haven't ridden in fifteen years.

At the same time she presses her weight down into her stirrups, sinking deeply into the heavily embossed western saddle. Although the pony is still careening sideways, she is now welded to his back and nothing short of a low-hanging limb—and they are out on the bald bare mesa in back of the pueblo, there're no trees in sight—can unseat her.

Cory shouts, and then Apple hears her sister's little roan mare pattering along in her wake, and thinks with her old pridefulness that her sister will never be able to catch her, her pony is faster as well as wilder than the sleek little mare Cory keeps at the pueblo for her own use.

Then she is abruptly drawn up—or the pony is—so abruptly she loses a stirrup, and Tony is jerking at the reins and the pony is tossing his head, foam flying from the bit.

Tony raises his whip arm and Apple cries out as he lashes the pony across the crupper.

As the pony leaps away, Apple begins to slide. She closes her eyes and breaths deeply, knowing that if this is the end she is ready to go.

Next she is lying flat on her back in the chamisa. A stone has grazed her elbow, she feels blood, and Tony is already there beside her, wiping the place with something surely unhygienic.

Cory, up above on her horse, is saying words Apple doesn't hear.

"I'm all right," she gasps, willing Tony and his unsavory rag away. Why doesn't Cory get down? But Cory continues to wheel and cajole overhead, her mare's hooves crushing the scrub near Apple's head.

"Come down here, Cory," she mutters, but Tony is sliding his arm under her, propping her up, holding a plastic bottle to her lips, and she drinks reluctantly.

Then she turns her head away and shuts her eyes. Once they

are closed, she can't seem to find the will to open them, and she smells Tony, smoky as a corncob-cured ham, and wonders how Cory stands that smell.

"Are you all right?" Cory keeps repeating, up above, and Apple wants her touch so much she lies still without saying anything or opening her eyes until she hears Cory jump down out of her saddle.

Tony's smoky flavor gives way to the sweet sharp smell of her sister's sweat, and Cory is asking her to open her eyes, with a hint of desperation, although Tony is repeating that Apple's all right, just a scratch on her elbow, he's taken care of that.

Apple presses her cheek into the soft dirt, and suddenly she wants them all to go away, even Cory, to leave her to rest and remember.

The darkness inside her eyes brings back the last time she was blinded: in the delivery room after they dragged Little Billy out, in the coldness and glare that were worse than the crippling pain of her long labor.

She closed her eyes then to the events that were occurring around her, inside and outside of her helpless body, and afterwards she couldn't open them, even when the O.B., dear old Dr. Lincoln, pleaded with her, even when Billy was allowed into the delivery room to try to make her see (as they said) reason.

"I remember when Billy was born," she says, and then she feels her sister crouching in the dirt beside her and hears her telling Tony to take the horses back, she'll find him later.

Apple can't believe her sister has actually dismissed that man (as she thinks of him, imitating, she knows, their mother). She can't believe anything she might have to share (Cory's new word) can equal the intensity of the Indian's presence.

His knee was near Cory's knee as they rode slowly, side by side, out of the coral and onto the mesa, silent together, deeply intertwined, while Apple followed along behind like an ignored child.

"Why'd you send him off?" she whispers.

"You started to tell me something." Then Cory is raising Apple's head to rest it, comfortably, on her knee. Apple turns onto her side, curved toward her sister like a nursling, and now her cheek is on Cory's hard knee and she feels the edge of her boot under her ear.

Apple says, "I'm going to tell you about when Billy was born because you've had a baby, too."

"It hurt like hell," Cory says, smoothing Apple's brushy hair back from her forehead.

"I thought I was going to die, and I wouldn't have minded it, just like now when I fell," Apple tells her.

"You thought you were going to die when you fell off the pony?"

"I let go, I just dropped."

"Is that what you want, Apple?"

"Yes," Apple says. "Just to drop. Let go. Just like when Little Billy was born."

Cory hesitates. "And never—with Billy?"

"No," Apple says, and for the first time, she knows, they understand each other.

"Why not?" Cory's question is as soft as her hand which is palming Apple's cheek, streaked now with dirt and tears.

"I wouldn't let go, it was my fault."

"Didn't he know, all this time?"

"No," Apple says. "I made enough noise, I wanted to fool him."

"I've tried that, too" Cory says, and Apple wonders how long ago, and why, and how. "I tried it with Tony. He won't let me, though. He knows it's a fake."

"If I could just let go and fall, again . . ."

"But then it'd be over, wouldn't it? Then maybe we wouldn't need them any more."

"You mean men?"

"Men, women . . . Love."

"'And the greatest of these . . .'"

"Not that," Cory says. "The love that bargains. The only kind I used to know."

Tears crawl from under Apple's closed eyelids. She can feel them cooling her hot cheeks. She touches her fingertips to her tears. "I haven't cried in ages."

"I know." Cory's hands continue to cradle her cheeks, to brush back her hair. "It's all right."

"It's too late now," Apple sobs. "Too late to get over what happened."

"Not if you want it badly enough."

"I don't know what you're talking about," Apple sobs.

"Taking a risk," Cory says. "They're all related, you must know that."

"You mean . . . this murder . . . And that Indian . . . And what you try to teach them and they don't want to learn, at Mabel's—"

"Yes. All part of the same thing. Taking the world on, then letting it go. You can't do one without the other."

"I don't want to take the world on, or let it go," Apple sobs.

"I know you don't. That's why you've never fallen."

It's not a nicer way of saying it, Apple thinks, it's the exact word.

"We need to get you some help," Cory goes on, "find a way to unload some of this. A sweat lodge, maybe—I'll talk to Tony."

"Don't tell Tony!" Apple sits up, opening her eyes to the brilliant glare of sun.

Cory swims into view, smiling. "Of course I won't tell Tony, Little Sister. I'll just let him know we want a sweat."

"I'm not going to think about that right now. I'm going back to Mabel's," Apple says, smearing her tears on the back of her hand.

"I'm a fright," she says, looking at her sister's beautiful face.

"Yes, you're a fright," Cory says, and then they are laughing and holding each other.

"That nursery—you remember—," Apple mutters, knowing that no one else alive remembers it. "Those blue walls. I had a crib in the corner, you had a white iron bed."

"Yes," Cory says. "It was safe, or we thought it was."

"I've been trying all along to get back to that," Apple says into her sister's damp neck.

"And I've been trying to get away."

Apple looks up at her sister.

"That nursery was false security—the only kind there is," Cory says. "I wanted it for a long time, I had to break myself of it—about the time of the sale."

"Why then?"

Cory turns her toward the corral where they can see Tony unsaddling the three horses. "I knew then I might have to go on without you. I knew then I could, if it happened."

"No more safety," Apple says softly, testing the words for weight.

"Yes, no more safety. It's the only way, for me. To take it all on, let it all go, breathe."

"I thought it was the money."

"No," Cory says, "although the money matters, of course. Mainly, though, I had to let you all know I could get along without you."

"But why didn't you tell me, then? All we did was fight over the price you were going to get for your shares."

"That was the essence of it," Cory says brusquely, and Apple realizes they have come as far as they can, for the moment.

Cory walks ahead of her and speaks to Tony, who looks up from the horse he's unsaddling, and Apple wants to scream because she imagines her sister reflected in that man's dark eyes.

Cory turns to look at her sharply, and Apple wants to take back everything she's confided, even her tears, to blame it all on the fall.

Before she can begin to do that, Cory is speaking, and it frightens Apple that Tony, unbridling the pony, is listening.

"You're going to have to let me tell you about Billy," Cory says.

☞ *9*

*A*fter lunch, Cory is talking to Conchita in the kitchen about the next batch of guests, five friends from Arkansas due to arrive later in the afternoon.

She leans back against the counter tiled with blue and white birds, Mabel's choice, the house is so birdy it'll fly away some day in a high wind, Cory tells Conchita, needing her smile, but Conchita is overworked this time of year and nothing Cory can say softens her fatigue.

As she talks, Cory sees Apple leaving the kitchen, balancing her cup of decaf, and wonders where her little sister is headed, her tears forgotten, her round face made up again.

Then she forgets Apple because Conchita is saying this is her last winter, she can't face another season cooking for so many people, and Cory realizes she's hearing an ultimatum and asks Conchita why.

She is leaning on her sponge, cleaning the blue and white tiles, and she tells Cory there's no reason except being too tired, isn't being too tired enough?

"But why now?" Cory asks, beginning to try to imagine

replacing Conchita who's run the kitchen since her grandmother served Mabel, who even held things together during the actor's disastrous occupancy (and she quit once then, Cory knows) and now through Cory's first triumphant (as she thought) winter season.

Conchita doesn't answer, but something in the renewed effort she's putting into her sponging reveals that there's a secret here, and Cory goes about prying it out carefully, as though separating an oyster from its shell.

After a while Conchita admits, Yes, there's talk at the pueblo, she's embarrassed, she doesn't know how to answer the questions.

"Tony," Cory says.

Conchita nods. "People don't like it, him being here so much."

"But I've seen Anglo women all over the pueblo." Cory doesn't add that she's often thought those bright blond ladies were prizes Indian men displayed, proof of their worth in the white world.

"This is different. Tony has a wife and kids," Conchita says, wringing her sponge out in the sink. "One more on the way."

Cory's first thought is that she doesn't want to seem surprised. "Will you stay if I deal with this?"

Conchita shakes her head slowly. "Tired," she says.

"Shorter hours, then. I'll hire you a helper, someone to take over at breakfast if you'll do dinner. That friend of yours, what's her name—"

"Maria," Conchita says, noncommittal. "I don't know. I have to talk to Juan. He wants me to quit," she says, turning to face Cory.

"But you need the money, five kids, Juan's been out of work how long . . ."

"He don't like all the talk," Conchita says, and Cory knows it was a mistake to mention need. Need is never the decisive factor here. There's a bald simplicity to Conchita Cory knows she's never encountered before, except in Frankie who preserved at the bottom of that particular totem pole—the south before integration—a determined belief in her independence from the white people she refused to call her family.

Conchita begins to measure out flour for the evening's loaf. She's proving there's no end to her work, morning to evening, and Cory realizes she has exploited this woman whom she's prided herself on understanding, overworked her just as Mabel overworked Conchita's grandmother in the time before women began to defend themselves— as our mother, she thinks, ran Frankie night and day till she dropped, as they all said at the time, in harness. As though that was the way it was supposed to be.

She can't blame anyone else. Tony, when he sits in a corner of the kitchen, hardly claims any of this as necessary for his well being. How different is Conchita's work in my kitchen, Cory wonders, from the endless labor of women at the pueblo?

But those women have a purpose, presumably, even though they're excluded from the kiva and the council and some of the dances; the embattled system their work supports benefits their brothers, their sons.

Cory goes into the Big Room. Sitting down on Mabel's old couch, she tries to feel the sharp edges of her disappointment. Without Conchita, she knows, it will be almost impossible to run Mabel's, and then she reminds herself, vaguely and obscurely, as though she's reading from a dim text, that this is not the only source of her disappointment, perhaps not even its main source, and wonders at the way her life is multiplying and dividing.

"Apple?" she calls, hearing her sister's voice in the office, and knows at the same time that Apple can't help; she's preoccupied with her own difficulties.

Cory sighs. Then she realizes Apple is talking on the telephone, and wonders if she's calling Billy again, trying to re-establish herself on that cracked rock.

"I'm going to town," she shouts, and she is scowling when Apple comes out of the office, folding a piece of paper, a message of some kind—and who does she receive messages from, Cory wonders—and announces she wants to ride into town, too.

"I'm going to see Tuttle, we've got to get cracking or the whole case is going to unravel," Cory says. "You'd be bored to death."

"I have a little errand, I'll just ride in with you," Apple says, and Cory remembers driving her to the ten-cent-store the summer she, Cory, first had a license and the use of their mother's big old station wagon.

"Riding you around again," she says, trying to make it playful, but the words have an edge and Apple winces.

"I can walk," she says with dignity.

"No, come with me. Conchita's threatening to quit, I'm worried. Forgive me."

Apple looks at her sharply as they turn toward the door.

"What is it?" Cory asks.

"I've never heard you ask that before."

"What—forgive?"

"Yes. You've never in your life asked me to forgive you," Apple says.

"I'm sure I've needed to."

"Yes." Apple is circumspect, buttoning her jacket. "What's the problem with Conchita?"

"She says it's too much work, but there's something else going on."

"Tony?" Apple asks, too quickly.

"There's talk at the pueblo. His wife's expecting, again."

Apple's arms are around her so quickly Cory is startled. "Oh, I'm so sorry," Apple says.

"About Conchita?"

"No, you idiot. The rest. All your losses."

"I don't think you understand my losses, Apple."

But Apple only tightens her grip. "I'd love to do something for you, Cory."

"Visiting me is something."

"More than that."

"Be careful, Apple. Remember that time you tried to get me out of hot water, with Mother."

"The time you nearly drowned?"

"Father threw me in."

"He didn't throw you in, Cory. You jumped in the deep end."

They are facing each other on the bridge over the acequia where, Cory remembers, she once imagined her guests having tea.

"Mother never would believe me," she says, "and now you won't believe me, either."

"Mother was angry at you for going swimming with nobody around."

"There was somebody around," Cory says bitterly. "He thought it was the best way to cure my fear of the water. The result is I've never learned how to swim."

Apple says patiently, "We have different memories. Maybe we have different pasts. But I'm going to do something to make the present a little brighter for you, Cory—"

"Oh, hush!"

"Yes, I am."

"Buy me the red satin shirt in the window at High Mesa. I love that red."

Apple laughs.

Cory looks back. Against the gaunt facade of Mabel's house, Apple looks cheerful as the child Cory remembers, the round stubborn smiling little girl who attached herself to her sister with arms and legs—

"like an octopus", Cory used to complain, detaching her, although when Apple asked, "What's an octopus?" Cory couldn't explain. It was a feeling—a wet clammy clinging.

"I'm sorry I used to push you away," Cory says, grasping the smooth rail of the bridge. "I know I did, a lot—I couldn't stand your clinging."

"Remember those experiments they did with wire monkey mothers?" Apple asks, looking out through the bare trees toward the mountain.

"The wire monkeys had everything the baby monkeys needed, but couldn't cuddle?"

"Yes," Apple says. "That was the trouble with us, wasn't it?"

"I was a wire monkey mother?"

"The only model you had. The only model I had, God bless her soul."

"There is the goddess, the warm and earthy version," Cory suggests.

Apple continues on toward the parking lot. "I'll never be able to believe in a female god," she says. "I'm stuck with the male version."

"Father didn't do much for us, but it's always Mother we blame," Cory says, behind her.

"He held me, God bless his soul."

"Do you always ask for a blessing when you mention them?" she asks, unlocking the door of the Jeep.

"Yes." Her sister looks up at her. "I want them both to rest, Cory, to be at peace. They had a hard life."

A knot of laughter breaks apart in Cory's chest. "A hard life!"

"Money doesn't fix everything, you ought to know that—"

"It's done a lot for me," Cory says, going around to the other side of the Jeep.

"And you paid the price."

Cory doesn't answer. Something is hanging from the door handle which she doesn't at first recognize; she steps back to study it. It's the head of an animal, neck tendons streaming, blood just beginning to coagulate. She sees the dipping ears.

"Apple—"

"What is it?" Apple is out, coming around.

"A cat, the head of a cat," Cory says. Now she recognizes the big half-wild Tom that lived outside the kitchen door, waiting for Conchita's table scraps. "Poor old Harry."

"Who did this?" Apple, angered, sounds like their mother, ministerial in the face of her helplessness.

"I don't know, though I could guess."

"It's that investigation—"

"Or it's about Tony."

Apple watches while Cory untangles the bloody strings that tie the cat's head to the handle. The head, surprisingly heavy, drops into Cory's cupped hands, and she turns it up and examines it although Apple is gagging. Harry's fur is clotted with blood, his eyes are glazed open. His ears are drooping, the tip of his tongue protrudes from his lips.

"Get rid of it," Apple begs, and finally Cory heaves the head into the bushes, knowing the coyotes will find it. But where is the rest—Harry's body, the tomcat's long slinking spine, crouching legs, switching tail?

No time to think of that, or of what she'll tell Conchita, who loved the old cat.

As Cory wipes her hands on a rag from the Jeep, her palm brushes the pistol butt and when she looks at it, she sees it's smeared with blood.

Apple is vomiting in the bushes.

Cory goes to hold her head, feeling bedeviled. Apple has always had a sensitive stomach.

"Sorry," her sister gasps. "Did you get rid of it?"

"Threw it in the bushes."

"Somebody's after you, Cory. That pistol hasn't done you a lot of good," Apple adds, and Cory snaps at her sister to get in the Jeep, they are going to be late.

"What's Tony got to say about all this?" Apple asks, quickly recovering, as they turn onto the main road.

"Nothing."

"Will you send him away?" Apple asks, and Cory lashes out, she doesn't know exactly what she's saying but it's something about putting up with Billy all these years. The words sink into Apple's thick silence and when Cory looks, her sister is wiping tears off her cheeks.

"You have to let me deal with this," Cory says. "It's not Tony's problem, or Conchita's. It's a question of what's right."

"But if you love him . . ."

"Maybe that doesn't figure, here."

Cory knows what she must do next: find a parking space on the plaza. Get out. Lock the Jeep although she knows it's useless, then walk to the stairs that lead to Tuttle's second-floor office.

Apple is wandering away in the other direction, consulting her note.

"See you back here in about an hour," Cory calls, and as Apple turns to nod agreement, Cory sees something strange in her sister's pretty face and wonders if it was there before the tomcat's head, wonders with a renewed sense of rage and helplessness what independent course her sister has taken.

She's never any use to me, never, she rages silently as she begins to climb the dusty stairs, and then the words of the commandment she believes in and tries to live by stream through her confusion and she repeats, over and over, "And the greatest of these . . . And the greatest of these . . ." But the final word won't come.

☞ ☞ ☞

Festiva Warren is looking at Apple as though she doesn't believe a word.

Apple has explained as much as she can without revealing her sister's identity; in a town as small as Taos, Festiva would immediately recognize the new owner of Mabel's house if any more clues were given. So Apple has stayed with generalities and perhaps, she thinks, this is the reason Ms. Warren doesn't believe her. "I'm not talking about me, it's not my baby," she insists.

Still Ms. Warren says nothing.

Apple clasps her hands on her knees, wishing she had one of her big sensible purses to open, producing credit cards, driver's license, proof of her existence, which this dark slight woman seems somehow to doubt.

"I know this must seem like a strange request," Apple begins again, but before she can continue, Ms. Warren is shaking her head.

"Not strange at all, we have people coming in off the street every day, there's a lot of interest in reuniting a child with its biological parents. I believe in it, in nearly every case, except of course when the biological parent is impaired in some way that would adversely affect the child."

"He's no child."

Ms. Warren reaches for a pencil, considering. "The real problem is we don't have the mother in here telling us she wants to find him. We really can't do anything without that."

"I'm afraid my sister is too well-known here to make this application herself," Apple says.

Ms. Warren looks at her with renewed interest.

"She sent me to protect her anonymity," Apple goes on. She's learning to use slight distortions of the truth; reality is just too flat, it has no handles. "I suppose I'm wasting my time," she says with a sigh, and begins, slowly, to get up. This is the riskiest moment.

"LoveSource doesn't turn anyone away," Ms. Warren says.

"Well then, tell me what I need to do to begin the process," Apple says, sitting down again.

"It would help a great deal if we had a birth certificate."

"That's impossible, obviously." As she seizes the advantage, Apple relaxes and looks at the framed diplomas behind Ms. Warren's head.

"Where was the child born?" Mrs. Warren is poising the pencil over a form.

Apple decides to guess. "New York City," she says, and remembers Cory making all those calls the day before Apple's wedding, remembers their father complaining, later, about the charges. All the calls had been to New York.

"Date of birth?"

Apple calculates quickly. Cory was barely showing, that June. "December, 1970."

"Father?" Ms. Warren's voice has developed an apologetic quaver.

Again Apple remembers a fragment. "Brian L. Connaught," she says, proud of inventing a middle initial. That adds authority. After all, even their mother when she was bewailing Cory's connection—as she called it—pronounced Brian's name in its entirety as though it was an expensive brand.

"They were married?"

"No indeed, my sister was married to someone else at the time, but estranged. They were divorced before the child was born."

"But he—the husband—must have known about the pregnancy."

"No," Apple says with absolute conviction. "My sister never told either one of them—the husband, or the father."

"Why not?"

Now, Apple thinks, Ms. Warren's stepping outside of her role, showing simple curiosity. "She was afraid her ex-husband would try to claim the boy—" And she's out on a limb now, she knows, but there's no way back. "She felt he was as unfit for fatherhood as she was, at the time, for motherhood. And so was the biological father—they were all children, really. An amazing act of maturity, giving the baby up for adoption, but you see, she really cared."

"That's something those pro-abortion people never understand. Every child that's born is a loved child—loved by God. It's always possible to find suitable parents." Ms. Warren's pencil still hangs over the form. "And the biological father—didn't he ask?"

"The biological father never knew anything about it," she says. "My sister made a firm decision to keep the whole thing a secret."

"In those days there was so much shame."

"Not for my sister. She knew it was the right thing to do."

"Why does she want to find the child, after all these years?"

"Change of life," Apple answers promptly. "She's never had any other children, you see."

Ms. Warren nods approvingly. "She understands now the sacrifice she made."

Here, Apple understands, is the key to Mrs. Warren's cooperation. She agrees enthusiastically. "She always thought the time would come when she'd remarry, start a family, but when she was ready it was too late."

"Reunion with her boy will go a long way toward mending her broken heart," Ms. Warren says, and Apple thinks she's home free.

There are more forms to fill out, more questions to answer, even a lecture about the wonders of the computer network that links all Desirers and Desirees, as Ms. Warren calls them.

Apple sails through it all, inventive, sprightly, a flush on her cheeks that reminds her of afternoon rides, long ago, in the last light, when cold air came up from the streams she cantered across and shadows lengthened on velvet lawns. The south, oh the south, she thinks, a refrain to these satisfying questions and even more satisfying answers, and she begins to look forward to her return home, in two more days, once her work (as she thinks of it suddenly) in Taos is done. "Work, for the night is coming," Frankie used to sing over her pie crusts, her rolls, her slowly-baking hams.

Now Ms. Warren stands up to shake hands. "This poor world needs love, that's what I try to do here," she says, and Apple reassures her that she is succeeding. She also asks her not to telephone; she will visit again in a day or so, before she leaves Taos, and after that Ms. Warren will be free to call her at home.

"This is going to be a long process," Festiva Warren warns her, and Apple almost says that she looks forward to the intricate reconstruction of this lost facet of reality.

"I won't give up," she promises Festiva, "no matter how long it takes," and suppresses the impulse to tell this delightful woman about her own travails—her son estranged now for more than two years, his stubborn bride the source, Apple believes, of this separation, as well as his addiction to the group that cured his addiction—but she controls herself, she only smiles and nods and goes out, closing the door behind her.

Desirers and Desirees, she thinks, smiling, as she goes down the stairs. Now, which one am I? The answer does not come at once, and she remembers Billy all those years ago on their wedding night in the little country hotel, sitting up in bed while she lay sleepless, her eyes sore from staring into the darkness. Hearing him turn over, she thought with satisfaction, Well, at least he can't sleep, either.

"I can't make you happy, Apple," he'd said, putting his hand on her bare shoulder.

"I know." She'd finished crying hours ago, and her voice was dry and papery.

"You're disappointed." He had leaned down and kissed her shoulder and she had flinched away. "You were raised to think marriage would fix everything. Nothing easier for me than to go on fooling you. It'd work for five years, maybe ten, who knows, and then one morning you'd turn to me and say, 'I've never been happy with you, Billy,' as though it should bring the house down, and it would bring the house down, and that's what I don't want."

"I don't expect to be happy," she'd mumbled, lying to save her pride, and his. She could still see, too clearly, the white satin mules she'd put on when she changed out of her travel suit in the bathroom, and the transparent white nightgown with lace all down the front— Frankie's gift, she'd sewed it by hand. All that was now lying, a discarded froth, on the floor at the foot of the bed.

"Sex probably won't work for us for years," Billy had said. "You've been trained out of it—" and even as she protested, noisily, her eyes filling with angry tears, she'd known he was right, she never even touched herself anymore, she hardly knew what she'd felt when Billy lay on top of her at the beginning of the evening. "I know some of it's my fault," Billy had said. "I tend to come too fast, other women have told me that—" and Apple had wanted to scream—"but I'll get better, age will help. First though you have to decide whether or not you want to be pleased."

Remembering that, Apple knows how to answer her own question. I'm a Desiree, she thinks, I always have been, after twenty-five years of marriage I still only know I want to be wanted.

She is standing on the stairs, staring at a stain on the wall that is shaped like Florida, and her life is all around her, buzzing in the chilly air: how often she wanted to fly at Billy with accusations and demands, but something always stopped her, forcing the words back down her throat, and it was not Billy—for all she knew, he would have accepted her complaints, tried to justify his long absences that were not just measured in time and space but in great blanks of the mind and heart.

She didn't confront him, she thinks now, because of pride, but as she stares at the Florida-shaped stain she is not proud, she hasn't a shred left.

But I loved him anyway, she thinks, and takes one step and stops again.

Yes, I loved him, and I love him still, and this is the truth neither Billy nor Cory nor anyone else I've ever known understands. Billy gave me a place in the world as his wife.

My whole life, Apple thinks, has been composed of what he needs, the parties, the friendships, the tennis games, all essential to his standing in the community—they even call it that, conferring together. Desire never had anything to do with our highly successful shared life, she thinks, and if there is any satisfaction, now, to rest on it is that I learned to love him and I continue to love him without desire.

Apple goes on down the stairs, stepping steadily, and now she sees herself as everyone else must see her, as Cory, exasperated, has always seen her: a pretty little woman who doesn't look quite at home in her blue jeans and checked flannel shirt, whose hands sway out from her side for balance as though she's walking a tight rope, as indeed she is and always has been, but without the flair of the true-born artist (that's Cory), without making a big deal of her risk.

It's been an ordinary risk, after all, she admits to herself, only the risk of loving, and wishes she was at home, sitting nicely-dressed in her polished year-old car, driving into town to have lunch with Billy, to present to their world the necessary united front—and only his smile as he orders her a glass of sherry will reassure her that they both understand, finally, the terms of their bargain.

And now, she thinks, I have to listen to Cory nattering on about unconditional love; Cory who gave away her own son.

In the street, she stands looking at the Christmas tree lights bobbing above the plaza. There's a manger scene in the middle, and she wanders over to look at it.

A blue-mantled plaster Mary is kneeling over a fat swaddled infant, the minor characters hovering in the background. An angel blowing a trumpet is suspended by a wire overhead; it sways back and forth, creaking in the wind. There's a star, too, swinging crazily. That wind, Cory knows, has come down from the sacred mountain, stirring the pine trees Roy died to preserve.

The wind brushes the blue mantel of the plaster Madonna, flicks a bit of straw over the Babe, travels on to the hiking gear store, the vegetarian restaurant, the overflowing garbage can, the woman jerking a crying child along the sidewalk.

Apple turns away, strangely comforted. As she crosses the street, she sees Cory coming out of a doorway and recognizes her tense, wild look, which their mother used to call A Horse at A Fire.

Cory is courting disaster again, she thinks, starting toward her with a firm step. Cory is once again acting on her convictions.

"What did you do with yourself?" Cory asks.

"It's a surprise, I'll tell you about it later." Apple takes her sister's arm.

"A surprise?"

"Curiosity killed the cat,"

"I haven't had a surprise in a long time. Not a good one."

"How did your meeting go?"

"Tuttle's scared, he got a threatening call again last night, and Andrew wants to alert the F.B.I."

"I thought you already tried that."

"We did, but Andrew thinks it's worth trying again, he has a new contact . . ." Cory looks at her sister. "Are you interested in all this?"

"Not really," Apple says. "I do feel sorry for Roy's widow, though."

"She told Tuttle the kid's too scared to go to school. What are you interested in, Apple?" Cory asks.

"Whatever it is you want to tell me about Billy," Apple says, and feels her sister's arm stiffen.

"I don't know if it's wise, now," Cory says, freeing her arm. She unlocks the Jeep and Apple climbs in.

"It never was wise, before, that's one thing for sure," Apple says after Cory has climbed in and started the engine.

Cory cranes over her shoulder, backing out. "What's changed?"

"I can stand it," Apple says.

"I'll think about it," Cory tells her, pulling out into the traffic, and the secret Apple has never before had the courage to ask for retreats like the gilded star over the manger scene in the plaza, a flash, then a hint of gold, then nothing at all.

10

*T*he family from Arkansas pulls in around dark. Cory hears them arrive as she lies in the tub in the upstairs bathroom, looking at D.H.'s red and blue birds, glowing on the darkening windows.

First, their voices—two brothers, their wives, and an uncle— rise up the stairs. Then Cory hears their boots in the hall, and Shoshona's explanations as she leads them into Tony's room, beyond the bathroom, and Mabel's, even further along.

"Those two didn't sleep together?" one of the men asks, and Cory smiles, knowing how Shoshona will handle that question, hands on hips, chin tilted up—they've discussed it before: "They wanted to preserve each other's autonomy."

The last word still sounds a little awkward. The definition is Cory's, she read it somewhere, and Shoshona will accept any statement about marriage that sounds harsh.

"Good idea," one of the women says, and there's the kind of quick laughter reserved for remarks no one wants to examine.

Cory imagines the woman's husband glancing at her; they both know something dangerous has passed close by. Let it pass! Let it pass!

Silence is always the best way.

Cory knows she's always said too much, too soon. Now she remembers—and it's the first time in years—how she finally decided to leave her once-husband (as the thinks of Buddy; he has no other definition, now), years after she should have, years before she understood anything about him.

It happened because she was determined to tell him something that he was just as determined not to hear, and when she finally forced her complaint down his ears—at a little French restaurant on Third Avenue, she remembers the rich oniony smell—Buddy went numb, his face a slab she was too young to realize concealed a pit of pain.

"Don't make me talk about that, Cory," Buddy pleaded, glancing around as though he was afraid of being overheard, but she forced, forced—and how she regrets it now, not for the sake of the marriage, which was by then unsalvageable, but for the sake of kindness, decency. "I don't know what to do to make you come," he whispered finally, leaning across their empty wine glasses. "I never have known."

And she admitted, "I don't know, either—" and they left it there, silence clotting into a gag of anger and pain that prevented them from talking for weeks.

Her ulterior motive was served, however, Cory knows now: she decided that night to leave Buddy because she believed a man, a husband—and Buddy was older, too, more experienced—should know how to do that for his wife, or to his wife, she wasn't sure of the terms but she was sure he had refused her something without which life was not worth living; and for the rest of their nights together, she turned her back to him in bed and jammed her hand between her legs (not that it did any good, it was years before she learned how to help herself) and chewed her pillow until the corner was as soaked with her saliva as it might have been with her tears.

Tears were what I should have shed, tears for our youth, our helpless immaturity that caused us so much pain, she thinks, sitting up in the cooling bath water to soap herself; and she looks with gratitude at her strong, straight thighs, her lean stomach with the little cup of flesh under her deep navel, her pale breasts. My body didn't know what it needed, but I could have learned, information was floating around in the early seventies. I chose not to learn, in order to have the exquisite (as it was then) sense of righteousness that occupied for so long the place I might have reserved for the Spirit, the Spirit made manifest in flesh.

My flesh.

My body as it ages finally into strength and wisdom is what I want to bestow now, she thinks. I have the freedom at last to give myself without counting the cost, that is what age has brought me. Tony takes me quietly, thoroughly, and goes back to his wife at the pueblo, and now she is pregnant.

Cory feels the knot of pain, and at the same time remembers Apple's question and wishes her sister was sitting on the edge of the tub as she sat so often when they were growing up, looking at her older sister's body, staring at the pale tuft (as it was then) of Cory's pubic hair, her delicate pink nipples breaking the surface of the water.

I didn't want her to see me naked, Cory thinks, but if she was here now I would share the secret about the locked place in our bodies that's really not a secret but a lump of hard, crucial fact we've never had the courage to put into words:

one of the simple facts of life, simpler and more essential than what I tried to teach her about who does what to whom.

Now she hears voices in the hall again, and someone is rattling the doorknob. She calls out to ask them to wait and stands up in the tub, and as she does so a flash of light from the setting sun penetrates a line of clear glass between two of D.H.'s red feathers, and her body blazes briefly before she covers it with a towel.

But what is it I've learned, she asks herself later, in the middle of her introductory speech to the Arkansans. The speech is already so familiar—respect for Mabel's house, for the old plumbing, the old floors, the old ways; the rest will come later—that she can keep her own monologue going underneath.

She looks at Apple, and wonders what her little sister really thinks about this evening's barrage of advice; she seems as subdued, as unreceptive, as the new guests, who are also entirely focused on their food.

If I try to tell her what I need to tell her, about Billy, the baby, the past, will I lose whatever slight connection we have? Is this connection, too, dependant on willed silence?

But without the truth, what is left? Triviality. Then she remembers her father's benign, well-weathered statement, "Tout comprendre c'est tout pardonner," and wonders if he believed it, and if she dares.

Stirred, she launches into the early part of her lesson, which she usually reserves for breakfast; better to strike while the iron is hot, while one of the men, at least—the uncle—is looking at her curiously.

"I've come to believe a few things," she begins, hearing their spoons scraping the last of the posole out of their bowls. "And I like to pass them along."

She expects silence—no one ever knows how to react—,but she doesn't expect Apple to speak up.

"Cory knows a lot of things," Apple says, a little too sweetly. "I advise you all to listen."

Faces turn toward Apple at her end of the table, and Cory realizes they may think this, too—Apple's interruption—is part of the program.

She goes on hastily, "Thank you, Sister. But of course I don't force what I believe on anyone; we have plenty of people doing that, these days. I'm not an evangelist, or anything like that—"

"Just awfully determined," Apple chimes in helpfully.

Cory thinks she will simply ignore these interruptions; Apple as a child used to do the same thing, drawing a whole roomful of grownups to look her way, even, sometimes, to smile. "You see, I've come to believe that if you act as you know you should feel, the feelings, usually, will follow."

"For example," Apple says, "if you hate the weird muck you've just been trying to eat, be sure to thank the hostess for it."

The strangers at the table are drinking water, glancing at each other, wondering into what madhouse they've tumbled; one of the chain motels would have been a surer bet, is there a chance of reclaiming their deposit and leaving now?

Cory smiles at them reassuringly. "My sister and I don't agree on a lot of things. I'm sure you're used to that, in your own families."

"My people are always feuding," the younger of the two wives pipes up. "Feudin', fussin', and a-fightin'."

No one laughs, and Cory thinks she is probably the one in the family who's assigned to put out fires. "Well, this isn't exactly a feud, is it?" she asks Apple.

Her sister faces her blandly. "Just go on, Cory."

"I'm trying to."

"It's such a lot of hot air," Apple says, balling her napkin. Conchita, who is passing the chicken, suppresses a smile.

"All ideas can be dismissed as hot air," Cory says; she is regaining her momentum now, she does not think Apple can stop her. "My idea is a simple one, but that's the reason it's so workable. You've all read these handbooks on how to save your relationships, improve your lives?" Reassured, her guests nod. "They're just about following directions, really. All I'm doing is introducing you to a slightly different set of directions, more old-fashioned, I suppose. Because after all, we can't go on forever blaming the past."

"Oh, can't we?" Apple asks, smiling.

"At least I don't find that very satisfactory. Whereas, if we give the energy we use trying to find explanations to behaving as we wished we felt, the feelings will follow. To give you an example—"

"If you have a sister you don't really like very much, keep smiling at her and kissing her and telling her how pretty she is, and maybe in the end you'll start liking her."

In the silence, Conchita begins to pass the sweet potatoes, and the guests take a long time helping themselves.

"But I do like you, Apple, I always have," Cory says.

"That isn't what I mean." Apple is layering sweet potato onto her plate, and Cory remembers she doesn't even like it. "I mean the way I feel about you."

This is more than the guests can be expected to put up with; the older of the two women excuses herself, and the uncle quietly follows.

"Even so," Cory continues evenly as Conchita stands, the serving dish in her hands, staring, "even so, it's possible to turn dislike into something less damaging, simply by expressing a moderate amount of affection. Maybe only a few smiles, and no kisses—" and suddenly she is choked by a sense of loss as palpable as a bone in her throat.

She stands up from the table, clutching her napkin, tries to say the usual words of dismissal, of apology, but cannot force them out of her throat, and leaves the room.

She has never done this, in her own house, in front of her own guests, and as she hurries up the stairs to the sun porch, she feels hurt, tearful, yet exhilarated: the future is opening, the past is falling away, at last.

Apple has spoken.

The Arkansas travelers, Apple thinks as they sit by the fire in the Big Room after supper, are embarrassed, almost frightened. All four of them are looking away, like birds on a wire facing out of the wind.

Cory has come back down the stairs. Calmly, firmly, she is finishing the evening lecture.

"The truth is," she tells them, standing in front of the fire, holding up the back of her red velvet skirt to warm her long johns, which gleam like pearls, "the truth is we don't feel anything after a certain age—twenty, eighteen, possibly even earlier, depending on when the world caught us; after that the best we can do is put on good manners and pretend. We all know what we ought to feel, don't we—" it's not a question, Apple observes— "in those crucial situations, love, death, whatever—"

"I didn't know what to feel when Mother died last spring," Maureen Connolly, one of the two women—wives, Apple thinks, most definitely wives, and realizes at the same time that she has moved a little outside that category—says to her husband, murmuring the words as though she expects their teacher, implacable Cory Mason, not to hear.

But of course she does.

"That sense of embarrassment at the great moments—it's a sure sign of what I'm talking about. If you stopped feeling anything for your mother years ago, and now she's dying, all you know is there's a set of appropriate feelings somewhere, grief, rage, it doesn't really matter what they are; but they're too far away for you to claim. Still, you can put on a black dress and a sad expression and get down on your knees at the funeral and pray. That counts, because it's appropriate, and appropriate behavior sometimes produces feeling."

"Sounds like a good solution," Larry Connolly, a big gruff man who's been silent all evening, admits to his wife, who smiles appreciatively. "As I recall, that's about what you did for your mom."

"Yes, but the children really did cry," Maureen says, as though that proves something positive about the parents.

"Dead parents produce live children, a miracle," Cory says, which creates instant silence. Into that silence, the younger couple plunges.

"I feel everything I want to feel," Ned Connolly says. He's a tall young man with his older brother's long, expressive face. "I never have any problem that way."

"It's the things you don't want to feel—" Cory begins.

"Society wouldn't work, if everybody acted the way they really felt," Ned's wife interrupts.

"If your commitment is to society, as corrupt as we all know it to be—"

"We have to have some kind of structure," Ned insists, and his wife is nodding before the words are out of his mouth," and all these feelings running around wild would create chaos."

"Of course many people decide to sacrifice their souls to the culture," Cory says carefully.

"You mean to say," Ned asks Cory, "you never made concessions to get along?"

"I did, years ago," Cory says. "I got rid of a baby." She glances at Apple.

"You mean an abortion?" Maureen asks, her voice sinking on the last word.

"No. I delivered him—I wanted to go that far. But I was ashamed. I wasn't married—to the father, that is. Yes, it was shame," Cory repeats, as though fingering a raised scar.

Relenting, Apple says, "Cory, It's not really necessary—" But before she can finish, the other two women have pushed their questions, like forks, into her sister's heart. How could she have done that, they ask, give her baby to strangers?

"I knew at the time I was doing the right thing for the wrong reasons," Cory answers, but the two women are not satisfied; one even has the temerity to mention a story in that morning's newspaper— "that woman who put her new baby in a garbage bag and threw it out, because she didn't want the responsibility."

"That's not what Cory did," Apple insists. "I'm sure she wanted the best for her baby." She's not prepared, she realizes, to allow these strangers to attack her sister.

"How in the world did you have him and give him away without your husband knowing?" Maureen asks, and again Apple raises her hand as though to shield her sister from a slap.

"We were separated by then. I went to a sort of rest home in the Virginia mountains—those places existed then, very comfortable, expensive and discrete; Buddy thought I was having a nervous breakdown. It was more like a conversion."

"To what?" Apple asks, in spite of herself.

Cory smiles at her, and Apple is amazed to see that now her sister is completely relaxed. "Why, to my own way."

"But that's selfish," Ned's wife exclaims.

Now the two men lean back in their chairs as though they're witnessing an amusing performance, a sort of sideshow, the women's hour.

Cory is silent.

"If it was selfish, my sister has paid the price," Apple says.

"How?" the younger woman asks, and her glance around the drafty old room where Mabel's mahogany furniture squats alongside a few painted pieces from Mexico makes her point: how can a woman as free as Cory is or appears to be lay claim to the suffering that is woman's birthright, her pride?

Before Apple can answer for her, Cory explains, "I made a commitment to a life alone when I let my baby go. That hasn't always been easy—" and Apple wonders if the other women noticed Tony, waiting in the kitchen.

"A life alone?" the younger woman asks. "You have people here all the time."

"But I'm alone," Cory says, with emphasis. "That's the price I agreed to pay."

"For what?" Ned asks with his slippery smile.

"For going my own way."

They are silent in the face of this revelation, which Apple, armed with a little more information, can't evaluate; is Cory being pathetic, playing for sympathy?

Even at the worst moments of the sale, when Apple and Billy were on one side of the long conference table with their lawyers and Cory sat alone, opposite them, she never by word or gesture asked for mercy.

Apple often hoped she would bow her head, wipe her eyes, let her lips tremble—anything to show Billy and the other men that she felt the misery of her outcast state.

But Cory held so firm Apple could never convince Billy she was suffering—"Bold as brass," he said at one point—,and so there was no hope of mercy from the other men with their agendas and their budgets, their cell phones linking them to what one of them actually called the real world.

And Cory, ten years younger then, ten years wilder, appeared one day in blue jeans, another in a pair of shorts, asking unflinching questions to which there were never any answers, questions that fell outside the realm of the acceptable. As Apple remembers, she wants to remind them—these strangers who don't appreciate her sister, don't understand how she was formed by her past—that there is such a thing as decency, kindness, silence, even.

Not that her sister has ever practiced those virtues, but she is at bay now, or at least Apple thinks she is. Cory is still calmly looking from face to face.

"Actually, my sister's rules—the ones she's trying to teach you— are our mother's," Apple says, as though that will placate the guests.

Cory stares at her. "You believe that, Apple?"

"Tipping your hat to ladies, holding doors—"

"I didn't only mean men—"

"Sending flowers on appropriate occasions—why, it's right next to that old rule about not wearing white shoes before Memorial Day or after Labor Day," Apple insists. She realizes she has the floor; even the men are attentive.

"If they are the old rules—"

"They certainly seem like it," Maureen says. "I thought women these days were trying to shake off all that."

"Even if they are," Cory says, "the aim is different."

"The end justifies the means?" Apple asks.

Again, Cory looks at her, as though surprised. "In this case."

"And what is the end?" Maureen asks.

"Honesty," Cory says.

"It sounds like lying to get there," Maureen says.

"Hypocrisy, at least," Ned adds, with a glance at Apple.

"The truth isn't always a good idea," Apple concedes.

"The truth isn't even always the truth. But we have to act as though it is, to have any simplicity or grace in our lives." Cory is summing up.

"Well, it sure is different," Larry says finally. "I mean, people claim to believe in honesty, but when it comes right down to it . . ."

"Why is insisting on politeness such a threat?" Cory asks, but before they can answer, Apple sees the fifth member of the group standing in the doorway—the older man, Maureen's uncle, who retreated right after the meal.

Ned makes way for him to sit on the couch by the fire.

"We're not here to criticize you, Ma'am," this man says—Duke or Dude, Apple thinks his name is. "We're your guests," and he throws a reproving glance in the direction of his nephews and their wives.

And so, spreading his knees, taking up every inch on the couch—Ned shrinks back against the arm—Duke or Dude assumes control of the situation in a way familiar and restful to Apple.

She glances at Cory, willing her to remember their father, a modest-sized man with a great capacity to impress, taking up a position from which he could both cajole and control a roomful of guests, swirling an inch of brandy in a snifter, glancing around, gauging the size of his opposition: an old-time southern liberal in the years before Vietnam and Civil Rights pulled the rug out, an old-time southern liberal, facing down whiskey Republicans, back-country tobacco farmers, the artillery of the past.

Oh for the old way, and the men who fought for it, Apple thinks, for powerful old men's voices, hoarse from decades of cigarettes, for the spread of their tough old limbs, their meaty thighs. And she realizes she is looking forward to the way Billy will spill out and spread with age, becoming weighty, occupying whole couches simply by spreading his knees. Already he has begun the process: when he appears, people shift, making room.

"I believe you folks have tired this lady out," the uncle is saying after glancing at Cory's smooth pale face.

And there, Apple thinks, is the lesson applied: whether or not this particular Arkansas traveler feels any compassion for the lady of the house is irrelevant. He has spoken the words.

As though relieved, the other guests rise in a flock and make their way to the stairs.

The old man lingers on the couch, studying Cory.

"You been running this place for long?" he asks finally.

"Just a little over a year."

"Seems like it's your bully pulpit," the uncle says with a chuckle.

"That's why I bought it," Cory says. "I need people to listen."

"Ever try preaching?"

Cory seems not to mind his intrusion. "Oh, I've tried everything, at one time or another, but it's hard to find an audience. What I have to say is not very popular or fashionable, right now."

"Most folks got over their manners a while ago," the old man says, "and here you are telling them they got to start saying Sir and Ma'am again."

"If they do, they might find it possible to respect someone," Cory says. "I think that's a feeling worth having."

"Pretty well gone now, and that's the truth," he agrees.

Apple realizes he is flirting.

"But why you try so hard with folks you're never going to see again . . ."

Cory smiles at him, looking a little dazed. "They're my family," she says.

Before Apple can object, Tony comes in with an armload of pinon for the fire, his excuse, Apple thinks, to see if the coast is clear; but Cory, with a gesture more imperious than Apple could have imagined, waves him away.

"Sorry if we've plagued you, Ma'am," the old man says, getting up—he has appraised Tony with a swift glance; and both men retreat at the same time, the old Arkansan to the stairs, Tony to the kitchen and the back door which Apple hears closing quietly.

Cory sighs and stretches her arms over her head. "Thank God that's over."

"I know it's late, Cory, but we have to talk," Apple says quickly.

Cory glances at her. "You said enough at dinner."

"That was just the tip of the iceberg."

"I'm worn out," Cory says. "But talk away."

Apple grows angry. There have been too many times when Cory has told her, Talk away, as though she—big sister, tormentor, beloved friend—has no part to play in the ensuing conversation, as though she is entirely free of her sister's preoccupations.

"This concerns you, too," Apple says with asperity.

"Then why not leave it till tomorrow." Cory leans her elbows on her knees, half-closing her eyes.

"All right," Apple says reluctantly.

Cory opens her eyes. Her appetite has been aroused; it is too late to turn back, her suggestion was merely a way, Apple realizes, of tightening the tension. "On the other hand," her sister drawls, "better to get whatever it is out of the way now, you'll sleep better."

"You'll sleep better," Apple says with emphasis.

"I'm usually up most of the night reading or thinking things out." Apple knows without being told that Cory plans her lessons during those long nights when the sacred mountain is lit by the moon and the morada south of Mabel's cast its darkest shadow.

"It's about your baby," she says quickly.

"I've said all I have to say on that subject." And now Cory is their mother, sharp, assertive, turning her face away.

Still Apple insists, "I haven't said all I have to say."

"What are you going to do now, blame me? Like those women?"

Apple shakes her head. "I wasn't any help to you, at the time."

"I didn't let you know."

"I could have found out."

"I wasn't reachable."

"There would have been ways."

"I didn't come back till a week after he was born."

"There would have been ways," Apple repeats.

"I didn't want to see or hear from any of you," Cory says in a low voice. "And don't ask about the father. I never saw him again."

"Brian?" Apple asks.

"Why does it matter?" Cory searches her sister's face.

"It matters," Apple says.

Her simplicity seems to soften Cory. "He was just a boy," she said. "A kid named Peter. I met him one dark night in the country, and then again one hot day."

"And you didn't use protection?" Apple hates the word but can think of no other.

"Buddy and I hadn't been able to conceive, and he had me convinced it was my fault."

"Why didn't you tell me?"

"It was nobody's business," Cory says. "But apparently the problem was Buddy's, after all. At least," she goes on in a lowered voice, her eyes on the tips of her boots, "I knew before it was too late I could have a baby. It meant something to me, at the time."

"Of course!"

"Of course to you, not of course to me. I'd already made the commitment to my own life, begun to pay the price."

"The price?"

"'Tears, idle tears . . .'" Cory smiles as she quotes.

"You could have raised the boy."

"Not well."

"As well as anybody."

Cory says, "I've thought about this a long time, Apple, don't come here at this late date and try to argue me out of it. That was the basis for my life, that giving up. I learned then that I can't hold on, even to a baby born out of my body, a love child."

"So it was love."

"I was in love with the act," Cory says, "not the man. I would have been in love with the raising, not the child."

Apple nods. She doesn't believe Cory—her logic is too seamless—but she understands how these arguments must have consoled her, over the years. "Don't you want to see him—your son?"

Cory gets up and goes to the window. She taps the chilled glass with her thumb. "No," she says after a while. "At least, not any more. Running Mabel's seems to satisfy the urge."

"That's why you teach people."

"Yes," Cory says, and laughs. "Ridiculous as it seems."

"Not ridiculous, but the audience isn't always . . ."

"Responsive? You think a child would have been?" When Apple doesn't answer, Cory says softly, "I know how hard you tried to teach Little Billy, and look where that got you."

"Drugs and alcohol," Apple admits, "and then the cure, and then that girl. I don't know which is worse."

"You measure it all in the distance it's created between you and Little Billy, but it has another meaning for him, I imagine."

"Yes," Apple admits, and as she says it, a cold draft touches her shoulder and she looks around to see that the door to the patio has drifted open. Someone is there.

"Cory—"

Cory has already whipped around, facing the door, and Apple sees her fingers slide the pistol out of her belt. She has her thumb on the safety, and Apple hears her call out a warning.

Tony steps in.

Cory puts the pistol back in her belt.

"Goodnight, Tony," she says.

Without a word, he turns and goes out.

Apple has a sharp sense of her sister's willingness to make sacrifices.

"I want you to see your boy," she says.

Cory turns. "Don't you dare."

"Why not?"

"Not your business."

"You surely don't mean to die without seeing him, at least once."

"I saw him once, when he was born. That's more than enough," Cory says. "Besides, there's no way to find him."

Apple knows better than to say that there are ways and ways, that she will try each in turn, and one of them will surely lead to Cory's son. She only smiles at Cory and says she believes it's time for bed.

As she goes down the hall to her room, she hears Cory knocking the last logs together, banking the fire, and wonders how much longer her sister will sit there, looking into the coals that flare up and die, believing, still, she holds her secret in her hand.

11

*A*pple starts for town early next morning while Cory, her Arkansas guests departed, is rubbing a broom along the vigas in the upstairs hall. Conchita and Shoshona are holding the ladder.

None of them noticed Apple getting into her warm jacket and boots and borrowing one of Cory's cowboy hats to keep the wind out of her hair; it turned cold during the night, there is snow on the mountain. Apple feels she is being brave and determined as she launches out on the road to town.

A dog barks shrilly from behind the subsiding adobe house Cory has told her was Andrew's before he moved to his shack on the mesa north of town. Passing the house, Apple realizes she is beginning to feel the presences of what she calls Cory's people—Andrew, Martin the astrologer, Roy who has been dead now two months, his unwilling wife Nancy, their son. Apple thinks Cory is surrounded by these invisible essences, planets circling her sun.

She stops to admire a set of curious painted plaster figures, set into the adobe wall—a mermaid, a fisher king, a moon and stars. The colors are soft, the details are almost worn away.

Apple wonders if Andrew set these figures into the wall before his departure; she knows he's gifted—Cory has told her so—but in the way of Taos, no explanation followed of how he is gifted, as though the fact itself is enough.

She turns out of Morada Road, imagining people looking at her from the safety of their cars, speculating about where this pretty, comfortable-looking woman is going on foot at such an early hour. Then she realizes that nothing about her is strange enough to excite much curiosity in Taos.

Some of these people certainly know Cory and, if they recognized Apple, would have stories to tell: how Cory has never mentioned any family except for her sister, and how this sister has now appeared, out of the blue, no one knows why.

Cory is surrounded by people whose motives Apple distrusts, and she is reminded of the way she felt about Little Billy's friends during the years before he finally left home, driven out by his father, who stood in the door repeating, "I will not have it. I simply will not have it," while Apple wept in the background.

Before that, Little Billy filled her house with vague, mild people, all addicted to good manners, lies, and illegal substances, the kindest and nicest young men—and a few girls—Apple has ever met, and with the most secrets.

Finally she began to pry: where did their money come from? What did they do all day? What strange smells were loosed in her house?

At that, they evaporated, apologetically, and Little Billy followed soon after. Then AA caught him, and other presences invaded the house, counselors who spoke a language Apple found incomprehensible. Everything, they tried to convince her, depended on honesty, but Apple knows—has always known—that honesty has its limits.

They were more opinionated, but they did not last longer than the druggies, although their influence apparently did. All these people shared a membership in a world Apple never imagined, or wanted to imagine, a world, she knows now, that claimed her son inexorably, sucking him down into profound distance, profound silence.

Stopping to peer into the doorway of a museum honoring the old Indian killer, Kit Carson, she is so blinded by tears that she can hardly make out the broken wagon wheel decorating the entrance.

Tears, idle tears . . .

What is the connection, she wonders suddenly—Taos and its threadbare magic, and the Indian killer honored here, and her son who has never seen a horizon, as far as she can tell?

She crosses the plaza, looking at the manger scene that has suffered from wind and snow; the straw has blown about and the gilt star has fallen into a bush. She wonders when the powers that be will decide to take the crèche down. Leftover decorations have always depressed her, like the Chinese lanterns still swinging weeks after her wedding. Coming back from her honeymoon, she saw them sagging, bleached by the sun, heavy with rain water. She went out right away and tore them down.

Now she reminds herself that she knows nothing of the ways of this town; at home, no civic body would be willing to sponsor a religious scene, the outcry would be interminable.

But perhaps this little old mountain town still crammed with Hispanics keeps its Christmas observances, she thinks; perhaps they have meaning, too, beyond mere decorations—and she wonders, again, about her sister and Tony, that strange pair, which may, also, have a hidden meaning, beyond the old one of breaking boundaries.

It would be comforting to believe they are symbols, only, replicating Mabel's marriage with the other Tony; but there is too much between them, too much anger and avoidance and silence, to fill a symbol.

More questions.

Where have the questions come from, she wonders, remembering years when there were no questions, when the reliable pattern of her life did not need scrutiny: Saturday night at the country club, a few dances with Billy and his amiable friends, full of compliments as though she was still a girl, a deb in trailing tulle; Sunday church with the same people, who, on their knees, looked a little too meek for what Apple knows of them, the divorces, the drinking, the other petty scandals; then Monday beginning with her shopping foray into town, always carefully dressed, behind the wheel of her freshly-washed car—and the regular treats Billy provides, weekends away, dinners out.

I am as outdated as the dinosaur, she thinks, and yet even as the economy collapses and women leave home in droves, the old model persists, she knows, in songs, novels and movies: the comfortable domestic life, ruled over by a goddess or at least her earthly equivalent, a woman who has decided to make the necessary compromises to hold the structure together—what Cory calls, bless her, the primary cell of capitalism: marriage, the family, nothing more or less.

And there are still, Apple knows, primary obligations that exist outside of time and change: especially the obligation of mothers to their sons. She was not surprised to learn, years ago, that Freud called that the most blissful of bonds.

She has reached her destination. She opens the door to LoveSource.

A few minutes later she is out again on the street. The snow in the peaks of the mountain flashes, blinding her, and the icy air gets into her bones.

She has found nothing, nothing either to resolve the question or to persuade her there is another route.

Festiva, simply, dismissed her.

There is no way, she said, of finding Cory's boy, and besides, Festiva hinted, Apple's motives are in question: why, exactly, does she want to dig up her sister's past?

So she's been turned away with a thin article called "Who Am I?" and the telephone number of a national organization that helps people find people—some kind of undercover group, she thinks angrily, unused to such a brief and brutal dismissal.

Still, she clutches the pamphlet, as though at least it proves she tried. For one of the things, she realizes now, she dreads is that Cory will one day accuse her of never having cared enough, even, to ask questions, of having been so absorbed in her own life she never thought to probe her sister's broken heart.

She begins to make her way back to Mabel's, wondering how she will get through this her last day. Cory has told her she will be busy cleaning house—something about the moon making this necessary, something Apple dismisses, abruptly, with a shrug.

Suddenly she knows she can't wait to leave.

What will it matter to Cory, after all? Apple has been a nuisance, an unwished-for messenger from the past. Their attempts to find common ground have ended in anger, exhaustion or silence.

She decides to drive her rented car to Albuquerque a day early and catch the jet home.

Marching through the streets, armed with determination, Apple remembers that she arrived with the hope of some kind of reunion Cory couldn't, after all, be expected to offer, Cory who is so much more absorbed in her old house and its itinerant guests than she has ever been in her sister, or her sister's life; and Apple allows herself a spurt of bitterness before she remembers that Cory is the unfortunate one, Cory is the sister who has lost everything.

"You stop this now," Tony is saying, and because the house is empty for the first time in weeks, Cory tells him to go on.

"You in bad trouble." He is kneeling beside the Big Room fire, rubbing her feet.

As he rubs, his thumbs press into the calloused pads under her toes, and Cory shivers with pleasure. For a moment it doesn't matter what he says; they are alone by the fire, and he will not be returning to the pueblo tonight.

"You forget all about it," he orders.

Cory glances at the Adams photograph of the other Tony, which Mabel commissioned in the forties; the drinking had begun by then, and its marks and the marks of their quarrels and disappointments are plain on the man's cheeks. She's propped the photograph on the mantel, over her Tony's head, and she wonders if he has ever looked at it.

"Your uncle used to try to get Mabel to stop," she says. "I don't think it ever worked."

He shakes his head, beginning on her other foot. "That woman crazy, drive my uncle crazy, too."

"The drinking."

"Then that shooting, you know what I mean."

"Mabel was interfering in somebody's marriage, and the wife tried to shoot herself in the bathtub—my bathtub," Cory says, with a laugh.

"Same thing happen to you."

"You mean I'm going to shoot myself in the bathtub?"

"Somebody else do it," Tony says, and for a moment he holds both her feet in his hand.

Then he stands up. "You no listen to me," he says, "but I know."

"You're hearing things?" Cory is alert now, slipping on her shoes.

"Nobody want to know what happen to Roy Cross."

"I do."

"Nobody else. You stick your nose in, somebody's going to get hurt."

"Why does nobody want to know?"

"Nothing to know. He died. That's all." Tony turns away.

"You mean whoever did it is powerful enough to suppress all the evidence? And nobody's even curious?"

"No evidence."

"I haven't been able to see his car, the police have it impounded, but Andrew heard there was blood—"

"No blood."

"How do you know?"

"I saw it."

He turns slowly to face her.

After a moment, Cory says, "All right, Tony. Tell me."

"I didn't do it."

She sighs. "I never thought you did."

"But if I had to . . ."

"What do you mean?" She stands up, facing him.

"Somebody got to take care of that kind of thing."

She searches for a reaction. "You mean, you believe it was right?"

"Right, wrong—" he shrugs. "Somebody have to stop him."

"So you stood by—"

"I held him," Tony says.

She crosses her arms on her stomach, pressing as though to hold something in. "Why, Tony?"

"He ruining everything for us—don't know what he's talking about, not even from around here."

"Ruining everything . . ."

"We got to cut," Tony says. "We got to have money. We losing everybody, now—all the young guys. No electricity, heat, running water—"

"I thought the pueblo wanted it that way, they prevented the electric company—"

"All the young men leaving now. Words die, stories die, dances die. We got to keep the young men, everybody knows that now. We got to make it so they get their hot showers, TV's, electric razors."

"So Roy was sacrificed."

"We did it the best way we could."

"The best, meaning . . ."

"We didn't hurt him none."

Now she is close to him, smelling his smokiness, and her fists come up and pound his chest. "Didn't hurt him! You killed him, Tony, you killed a decent man—"

He grabs her wrists and holds them, easily, in one hand. "Quit that, now."

"So the pueblo matters more to you than life. Human life."

"Say that if you want." He is staring at her, holding her hands together. "I know what went on between the two of you."

She sighs. Someone must have seen her with Roy, and noticed how it was between them. "That isn't the reason I'm doing this."

"Doing it?" He glares at her. "You going on?"

"Yes."

He curses, under his breath.

Cory feels herself drooping like a broken branch from his hands.

He lets her go abruptly, and she drops onto the couch.

"I can't take this." Her voice is dry in her throat. "I can take your situation at the pueblo, even the new baby that's coming." He ducks his head." But this—no. Not murder, Tony. Not you holding him so they could—"

Tony has turned toward the door.

She wants to call after him, raise questions, doubts, ask for more answers. How did they kill him without hurting him? Did Roy know what was happening? And how many men, and exactly when, and who decided? And was Tony maybe just there by chance—but she knows that could not be.

All her questions drift away as Tony opens the front door.

⊂⇝ *12*

Coming into the house she had always thought of as home—my home, our home, that special place—Apple stopped and stood listening.

Silence, an invisible barrier, held her in place.

Where have they all gone? she wondered, although the house had not been full since her parents' deaths. I have only one child, after all, she thought, one husband, and one part-time helper who rotates annually as other options or responsibilities present themselves (hiring at the GE plant south of the city, or a daughter with a new baby). That hardly constitutes a crowd.

"But I wanted a lot of babies!" Apple protested to Billy when she turned forty and realized it was probably too late—too late for many reasons, only one of them having to do with her body, finally quieting, finally settling down.

When he looked startled, she said, "You know I always wanted more than one!"

Then Billy with infinite kindness had mentioned the miscarriages, the agonizing stillbirth, and Dr. Carrel's final, firm decision—"No more"; which spared them both, Apple knew, from thinking about the other reasons—their failure of faith, their failure of hope.

Was that when it all stopped, she wondered?

Stopped like an old-fashioned wind-up clock?

Standing stock-still at the foot of the stairs, she remembered asking her mother, the day before the wedding, how it was done: marriage. Love. It had not occurred to her until much later that perhaps her mother hadn't succeeded in doing it, that perhaps she was sacrificed.

She set her suitcase down.

But Billy and I have succeeded in doing it, she insisted to herself—raised a son, made a life.

She looked at the sunlight patterning the wall and remembered her mother as she lay dead, still as hardened wax. Why does it matter? she wondered, taking one step toward the stairs. Why does any of it matter when we come, in the end, to that?

But she remembered a flicker of light, of life, at the wedding—my wedding, our wedding—and for quite a while afterwards, the brightness of infinite possibility. Or had that only been Cory, prancing on the garden wall?

She went up the stairs and into the big peach bedroom (my bedroom, our bedroom.) Cory's picture, taken on the day of the wedding, stared at her from its silver frame.

My God, she was bold then, Apple thought: Cory, shouting at the wedding (my wedding, our wedding), disrupting the service, then strutting in her bursting dress on the garden wall.

Cory's photograph had pride of place, Apple thought as she straightened the picture. Even the photograph of Little Billy was smaller, quieter—taken, admittedly, when he was smaller and quieter, too. She compared the two expressions, Billy beaming over a giant Easter egg (he knew how to beam, then), while Cory . . . Well, so be it. Her sister refused to smile for the photographer—to smile for anyone.

Looking in the mirror, Apple saw her own smile, cropping up as dependably as a dandelion.

Standing there staring at Cory's pale face (no make-up, either, it was taken long before she discovered her role, in Mabel's house, as Mabel's replacement), Apple wondered if they were two halves of one whole, split before birth, never to be reunited.

What a thought, she chided herself in their mother's practical voice; what a piece of nonsense! And knew it both was, and wasn't. Practical wisdom proved more and more limited as life wended its winding way. Oh no! she thought, unzipping her suitcase and letting her hands drift through layers of slightly soiled clothes. That's not the answer.

But then what was?

She blamed the desert, now, for these endless questions. Why had she submitted to its harsh light? More than Cory's curious example—and Cory's example had always been curious—more than her own recurring doubts, the light of the desert had stripped her bare. This is how it is to accept old age, Apple thought, taking a wrinkled shirt out of the suitcase. This final stripping.

Yet THEY don't care, or even notice, she reminded herself as she dropped the shirt into the sink, for soaking. (And how reassuring these small tasks were, although no longer really necessary, as Billy sometimes reminded her; everything could be sent out—but essential in another way.) Men don't. They listen, sometimes—certainly Billy listened—when we make our moans. But they don't care, not out of callousness but because their view of the world is different. They know what counts.

Whereas whatever counted for our mother—and Apple realized she didn't know what that was—never left a mark on her years, her times (for what had she changed? Effected, even?), although all those petty preoccupations had engraved themselves on her face so that Apple, sorting old photographs after the funeral, had sobbed over those images from a lost time: the dear, soft face, full of foolish hope and expectation, which life, even her mother's most fortunate life ("Loving and beloved," Father Michael had said at the funeral) had inevitably dashed.

As mine were—are, Apple thought, taking out her walking shoes, still caked with Taos mud. I went up there with a few of my hopes still intact, went to see my sister in good faith, and came back stripped.

Now Apple wanted to blame.

But not Cory. She never could blame Cory. She loved her, in a seamless unquestioned way. It was what Cory represented that disturbed her, not what Cory was.

She lifted out the skirt she'd worn at the pueblo on the day of the dances, when she'd first felt how completely her sister had gone over—to them—how completely lost she was. That should have prepared me, she thought, for her relationship with the Indian.

Question not, their mother had said once, or words to that effect, you won't like the answers. Life is indomitable, bend your backs. But Cory had not bent, or broken. Even the astonishing sums of money from the sale had caused her neither grief nor happiness; she bought Mabel's old house and fixed it up, a little. That was all. She was indomitable, not the money.

I'm exaggerating, as always, Apple thought, and stopped to look around the room (my room, our room), freshly redecorated with the help of that charming Missy Chung—first of this new breed, perfectly Americanized Asians, coming to the south from eastern and western ports-of-first-call. The chintz not too chintzy (Billy slept here, too), the armchairs downy as nests, the great bed, embarrassingly large ("You deserve it!" Missy had cried), layered with lace pillows. How Mother would have hated all this ostentation and frivolity, Apple thought with the relief of finally letting the perception through; Mother who seldom lay down in daylight for fear of wrinkling the white blanket cover.

But all we have is ostentation and frivolity, she would have told her mother. All we have is what we can buy, or what comes to us, willy-nilly, as a result of Billy's position, his success—the sale.

"And what does Billy do all day now?" her mother had asked, with asperity, one molten summer morning a year after the sale. For she had been opposed, bitterly opposed, to the whole business. "How does he use his time now that you've snatched the business out from under him?"

Apple had protested, of course; it was a shared decision, arrived at after long and careful discussion (for Apple, after their father's death, became Billy's chief confidant, the only person he, as chairman and chief shareholder, could afford to talk to frankly, for Apple had his interests at heart.) Only life strips, not the decisions we make, she'd have liked to tell her mother, now.

She took out her soft warm nightgown and crumpled it against her face. It smelled of long nights and pinon smoke in that cold, dry room in Taos. Where will I go now? she wondered, as though before Taos there was still possibly some hiding place, as there used to be in Frankie's arms, against the bib of Frankie's apron.

There was no escape now, she knew. She would have to continue to tend to Billy's career—all those late night sessions when his confidence sank as low as a candle flame!

No one knew about those late night sessions. Or would ever know, she thought fiercely; it wouldn't be fair to Billy—so brushed, so smooth, so certain during the day.

So no one would ever know how, late on a few, a very few nights, Billy had wept with his head in her lap, insisting everything he did, had done—more than thirty years, now—was only for HER benefit, to maximize HER profits—which was as close as they had come or would ever come to discussing why Apple's father had turned the business over to Billy shortly after he married Apple.

That was something neither of them would ever touch.

A businessman, a nice little businessman, she'd overheard her mother describing Billy once (as though she, Mrs. Mason, had only consorted with poets and philosophers), but she didn't know, didn't deserve to know, how Billy had wept, and how agonizingly sure Apple had been, for one unbearable moment, that he had done it all for her: building up the company, organizing the sale (with her help, of course, her devoted, essential help.)

"Men don't understand," she repeated over and over as she took out her comfortable flannel robe and her big fluffy slippers. "They never have understood, and they never will." How soothing an assumption that was, compared to the other: that they understood everything, and kept their council.

Stop that, she commanded herself, using their mother's voice. You have things to do, telephone calls to make.

But it was too late—she couldn't reassure herself, reassemble the old certainties (Taos had destroyed them) and when she went to telephone her son, leaving a message to upbraid him for something or other, she heard that fatal hesitation in her voice. For after all, what did it matter, the unpaid bills, the unreturned telephone calls? And she knew Little Billy would hear that hint of falling off, that touch of defection. The tape, more reliable than his ear, recorded it.

13

*I*t was not, it could not be enough: Billy acknowledged that to himself unwillingly as he drove out from town. He'd kept the illusion of sufficiency since the evening before when, returning late from Beaver Cove, he'd met the soft, shifting silence of his wife's bulk in bed—not asleep, far from asleep, he knew—with a reassuring if somewhat mechanical pat. She'd sighed then, relaxing—forgiving? It was a week after her return.

But what was there to forgive, he'd wondered, waking in the cool grey dawn with the first birds. After all this was the life they'd constructed together. They both had their inevitable, their essential escapes: her garden, always, and now perhaps visits to her sister (no more of that, he told himself sternly, as visions arose of the woman he never allowed himself to name), while he had his work—although what it was precisely, now, he didn't know; his secretary however seemed clear about it. It was the Foundation, of course. And he had his every-other-week evening at Beaver Cove. He was always home well before midnight.

Those evenings were supposed to be his poker nights. Apple

was so complicit in the deceit she sometimes claimed to smell tobacco smoke in his clothes when he came back.

Billy didn't smoke, didn't drink, as Apple knew.

As he drove in a long snake of traffic along the river road, he wondered if his abstinence had prevented him from forming the sort of friendships he'd expected with male colleagues, forged, it seemed, over shot glasses of Bourbon, fumigated with burley-tobacco smoke.

He remembered, now, certain looks, certain hesitations—in the bar of the Kenilworth Club, when he ordered a club soda, or in his box at the race track when he'd poured Vieuve Cliquot for his out-of-town guests, big-shot hardware dealers and manufacturers from Milwaukee and Des Moines. Some intimacy was missing, and missed, in these exchanges; his friendships had an automatic quality; no one confided in him. "You don't EXIST, man," Little Billy had shouted at him, years ago, but that was liquor talking, before the boy disappeared into marriage and AA. Why remember that now? Billy wondered, disgusted, and tried to distract himself by staring at the mass of greenery that had sprouted on the huge bulk of the old dump. That existed! The dump even had a name—Apple would know it.

He began to ruminate again.

Hammond Mason, Apple's father, had never had any complaints about Billy's performance, as he would doubtless have called it. The Old Man—Billy had begun to use that title a year after his marriage—was always bending an ear in the elevator to hear some receptionist's complaint: the air-conditioning was turned up too high, that kind of thing; and then he'd be on the phone at once, making the necessary correction.

But why did the receptionist or whoever it was speak to the boss in the first place? Hammond Mason was a formidable presence, especially in old age, when deafness and blindness had turned him into a monument, steered by Billy down corridors and in and out of elevators.

"You look like a tugboat, Dad, pushing Grandpa around," Little Billy had said once—now why remember that? But even then some worker would pierce the Old Man's earned reserve with a complaint or even a piece of good news—the birth of a grandchild, something like that. As though the Old Man cared.

But he had cared—there was the riddle. He'd sent flowers for funerals, silver bowls for weddings, blue or pink baskets of flowers for births—and meant every bit of it, even the ridiculous doggerel printed on the greeting cards he chose with such care. "A little bit of heaven come down to earth—" Billy remembered that one.

He'd remonstrated, occasionally, he'd tried to remind the Old Man of his position, his dignity, but the Old Man had insisted that these people loved him, insisted with an intensity, a naïveté, that had left Billy silent. For after all they were Mason Hammond's employees. As Billy was, as he had always continued to be.

Even after the sale, when Billy was guiding the Old Man down some street in town, an individual would come puffing up, having sighted them from afar, and begin to blabber something about the old days.

"Like being part of a family—" they always said that, even Clarence, the sour black janitor who'd been so unhelpful about staying late or doing jobs he considered beneath him. "Just like a member of the family"—Clarence had actually said that, on the street outside the Lobster King when Billy was taking the Old Man out to lunch; for he had to be saved, after the sale, from spending all his time with his wife. And the Old Man had chuckled and beamed, forgetting all about old Clarence's sourness and unwillingness, now that the business was sold and someone else was worrying about reality—that someone else, of course, was Billy, retained, almost against his will, by the new owners, that pair of cormorants (as he thought of them, although uncertain what cormorants were) from Chicago.

The Old Man had had the gift of—what was it?—politeness? No, it was more than that. He'd gleamed, he'd glowed with the luster of gathered confidences, although he'd never, as far as Billy could remember, spoken intimately about himself.

A gent of the old school, Billy thought, trying to put the memory behind him, for the thought of his father-in-law still kept its sharp edges, unlike the other people in his life—Apple, whom he almost never named except by her title of wife, Mrs. Mason, who'd hardly existed except as his mother-in-law, and that other, the fourth wheel, as he tried to think of her, the sister, who flourished independently of both name and title.

And what title, he began to cry to himself, there on the winding river road, could he have given to her anyway, after all these years, after all this hopeless silence—and heard, Billy Long heard, at fifty-three and in the prime of his life, a child crying at the end of a long hall, a little boy closed up alone in a room, and thought again, Of course it's not enough, life is not enough; or is it somehow too much? He glared out at an entrance he was passing as though it had challenged him, pale limestone pillars flaunting themselves at the side of his road.

But had Mason Hammond ever really trusted him?

Billy remembered the day they'd announced the sale, or rather, Hammond had, as former chairman of the board, Billy standing at his elbow.

The news conference was held in the cafeteria at the plant, employees standing around gaping, their early lunches disrupted. There'd been rumors, of course, for months—everyone noticed the lawyers flying in from out of town—but no one had believed that the company would be sold. The triumph of that moment, of the announcement, had been diluted, for Billy, by the smell of steam-table Brussels sprouts.

The cook, old Betty, had been weeping—one of the first to be laid off, of course; the new owners hired minimum-wage girls in striped dresses that barely covered their thighs. No one belonged to a union, it had never been needed, and so the lay-offs were accomplished quickly and with a minimum of fuss. But old Betty had seen Billy in the corridor, her last day of work, and laid her sob story on him; he remembered that—his discomfort and gathering irritation. The woman hadn't understood there was nothing he could do.

Now he was passing the country club where he and Apple went nearly every Saturday night. He craned at the tennis courts and recognized Hoyt Winston, that no-account, playing a game of singles with a blond, at five o'clock on a work day—Hoyt who had family money and had never held a job in his life.

Billy tried to suffuse himself with scorn, but felt it fade. Hoyt, and the pretty lady, and the perfect white lines of the well-maintained court: perhaps that was what Mason Hammond would have trusted, after all, rather than the nose-to-the-grindstone loyalty of his second-in-command, whom he'd never called anything but Billy.

Ridiculous name for a full-grown man, but Billy had accepted it, taking it for himself until now if he'd been wakened in the middle of the night and asked his name, he'd have said, "Billy. Billy Long."

He forced himself to focus on the past that for a moment seemed less painful than the present.

The sale, he recounted to himself, had been the event of the year in their little community. Three generations of Mason men had owned the hardware company, and its passing to "foreigners," as someone interviewed in the street had called the people from Chicago, was viewed as exciting yet destructive, like a four-alarm fire.

People spoke, Billy remembered, of the fabric being rent (whatever that meant) and did not seem reassured by the very handsome price Billy, after endless negotiations, had secured for his adopted family—for when the chips were down, Mason Hammond had acted quivery, old, confused by terms and numbers, and so it was inevitable that Billy, as second-in-command, would take over. Mason had even accepted, with bewilderment, Billy's assertion that he must have his own attorney, Millicent Tandy, to represent his interests—"As though," Mason had said, pitifully, "your interests ever were, or ever could be, different from mine."

And so Millicent Tandy had come into the picture and ten years later was still in the picture, although in a slightly different position.

But had Hammond Mason ever trusted him, even when the multi-layered papers were signed and the first, symbolic check was handed over?

That was always the question, always would be the question, Billy knew; and now his father-in-law was dead.

He thought he remembered an odd sort of merriment in the Old Man's eyes, on the day of the sale and for some time after, a look of profound unconcern that had shocked Billy, as though Hammond had long since relinquished control of the situation and so could enjoy all the shenanigans—as he doubtless called them, privately.

"Crooks, every one of them," the Old Man had merrily described the Chicago buyers, as though that was all he, or anyone, could expect.

Not that they'd done a bad job, the people from Chicago, in spite of the inevitable lay-offs and the disappearance of the trademark logo, among other things. Billy, knowing his initials would never appear in that dark-blue wreath, had not mourned its passing.

True, the pension plan had been used to leverage funds for a much-need renovation, and some of the old-time employees had squawked, on principle, but even they could hardly hold it against the Chicago people when, once the building was renovated and the staff trimmed—and Hammond Mason safely dead—,they'd sold the company to a hardware chain for twice what they'd paid the Masons.

That was business, American style, Billy thought; it was in fact one of the now-rare success stories of low interest rates and plenty of free-flowing capitol that had made it vividly clear in the mid 1980's that the system still worked.

Perhaps it was fortunate, though, he admitted to himself, that the Old Man was in his grave when the next sale transpired; for of course it had been followed by more lay-offs, and Apple had taken it upon herself to complain, "Daddy would be appalled," as though the chains were the devil's handiwork instead of a more efficient way to manufacture and distribute a no-longer distinctive line of hardware. But Apple, finding a rough place on the handle of one of "our" rakes, had claimed the product was ruined forever.

At the house—Billy had driven blind for the last few miles and was surprised to find himself suddenly at his own door—he parked and climbed out of the car.

The late-winter evening was chilly, and he noticed it keenly as he made his way slowly to the front door. The place had never been particularly lively except during one eventful year of Little Billy's adolescence when hairy young males and intolerably loud noises had taken up all the space, all the air. Now the house seemed almost forlorn. He thought it was the quality of the silence.

There had been a moment, he remembered, at his mother-in-law's funeral when Apple had whispered, "Maybe we ought to sell the place, try building our own house," but when he'd asked her, later, what she meant, hoping against hope that she actually had a plan, she'd looked at him blankly. It had only been a moment of anguish, of wild surmise, he realized, and it would not come again.

He hesitated at the door, knowing exactly what he would find inside. His private secretary would have left a pile of typed letters to be signed, each neatly clipped to a stamped and addressed envelop, and there would also be a list of reminders, as she called them, written out in her cautious hand: a dentist appointment, his light-weight woolen suits to be tailored—for he'd lost weight, of all things, since the thinking began.

When did it begin? He couldn't remember—in the past year or so. It had definitely become worse during Apple's absence; she tended to distract him, a low hum that kept his mind partly occupied.

But was it thinking at all, he wondered, or just a sort of mental degeneration, the powers that had fueled his career now dropping off into depression, apathy? For he had never wanted to retire.

The people from Chicago had been adamant about that, and he had been forced by sheer weight of logic to agree. It wouldn't have worked for an executive from the old regime—they actually called it that—to stay on after a time of painful if necessary changes; it would have caused a split in the command.

He'd have scorned to arrange something for himself beforehand, especially since he assumed his value to the new owners would be obvious. It was obvious, they'd said, but unusable, under the circumstances, and they sent him on his way with his pension and an expensive set of golf clubs.

He unlocked the front door, worn carved wood his mother-in-law had often spoken of replacing.

Inside, the house was empty and cool, waiting for his reviving presence as Apple, filing her nails in their bedroom, would be waiting. Empty, and cool.

Too much responsibility, Billy thought, shearing off toward the garden. Can't anyone exist without me? And he thought, briefly, of his wife and her house nested one inside the other.

Then he saw Apple. She was on her knees at the edge of the border, scratching at something with a short-handled rake. He went closer.

She was planting seeds.

The dirt, he imagined, was still half-frozen. There were orange clods turned up beside her knees. She was breaking them methodically, first with the tool, then with her naked fingers. She never wore gloves, loving, she claimed, the feel of the dirt (and its smell, he knew, and perhaps even its taste.) That was his wife—dabbling in dirt like a child. Now and then she scattered a few seeds.

Why did we only have one child? he found himself wondering. There were all those problems, and then the doctor's pronouncement. But we never really decided; we only accepted, as though there was no choice, as though it didn't really matter.

It was the garden, he thought, recognizing his own irrationality. She was always obsessed with the garden. It got in the way.

He watched her for several minutes before she became aware of him. So much for telepathy, marital instinct, he thought, even after all these years—but a useful blindness, he knew, given the situation at Beaver Cove.

"Why, Billy!" she exclaimed. As she turned to him, he saw her childish, her impossible exhilaration burn off, leaving her poor old face bald, the face of a capable, if limited middle-aged woman—a stranger. "I didn't hear you." She scrambled awkwardly to her feet, ignoring his hand.

"You haven't finished," he said gruffly, indicating the scattered seed packets.

"Time got away from me. I need to change, start supper."

He had a sense that something precious and irreplaceable was passing. "Finish what you're doing," he said. "I'll help you."

"But you don't care anything about my garden," Apple murmured.

He crouched down and picked up a seed packet. "Marigolds. I remember them, last summer—a row along the path. They have a strange smell."

She was staring at him.

"The nasturtiums were in the big blue pot by the gate." He picked up that packet. "One hard rain drowned them out."

"I never knew you noticed."

"You cried—or at least you were terribly disappointed."

"I never knew you noticed," she repeated.

"My mother always grew nasturtiums in a window box, all the space she had."

Apple nodded. "She objected to the bright colors, though"— at the one lunch, formal but quite easy, they'd all shared after the wedding, when the talk had been mostly of flowers. How their memories clacked together, Billy thought, wooden yet comforting.

"I always grow at least one variety of everything Mother loved," his wife was murmuring. "This garden is her best memory."

Ordinarily Billy would have corrected her. The sentence was imprecise; Apple would have reworded it, with a smile. Standing there in front of her, though, he felt cowed: the garden was her kingdom. "Maybe I'll help you Saturday, weed or something." he said.

"Oh Honey, you have your tennis game Saturday." She passed her arm around his waist, refraining from mentioning, he knew, that now he could help her any day, he had so few demands on his time.

"The game's in the morning," he said. "I could help you in the afternoon. Or maybe you don't want me."

"I want you, Billy, I always want you," she murmured, tightening her clasp as she turned him toward the house. "It's just kind of hard to believe, after all this time . . ."

"I missed you," he said suddenly, "when you were off in Taos." Something hovered between them, then sped away.

"We need to try doing new things together, for our old age. We're going to grow old together." As he said it, he knew for the first time it was true: his future. Their future. With something silent and unspeakable at the end.

"We're already growing old together," Apple said comfortably.

But perhaps, Apple thought later, dozing with her hand on Billy's hip, perhaps I don't want to share, after all.

My garden was always mine—the only thing that is mine, she'd thought, with some bitterness, more than once over the years. When I bury myself there, no one can reach me. If Billy comes to me there on Saturday, looking for help, I may find it's more than I can deal with, comfortably—and comfort, she admitted to herself for the first time since her trip to Taos, is very important.

For how much of her misery with Cory was due to that dark cold room, the Kiva room, at the end of that dreary hall?

Also, she thought, there is a kind of reassurance, after all, in mild, continuous, familiar disappointment; she expected nothing of Cory, and not much, she realized, of Billy.

Comfort, she thought, with some asperity, is far more important to me than I'd realized, and I had to go all the way to New Mexico to find that out.

Remembering her acute sensations during their increasingly-rare love-making, Apple wondered if she might have, could have chosen the other way—the way of relentless sharing.

We did have that for a while, she remembered, during the sale; she'd kept lists on yellow pads, she'd taken notes on telephone conversations, she'd forgotten to eat during the most intense of the negotiations—and Billy had told her she'd been very helpful.

She'd even mastered her fear of her mother's disapproval, for Mrs. Mason had been vigorously opposed. "The company is our family," she repeated, over and over, frowning at Apple, whom she accused of somehow masterminding the sale. Apple knew her mother couldn't bear to believe that her husband, on his own, had taken the first step, calling people he knew all over the mid-west who might be interested. Apple had tried to bear the blame, but had succeeded, finally, in blazing out at her mother: "Daddy wants this, I'm only going along." She'd done it because she felt she was helping Billy.

Finally one morning her face in the bathroom mirror had looked almost as feral as the face of the young female attorney Billy had hired to represent his—their—interests.

The sale was accomplished in time. Then she had dropped back into her comfortable sense of slight disappointment: that her marriage, her life had not quite worked out—whatever that meant.

Apple slid her hand up to Billy's waist. Her fingers were so used to the consistency of his skin she hardly needed to touch him; and yet she did touch, did feel. Then was there an objective reality to touching, to the tangible, that had nothing to do with gathering information?

At least I won't be pegged anymore as the silly one, the superficial one, Apple thought, moving her hand to Billy's thick shoulder. I'm too old for that now, too complicated, to be treated as a simple puzzle, a question with a single answer—as Cory, she thought now, had always treated her.

She tried to remember when Cory had begun to treat her as simple, as superficial. Immediately she knew it had been at her wedding, when Cory made her disturbance: "Speak now or forever hold your peace"—that had been Cory's cue.

She remembered staring at the alter where their mother's arrangement—bridal wreath, lilies—had quivered, knowing she would never see her sister in the old way again, as accomplice, fellow victim, but would imagine her instead wrapped in the silvery sheen of armor: armed, as in fact Cory was now armed, with her pistol.

Cory was easier to deal with when she was a victim, Apple thought, shifting her hand to the back of Billy's neck, faintly damp, and warm; I could feel sorry for her then. But that was years and years ago.

Apple knew as she kneaded the tendons in Billy's neck that she'd stayed away from her sister not because of the sale and their disagreements about it (which was their shared, their silent excuse) but because of Cory's silvery shine.

I can't take up arms, either with her or against her, Apple thought. Let her be pitiful again.

And knew Cory never would, or could.

She touched Billy's ear with her fingertip, and he stirred. Perhaps he felt the vibrations of her thoughts. But no—he was too deeply asleep for that.

She passed her arm around him, sliding her hand down to his belly, now slack, drooping. How defenseless he was, finally, in his sleep.

Why do all men fall asleep right afterwards, she wondered. It was not a question. But then, she reminded herself, I don't know anything about all men, I only know Billy—and wondered, in spite of herself, if Cory's Indian sank away this fast, or did he have some magical way to stay conscious?

She dropped her hand, lightly, on her husband's penis. How small he was, shriveled, in the aftermath. "Do you notice, we say 'he' as though the penis was the whole man?" Cory had asked her once, years ago, when they were both girls and could still—within limits, of course—mention that kind of thing. "As though when it's little, he's little, and when it's big, he's big?"

By now Cory must have an answer to that question, an answer Apple didn't want to hear. And she felt their parents' bedroom (as it was; she and Billy had moved into the house a few months after her mother's death) inviolate around her, around Billy, a safe fortress against everyone and everything, even her sister. For really Cory had no right.

There are certain questions, Apple thought drowsily, fingering her husband's penis, that can't be asked, or answered. Intimacy is so rare, so precious. She remembered after all this time their parents' door, closed firmly against both daughters all night long and sometimes on Sunday afternoons as well. That was marriage. That was privacy. The two were entwined.

She tried to slip her fingers between her husband's thighs. Billy slept as always with his knees up and tightly clenched together so that, knowing what she knew about his mother—her flowers, her fusses—Apple thought he'd probably lain that way in the womb, his knees defending him against her contractions.

But why did he still sleep that way, clamped?

He was a success, everyone said so. Only a month earlier, there'd been a story in the local newspaper, a respectful recounting of the first sale: one of the major events in the small town's history. The second sale had hardly been mentioned.

Now that Hammond Mason was dead, Apple knew, credit could be given where credit was due: the news story called Billy "the main player," even "the architect" of the sale—Billy Long who'd started as a stock boy and worked his way up in the good, solid American way. And she knew her love had helped him.

But Billy was somehow still innocent, still vulnerable. As she cradled his penis in her palm, she longed to protect him, in his sleep. Billy Long was neither vulnerable nor innocent, awake, but sleep drained him of his history and scattered his defenses. At such moments, she knew he was hers. She began, gently, to massage him.

We've had nearly all our most important experiences together, she remembered with a nostalgia only slightly soiled by her perpetual sense of disappointment.

And if I've lived too little, Apple thought (that was one of Cory's silent observations, she knew), I haven't missed anything really important.

I learned to give myself to Billy (how Cory would howl at that expression)—something of a miracle, considering how we were raised, with that fear and distrust of anything having to do with the body. Billy patiently and slowly over a period of years undid my reserve, although it wasn't until after Little Billy was born that I had my first orgasm, alone, when Billy was away.

His penis was slowly stiffening under her fingers. He shifted a little, and sighed.

Oh yes, I did it finally for myself, Apple thought, and knew how Cory would applaud that, how neatly it would fit all her preconceptions. I did it for myself, with oil and candles and music: sesame body oil, camellia-scented candles, and the hard-driving rhythms of Paul Simon's band. I danced naked in this room before that mirror; I looked at myself for the first time, spreading my thighs. The bloom of it startled me—that profound secret, suffused with color, under everything. "What you sit on," our mother called it.

Vagina, she thought, stroking Billy's penis. Vulva—more accurate as well as prettier. Labia major and minor. Clitoris winking under its little hood. We were never given those words when we were young; they were kept from us. Even masturbation—I never heard that word. Our mother said, "You must always make sure to wash, down there"—as though there was something evil hidden in those rosy folds.

As there was—is. The devil. A pink devil. Wonderful.

Billy groaned and turned toward her. Apple cradled him in her arms and felt his stiffened penis against her full belly. In a moment, they would begin—their practice, their dance. Already he was feeling for her, separating her thighs. "Never say no," her mother had warned her. "Always give him what he wants. It's your only insurance."

Not looks. Not health, or intelligence. Not even money. All that, her mother had said, was meaningless or transitory. Looks (especially Apple's brand of blond prettiness) fade, health collapses, intelligence dims, money is spent and buys little. But the ability to please, to say yes, is solid gold. He won't get that anywhere else, their mother had said, because times have changed and women have lost the gift.

The gift, she thought, lifting one thigh onto her husband's hip. That's what Cory refuses to understand: the gift of giving. It sounded ludicrous, but Apple clung to her conviction—her legacy. It had come to her from their mother, along with the house and the garden and the very bed they were sleeping in, and would, with luck, sleep in for the rest of their lives.

She shifted, and welcomed Billy in. She held him, cradled him, rocked him. Urgently, he pressed against her, toppling her over onto her back. She lifted her knees. Cory would never know this—the bliss of absolute surrender, downy and quick. Cory would always demand.

I did that once, too, Apple thought, but I learned the error of my ways. She slid a big lace pillow under the base of her spine.

This time, Billy remembered to do what she needed him to do, and she came, with a twittering cry.

⌫ *14*

*C*oming home the next evening, Billy found Apple talking on the telephone.

She was pacing the hall, the cordless phone in her hand, and he was struck—absurdly, he knew—by the notion that she'd grown taller.

She was speaking to their son.

"Eight o'clock this evening," Apple was saying. "Both of you."

Billy took her in his arms. Immediately, she put down the phone. The surrender of her body was too quick, he felt, to be authentic. She had merely willed it.

As he kissed her, her mouth became moist and familiar. Why do I know her so well? Billy wondered as she tightened her arms around his neck. He did not believe she knew him so well, but that was surmise. He felt that he was more complex, stranger, that it would take more than a lifetime to know him; but then, perhaps he was mistaken— perhaps everyone was permeable, and intimacy was only one of many ways to see in, to see through. The thought terrified him.

They went hand-in-hand into the living room, and the simple

touch was restorative. Billy wondered what it would be like to renounce the rest of it—embrace old age, and rely on hand-in-hand only from now on.

He was astonished by the thought, then shamed. It seemed to mark a collapse of virility. He had no reason to fear that, as the week Apple was away in Taos had proved. No; it was only his reaction— enfeeblement—to familiarity, to her too-easy giving.

All this time Apple, it seemed to Billy, was talking on and on, but her description didn't match what he knew must have been the reality of her visit: Cory, running some kind of bed-and-breakfast dump, dried, by now, over it all, by now: her juiciness. Apple had already described that in terms he could understand, but now she was adding something new.

A fragment from a prayer floated up (for they were church-goers, it was expected), something St. Francis—was it?—had asked: to love, not to be loved.

Why had that come into his mind now, when he was once again fending off unwelcome visions of Cory? All any woman ever wanted was to be loved, on and on. On and on. On and on.

He didn't think St. Francis had spoken for them.

Or for the birds.

Billy remembered hearing that the birds had flown away once when the saint was preaching. We don't hear, we don't see, Billy thought, and promptly reminded himself of his tennis game, the next day. For life does have to go on. On and on . . .

Why? he began to ask himself later, over their special dinner (and it was special, he knew: quail on toast with lingonberry sauce, a whole afternoon's labor.) Why?—with Apple still going on about Cory, how she'd worn something called a broomstick skirt and preached to her guests (the birds, again—most unwilling). Why not stop life now, in early middle age, a reasonable amount accomplished? Let go of the

Foundation. Turn the house over to someone else: but no one would take it, least of all his son—it was old-fashioned, would need a lot of work. And it would be wrong to sell it. The house was an heirloom.

Billy did not let himself speculate further in that direction.

At that moment, as she chewed the meat off a tiny quail leg, Apple said something Billy couldn't believe.

He drew a breath, and stared at her. Then he asked her, quickly, to repeat herself, and she did.

"I don't believe it," Billy said evenly.

"I didn't want to believe it, either, but I heard them, one night."

Billy balled his napkin in his right hand. "It can't be."

"I'm afraid so, Darling. She probably moved to Taos just to find him. You know, the Indian lover who solves everything."

"That's ridiculous. She wouldn't want that kind of complication—"

"She's changed."

"No!" Billy's voice rose.

"Honey—what's wrong?"

"Nothing," he muttered, jerking at his tie, which was strangling him. "I just need some air"—and he rushed out of the house to stand in a cool cleared space by the forsythia while Apple went on sitting between the two lighted candles, alone.

This is intolerable, he thought, this is the last straw—Cory, who gave it all up—family, possibilities—to retreat out there, to the trackless Southwest (as he'd always thought of it) and now a preposterous liaison, as though she was still a wild, flitting girl. With an Indian, of all things.

I won't accept it, Billy thought. I won't believe it—which was after all the same thing. Apple is dramatizing; she heard something, and made a whole history out of that.

It was only a little while later, ten minutes, maybe, Billy calculated, when he heard the smooth roar of their son's sports car at the foot of the hill.

Billy hurried inside, touched his wife's rigid shoulder, smoothed out her expression with a few kind words—for Little Billy must never find them having something as unlikely as a spat.

They went to the front door arm in arm. What was it about Little Billy's dissipation (to use Mrs. Mason's old-fashioned word) that united them—was it to prevent, Billy wondered now, any hint of understanding, even of familiarity with their son? An understanding, a familiarity that might threaten their own bond.

Billy knew from his own experience all the ways their son had tripped and stumbled, all the dark passages he'd wandered down to find an explosion of fireworks at the end. Like father, like son. Only their means, not their ends, were different.

All men know this, he thought, but we can't afford to admit it to our sons, it would unfit them for the world, for discipline, ambition— the essentials; it would seem to be condoning anti-social behavior. We can no more admit to understanding than we can admit to the first wild stirring that brought us to our nice middle-aged wives.

We don't see, we don't hear, Billy thought again, reminded of his golf foursome, his tennis partner, all the dear sharers of the essential subterfuge; and then his son sauntered into the house.

The girl—Little Billy's wife, Maureen, what a name—was with him, as she always was, as thought the parents might get to Little Billy (and indeed they would have tried) if she was not there.

Some greetings were exchanged.

Billy followed the twinkle of his daughter-in-law's pale legs down the hall to the dining room, wondering why a pious church-goer wore such short skirts.

Oh yes, he thought, she must have her attractions, Maureen. Little Billy had been dating her, as the term went, since they were both in middle school; they had married right after high school graduation, like a pair of hicks, a couple with no future except a mortgage and too many children. No children yet, but surely before long—Billy had heard Maureen's mother was already hinting.

The young couple went ahead of him into the dining room, where Apple was spooning strawberries into bowls.

Maureen sat down at once, and Billy, standing near the door, watched her eat. She sucked her strawberries from their stems as though they were cherries, with a greedy smack.

He did not look at his son. Little Billy was talking to Apple.

What after all was the use of looking at him, or listening to him? He was handsome in spite of his long curls, Billy thought, and his forearm, lying along the table, was well-muscled. The tattoo, cause of a memorable scene, had faded a little; the heart looked less red, and the initials worked into a banner across it were now too dim to read. But Billy knew what they were. Maureen had gotten her teeth into him early.

Little Billy's voice was modulated, but the story he was telling his mother was always the same—Billy picked up a word or two, all he needed: an unfair supervisor had fired him from his latest menial job—"For tardiness," Little Billy sneered, "like I was still in school."

"As though," Apple corrected, playing with her fork. "As though I was still in school."

"You were tardy often enough then," Billy muttered from his position near the door.

"Billy, please." Apple frowned at her husband.

Maureen was still gobbling her strawberries, for once oblivious.

"Dad, you're always the same." Little Billy leaned back in his chair, which creaked under his weight. He had the heft of a full-grown man, his father thought; fists that could cause damage, teeth that could bite and tear, genitals certainly capable of rape and reproduction. "It's just like my councilor says," Little Billy went on. "Expect failure and you get failure."

"When did my expectations ever mean anything to you?"

"Billy," Apple pleaded.

"OK, Dad, I get it. Because I'm not like you, nose to the old grindstone—"

Maureen spoke suddenly. "Your father's job was a sinecure," she said, and bit into her last strawberry.

Apple and Billy stared at her. "Where'd you learn that word?" Billy asked, amazed.

"Everybody knows you married into the hardware business," Maureen said, glancing at her father-in-law. "What's so nose-to-the-grindstone about that?"

Little Billy chuckled.

"No, I mean the word," Billy said, coming to the table. "Where'd you learn that word?"

"You think I'm ignorant," Maureen said.

"That's something we're discussing with our councilor," Little Billy added. "Your attitude."

Billy leaned on the table. The muscles in his forearms began to quiver, as though they were supporting a much heavier weight. "Councilor? Is this something I'm going to be expected to pay for?"

"If it helps—" Apple began.

"Don't worry, Dad," Little Billy said. "Maureen's folks have agreed to pay."

"They couldn't possibly afford . . ."

Little Billy and Maureen exchanged an amused glance.

Billy's tongue was thick; he could hardly get it around his next words. "I'm glad to pay for anything, within reason, but how many councilors and psychiatrists and assorted social workers by now—?"

"Everybody needs help at some point," Maureen said. "Even you, Mr. Long, if you could get passed your denial."

"Denial is not a river in Egypt," Little Billy intoned.

"You think I'm in denial?" He stared at his daughter-in-law.

She nodded. "Everybody knows the stress you're under, these days."

"The stress . . ." He realized he was numbly leading her on, but he could not stop himself. It seemed suddenly that this plain, greedy girl knew something, possessed a secret, or an answer.

"With your double life, I mean," Maureen said.

Apple said something, and knocked over her glass of water.

Billy watched the water spread across the mahogany table, draining into a crack. "What do you mean, Maureen?"

"Billy!" Apple's voice was far away.

"You really don't have to get into this, Dad," Little Billy said.

"Oh yes, he does." Maureen had locked her eyes on her father-in-law's face. "He's always accusing you. Even when he doesn't say anything, he's accusing you—"

"I don't spend my time breaking the law," Billy said. He could feel Apple fluttering around him. Annoyed, he put off her hands. "We might as well have this out," he said, and then remembered how, only minutes earlier, he'd said to himself, We don't see anything, we don't hear anything.

"You are breaking the moral law," Maureen said.

"I will not allow this at my table," Apple told her. "You have no right to come here causing this kind of trouble."

"What about the trouble he's caused us?" Maureen asked. The two women were facing each other now, across the table, and Billy realized that there was a similarity to the set line of their jaws. "He's ruined Billy in this community, with the stories he tells. Billy'll never be able to get a decent job here; all his father's friends think he's a druggie, a criminal. And for what?" Maureen leaned across the table. "Smoking a little pot? Drinking a little too much? Getting picked up for speeding?"

"I learned how to work when I was a kid," Billy said. "I didn't lie in bed all day—"

"You think I lie in bed all day? I had to be at the warehouse at eight!" Billy protested. "The next job I get—"

"I had a goal—"

"Yes," Billy said. "Taking over Grandpa's business and then selling it. You succeeded, Dad, you really did. And now I can't get a job. Grandpa would have taken me on at the company—he told me that once."

Apple wailed, "We thought about you—we really did—when we were negotiating the sale—"

"I'm sure you did." Her son looked at her. "You set up that trust fund with money from the sale of my stock. I'll get the income when I'm, what is it, forty-five?"

"When I was your age, I got up in the morning, I went downtown, I had a mother and a sister to support," Billy was saying.

"Good for you, Dad." Little Billy twisted around in his chair to look at his father, still leaning on the table next to Maureen. "So I should be satisfied to work minimum wage? Is that what you mean? How many years did you work minimum wage in the stockroom before Grandpa promoted you?"

"I will not have this at my table," Apple said again, sinking into a chair. Her voice was reedy with exhaustion.

"Your table?" Billy wondered aloud. Then he realized what he had said and reached to pat her arm.

She jerked it away. "What do you mean?"

Billy looked at the shined silver, the glasses, the blue glass bowls of strawberries: where had it all come from? Who had paid for it? Wedding presents, probably, he thought. Ill-gotten gain. "I don't know what I mean."

"I guess you bought everything here, right, Dad?" Little Billy said. "But it was with Grandpa's money, wasn't it?"

"Go to hell," Billy said, and he thumped the table with his closed fist. The glasses jumped.

"No," Apple said, putting her hands over her ears.

Billy looked at Maureen and saw with satisfaction that she flinched slightly. "And you, daring to bring that up—"

"Bring what up, Dad?" Little Billy asked.

"Oh no, Honey," Apple said. "Please."

"We might as well get it out on the table, everybody in town talks about it, Mom."

"We will not discuss that," Billy said, and he thumped the table again. A plate jumped and slid toward the edge.

Little Billy put out his hand to stop it. "So everyone in town can gossip about your mistress but when we try to bring it up—"

Billy grabbed a glass and threw it against the wall. Apple screamed. The glass crashed against a tulip-shaped sconce, splintered, and fell in pieces to the floor. Water trailed down the brocade wallpaper in a widening stain.

"Get out of here!" Billy shouted.

He kept his trembling hands clamped to his sides while the two young people glanced at each other, glanced at him, and continued to sit at the table.

Apple was sobbing. He heard the sounds from a distance, and wondered, briefly, what they were.

After a while Billy went to her and leaned his hand on her shoulder. He caught sight of their reflection in the French window that lead to the terrace and realized that they were posed the way couples used to be in old-fashioned daguerreotypes, the wife sitting, the husband standing with his hand on her shoulder.

But Apple's head was bowed.

Billy stood looking at their reflection for a while. Then he slowly removed his hand from her shoulder and left the room.

In an instant, his big comfortable car was taking him where he knew, instinctively, he must go, where it was only right, he thought, for him to go at this juncture. He sank down into the leather seat and gripped the steering wheel, shifting gears smoothly, accelerating, leaving them all behind: and he imagined their faces trailing behind him, tin cans tied to his bumper.

Let them shear off, disappear, he thought. What is love, compared to this frustration—years and years of it? It had started, he realized now, when he first saw his son at his wife's breast and knew there would be no separating them.

In a while, when he reached the familiar place—the town house, as she called it, on the dead-end street, Beaver Cove—Billy felt as though he had cut his family off neatly and cleanly, slicing them away with surgical precision so that he could be a young man again, unencumbered by all he had wanted and won.

But when he was finally where he needed to be, and felt the hard skin of her heels grating his back, he knew he had, at least in the moment before orgasm, exactly what he deserved: a beautiful young woman who slightly, poetically resisted him, with a shade of surprise, a coloring of rebellion, even, so that each time he overcame her and pressed into her (and it had been how many thousands of times, now, over ten years), he felt he was snatching a prize—his youth, life itself, from between her thighs.

While at the house, the Masons' house, his house, Apple's house—maybe one day Maureen's house, who knew?—three people sat silent among blue glass bowls of strawberries until Apple cleared her throat and began once more to explain: "Your father is under stress, you must understand, he comes from a different time"; while the young man and the young woman, linked, firm and justified, glanced at the woman alone and suddenly old even in candlelight, then looked away.

I am standing in the courtyard, feeding Mabel's pigeons. We had snow during the night, and their pink feet cross-hatch it as they gather around me, fluttering down from Mabel's birdhouses which jut at odd angles against the clearing sky.

Tony comes across the bridge over the acequia and stands watching me, and I wonder what context he puts me in, what frame: a white woman feeding expensive corn to pigeons.

"Boy or girl?" I ask when he comes closer, and realize how easy it is to say what needs to be said.

"Boy." He smiles.

"That makes three of each, doesn't it?"

He nods.

There is nothing more to say. I scatter another handful of corn.

"Cory."

He has never called me by my name; there has been no need.

"Yes?"

Again, the obvious comes easily: the patient look, the patient waiting. I throw another handful of corn.

"Those birdhouses look like they about to come down."

"I'll ask Manuel to do something about them after he finishes with the roof."

He wants to know about the roof, and I tell him. I leave out Primrose's contribution. Tony is skeptical of her powers.

As I speak, I see his eyes. We are both in the same place, suddenly, mouthing words.

"Last night—" he begins.

"It's all right. I know they're angry at me."

"How come you went?"

"They said you needed me. Whoever called."

He shakes his head. "Well, I done what they said. I stayed."

"You would have stayed anyway."

He nods.

"She's all right?" I clap my hands and the pigeons fly up.

He nods again. I know he is not interested in discussing his wife; they sleep together, she has a baby every year or so. It would have been the same with me.

"Cory."

He says it again. The way he pronounces it sounds strange to me, as though he is translating my name into another language.

"Yes?"

"I come tonight."

He has not made it a question and yet he is waiting for my answer.

"Yes," I say.

It is not what I intended, but there comes a time, for me, when intentions fall away.

I know what Tony did, on the Raton pass, or somewhere near there, that cold night two months ago. I don't know the details, but I have no need to know them. He helped Roy to die, in whatever way the pueblo had decided he should die; and he would do it again. Perhaps he is restive, now, under the rules the council is laying down for his behavior; perhaps his slow pride is starting to rise up, to reclaim the authority he's lost. But still, if his people were threatened, he would do whatever he was told to do. They come first. They will always come first.

Perhaps that's why I always feel so light with him, so airy.

I turn to go into the house. Conchita is waiting for me to go over the menus with her.

Tony is gone when I look back.

In the kitchen, Conchita is inspecting the big refrigerator, checking her supplies. I see we have several pounds of butter, three boxes of eggs, two quarts of milk.

"I want you to try something new at dinner tonight," I tell her.

She turns, wiping her hands. "I thought chicken mole."

"I know that's what we usually have on Thursdays. But I want you to try something new. We'll need a pressure cooker, some brown rice, dark sesame oil—"

Conchita says, "I don't know how to cook that stuff."

"I'll teach you. We'll do it together, till you get the hang of it."

"You always like my food."

"I still like it. But it's time for a change. I've been reading some books about nutrition—"

"Just like everybody in Taos."

"We might as well try to be healthy," I say.

"People been living off my food a long time. This is the way we eat here."

"I know. All I'm saying is, give this a try"—and I begin to pull things off her shelves, white sugar, salt, a big blue can of lard.

The truth is, I need to try something new. Apple has left, Tony is leaving, and at dinner last night my own words sounded flat: I've preached the same lesson a few too many times, my oratory is dulled. At dinner Conchita's good food tasted like cardboard, and I remember that this always happens when I lose people I love: food loses its savor.

When they took the baby, I didn't eat for a week—just a week, so little time, to measure the loss. But I remember that week: the gradual clearing out of my head, the gradual increase in my peace of mind. Starvation is not the answer, I know now, but a change in diet may be.

I get several of my books on nutrition and stack them on the counter for Conchita. I know she will not read them.

She is offended, banging through her pots and pans, and although I try to reassure her, my heart isn't in it. Big changes are on the way. They are always heralded by something that seems trivial, like throwing out the salt.

But Conchita is going to stay. That much is sure. I've upped her wages, but she is not staying because of that. She knows I need her.

15

*A*fter seven words on the stairs—"Why did you go?" Apple had asked; "I had to," Billy had replied—they'd undressed for bed in silence.

As she lay on her back in the dark, Apple remembered how many nights she'd spent staring at shadows the light cast through the maple near their window. Many of the nights of her life, she'd watched those shadows.

She had been alone under the weight of the hours. The pain of that realization was so sharp she tried to blunt it with reasonableness. All marriages have these times, she thought. Anger is impossible to control. Two people even as well-matched as Billy and I have our disagreements.

But while reason had once provided a shabby solace, now it seemed worse than the clutch of panic, and she remembered, against her will, her sister's cry in the dark house in Taos, the cry that had winged its way to Apple's icy room like a bird seeking the light.

She'd heard nothing from Cory in the week since they separated, which was not surprising. Cory seldom wrote, never called, and the silence that was as much a trademark of their stalled sisterhood as it was of Apple's marriage had already closed seamlessly over the small mark made by her visit.

Why did I go to Taos? Apple asked herself, and the pain of the question, the rejection of hope it implied, twisted her like a cramp. She stuffed a corner of her pillow between her teeth. The pain of a lifetime of losses usually seemed ordinary, flat—a son, a husband, parents, a sister—even Frankie; but in the darkness and the silence orchestrated by Billy's deep, relentless breathing, Apple felt the pain unsheathed. Lost, all lost.

She turned over on her side, the pillow corner still stuffed in her mouth, and reached one finger toward Billy's back. He always wore pale-blue cotton pajamas, winter and summer—had done so even on their honeymoon—and after her confusion and resentment passed (Apple slept, had always slept, naked), she realized it was his way of safeguarding his life, as essential as a life-preserver, a fire extinguisher, the whole panoply of survival.

Now with her finger, she lifted the pajama top an inch and touched his warm back. Billy shifted away.

It was Cory she needed, Apple realized. It was her sister's voice, traveling the miles from the terrifying, inhabited darkness of the old house in Taos.

Apple climbed out of bed.

As soon as her bare feet touched the chilly floor, she knew this was ridiculous. But she went on, crossing the darkness, wondering if she had ever before in her life acted unreasonably, at least when she was aware of it. And she remembered, perhaps for the last time, Cory's voice at Apple's wedding, so many years ago, lifted in celebration of unreason, lifted to bring down institutions, lives; and Apple accepted, as she had never been able to accept before, her sister's act.

Cory was not responsible, had never been responsible, for her peculiar insights (something wrong where nobody else saw anything wrong, and so forth), or for the energy that drove those insights into action.

She was a force, a wind, and Apple remembered the Indian in his corner of the kitchen, waiting, watchful, silent, knowing his turn would come—Cory, the wind, in his arms.

She walked across the living room, so used to the placement of the furniture (all her mother's except for a comfortable armchair Billy had requested) she did not need to turn on the lights. Her hand felt for the telephone on the desk, and she lifted the receiver. A voice spoke in her ear before she could dial.

"Is that you, Mother Mason?

The title made her smile, even now.

"Yes, Maureen. I didn't hear the telephone ring, I was picking it up to make a call."

"It didn't ring. I just called you. Must be telepathy."

Where had Maureen acquired the new words in her vocabulary, Apple wondered, then remembered she'd enrolled in a communications course at the community college "to make better use of my time": even that had an elegant ring.

"I didn't want to wait till morning," Maureen said. "Billy told me it was too late, but I said some things that can't wait."

"What things, Maureen?" Apple sat down on her mother's needlepoint stool, knocking the telephone book off, and wished for the first time in her life she had a cigarette.

"Some things that came up at dinner. I'm glad they came up," Maureen added, as though to forestall Apple's murmur of protest. "They needed to. High time. We haven't talked in months."

"Years—if ever," Apple said wearily. "Do we really need to, now?"

"Oh, yes," Maureen insisted, with an assurance Apple believed she herself had never felt, and she imagined her daughter-in-law, sturdy as a column in her thick fleece robe, standing at the window on the landing where the telephone lived in a special table with a shelf for the book and a receptacle for pencils and paper—the type of furniture Apple would never have considered buying because it was made only for one purpose and proclaimed the importance of that purpose: to talk—communicate, Maureen would certainly say, now that she was enrolled at the community college.

"What do you want to tell me?" she asked Maureen reluctantly, and again she imagined her daughter-in-law in all her absurd strength and simplicity, sitting on a spindly chair as though it was a throne.

"I feel bad about what happened tonight," Maureen said. "I told Billy on the way home I needed to apologize. The Program teaches you that: to make amends. I want to make amends to you."

"What if I don't want your amends?" Apple asked, with harsh glee. "What if I'm glad you said what you said?"

"The point is for me to say I'm sorry. Your reaction is not my concern," Maureen said in her stiff, textbook way.

"Well, I guess I can't stop you."

"I'm very sorry I said what I did about Mr. Mason. I know it must have caused you a lot of pain."

"Oh, did you."

"Yes. That wasn't my intention. I believe in being honest with people I love."

After a while, Apple asked, "You love me?" It hardly had the inflection of a question.

"Why, yes, of course I do. You're Billy's mother."

After that Apple didn't hear anything for a while. Her mind was filled with an unaccustomed tumult, as though she had been caught up in the noisy edges of a hurricane.

When she began to hear again, she realized that Maureen was making another momentous announcement. Embarrassed, Apple had to ask her to repeat it.

"We're having a baby," Maureen said, patiently.

Apple wanted, at once, to remind her that only she, Maureen, would have the baby. Only she would stagger along under the accumulating weight; only she would lie, groaning and alone, in a bed in an antiseptic room; only she would feel the cruel fingers and instruments prying into her suffering flesh; only she would be instructed to Push, Mother! Push! when the last vestiges of her strength and courage were gone.

She said vaguely, "How nice," then heard her own voice and quickly added, "How wonderful! Is Billy pleased?" she asked, after a moment.

"Absolutely over the rainbow," the astonishing young woman said. "But I guess it comes as a surprise to you, Mother Mason."

"Why of course not, the most natural thing in the world, you've been married almost two years . . ." She ran down, then started again, goaded by Maureen's doubting silence. "I just wonder how you two are going to support a family, with Billy out of work and you back in school."

"We'll manage," Maureen said. "We don't expect help from you or Billy's father."

"Oh, but we'd like—" Again, Maureen's doubting silence stopped her. "I'm sorry," she said. "It's been a hard night, I guess I'm low on enthusiasm." But why does she have to go through it all—this girl I hardly know and yet who seems somehow worthy of protection, even of protection from life?

As no one ever protected me, Apple thought, or even dreamed it might be necessary.

And there she found the essential, buried link with her sister.

"Billy warned me you'd be too upset to care, but I wanted to tell you tonight for my own reasons," Maureen was going on. "I wanted you to have something really nice to think about when you wake up in the morning."

Once, Apple would have protested that she had many nice things to think about when she woke up in the morning. Now, she sat in silence, listening to the humming wires, until her daughter-in-law told her goodnight and hung up the telephone.

I don't deserve her, Apple thought. Maybe I don't deserve Billy either. As for this baby...

But she could not think of that, it was unbearable, the future bursting into her life before she had made her peace with the past.

She had to turn on the light to look up Cory's number; for several years now, Apple hadn't been able to remember numbers, which was, all things considered, a relief. She believed that freed her mind for more important things, although what they were, she couldn't say.

The telephone rang and rang. She thought she'd hear the answering machine click on, and Cory's professional voice detailing the bed and breakfast's amenities and costs, but Cory must have turned off that instrument of her professional commitments; the telephone went unanswered for a long time.

Apple realized she hadn't heard a telephone ring twenty or thirty times in ages—answering machines took care of that—and recognized the late-night claxon of emergency, accident, sudden death.

Her own apprehension increased to match what she imagined Cory would feel, hurrying down the stairs in her nightgown (did she own one?) to answer. In Taos, it would only be eleven, but Apple knew the inhabitants of Mabel's house went to bed early.

"Yes," Cory said abruptly in her sister's ear, and Apple knew she hadn't wakened her.

"It's me," Apple said. "I haven't heard from you since I got back."

There was a horrifying silence.

Then Cory said, "Some things have been going on here. I was planning to write you, as soon as I caught my breath."

"What things?" Apple asked, instantly alert.

"A break-in, we're calling it."

"In your house? Was anyone hurt?"

"I was," Cory said flatly.

Apple pressed her free hand to her breast. She thought she could feel her heart. "Are you all right?"

"I wasn't hurt, physically," Cory said.

"Why didn't you call?"—but even as she asked, Apple knew the reason: hours of accepted separation, adding up over the years to a life-time of days and nights.

"I was going to write," Cory repeated, "but it's not the sort of thing to put in a letter. Don't be alarmed," she added.

"But I am, of course I'm alarmed." Apple clutched her breast, as though to keep her heart inside. "What in the world happened?"

"I'm not comfortable discussing it on the telephone," Cory said in her professional voice.

"Then I'm coming out," Apple said.

Whatever they'd discussed on the telephone, Billy thought next morning, was not nearly as interesting as Apple's decision, just announced, to go back to Taos.

He stared at his wife as though he'd never seen her before, and Apple, embarrassed, looked away.

"There's another thing," she said, stirring her coffee.

"No more surprises." Billy sank back on his spine in the straight breakfast-room chair and closed his eyes.

"Don't you like surprises?" she asked, as candidly as though they were strangers meeting for the first time in an anonymous public place.

"No," Billy groaned. "I never have, you know that."

"I didn't know that," Apple said, with her new, cool judiciousness. "Remember that surprise party I gave for your thirty-first birthday?"

"Oh God, one of the worst," Billy groaned, and wondered why it had taken him so long to make that admission.

"Well." Her tone was final, even dismissive. With his eyes closed, he heard her stand up. "I don't want to get sidetracked, we can talk about all that later. . . . The unwelcome surprises."

"I don't want to," Billy said, opening his eyes. "What's the other thing?"

And there she was—Apple, the woman he'd known longer than anyone except his own mother, standing transformed in the yellow light from the window, poised as a butterfly on a branch tip. "You're leaving me," he said.

"Just for a few days." She glanced at him, over her shoulder, and he noticed again her perfect poise. She'd brought that back from Taos—the grace of another life. Another unwelcome surprise, Billy thought, then wondered if he could even tolerate Ms. Tandy moving her blue robe from one hook to another in the polished prism of her bathroom at Beaver Cove.

"She's having a child," Apple said.

"Cory?" Billy yelped.

"Of course not." Apple's tone was dry. "Maureen. And your son. She called me last night, to tell me. Couldn't wait."

She'd never called Little Billy "your son" before. "Don't assign him to me," Billy grumbled, "especially not now when he's made another bad decision. He's at least as much your creation as mine."

"Maybe it wasn't a decision."

"Then it should have been."

"Aren't you going to ask about the baby?"

As he reeled out the expected questions concerning due date

and the state of his daughter-in-law's health, Billy realized that he was living—had always lived, he thought now—in a world that had closed sometime in the summer of 1970: the world of his wedding, of his last encounter with Cory, of the birth of his hopes and expectations as an adult, about to acquire nearly everything he wanted.

"I'm stuck," he said, suddenly.

Apple turned. Her light eyes considered him thoughtfully, as though, he thought, he was an insect in a jar.

"Yes," she said. "You are."

"You knew it?"

"For a long time."

"Why didn't you say anything?"

"There wasn't anything for me to say"—and Billy remembered, with a spasm of resentment, that she'd gone to all those support groups when Little Billy was in trouble; she'd learned their useful lingo, although she'd never used it before.

There had been no need.

"Do you care?" he asked, under his breath, and felt his hand moving toward her, as though of its own accord.

She reached to grasp his fingers, and he felt the strength of her hard little hand and remembered that this was Saturday, the day he'd promised to help her in her garden—the first time, he realized, in all these years, he'd made such an offer—and now she was leaving. "Don't go," he said. "At least put it off."

"I can't. Something's happened to Cory."

"She's hurt?"

"Yes. I don't know how. I have to go to her."

"But you're just back," he mumbled, ashamed.

"Remember when your mother took sick, and you had to go in the middle of the night?"

"Yes, but I hired nurses the next day—"

"I can't hire nurses for Cory," Apple said abruptly, adding, "I don't think it's that kind of thing. Cory's not dying."

No, she's not dying, Billy thought, that's one thing for sure. Cory would outlast them all. His mother had withered away into a death as small as her life, as suitable, after his sister had moved to Cincinnati "for the possibilities"—a man with a steady income—and a rocky marriage, as it turned out.

"Why don't you care about this baby?" Apple asked, and again her light eyes rested on him with a certain weight.

"It's too soon for a baby," Billy said. "I'll have to increase their allowance."

"Maybe Little Billy can get a job at the library."

"What, shelving books?"

"To start out. Oh stop that, Billy," Apple said, turning away with a flick of her skirt—the tailored suit Billy hadn't seen her wear in years, but then, she was off to the airport in an hour, which gave her the insouciance of travelers, so galling to those left behind.

Of course there would be consolations.

Billy tried to look forward to more time with Ms. Tandy, extra time, only slightly poisoned by the fact that she would expect him to spend it all with her, including the nights when he would so much prefer to be alone, stretching luxuriously in his own big bed.

A little later, he helped Apple carry her things to the car—a warm coat, it would still be chilly in Taos, and a suitcase that seemed to him suspiciously large—and kissed her goodbye.

She was already pointed toward her departure, preoccupied, but she relented after giving him a dry kiss on the cheek and turned her full, soft mouth as though she was going to collapse in his arms.

My God, Billy thought, that hasn't happened in a long time— decades, he couldn't be sure—a collapse of her will and a quick trip to their warm bed. He knew that she had finally gone into a dry, harshly-lighted adulthood where he could not follow—did not even wish to follow. And she had always been, for so many years, so young.

He stood at the end of the stone path and watched her drive away; politely, she flipped her hand out the window, waving. How would he hold her now that she was grown? he thought confusedly, and remembered with relief that Ms. Tandy might be available that evening, especially if he promised to bring dinner and a bottle of champagne—for she would want to celebrate these unexpected days of freedom.

Freedom, Billy thought bitterly, making his way to the house. What a taste.

Still, he went at once to the telephone, partly because he knew his secretary would be arriving soon, and that would end his privacy.

Melissa Tandy's assistant at the law firm put him through at once.

"I've had a reprieve," he said, and hoped he sounded joyful—one of Ms. Tandy's favorite words. When she was disappointed, she often mourned that her life lacked joy; Billy had never been sure what she meant. She seemed to him to have everything except the marriage and children she'd told him were never part of her plans.

But Melissa had an engagement for dinner, which she refused, in her business voice, to break, and Billy heard himself pleading, to no avail.

He hung up and sat looking at his hands, noticing for the first time the spots of dark pigment that rode the lumpy veins. Perhaps, he thought, old age when it comes will bring some relief.

As he stood up, he saw Apple's gardening hat and gloves lying on the hall table. He remembered his promise gratefully; it gave a shape to the day.

Picking up her gloves, he started to the garden, and when his secretary pulled into the driveway half an hour later, she saw him on his knees in the mud, scraping at something.

She was not surprised when he came in, half an hour later, ready to dictate ten or eleven letters while he removed, with an orange stick, the dirt beneath his fingernails.

16

Cory left early that morning to see Father Visconti at the Ranchos de Taos church where Roy Cross had been a parishioner.

She had a reason, this time, a justification beyond asking Father Visconti questions to which he could only answer by shaking his head and sighing.

Earlier that morning, when the smoke from Manuel's first fire in the Big Room fireplace was beginning to curl up past Cory's sun porch—her signal that the day has officially begun—and the five guests in residence were scraping their chairs back in the dining room, preparing to sit down, Conchita came up the stairs and tapped lightly on Cory's door.

This never happens.

Cory's orders are explicit.

She put on her robe and slid her cold feet into her slippers.

At the door, she glared at Conchita. The sweet smell of pinon from Manuel's fire drifted up the stairs behind the frightened girl.

Conchita slipped a thick envelop into Cory's hand.

"Where does this come from?" Cory asked.

Conchita shook her head, face averted, and flew back down the stairs.

Inside her room, the door securely closed, Cory wished for the first time she had a fireplace to go to, a leap of warm flame to warm herself at before she opened the envelop.

Her name—her first name only—was scrawled in big black letters across the envelop.

Inside there were four strips of negatives, folded.

She turned to the window, flooded with cold still light from the mesa, and held up each strip, trying to see the images. Several were of groups, whose faces emerged as small, featureless blobs from the mass; others appeared to be of people standing alone against a familiar landscape—distant mountains, the mesa. She guessed they were taken at a celebration of some kind, perhaps a party out in the desert. There was an air of festivity, although without the usual bottles and flowers.

In the background of one of the negatives, a pack of cars was parked around a pinon tree, as though tethered. After staring again and again at this one, she thought she saw Roy's old van.

She dressed quickly and went downstairs to tell Consuela she was going out. The girl stared at her anxiously, guessing the envelop had caused this unusual change in Cory's routine—she always worked at her desk in the morning.

"The guests will be fine till dinner, I gave them an earful last night," Cory reassured her, remembering how this particular bunch had stared when she talked to them about her theory of conception: a form of prayer, she called it, and like all prayers, most effective when we don't know whether or not it's working—a speech she would never have given in Apple's presence.

Out in the courtyard in front of Mabel's, Cory glanced at her patroness' birdhouses, and remembers that Mabel forbade the courtyard to cars, to protect her precious pigeons.

Birds for her, people for me, Cory thought, and felt it is a worthy replacement: one form of care-taking for another, but at least her form might seem more elevated. (Although when she remembered Apple and that dog, that old snoozer, whose last illnesses her sister attended with tears of despair . . .)

Shuffling that thought away—Apple is gone, after all, and not likely to return, although what exactly went wrong between them (again) she was not sure and did not really want to know—Cory crossed the footbridge to the parking lot, unlocked her jeep (no hideous reminder, this time, of her foolhardiness) and slid onto the cold seat.

She was driving into town before the rush of early morning traffic, and the quiet road reminded her that two years ago it was usually empty. Now there was talk of widening it, taking out a thick hedge of pinons, there since before Mabel's time, when the road was dirt. Cory knew she would be called on to oppose this so-called improvement, and felt exhausted at the prospect: speeches, protests, more speeches, more protests, and in the end, almost inevitably, the big earth-moving machinery.

In town she parked at the curb and ran in to the photography lab that had stolen a few feet from the La Fonda Hotel's lobby. The lab would not open for another hour.

Brooding over this, walking up and down on the pavement outside, she wondered for the first time why she was given only the negatives.

As a device, it seemed transparent: to afford the giver a few hours, before she has the negatives printed.

She decided to take the photographs directly to Father Visconti. He would perhaps help her to identify the faces; he knew Roy for years and regularly heard his confession.

Thoroughly chilled, she went back into the hotel lobby to see if she could find a cup of coffee. The man at the desk, who was trailing an oxygen tank, offered her his styrofoam cup, half-full of something dark, but Cory, in a fit of fastidiousness, refused it.

"Not clean enough for you?" he inquired with a leer, and she turned away sharply. "Sorry," he called after her, and, affected by the crushed quality of his voice, Cory turned back. "You waiting for somebody?" he asked amiably.

"The photo lab."

"You got a while. They trying to get their new machines sorted out—brought them up from Albuquerque last week." He made an elaborate job of studying the clock hanging behind his shoulder. "Be another half hour, anyway. Want to see the pictures? Nobody's up yet, I can leave the desk." Already, he had dug a large key out of a drawer.

Cory protested—she'd heard something about the pictures— but he was already wheeling his oxygen tank toward a door to the right of the reception desk.

As he unlocked it and flung it open, the oxygen tank pattering along behind him, Cory smelled the stale air.

He was ushering her into a windowless room, papered with framed drawings and paintings. At the bottom of one wall, a long row of small, shined shoes stood as though waiting for feet to be put into them.

"D.H. was a great painter," her escort said, sitting down abruptly on a chair near the door. "But they never would show his paintings in England. Banned. Indecent, according to the authorities back then."

Dutifully, Cory began to study the paintings: unfinished scrawls, showing arms and legs and backs in profusion; a great, simplified energy, like a bolt of electricity, seemed to animate them.

"You like 'em?" her escort asked with a lasciviousness that was mostly just hopeful, she thought.

"I don't know yet." Cory continued her study. A great black oil of entwined bodies made her shake her head, amused; the painter was struggling, obviously, with many demons, and his lovers had the appearance of writhing snakes.

Yet a landscape with horses was as childish as a sampler.

"How could anyone find these indecent?" she asked. "They're so innocent it's embarrassing"—and she remembered the red and blue birds on her bathroom windows.

With a practiced gesture, he indicated several dangling penises and a bunch of breasts, scattered randomly throughout the paintings. "Nudes," he said, "that's the problem."

"There've always been nudes, in paintings."

"Not doing those things," he explained triumphantly. Heaving himself up, he dragged his tank to a large painting where two bodies were copulating; as he began to point out the details, Cory left the room. He called after her, urgently: she owed him five dollars, for the viewing. She left the bill on his desk and heard him hurrying along behind her, pulling his tank, explaining.

Out on the street, she decided to walk down the block to the pastry shop that was usually open early, past the tourist joints that sold t-shirts and fake Indian blankets and turquoise that was often painted plastic.

In the coffee shop, warming her hands around a mug, she thought of D.H.'s scrawls with dawning affection. That same innocence and energy charmed her in Lawrence's novels, when she read them years ago; as though a child, an exceptionally clever and sensitive child, had set out to create a world.

The paintings were only a cruder version of his Paradise, she thought, and of course it was largely inhabited by snakes. No one from that period could escape the coruscating Puritanism Lawrence battled all his life—

And she recognized a link with Roy.

So innocent, too, somehow. So energetic. Selling his Navajo blankets up and down this spine of the Rockies, never more than a few dollars in his pocket, and contributing all the rest of his time and energy to sermons, pamphlets, meetings.

No one believed he could change what was happening to the forest up on the mountain; no one believed he could save the Grandfather trees.

Now he was buried under one of them.

Cory felt his loss like a cold draft and took a swallow of coffee, distracting herself by wondering when lattés and cappuccinos first made their appearance in Taos.

Innocence. Why do I value it? she wondered, a little later. Innocence always goads me to action. Without that as a spur, I would be content to let the mysterious cycles of the universe have their way—as indeed they do, whether I strive against them or not. Apple knew this, floating in the warm passivity Cory always found so objectionable. Perhaps it was after all a form of wisdom.

She knew she would not be pursuing Roy Cross' murderer if it was not for Roy's innocence, his eternal belief in the possibility of change—as though, she thought, finding out what happened to Roy would keep her own feeble faith alive.

She didn't think about Roy himself much anymore; what might have been her grief turned into the determination to avenge him which she could express to no one. It was as out of control as her feelings were, two years ago when they came, briefly, together.

He couldn't stay.

It was not so much his marriage, although he honored that bond, as it was his obsession with the Grandfather trees. No one at the pueblo called them that, but Roy did, to express his reverence. He thought they were essential to a ritual from his own tradition: the Beauty Walk.

Cory asked him once late at night, after much drinking and love-making, what exactly the Walk was.

It was a form of graceful acceptance, she decided, after she listened to Roy for a while.

A dance-like resignation, without the bitterness implied by that word.

A fluidity essential to survival for a hard-pressed people—Navajo, Pueblo, what difference did the tribe make?

It was, she thought later, the softening of her tough body under his, the blessed willingness to receive.

With a renewed sense of mission, she walked out onto the street and back up to the hotel, where the photo lab was finally open.

Turning the negatives over to a girl in a white coat, she began to worry that they might go astray; she cautioned that these were important, then recognized the girl as one of Juanita's many daughters and wished she had been more discreet. Everyone in Taos, it sometimes appeared, was interested in her activities.

With an odd look, the young woman took the negatives and disappeared into a back room; the reek of chemicals was strong, and Cory wondered if the young woman worried about their effect.

Then she remembered that not everything in modern life was her responsibility—a lesson her sister has learned if anything too well—and left to get through the next hour.

Back in the La Fonda lobby—she saw her guide glaring at her from behind his desk, heard him give his oxygen tank a jerk so that it rattled protectively toward him—she decided to call home.

Answering briskly on the first ring, Consuela sounded as professional as she should: "Mabel Dodge Luhan House? How may I help you?"

Perhaps, Cory thought, the greeting was a little too professional; they were not the Taos Inn after all, or any of the other official tourist establishments.

"How is everything going?" Cory asked.

"Fine. Your sister called."

"What did she say?"

"She's coming back. She gets to Albuquerque this afternoon."

Cory was silent.

"She wants somebody to meet her."

Still Cory had nothing to say.

"Manuel was going to fix that hole in the roof," Consuela reminded her. "And somebody has to go shopping, nothing in the house for supper."

"Tell Manuel to meet her," Cory said, thinking only now of the hours she had left to get used to her sister's return.

"When's he going to fix the roof?"

"He can fix it this morning, I've told him where to look. I'll do the shopping myself, later on."

Eight hours, she figured, looking at her watch, wishing with sudden vehemence she had not decided to give in and wear one; as though the watch itself had brought on this unwelcome second invasion.

Something about the nature of time, she thought, standing in the lobby—the man behind the desk was still staring at her—was bringing Apple back; as though both of them realized, now, that time was short.

She walked into the plaza, beginning to fill up with cars. Men spoke, nodded and lingered, women hurried along with preoccupied faces, a few Indians from the pueblo were clustered in front of the window of one of the tourist shops. Around the bandstand, a group was taking down the Christmas decorations—at last. The scene seemed trivial to Cory, tawdry, almost; and then she caught sight of the mountain, gleaming with snow above a tangle of electric wires.

There it was, as always, winter or summer.

Then she saw her lawyer going into his office, one arm loaded with papers, and crossed the plaza to speak to him.

"Anything new?" she asked, surprising him.

"You'd have been the first to hear." He had a shaving cut on his chin; it was bleeding. Cory reached into her pocket for her handkerchief and quickly blotted the drop of blood.

"Why, thank you." He stared at her, embarrassed. She had never done anything like that before.

"I always carry a clean handkerchief," Cory muttered, a little taken aback herself. "Just so you know: I got an envelop this morning. Someone left it at Mabel's during the night." She showed him the envelop with its angry scrawl. "Recognize the handwriting?"

He took the envelop. "Afraid not."

"And the gall to call me by my first name. I believe I'll take it to Martin, later."

"What was in it?"

"Negatives. I'm having them printed."

"Bring them over later, if they amount to anything. Be careful, Cory," he said as she turned away.

As she crossed the plaza, a cold wind from the mountain whipped the edge of her jacket and she clutched it closer, wishing she'd worn a scarf and gloves.

Time to go again to Martin, she realized, and for more than the deciphering of handwriting. He set her expectations in order two or three times a year.

In the photo lab, Juanita's daughter was waiting for her with a curious expression on her face, half anticipation, half chagrin. "They're in the machine." She gestured behind her.

Cory saw photographs passing slowly through the viewer on top of the new developer.

At once she recognized Roy's van, parked beside a road.

She stepped closer, conscious of Juanita's daughter just behind her shoulder.

The photographs were amateurish, out of focus; some showed turned backs, averted faces, as though the photographer was circling the edge of the crowd.

Now and then a face flashed out, and Cory studied it, looking for someone she knew, but they are all strangers.

There was something going on, she realized, a gathering of some kind—the crowded figures told that much; but what kind of gathering she couldn't imagine. The stripped trees showed the photographs were taken in cold weather, probably last fall, shortly before Roy died.

She studied a photograph of parked cars—who would take such a picture?—but the van she'd thought was Roy's was indistinguishable from most Taos vehicles, mud-encrusted, a big dent along one side. It could be Roy's or anyone else's. She'd been misled by her own hopefulness.

"Thanks." She took the prints and asked how much she owed.

"Nothing," Juanita's daughter said.

"What do you mean?"

"You're trying to do something for Nancy—she's my aunt, my mother's sister."

Cory had not known this, although she was not surprised. Everyone in Taos was related.

"I'm not having much success," she said, pocketing the photos.

"You're trying. Everybody else has quit."

Thanking her, Cory wondered if the girl had noticed something in the photos. "Did you see anything?" she asked.

"Some party, it looked like," Juanita's daughter said, turning away.

Enough is enough, Cory thought, and she went out to the Jeep. Sighing, she started the engine and backed out. Looking over her shoulder, she saw a woman she didn't recognize staring at her from a doorway.

Then she was driving along the strip with its hideous accumulation of gas stations and discount stores—the development that ruined Taos for people who knew it, before.

After a few miles, she emerged onto the mesa. Far away to the right, some benighted soul was building a golf course, and she could see the looming hulks of new houses on its fringes. A vigorous attempt to preserve their meager water supply from this usage failed, a year before; it was the only fight Cory led. Not the defeat so much as the stripping away of her privacy, the interviews, the press photos for their little weekly (even a threat, never fulfilled, of a visit from an Albuquerque TV crew) convinced Cory she must work in another way.

Quietly, quietly.

Although some of her guests, she knew, would hardly call her method quiet.

The Ranchos church turned its broad backside to the street; a gallery of little shops, most of them closed, circled it. Cory pulled into the dirt courtyard behind the church and parked, locking the Jeep.

She took the pistol out from under the seat and pushed it in her belt; she'd given up wearing a holster after the word was painted on the windshield. It took too much time to get the weapon out.

Knowing the priest would object, she pulled out her shirt, covering the pistol.

A man leaning against a wall watched her, and several stray dogs, frolicking in the dust, turned to follow. She warned them away. Dogs in Taos were common as fleas in warm weather; she had learned never to allow them to follow her, for fear they would win her heart. There was no space in her life for a dog, she knew, scarcely for a human, and remembered Tony.

Tony comes and goes according to some mysterious current in his own life, she thought. Really it has very little to do with me. A rationalization, perhaps, but useful. She refused to associate Tony with any form of guilt, with any form of responsibility. That would spoil it.

She crossed the little graveyard.

A few of the wooden crosses were hung with artificial flowers, the blue and pink roses O'Keeffe turned into febrile decorations. Most of the graves were too old for such remembrances.

How plain, how bald death is here, she thought as she pushed open the heavy carved church door. On the Day of the Dead, she always bought sugar skulls and little dancing skeletons as though she, too, had accepted the fatalism that made its way north from Mexico. In fact, the blurred image of a redeeming Savior, a golden-haired Christ with a lamb in his arms, still intervened at times and blocked the colder shadow.

Inside the church, she dipped her finger in the holy water font and crossed herself, claiming the place. All forms of worship were the same at the root, she believed, and she refused to play the infidel because she was only a baptized, not a practicing Christian.

She walked down the narrow aisle between the hard wooden benches. A sign on the wall in Spanish warned non-Catholics not to partake of communion—another prohibition Cory chose long ago to ignore.

The stations of the cross, small steel plates painted in pastel colors, were fixed at regular intervals on the whitewashed adobe walls. Ahead of her, the retablo with its enigmatic carved images loomed like another great closed door.

An old man was sweeping the area around the alter. Cory called to him; she felt his fierce defense of the sanctuary as he turned, frowning.

"Is the priest in?" she asked, in Spanish.

"Sí." He sounded unwilling.

"Would you get him for me, please?"

He nodded brusquely, laid down his broom, genuflected and crossed himself as he passed the alter, then disappeared through a side door.

Waiting, Cory shivered. The big wood stove, stoked and lighted for mass, was dead; the towering nave was packed around a cube of coldness.

Father Visconti, a young man with a lean face and dark eyes, appeared in the doorway.

He glanced at her sharply, and then, with a slight shake of his head—he expected a parishioner, she felt sure, someone he could legitimately counsel—he came swiftly toward her, his boots slapping the hardened mud floor. He wore workman's clothes, rough and serviceable.

"Good morning," he said with a half-submerged sigh.

Without asking her the reason for her visit, he turned and led her through the door to the little office.

A mug of coffee sat cooling on his crowded desk; an ancient telephone, its round dial gleaming, was perched on top of a pile of papers.

He moved books from a chair so that Cory could sit down. Still he did not speak, and she found herself waiting for a signal.

He sat down behind his desk, leaned on his arms, and looked at her.

She held out the package of photographs. "I wonder if you would help me with these."

He waved them away. "Signora, I have something to tell you," he said in his slightly accented English.

"Please." She was all attention, the photographs resting on her knee.

"Mrs. Cross came to see me yesterday. She has asked me to do all I can to persuade you to stop."

"More threats?"

"Her boy is afraid to leave the house. She's been forced to ask her sister to come and stay with him when she goes to work. You are creating great hardship for this woman."

Cory could no longer meet his gaze. She looked at the crucifix hanging behind him. "I want to find out who killed Roy."

"His widow wants you to let her husband rest in peace."

"What do you think, Father?" she asked. "Is it right for whoever murdered Roy to go unpunished?"

"Judgment is mine, says the Lord. Roy is dead." He crossed himself. "Finding the murderer changes nothing."

"Perhaps it would prevent another death."

"That is not within our power."

She felt the weight of his certainty.

"We must accept the will of the Lord, even when we do not understand it," he said with the same leaden assurance. "You are not a believer, Signora. If you were, you would stop what you are so stubbornly insisting on doing. Who here supports you?" he asked, raising his voice, and with a sweeping gesture of his arm, he seemed to indicate the whole town, the whole county.

"Nobody," Cory admitted. "My own lawyer wants me to stop."

"So why do you not—?"

"I believe in the truth," she said quaintly but with utter conviction. "Now will you take five minutes and look at these snapshots?"

She handed them across the desk. Father Visconti took the package with the tips of his fingers. "Someone left the negatives at my house during the night."

He glanced at her skeptically. When he did not open the packet, she took it back and opened it for him, spreading the photographs out on the crowded surface of his desk.

He tipped his head, glancing at them unwillingly. "I do not know any of these people," he said after a moment.

She began to gather up the photographs, satisfied that he had been willing to look. She wanted to believe that authorized her to continue. "I'm only trying to find out what happened," she repeated.

He stared at her, and she sensed the limit of his patience. She was, after all, from a world he had been taught to distrust, the world of entrepreneurs, developers, retirees, godless emigrants from the ruined cities of the earth, flocking to Taos (but not to its churches) like the Biblical horde of locusts.

"I beg you to reconsider," he said.

"What?"

"Your own safety," he explained in a lowered voice.

"Why do you care?"

"We don't need any more violence here—"

"You means the deaths of women. The unresolved murders of women."

He sighs.

"Five, since I've been here," she said. "Sophia Cardinale, behind the Desert Bar. Tina Mendoza left in the ditch by the road. The two Hernandez sisters—"

He held up his hand. He presided, she knows, at those funerals.

"Don't worry, Father. I'm here to find out the truth, not to die for it."

"You have no way of preventing that," he said, and she felt, for the first time, his concern.

"I'll take good care of myself," she promised him. "But I can't rest till I find out what happened to Roy."

He sighed. She waited a moment. He had nothing further to say. It was all the vindication she needed.

Yet it may happen, Cory thought as she left the icy church, that we will destroy this place, not only with our golf courses and two million dollar houses and expensive restaurants but with our insatiable appetite for the truth.

Or that version of it that matches our preconceptions.

She realized as she drove away from Ranchos that she had no way to comprehend Nancy's resignation. The priest must know its source and structure. He and his church were agents of that resignation. But Cory, who knew only how to fight (as she thought, the useless wad of photographs on the seat beside her) refused to recognize the meaning, or the way, of resignation. That would bring me to bitterness, she thought.

There is no other will than mine, she said to herself, an ironic mantra, as she drove into Taos and took the turn to Mabel's, no longer on two wheels now and obeying the speed limit.

Parking, she saw Manuel on the roof, a small figure hunched against the sky. It was clouding over, and she guessed the afternoon would bring snow. She must relieve Manuel of his duties so he could get an early start for Albuquerque. The road through the pass would be treacherous once the snow began.

She walked up the path to the footbridge, her eyes fixed on Manuel, who stopped work, watching her.

"You better leave soon for the airport, it's coming on to snow," she called.

He nodded, and climbed down the ladder. "I got the hole fixed, enough to hold for now," he told her,

"What's that?"

He was holding something in his hand.

"I found it up under the vigas." He handed her a small book, bound with faded red covers. "Water got in and ruined some."

She opened the book and recognized the deeply slanted, darkly inked writing. "Thank you, Manuel," she said, turning away.

"You want me to take the Jeep?"

"You'll need it, coming back over the pass." Her voice trembled. She could hardly wait to get to her room.

She heard the ladder scrape as he took it down, behind her.

In the hall, she hurried past Consuela, who handed her a shopping list—"Later," Cory said—and ran up the stairs to the sun porch.

She closed the door, panting, and sat down on the side of her bed.

Then she opened the diary at random. She read the date: "October 21, 1952": three years before Mabel's death.

She began to read. The daily account, nothing more, for several pages.

She went to the bathroom.

As she stepped inside and closed the door, something crackled under her shoe.

Looking down, she saw the floor covered with red and blue fragments.

The window, D.H's window, was gone.

Cory knelt down and began to gather up the painted pieces of glass.

And then she was crying.

Three hours later, Apple is standing in the glaring late afternoon sunlight at the Albuquerque airport. She wonders as she has all the way across the country why she is coming back, why she is willing to visit Taos, and her sister, again. The apprehension that assailed her earlier in the day, wordless, without an obvious cause, has faded away.

She shifts her heavy suitcase to her other hand.

Cory will realize Apple means to stay a while when she sees the size of that suitcase.

Well, let her. Better that way than with words.

Apple expects to be met—that was the message she left at Mabel's—and she is not in the habit of being disappointed, in that department.

All her life, she has been ferried back and forth to airports. It is a form of politeness, she thinks, to see a woman off on her journeys and welcome her back. Perhaps even, she thinks, a form of protection—but from what?

The agents of strangeness.

Then she sees the man who works for Cory coming toward her with his loping gait.

"How are you," she says amiably, giving him her suitcase. He lists sideways under the weight.

Now she begins to dread the long drive up into the mountains. What will they talk about? And she realizes she has hoped that Cory would come for her, providing a nice secure space for conversation.

But Manuel is resourceful. He turns on the radio as soon as they are settled in the Jeep, then the heater, which emits a steady roar. Before they have reached the throughway north, Apple, exhausted by her premonitions, is asleep.

When she wakes, almost an hour later, they are driving through the narrowing plain that leads into the first mountain pass.

She sits up, an apology for her inattention on her lips, which she represses. "Where are we?" she asks, yawning.

Manuel turns down the radio, which is playing an insistent form of rock—Apple remembers it from the days when Little Billy filled the house with that passionate, irascible music. "Velarde," he tells her. "Apple orchards, here"—and points out the spindly bare trees down in the valley.

A mass of clouds is boiling up from the north, over the first purple peaks. "Looks like bad weather," Apple says.

"We get there before." His hands on the steering wheel are small as a child's, she notices, but wiry, each finger dense with black hair.

Searching for conversation, she asks, "You're from the pueblo, aren't you?"

"My father." He seems reluctant to go on. "Born there, but he left early. I was raised in town."

"Your parents go back to the pueblo for the feast days?"

"All of us. My grandmother has her house there. We cook a big meal, invite friends."

Apple remembers her discomfort, a week ago at the dances. "You don't really want us at your dances, do you?" she asks.

He glances at her, his narrow face shadowed. "Some people don't know how to act, taking photographs, talking to the dancers. One woman last winter climbed the ladder to the kiva." He blows out his cheeks. "They don't understand."

"But I understand," Apple insists. "My sister taught me."

"Some people is all right," Manuel says, but he sounds reluctant.

"Wouldn't it be better if you just closed the gate and posted a keep-out sign? Then you wouldn't have to be bothered. Of course you'd lose the entrance fee we pay, and nobody would buy your crafts."

He glances at her again. "Some of the old people want that. It's not the money," he adds.

"I thought you honored old people. If they want to close the pueblo, why don't you do it?"

"The governor and the war chief don't like it. They say we got something to give ."

"What is it?" Apple asks, looking out at the ice-crusted stream she remembers passing on her first trip up.

"The spirit," he says, embarrassed.

"But maybe we can't appreciate your spirit."

He shrugs. She waits for a bit, then asks him some direct questions about the meaning of the dances, but now he has closed stubbornly against her, he wards her off with obvious bits of misinformation.

After a while, he points out a bridge and a grove of cottonwoods: "Embudo Station. Mabel lived there at the end."

"Why?" Apple asks, surprised.

"Wanted to get away from the big house, too much going on up there, I guess."

"Tony went with her?"

"Seems like." Again, he is concealing something.

"What did your people think about that?"

"Didn't like it."

"He had a wife in the pueblo, didn't he?"

Manuel nods.

"So why did they tolerate Mabel?"

He looks at her, and she remembers her sister and the other Tony. "And now," she begins, "with Cory . . ."

Manuel's silence seems to have grown points.

Apple wonders if she is being disloyal to Cory, then realizes the question itself is irrelevant. If the bonds of loyalty held her, she would still be at home, waiting for Billy to come back from his half day at the Foundation. She would be putting on lipstick and brushing her hair.

She tries to imagine what he will do when he finds her note, propped on the pillow, but she is not interested enough in his reaction, now, even to imagine it. She has slipped out of harness, she tells herself, with a submerged laugh. She has done the wicked thing she never believed she could do. And she does not even know why.

Hung for a lamb, hung for a sheep, she thinks. "What's all this about Roy Cross' murder?" she asks Manuel, so brusquely he stares.

"I won't tell Cory," she adds childishly, but with emphasis, then laughs to let him know they are conspiring together—like two kids hiding in a closet, she thinks, waiting for the all-in-free.

Manuel shakes his head. "She better watch out."

"I know," she agrees, vehemently. "They killed her cat—"

He nods. "I buried him, back of the house."

"And wrote that word on her Jeep." She realizes she doesn't want to tell him what it was.

"Took me an hour to get it off." He goes on, slowly, "Your sister do a lot for this place, but she don't understand. People here don't like it. They take care of things their own way."

"Even a murder?"

He stares at the road. "Nobody knows what happened," he mutters.

"You think Roy died of drugs, the way the police are saying?"

He shakes his head, then mentions that Roy's various activities "got on people's nerves. We got to cut them trees, we need the income. We don't have a casino—the governor won't allow it—and we don't store nuclear waste, the way the Mescalaros are getting ready to do. So we got to cut the trees."

"But aren't they important?"

"That owl." He puffs out his cheeks, dismissively. "No owls here."

"I thought the trees were connected to your dances."

"That's more the Navajo."

"But what's this Cory told me, something about walking in beauty?"

"We got to have schools for the kids, health care, jobs. We not thinking too much right now about beauty. Roy didn't understand," he says bitterly, "he just see the way he thinks things ought to be. We don't act that way. We got to agree, put things before the council, listen to the governor, or the war chief. Roy want to go his own way."

"Well, he paid the price. You think it was somebody from the pueblo—"

"Tell Cory to stay out of this," he interrupts her. "She don't know, she don't understand. Anything can happen in Taos."

"You mean she's in danger?"

"Tell her!" he says, insistently. "She won't listen to us, just laugh, go on. Maybe she listen to you."

"Something's already happened," Apple says.

"Since you been gone?"

She nods. "Something happened yesterday."

Now they are driving through the gorge. Steep mountains cut off what is left of the daylight. The darkening sky turns lavender, then purple, and the first stars wink out.

Through her window, Apple sees the moon.

After a long silence, Manuel begins to tell Apple about the villages they are passing, but either his information is uninteresting or Apple has lost the ability to listen; in any event, she is dozing again.

Half asleep, she wonders for the first time why all the opportunities money opened to her—the visits to spas, the tasteful jewelry, the opera, theater—never meant anything, although there were times when, sitting at the symphony beside Billy, she felt her eyes fill with tears.

She knows now as she wakes up it was only the ordinary moments that are available to most women—nursing Little Billy, cooking a favorite recipe, having her hair done, weeding her flower bed—that gave her joy. The privileges she fell heir to were interesting, perhaps, but cold comfort.

She plans to talk to Cory about this realization, then remembers that something has happened to Cory, something she may want to hide from Apple.

If Cory is angry, it won't be the first time, she thinks. We will survive. Our relationship will survive. After all, it has already been tested in the fire.

But she knows it is different now. There is even more at stake: Cory's independence, her ability to cut off the past, and go on. Apple's own independence.

She nearly laughs. She has never been independent, or even wanted to be; and she remembers the great outcries of the seventies, when she was absorbed in her young son. She was shocked when, as a result of those outcries, abortion was made legal, and women stopped wearing bras. She never considered either an option.

But she knows now that Cory would have chosen abortion, had it been legal then; and Apple's present crusade—she recognizes it as that, now—would never have happened.

Would the loss have been for her, or for Cory?

A strange question.

As Manuel drives up the hill, Apple looks out over a long, purple plain, leading to the crested curve of the Rio Grande gorge. In the far distance, the Taos mountains are closing darkness into the valley. The lights of the town are just coming on.

Manuel sighs, as though relaxing at the sight of home, and Apple begins to ask him about his life—his wife and children.

As he talks, she wonders suddenly if he would understand her passion for the rituals of marriage and child-rearing, or if his wife would, washing clothes by hand and hanging them on a line behind their little adobe, pounding tortillas the way her mother and grandmother did before her.

This couple would never have given away a child.

They turn into Cory's drive, and Apple sees the bulk of Mabel's house ahead in the half-darkness.

There is something unknown there, she thinks. Something that can't be fitted into what I already understand, although what I already understand is substantial in its way and cannot be discounted.

Manuel parks the Jeep, and Apple sees her sister, standing on the footbridge that crosses the acequia.

17

"*W*hy did you come back?" Cory asks.

Manuel is carrying Apple's suitcase into the house.

"Something's wrong," Apple says calmly.

Cory looks away. Then she wipes her nose across the back of her hand.

"What happened?" Apple asks.

"They shot out D.H's window."

"Oh, Cory . . ."

"The window lasted eighty years, and now it's gone."

She sobs, once, as though the sound has been wrenched up out of her throat.

Apple carefully reaches out and touches her sister's shoulder. "But you're alright. You weren't hurt."

"You don't understand. The window is gone. They shot it out."

"You have to stop now, Cory," Apple says, and at once her sister turns away, toward the house.

"I'll never stop," Cory says.

Manuel is waiting for them at the front door. "Kiva Room?" he asks Cory.

She nods.

As Manuel goes off, Apple says, "I'm not trying to interfere. I love you, Cory. I want to be here. I'll see it through with you."

Cory does not turn around. Apple sees her bow her head, and suddenly Cory is sagging, as though she can hardly support the weight of her own body.

"I'm very tired," she says.

"Come in, sit down." It is Apple, now, who is deciding.

She goes to the kitchen and asks Conchita to make some tea. When she comes back, Cory is leaning her face on her hand.

"Are you tired enough to stop?" Apple asks.

"No."

"You were in love with Roy, weren't you?"

"I was in love with everybody," Cory says.

Conchita brings in the tea and goes out, quickly.

The room is full of doors, and Apple knows someone else will appear, in short order. "A lot of people get murdered—you told me that, yourself. But it's Roy you care about."

"Roy wasn't drunk in a bar, killed in a fight. He died because he was trying to accomplish something."

"You sound just like Mother." Before Cory can object, Apple goes on, "And Tony? Does he stand for something, too?"

"Yes," Cory says.

Apple smiles. "What does he stand for, Cory?"

"How in hell would you ever . . ."

"And your son? Did he stand for nothing at all? Is that why you let him go?"

"Go to hell, Apple."

"If you like. But I see the thread, finally—it's taken me a while. I've lived my life for love—oh yes, I have, and I know you find that ridiculous, because you believe, dear Cory, that you've lived your life for principle."

"You think—"

And then the guests come in, and Apple goes quietly away to her room, to wash her hands and brush her hair, for dinner.

If the woman doesn't want to listen, Cory thinks, of course there's no way to coerce her, but she is biting her tongue and staring at that bright, painted face—too bright, too painted, she thinks, why does this sort of woman bother to come to Mabel's?

The other two guests are silent on their side of the table, still pushing at the remains of Conchita's custard. Even Apple— unpredictable Apple, Cory thinks—is picking at the hem of the tablecloth as though she needs distraction.

"Of course I respect your opinion," Cory says, trying to get them started up again, for anything is better than this heavy silence. "I'm sure you've earned a right to it," she goes on.

The woman, Mirabel Kelly, returns her look directly. "Yes, I've earned it. I had an abortion when I was seventeen. It was the worse experience of my life."

"As I said, I respect your opinion, and I'm sorry you had such a bad time." It sounds weak, and she wonders what Apple is thinking. "But that's no reason to make abortion illegal."

"Women shouldn't be exposed to that sort of thing." Now it is Mirabel's husband, Raymond Kelly—a lawyer, isn't he?—weighing in. The protector, Cory thinks. What we all need.

"We have a right to chose what we want to be exposed to," Cory says.

Another woman, older, with a distinguished profile and grey hair knotted unfashionably on the back of her head, speaks up in a strange, squeaking voice. "I have never expected to take part in discussions like this at a bed and breakfast, and I assure you I have been to a great many, in all parts of the world."

Apple breaks in, to her sister's surprise, "I happen not to agree with Cory, but I understand her need to get this out on the table."

"What—?" Cory gasps, before she can stop herself.

Apple goes on coolly, "My sister has always believed in total honesty. Yet here I find she's leaving out something essential, from her own history." Now she looks at Cory, squarely. "Of course you're in favor of abortion. If it had been legal all those years ago, you would have gotten rid of your baby instead of giving him away."

So this is why Apple has come back: to have it out, all of it. Cory looks down at her hands, clenched on either side of her dessert plate.

Mirabel Kelly is nodding as though now she understands, and the older woman, fascinated, is leaning toward Cory. "It must have been heart-breaking," she asks kindly.

Kindness always tastes bitter. Cory snaps back, "To tell you the truth, I hardly remember it."

"Twenty-four years ago," Apple puts in. "He's a grown man, now. We don't know where he is."

"You never even saw him?" Mirabel asks.

"I saw him the day he was born." Cory is nerving herself. "I knew he would have to be put up for adoption."

Now Mr. Kelly feels called upon to express his unwanted sympathy. "In those days there was so much shame . . ."

"I wasn't ashamed. In fact, I felt quite proud of myself, going through all that alone. But I knew I was too young to raise a child. I had other things in view."

"What were they?" Apple asks.

"You know," Cory says.

"But your guests don't."

"I wanted to be free," Cory says. "I was willing to pay the price. I still am."

"Free, or paying the price?" Now it is the grey-haired woman asking, with an insidious smile.

"Both." Cory gets up from the table. The conversation has gone far enough. "Coffee in front of the fire," she says, in her hostess voice.

But she is trembling.

Apple takes her arm on the way out of the dining room, and Cory knows Apple feels her agitation.

Let her try to force me into something, she thinks grimly, snatching her elbow away.

Then she leads the way to the fire and sits on the edge of the back-broken couch, remembering their mother sitting like that, perched, a bird on a bough. Now all I need is a lapful of needlework.

As though in response to her sister's irony, Apple has pulled out a bag of knitting—when did she become a knitter, Cory wonders?—and is asking Raymond Kelly to loan her his hands.

Cory watches with astonishment as the burly man kneels at her sister's feet and extends his hands.

Rapidly, Apple casts a bright blue skein around his fingers and begins deftly to wind more wool around them.

"What are you making?" Mirabel asks, hovering.

"A cap for my grandchild."

Cory stares.

"My son and his wife are having a baby next fall," Apple goes on. "They told me when I was at home—couldn't wait, even though she's barely started."

"Apple!" Cory exclaims, but her sister continues to weave her wool around Raymond Kelly's hands.

"Lovely," the grey-haired woman exclaims. "I have five grandchildren, all girls, the lights of my life."

She and Apple begin some kind of a duet about grandmothering. Cory doesn't hear, can't hear; the conversation has been swept away, and she feels as though she wants to creep off to bed, unnoticed.

All this ends with a knock on the front door.

Conchita, drying her hands, flies to open it. Cory is surprised that she has heard the knock all the way in the kitchen, yet it seems appropriate that even Conchita is behaving in unexpected ways, revealing new powers.

The man she ushers in is bundled to the ears; his fur hat is flaked with fresh snow. Between its brim and his collar, a pair of round, dark eyes peer out, over a dark moustache that is also glittering with snow.

Suddenly Cory wishes Tony was sitting in the kitchen.

"Come in," she says in her practiced way, standing up to give him a seat on the broken sofa. Then they all watch as he stamps snow off his boots on the skiers' mat and strips off his coat, hat and gloves. Conchita stands by to take them and stack them on a chair.

Out of his coat, the man is short, stocky, powerfully built, one of those men, Cory thinks, whose skin seems to slide over his muscles loosely, like a bear's.

"Sit down," she says, then introduces herself and the others. To her surprise, the stranger doesn't tell them his name.

Who am I welcoming here? Cory asks herself a moment later.

Who is this stranger?

For he has launched into a monologue that leaves them all speechless, his authority as potent as his smoky smell, released by the heat of the fire as it dries his damp knees.

"It's a mistake to confuse our forests with Brazil's," he begins without further introduction, fixing his round eyes on Cory's.

Everyone seems to move closer, huddling together.

"The Southwest is entirely different. I manage nearly three thousand acres of forest land, up at Chama," he goes on. "I've mastered a technique that preserves what is unique to the forest while sensibly harvesting weak or disease-ridden trees. My technique can be applied anywhere—even here."

"We don't have your access to unlimited timber," Cory begins, assembling an authority to equal his. "There's not much left on our mountains after generations of firewood cutting and grazing."

"It's not a question of the scale of the operation," her guest continues, his eyes searching the little group for support. "We do not clear cut. We protect riparian areas. We promote old-growth trees and we retain dead snags."

"What's that?" Apple asks, but the stranger rides over her interruption and goes smoothly on. He is not interested in questions. In that, Cory realizes, they are alike.

"We go so far as to mark each tree individually. We consider where it will fall, how the tractors will remove it, where the trucks will load it," the stranger says, and Cory wonders why she cannot interrupt him, demanding an explanation.

"And at the same time, we operate a recreational service for hunters, hikers and fishermen—"

"No one's allowed to hunt on the sacred mountain," Cory interrupts, but again he rides smoothly across with a barely-perceptible raised eyebrow:

"I believe I've proved to my own satisfaction that forests can be maintained in a healthy condition, to the benefit of all species concerned, including the spotted owl, and yet be skillfully harvested in a way that benefits all."

Satisfied with his conclusion, he sits back, his hands on his knees.

"Is there some kind of dispute, around here?" Raymond Kelly asks. "Some kind of local disagreement?"

The stranger nods. "So-called do-gooders interfering in what we know is best for these forests."

"This is not Chama," Cory reminds him. "You're much higher there, it's a completely different habitat."

"Still, the principle holds. Harvest what is best for the forest, and allow multiple use."

"Coffee?" Apple asks, reaching for the silver pot, but this is going too far; Cory raises her hand.

"Have you come here for something?" she asks finally.

He frowns. At that moment, she senses rather than sees that someone else has come into the room.

It is Tony, leaning in the doorway to the dining room, his hands in his pockets.

For the first time since she's known him, for the first time in her life, perhaps, Cory wants to say, "Yes, come on in, take charge of things."

Not because she is afraid—there is nothing particularly intimidating about the intruder—but because the evening has slipped out of her grasp.

She stares across the room at Tony, willing him to come closer. And, unbidden, a memory comes to her of the photograph of Mabel's Tony, sitting majestic and silent on a straight-back chair in the midst of just such a gathering, around the same fireplace.

Perhaps her Tony has seen the photograph, Cory thinks. Perhaps that is why he never sits down in this room.

Now Apple has seen fit to try to begin a general conversation, into which the stranger—if Little Sister has her way—will disappear without a trace.

But this is Taos, Cory thinks, this is Mabel's house, and there are no general conversations here.

"I believe there is something more to be said on the subject of cutting our forests," Cory inserts into Apple's soothing monologue—something about babies, again—and she feels Tony stir by the doorway. "The pueblo has a special relation to the old trees. Their religious rituals—"

"The pueblo supports clear-cutting," the stranger interrupts.

"Well, they could be mistaken. Short-term interests—"

"Indeed." Where, Cory wonders, was this man educated? "But it's the opposition that drives the Native American populations to extremes. Left to themselves, they'd be willing to heed prudent suggestions, especially from people who've actually been involved in successful timbering."

"But what about the Grandfather trees?"

The man smiles. "Strangely enough, I've never heard them called that, except by Anglos. Aren't you thinking of the Navajos?"

Now Tony, in the doorway, speaks up. "Yes, the Navajos," he says.

"That young man who died of the overdose. . . .He was a Navajo," the stranger continues gently. "He should have gone back to his own people, practiced his principles there." Then he crosses himself, to Cory's dismay, drawing on another potent form of magic.

"Too late now," Tony says.

"Yes." The stranger looks at him, and Cory realizes they know each other.

"He's buried under one of them big trees, back in Navajo land," Tony says.

The stranger nods. "Why did he leave there? "

"Came here trading, never went back to his people. Married here."

They are beginning a duet.

Exasperated, Cory asks sharply, "You two know each other?"

They are silent.

Cory stands up. "This is my house," she announces, as though there might be some question. "I insist on knowing how you two are connected."

Tony turns back to the kitchen. The stranger, standing up, begins to put on his coat.

"Is it snowing?" the grey-haired woman asks, to fill the silence.

"Five inches before morning." He pushes his hat down on his head and buttons his coat. "Thank you," he says formally to Cory, and extends his hand.

She will not take it, she turns impatiently away. What lesson, she wonders, have they all learned from the evening? It is not a lesson she planned, nor will she look back on it with any degree of satisfaction. By the law of unanticipated influences, which she believes in, something positive should have come from this intrusion, which is why she permitted it; but nothing seems to have come of it, the stranger will leave without even having explained himself.

After he goes, the three guests hurry off to their rooms, propelled by discomfort, Cory thinks. That has happened often before, but only as a result of her own challenges.

Apple lingers.

"Goodnight," Cory says brusquely.

"I'd like to talk."

"Not tonight." Cory is already at the foot of her narrow stairs.

Then she turns around. "You think I delude myself," she tells Apple, and her voice is thick. "You think I believe I only act on principle."

"Yes," Apple says.

"If that was so, Tony would never come here again." And then she is hurrying up the stairs.

Passing Mabel's room, she hears voices, and knows the Kellys are discussing their surprising evening.

No wonder I never have repeats, she thinks.

In the sun porch, she turns on a light and sees Mabel's diary lying on her bed. She sits down beside it.

"*O desolation,*" she reads, in Mabel's intense scrawl. "*O the end of the end. I am leaving my house, I am going out into the desert like the Biblical Ruth. After all these years, it is dust and ashes in my mouth.*"

Cory turns the page. There are only a few more entries before the water stain begins, blurring the remainder.

"*I believe Embudo is the best I can do, at this juncture,*" she reads on the next page. "*We will be away from the guests, we will be alone together at last, and maybe together we can stop the drinking. Everything I tried to do has come to nothing. I believe it was Lawrence's death that turned the tide. Somehow after that nothing prospered. And Tony's drinking. And my drinking—our great bond, now. And that terrible incident in the bathtub—.*"

"*The house seems full of sadness now,*" the next entry begins, dated a few days later. "*All the life and hope and energy I poured into it, all the life and hope and energy all the others poured into it—Lawrence, Frieda (Bless her Soul), Brett, Caddy-*" the list goes on and on, Cory is skipping—"*all of them to a greater or lesser degree shared what I was trying to create: to bring strangers into this magical world, to expose them to its influence. And now all gone, all destroyed—and Tony with it, gone down into destruction, and I am to blame.*"

"*When I remember,*" another entry begins, "*how I first saw him, how my heart beat, for no reason I understood. . . . A figure standing motionless by the gate, round, tall like a lilac bush—like a still column, wrapped head to toe in a grey blanket. He looked at me and said, "You do not see me if I don't want you to." It was half a joke. I invited him inside.*"

"*Always, after that,*" the page goes on, "*I thought he was so poised, able to take care of himself—like a rock balanced on the edge of an abyss. I never worried about Tony—never until much later.*

"*But once he said to me, "I lost here. This not my place," and after that he would go off wandering into the night, two or three times a week, and not come back until morning. And he never would let me plait his hair, in the old way, for the dances; he went back to the pueblo, to his wife, for that. "Let me plait your hair," I used to plead, but he wouldn't, he wouldn't even explain why. And little by little he shut me out, and then the drinking began, and after a while it was the only thing between us, the only passion we shared.*"

"*It was the pueblo,*" Mabel had written in stark letters on the next page. "THE PUEBLO GOT HIM IN THE END."

Cory turns another page, skips a big splotch, purple as a bruise.

"*He never sang anymore, after that,*" she reads. "*And I remember the first evening, when he asked for a drum, and we didn't have one, and he commenced to sing, anyway. He drew his breath from deep down, and sent the sound out into the room, and soon the room was full of it. Again he drew his breath, from deep down, further down than I'd known breath could be drawn. And brought it up, and with it the song that went around the room, all around the room, like waves. None of us had ever heard singing like that before, even though we'd been in Europe, in Paris and London, and gone to symphonies and operas, for years. No one knew how to draw the breath deep out of the lungs, out of the belly, and send it forth in sound.*"

Cory closes the diary. She wonders, suddenly, what right she has to read what Mabel hid from all eyes many years ago.

What right?

The question of right, she realizes, has never concerned her.

Now she goes to the door, opens it, and listens. The house is quiet; she can't hear any of her sleepers breathing.

But it is not her guests she wants now, not even their attention, their surprise, their dismay, their rare unwilling agreement. It is not Apple's warm arms, her smiles, her explanations. It is the man who stood in the dining room doorway and, so rapidly, disappeared.

She goes down the stairs and through the dark house, looking for him.

But Tony has gone.

Apple, tossing in the cold night, knows from past experience that sleep has left her suddenly and finally. She sits up in bed and turns on the light.

Immediately she remembers Billy shading his eyes and complaining, "Do you have to do that?"

For years they spent every night lying peacefully side by side, falling asleep and waking at almost exactly the same moment, so that she did not even know what his breathing sounded like, once he was deep in dreams.

Turning forty, Apple realized that she was sleeping in a different way. She lay awake a long time most evenings—except when she had a glass of wine at dinner—listening to Billy's breathing grow deeper and deeper, with pauses between so long she sometimes nearly shook him to see if he was all right.

At Mabel's, there is no one to be disturbed by her lamp.

She looks at her watch; barely midnight—and feels the panic that comes with all changes. So many hours of darkness left; and she is, once again, at the far end of the house, in the Kiva room, remote from the others.

Not that she could have drawn much comfort from the company of those strangers, she realizes, after what went on at dinner;

and who was that man who came in the door, whom Cory welcomed as though she knew him?

But of course he was a stranger, too, Apple thinks, like everyone else here. Cory welcomed him without questions because she is always welcoming strangers. The easier way.

Apple gets out of bed and puts on her terrycloth robe. Packing hastily that morning, she almost decided to leave it behind, to make space for her boots, but then she remembered the comfort she derives from its familiar smell and feel, and knew it would be cold, ever colder, at Mabel's as January draws toward its end. She realized then she did not know how long she would stay.

Not long, if none of these mysteries are solved, she thinks, if Cory goes on avoiding me, as she has from the moment I saw her on the footbridge across the acequia. Hardly a greeting, even.

For of course her sister was not glad to see her.

Apple feels a stab of pain.

In spite of the thickening of all her feelings, the dulling accomplished by years of restraint, the stab is sharp, and she knows she still hopes for something essential from Cory. My sister, my only sister, she thinks. Cory is essential to her now their mother is gone.

This is something we must talk about—our memories of her, she thinks.

I know she was different for Cory, disappointing in other ways.

We must talk about that, Apple decides.

She recognizes the thrust of energy that comes with the decision, and the welcome clarity.

I'm not going to sit here in the cold all night, she thinks. I'll go and make myself a cup of tea.

She pads down the long dark hall, a light shining from the office at the far end. Passing Consuela's desk, she wonders what happens if a guest comes in late, after everyone has gone to bed. Perhaps there's a bell somewhere to ring.

In the big room, she sees snow falling outside the windows, flakes dancing in the beam from the light over the door. She goes down the three steps into the long, shadowy dining room. A wall light has been left on, casting rays through pin holes in a curved tin shade.

At the kitchen door, she hesitates, realizing someone is sitting at the big table.

That Indian.

She immediately corrects herself: Tony. But what is he doing here?

He has a light—a big flashlight, she sees—and he is intently peering at a paper spread on the table.

She nerves herself to step into the kitchen, knowing he will be surprised. But he turns toward her as though he is expecting her.

"I need a cup of tea," she explains and goes quickly to the huge black stove where a tin kettle is waiting.

Striking a match, lighting the gas burner, filling the kettle with water, she knows he is watching her and moves with self-conscious grace. I am a woman, after all, she thinks defiantly, even in this thick ugly robe, even in the presence of this unrecognizable man who is my sister's lover.

"Would you like a cup?" she asks him, but Tony shakes his head. He has returned to studying his paper—a letter of some sort, she sees now—with the help of his big flashlight.

Apple goes to the wall switch and turns on the harsh overhead light. "No need to blind yourself." Then she sits down at the other end of the table to wait for the kettle to boil.

"Don't need light."

She is astonished by his brusqueness. I am Cory's sister, she wants to remind him. Treat me with due respect.

Then she guesses his tone has nothing to do with respect, or the lack of it. He is simply stating the obvious.

Apple goes to the wall switch and turns off the overheard light.

At once they are closer, in the beam from the flashlight and the blue glow from the gas burner. Even the bubbling tea kettle has taken on another, more intimate note.

I came back to Taos partly to surprise myself, she remembers. I can't run from strangeness anymore.

I've done that my whole life, she thinks as she pours boiling water into a thick mug and drops in a tea bag.

The tea, she knows, will be insipid—Cory only stocks the herbal kind—but that is appropriate. My whole life, except for Billy's birth, has been healthfully pale and thin, like this Lemon Springer tea. She lifts out the teabag and asks Tony what he is reading.

He slides it toward her.

Apple sees a page black with handwriting she can't decipher. "I can't read it," she says.

He begins to read it to her, without comment, as though, she thinks again, he has been waiting for this opportunity. With his finger, he underlines each word.

There is some legal language at the beginning which he garbles and passes over quickly. Coming to the body of the letter, he slows down.

"My husband Roy Cross never used drugs in his life, except sometimes for his headaches. He was a runner, an athlete, a man concerned with his own health and with the health of our people. He spoke out against drug use on many occasions. The explanation of his death offered by the D.A. and the Taos police makes no sense to me. It never will."

"Who gave you that?" Apple asks.

"Nancy Cross. She say, "'Give this to Cory.'"

"Why didn't she give it to her, herself?"

Tony shrugs. "Maybe she think Cory pay attention, if I give it to her."

"Cory doesn't pay attention to anybody who gets in her way," Apple says stoutly, and realizes how proud she is of her sister.

"This time, maybe," Tony says, brooding. Then he continues to read:

"Even though what the police say hurts me, and hurts my husband's memory, I want all who cared about him to let things alone. There is nothing more to be done. Nothing will bring Roy back. I want to get on with my life, in peace. I want to raise my son without all this trouble."

"What's the trouble?" Apple asks.

"The committee in D.C.—Department of the Interior. They still want somebody to testify about the owl and the old trees."

"Roy's dead. There's nobody to testify," Apple says.

"Your sister."

It is the first time, Apple knows, he has recognized her relation to Cory, and this means even more to her than his startling bit of information. "She hasn't said anything to me."

"She don't talk to nobody," Tony says, and Apple hears his pride in her sister, underlining his gruffness. "She's thinking about it, you better believe. She make up her mind, she'll just go. Nobody'll know anything till she's gone." He folds the paper.

"You want me to stop her," Apple says with her newfound clarity. "That's why you were waiting here."

"Yes," Tony says, looking at her quickly. His dark eyes flash out. Something that is usually hooded is revealed—an intent, its steel edge. Apple wonders if her sister is ever afraid of him.

"I love her, but I don't tell her what to do. I never have."

"She get hurt, maybe. Maybe get killed."

"You tell her not to go, then."

"She don't listen to me." Again, it is a statement of fact, free of any personal intimation.

Suddenly Apple has a flash. "Who shot out that window?"

He stares at her, silent.

"She could have got hit," Apple says.

"She in town, when it happen."

"Cory has to do what she feels is right," Apple says after a minute, standing up.

The man's silence is at her back as she washes the mug out in the sink and turns it upside down in the drainer. She thinks he can hear the faint patter of her uncertainty, like the snow falling outside on dry leaves. Is he really, she wonders, asking her to save her sister's life?

But how could she do such a thing—how could she even imagine it?

She has no strength to match Cory's determination. Even now. She has words—but Cory is expert at turning aside words.

She faces the Indian. "You tell her," she says. "I can't do it. I'm the little sister."

"I try. No good. Something about Roy." Again, he is stating facts, without the coloring of jealousy Apple expects. "Something she don't want to let go of."

He stands up.

How solid he is, Apple thinks, planted on his feet, and she wonders if it has come down to him, this hereditary pride of place, as though bequeathed by his great-uncle. That Tony built the kitchen, after all.

"What about your wife?" Apple challenges him, as though, she realizes, she must reclaim the kitchen—the whole house. Reclaim it for her sister, who is not here to defend herself. "Doesn't she wonder where you are?"

He looks away.

Apple is ashamed. If this is the way to protect Cory, Apple can't do it, anymore than she could intrude on Nancy's privacy, insist on her right to know.

Yet shame is clarifying, too, as though each emotion, this dark night, is a light turned on in another small room.

I feel Cory needs protecting, she thinks, and I've never felt that before. It's not just this man's urging. This new feeling comes from a vision of my sister sleeping alone at the top of the house, in that cold sun porch, watched over by those odd painted roosters the English writer put up to protect Mabel's privacy. Now shot away.

Mabel didn't want her privacy protected; she laughed at the roosters. But she left them there.

All these years, Apple thinks, men have been doing things to protect Mabel, to protect my sister. But they have never been the right things. They have tried to prevent revelation.

Revelation is what my sister wants, and she does not worry about the consequences. That fear was burned out of her early.

At the same time Cory's instinct for self-preservation was damaged, as though only those women who feel shame live long lives.

The Indian is watching her.

"All right," she says. "I'll try."

☞ *18*

Cory wakes early next morning to the scrape of Manuel's shovel, down below in the courtyard. She jumps up and looks out the window.

Manuel has already cleared a path through the snow to the footbridge and the parking lot. Sunlight flashes off the stone pillars by the bridge, off the tilted white crests of Mabel's bird houses and the bronze reindeer in the center of the courtyard, saddled and wreathed with snow.

A beautiful day! Cory thinks, pulling on her clothes.

She smells Conchita's breakfast bacon and knows for the first time since she's owned Mabel's that she'll skip breakfast and her usual morning oration to her guests. There's something else she wants to do.

Maybe that stranger frightened me yesterday, she thinks, hurrying down the stairs.

But she knows it is not fear that is driving her away from her own table—now she is in the Jeep, enclosed in its cold—but a vivid awakening sense of something new, something even more important than her teaching.

She is halfway into town before she has decided on her actual destination; the sense of urgency is enough. She is delighted to have no sure direction, for once, especially when she remembers that Apple is back and probably already at breakfast, perhaps even assuming Cory's place at the head of the long table.

Why has she come back? Cory wonders, exasperated. She says she knew I was hurt; but neither of us knows what to do with that information.

It's too late for us to understand each other, too much has come between.

We tried, and it didn't work. Better to accept the situation as it is: polite alienation is easier on the spirit than painful struggles to understand.

She pulls up at the curb in front of the Cafe Tazza. It's early enough, still, to find a parking place, and she takes that as a sign.

Inside, Coral is pouring a demitasse of espresso into a mug of whipped milk.

"The usual?" she asks, when they have said good morning and commented—there will be comments all day—on the fresh fall of snow.

"Yes," Cory says, and wonders when it became the usual; has she been going to the Tazza for months or for years? Sometimes these days she feels as though she's lived in Taos all her life.

"Martin's in there," Coral says, shrugging her shoulder toward the back room where, in summer, groups beating drums or wailing along with guitars entertain the tourists. In winter, the room, which is unheated, is seldom used, and Cory wonders why the astrologer has chosen to sit there.

She carries her hot mug of latté back.

Martin is opening the glass door onto the terrace where a handful of sparrows is picking at the snow. "Too cold in here. Lets' sit in the sun."

Cory follows his narrow back.

With his sleeve, he clears snow from a tile-toped table, tilts two chairs to unload them, and invites her to join him. "I expected to see you today," he says.

Cory sits down, facing him.

The astrologer has been in Taos since the old days—the good old days, as some, though not Martin, call them—when the well-known dilapidated actor was making a spoils of Mabel's house, when the town was full of motorcycle riders and the hills of city refugees plowing with mules.

Martin feels no nostalgia for those days; he stayed on after the invasion passed, with muffled drums, to another frontier. Now he lives quite comfortably in an apartment over the toy store—a fitting location, people often say, for a dealer in more-or-less plastic visions and dreams.

But Cory believes in Martin.

When she was failing to proceed with the purchase of Mabel's, caught up in quarrels over details and problems with the mortgage, and again when she was losing confidence in her ability to teach her guests, Martin came forward with star support to guide her. She is, he has always said, a born teacher; he has also told her she is one of the few who has a genuine mission in life.

"Snow got me out of bed early," Cory tells him now, feeling the icy table under her palm. "What's your excuse?" Martin is seldom seen around town before noon.

"I knew you were coming."

"Well, here I am."

They lift their coffee mugs in unison. Martin's blue eyes, vivid under his bristling brows, meet hers over the cup rims.

"Go ahead and do it, Cory," he says.

"What in the world are you talking about?"

As he shakes his head, sets his cup down and huddles himself into his faded nylon parka, Cory thinks he looks like an old hen, ruffling feathers against the cold. Under the table, she knows, his skinny knees are pressed together in jeans torn here and there to display none-too-clean long johns. He wears thick sandals with a pair of purple socks that will be dripping wet by noon.

"Please explain," she asks patiently, knowing he never does.

"Go ahead with what you're planning."

"I'm not planning anything."

"Of course it's dangerous, to a degree, but that's not the issue, although that preacher-voice you carry around inside of you will try to insist that it is. Already has, I expect."

"Yes." That part of his prophesy, at least, she knows is true.

"Well, don't pay any attention to it. This is your chance to settle a lot of old scores."

Now she no longer wants to equivocate. "By going down there and—?"

"Yes." He nods, and she sees his white moustache quiver; the thread-like hairs are beaded with moisture.

"What about Apple?"

"What about her?" Again, he gives her his bland look, without curiosity, she thinks, like the supercilious gaze of a pack-llama, waiting to be loaded.

"She wants something from me—that's why she's come back. I don't know if I can just leave her," Cory says.

"She wants something you can't give her, Cory."

"What's that?" she asks reluctantly, feeling protective of her sister, who has never been blasted by too much truth.

"Her love for her husband—focus of her life, you know that. Leo and Libra, marred twins, made for each other. She'll find her way back to him, or not, on her own. Or he'll come get her, in time, and that's probably all either of them needs, to make it work again. She's not you, Cory," he says.

"Of course not. But I feel for her. She's suffering—something unusual."

"Then let her suffer, boss lady. The best thing for her, evidently. It ever occur to you she's come back to Taos simply to let that happen?"

"What?"

"The suffering. They don't allow it, most other places. She's not here for any of your so-called cures." He grins, and she wonders how long he's going to be able to keep his pointed yellow teeth; Martin doesn't believe in dentists.

"So you want me to go to Washington." She turns the warm mug in her hands.

"Hold on, there. I don't want you to go. It's none of my business. I'm telling you what's in your chart. I looked it up before I came over. How's Tony?" he asks, as though there's a link, and Cory knows, and fears, that there is.

"I haven't seen much of him recently. Too much going on, up at Mabel's—he tends to disappear."

"Yes." He is watching her, waiting for more.

"He brought somebody in to talk to me last night," she says. "Somebody to warn me."

"Yes."

"You knew?"

"Sure."

"I'm angry at Tony for trying to warn me," she says, lowering her voice; other people are coming out onto the snowy terrace.

"Tony's worried about you," Martin says, oblivious to the newcomers. "He wants to keep you around for a while."

Cory says nothing, admiring the gnarled and grizzled face of an old painter, well-known in the community, who is striding by, flipping his grey-and-white pony tail over his shoulder. He sits at the next table, knocking aside the snow.

"Tony's wife just had a baby, another boy," Martin says.

"I know." Cory's eyes are still fixed on the painter. Then she looks, hard, at Martin. "What does that have to do with anything?"

"Be careful, there, Cory. Don't interfere."

"Interfere!" she exclaims. "Here you are urging me to risk my life—"

"Hardly that. Just a short trip, a couple of days."

"Nobody on that committee knows who I am."

"You'll be summoned," Martin tells her. "Good time for you to take off, get away from Mabel's for a while."

"Why?"

"Your sister, Tony, the baby. None of it's going to work, now. Mercury's going retrograde tomorrow, everything's going to be stuck. Don't worry, Cory," he adds, watching her, "I know how you feel. You want all those lives, as well as your own—lives you never worked for. Your sister, all safe and snugly back home in the south, with her son problems, her grandchild problems, whatever. Tony with his double life—as we call it, right?—a loyal lady at the pueblo and all those relatives, handy for the kids, and every now and then an adventure with you at Mabel's."

"Oh, stop!" She stands up. The group at the next table doesn't even turn to stare.

"It's perfectly all right to want all that, Cory, your stars make you basically unable to be satisfied. But you don't bring it up into consciousness (pardon the expression, I admit I'm a ragbag where theory's concerned). Just remember, Cory—"

But she is already striding though the open gate into the street.

This is not really anger, she thinks, this is simply that hot-blooded feeling I get, and enjoy, whenever someone with a certain amount of natural authority (and it happens so seldom, too seldom) seems to know me better than I know myself.

She strides toward the Jeep, kicking lumps of crusted snow out of the way.

It's not really true I want all those other lives, she thinks. If I wanted them, I'd have them—and pay the price. The trouble with Martin is he tends to accept old notions about women—basically unsatisfiable, is that what he said?—or else the stars are organized around those same outdated formulas.

Already the rooftops are melting; water runs in little channels beside the path. By four o'clock everything will begin to ice over again, and Cory knows she will need to be through the pass by then.

But it's still early.

Martin even had the nerve to mention Tony's new son.

But I never wanted that! she cries to herself as she jumps into the Jeep (undecorated, this time, it's too early in the day for those folks to be at work), jerks it into gear and heads for Mabel's. Apple is most wrong of all about that. I never wanted that—love-and-babies—and I worked efficiently and with some sense of sacrifice to be sure I never had it.

And now never will.

⟛⟛⟛

Apple sits at the foot of Cory's table and realizes it might as well be the head; all seven guests are turning in her direction, like sunflowers.

The blond family from Utah—Mormons all, she supposes—actually looks a little like a bunch of tall sunflowers, their crowded dark features set in haloes of blond hair.

As for the couple from France, they are caught in the web of their own language—Apple understands only a few words—and hardly glance at her.

"My sister left the house early," she told them all when she first sat down. But the guests don't seem to realize who her sister is; they arrived the night before, just before the storm, and so they do not know what they are missing: the morning words, Cory's way of starting the day.

Now they are asking her the standard questions about Taos—where to go, what to do—and Apple feels herself expanding a little in her new-found authority.

She is better than a guidebook, at least, she thinks, as she recommends the Martinez hacienda—what will they make of its coldness, its starkness, its unrelenting exposure of a cruel life?—the Millicent Rogers Museum, pretty as a postcard in its setting on the mesa, with all that fine Navajo jewelry as memorial to its fascinating founder—and the pueblo, which is far beyond Apple's power to describe.

After the guests troop out, Conchita comes in to take away the battered covered dishes of bacon and pancakes.

Perhaps Cory would enjoy having their mother's silver serving dishes, to replace those, which look as though they came from a camp—and then Apple remembers that Cory has never wanted anything of their mother's, that they have never even talked about her in the years since her death.

Cory invents her own past, Apple thinks with asperity, or at least she has, until now.

Getting up, she realizes that Conchita wants to ask her something—some practical detail, she expects.

"Cory gone somewhere?" Conchita is balancing a big battered dish.

"I heard the Jeep start, a while ago. I think she went to town."

"Somebody been calling for her; Consuela went out to see could she find her."

"Who?"

Conchita shakes her head. "Consuela say he don't want to give his name. Somebody needs to talk to her right away."

Another warning, Apple thinks, as though Cory is ever going to listen to any of them.

"A man?" she asks.

Conchita nods.

"Where'd Consuela go?"

"Took Tony's pick-up and went to town. About half an hour ago. I got to get the phone," Conchita says, setting down the dish and hurrying toward the office.

Apple follows her.

The young woman is frowning as she tries to explain to the caller that no one knows exactly when Cory will be back.

Apple gestures at her. Conchita hands the receiver over. Again, Apple feels the authority that has something negative at its core.

The voice Apple hears is still blurry with youth, and yet she does not think it belongs to a very young man.

"This is Apple Long, Cory's sister. She's gone out for a while," Apple says.

"I need to speak to her as soon as possible."

"Who may I say—?" Their mother's formula for an unacceptably direct question.

"She don't know me."

"Then I'm afraid I can't leave her a message."

"Just tell her, Martin."

"You're Martin?"

"Just tell her, he told me, call her, call her today."

"What is this in reference to?" But the line has gone dead; the young man has disappeared back into the vacuum.

Conchita is hovering at her elbow. "Who—?"

"I don't know. Have you ever heard that voice before?"

Conchita nods. "Two, maybe three times."

"Who's Martin?"

"That man Cory goes to."

"Goes to for what?"

"He tell her what's going to happen, maybe."

Another meddler, Apple thinks. "Do you know how to reach him?"

But Conchita shakes her head and heads for the kitchen.

So a fortune teller is now stirring the pot, Apple thinks as she heads down the hall to the Kiva room. She wonders if Martin is also a friend of Tony's and of the man who came the night before. Why do all these men try to protect Cory? Cory has never wanted protection.

It's something about her strong appeal, the visible current of her energy, Apple thinks as she walks down the hall. Something lively and liquid that people, especially men, think they can scoop up in their tin cups and use for their own purposes.

The image startles her. She doesn't usually think in images.

Then she remembers when the image of Little Billy was at the center of her attention, draining her of every molecule of her ability to observe and interpret.

She didn't understand until much later Billy's lingering resentment of the baby's hold.

That is just the way things go, Apple used to think contentedly, even enjoying Billy's discomfort, for were not all men at heart boys deprived of their mothers' unconditional love? The same love, in its truest sense, she has always given to her son.

But Cory has foresworn all that, and so it is in the nature of things that other people—strangers, men—should be drawn to the untapped stream of her energy—untapped, that is, for any other purpose than her own.

Apple knows now she will never redirect her sister's energy. There is no way to find the boy, the lost son.

The man who called, Apple realizes, the man with the boy's voice, is only the latest in a long procession: men who want to make use of what Cory won't give away.

She decides she will not tell her sister about the call. Let Conchita tell her, or Consuela. They are probably still capable of turning the message into another warning. Now that Apple understands the uses her sister makes of danger, she knows she can no longer warn her against it.

Danger is Cory's family, she thinks, discomfort and risk people her empty life.

She hears Manuel chopping firewood under the portal, a comforting sound, and sits down at the uneven little desk to write a letter home.

She realizes with satisfaction that it is the first time in her married life she's relied on writing, rather than telephoning. The urgency that has driven her all these years is gone, dried up like a trickle of snow water in the sun. Now it seems she has all the time in the world to write Billy a letter he will probably not want to read.

Outside her window, water drips straight down from the roof of the portal, pattering like a waterfall.

"Cory wasn't really hurt," she writes, after the usual greetings, "although someone did shoot out the window in her bathroom with the birds on it. But it didn't scare her, or stop her. She's going on with this crusade—"then remembers she hasn't told Billy what Cory is trying to do.

I've kept Billy out, she thinks, amazed. I've kept him away from Cory.

What a revelation, she thinks, as the sun comes through the little window over the desk and glares in her face. I always thought I told him everything.

Yet it's with an extraordinary sense of freedom, of recklessness, even, that she crumples the page and throws it in the waste-paper basket.

A knock at the door startles her a few minutes later when she is washing her hands in the sink.

"Come in," she calls, expecting Conchita or Consuela, with news.

Cory sticks her head in the door. "May I?"

Her tone is so unexpected Apple laughs. "When have you ever asked, first?"

"Not often." Cory strides in and sits down on the side of Apple's unmade bed.

Apple dries her hands.

"Where'd you go?" she asks her sister.

"Did anybody ask for me?" Cory counters.

"No. Those new guests only wanted to know what to see; I told them the usual. I didn't think it was a good time for a lesson, they all seemed in an awful hurry. But I wondered," she adds, softly. "I wondered if there was more I should say."

"Did anybody call?"

Apple thinks her sister looks unusually intent, even for Cory. "A man. He wouldn't leave his name."

Cory shakes her head impatiently. "Conchita told me it's the same one that's been calling, for days. Ever since you first came," she adds, shrewdly.

Apple sits down on the other side of the bed. The rumpled sheets are between them. "You mean I stirred up something?"

"Seems like it. I never got that kind of call before."

"What in the world could I stir up, Cory? I don't even know anybody in Taos."

Then Apple remembers Festiva Warren.

"You've been acting awfully mysterious," Cory reminds her, "coming and going without even bothering to tell me."

"I had to leave, before, to go back to Billy. I felt as though something was going wrong, at home."

"Was it?"

Apple realizes her sister has no way of visualizing Apple's house or the way she lives or the urgency she feels, or felt, about all that goes on there. "Just another little discussion with Little Billy and his wife—we have them all the time," she says, with a calmness that is not assumed. "And then Maureen told me she's going to have a baby."

"Good for her."

"You don't need to sound like that. For me, it's wonderful news," Apple says, patting a crest of sheet down.

"So you're going to start that whole damn business again?"

"What business?" Apple is aware suddenly of the coldness of the room, of the wind down the chimney, stirring the dead ashes on the hearth.

"I remember it well enough, with Little Billy. You won't be able to see, think, or hear once that baby's born."

"You're bitter, Cory."

Cory's eyes are fixed on Apple's face. "I tried to warn you, Little Sister."

"The way you behaved at my wedding—"

"I wanted to spare you all that."

"All that is my life!" Apple says, her voice rising. "What right did you have to try to spare me my life?"

"And I didn't want us to lose each other," Cory says, leaning across the bed. Apple feels her warmth, and smells her odd patchouli perfume. "Was that part of your deal with Billy?"

"I never had a deal with Billy," Apple says, leaning away.

"You quit on me, Apple—soon as you two were married. You abandoned me." And suddenly Apple hears a sob under her sister's voice, nearly submerged.

"I didn't know it mattered." She reaches across the sheets and lays her hand on her sister's.

Cory jerks her hand away and stands up. She begins to pace between the bed and the fireplace. "How could you think it didn't matter?"

"You never told me."

"And I needed to tell you? After what we went through together, growing up?"

"What did we go through together, Cory?"

Cory glares at her. "We never had anybody except each other. Isn't that what you remember?" she asks. "Or have you rewritten all that, too?"

"No."

"But it didn't matter enough to . . ."

"You have so much else, Cory. You always have so much else. How could it matter, what I did with my life?"

Cory strides toward Apple, who shrinks back. "Are you that dumb? You really think all this—"and she waves at the room, the house, the whole of Taos—"somehow makes up for what I lost—for what we both lost? You'll never convince me whatever it is you have with Billy—"

"Stop, Cory!" Apple sits up straight, determined not to cower.

Cory is looming over her. "We have to have this out, sometime before we die. I've known that since Mother's funeral."

"You were included in all those arrangements," Apple gasps. "You can't claim anything else. We did everything we could to make sure—"

"Yeah, and put my wreath way over on the side, and made me sit in the wrong pew—"

"Nobody made you—"

Manuel's shovel is scraping nearer the window; both sisters fall silent and glance outside. They see his hunched shoulders and dark head.

"Never mind him," Cory says harshly. "We both use every excuse—"

"I don't."

"You do! You do, too!" And they are girls again, arguing across the width of the rumpled bed.

The humor of it breaks upon them both at the same time. Apple laughs, wiping her eyes. Cory barks, once. They stare at each other, their smiles freezing, and Apple sees a bleakness she's never seen before in her sister's eyes.

"I really did the best I could at Mother's funeral to make you feel welcome," Apple says.

"I'll never be welcome there."

"Are you happy here, Cory?" Apple asks.

Cory leans toward her and for a moment Apple sways away, frightened. Then she sees her sister's expression and holds out her arms.

Cory's head is on her shoulder, her unexpectedly firm and heavy body is leaning against her. Apple props herself with one hand behind her on the mattress. Cory is sobbing.

Apple pats her back. She says the soft meaningless things she said, once, to Billy when he feared the sale of the company would deprive him of his hard-won identity; she repeats the same endearments she once lavished on Little Billy, years and years ago.

How dry my life has been, she thinks, with astonishment. How complete, and how dry—and she wonders, suddenly, if Maureen will allow her to be present at the birth, to refresh herself in those terrifying streams. Blood, and tears, she thinks, all Cory and I have denied ourselves, all our lives have been constructed to deny—and thinks of the Indian, impenetrable, in the corner of the kitchen.

"Why do you take all these risks, Cory?" she asks when her sister finally sits back, wiping her nose on the back of her hand the way she always did, in spite of their mother's remonstrances.

"I have to," Cory says simply. "I think I'm here to take risks," and for once, Apple doesn't argue.

"Then let me take them with you," she says, unthinkingly. Then she hears her own words, amazed. She has never said anything like that in her life.

"Take my risks with me?" Cory is smiling, but it is not the grin, edged with sarcasm, Apple fears. "Then they wouldn't be risks, Little Sister."

"I'm trying," Apple says slowly, "to understand what the risks do for you, how they make up . . ." She hesitates. "How they make up for what you've lost." And now she doesn't need to define it; they understand each other, at last.

"The risks make me feel alive," Cory says.

"And is that why . . . With Tony . . ."

"I come with Tony. I've never come with anyone else."

Apple holds her breath.

"Do you come with Billy?" Cory asks.

"Of course," Apple says, hastily.

Now silence thickens between them.

"Tell the truth, Little Sister."

"At first I didn't."

"At first nobody does."

"Why does it matter, Cory?" She looks at her sister pleadingly.

"Because it's at the heart, at the core."

"And we have to share that—?"

"If we're ever going to understand each other."

"So you've figured all that out, too?" Apple asks bleakly. "What it all means?"

"I think you have too, only maybe you don't want to think about it. We went through the same experiences, growing up. The surfaces were all we could hope for—take them, or leave them. The expressions of affection that were without heart, without soul. Remember how Mother always used to say, 'We love you' after she'd heard our prayers? I never knew who the you was."

"But that was so long ago, Cory, isn't it time we—"

"'We love you,' and neither of us ever knew who the 'we' was. God, maybe? God was three persons, after all. Or Mother and Father? But that didn't make sense. They never mentioned love when we saw them together. And how could she speak for him, when he didn't speak for himself?"

"I tried to believe what she said," Apple says.

"You needed to believe. I did, too, for years. I started holding my breath, counting to ten—believing. It's all about holding your breath, isn't it, Apple?"

"I don't know what you're talking about."

"Yes, you do, Little Sister. I saw it, all those years ago, how hard you tried to believe. But if that's love, Apple—if that's what we need, to live—then I'd rather eat sawdust. I'd rather roll in a bed of cactus. I refuse," Cory says, her voice rising to the vigas; Apple looks up, instinctively, and sees a patch there. "I refuse to accept that. Either the real thing, or nothing. You go for compromises."

"And have you found the real thing?" Apple asks, her eyes fixed on the patch behind the furthest viga.

"No." Cory's voice is harsh, final. "I haven't found it, and I probably never will. But I do breathe. I do come."

"With your Tony—"

"With Mabel's ghost, with her Tony, with what the past—this particular bit of it—means to me. But he's not my Tony, Apple. He never has been, he never will be."

"How desolate," Apple says, "how discouraging—"

"Those last years, when Mabel and Tony moved to Embudo to get away from all the goings-on here, the daily dramas, Tony was in despair. He was drinking all the time, and so was Mabel. The experiment—what they tried to do, together, uprooting him from the pueblo, incorporating him into her life—it ruined him, it killed him. He died in great bitterness, cursing her. That's why he's buried in the pueblo, and she's alone, up on the hill."

"How do you know all that?" Apple asks, awed. "Is it in the books?"

"Oh no. The books paint a different picture. I found something. Or rather, Manuel did, when he was fixing the roof." And they both look at the patch. "She hid her diary from the last days in there."

"You read it?"

"There are no secrets, Apple."

"But your Tony—it's different—"

"He'll lose everything, too."

"But you love him," Apple says.

"Yes, I love him, Apple, but Mabel loved her Tony, too."

"Oh, Cory, oh, Honey—"

"It's better to know," Cory says. "It's better to see the limits. Tony has done something I can't accept. Of course I have help," she adds, as Apple begins to protest. "I have the mountains, over there beyond the pueblo, I have Primrose, and Andrew, and Martin, and all they see and show me. I'm not alone here, Apple," Cory says. "I don't come to these conclusions, or face them, alone."

"So it's principle, again," Apple says.

"Yes, it's principle, among other things."

"Is that what Roy Cross meant to you? Principle?" Apple asks.

"Yes. I loved him, too, Apple—and yes, it's possible to love two men, or more, at the same time."

"You were—?"

"Yes, Little Sister. Very happily, and very briefly. Roy had the ability—I've never found it before, or since—to give himself completely, and then to let go."

"Because he was married," Apple says, quickly.

"I don't know."

"Because he was married," Apple states, and Cory doesn't argue. "So that's why you want to go to Washington."

"How do you know I want to go to Washington?"

"Everything points that way," Apple says. "All these calls, these warnings. They wouldn't need to warn you, if you weren't planning—"

"Considering."

"Planning to go."

"Nobody's even asked me," Cory says, circumspectly.

"They will."

"The subcommittee meets in two days."

"Today, or tomorrow at the latest, you'll get the call."

"Well, we'll see."

Now it's Apple's turn to smile. "I know you, Cory, I know you make things happen."

"And you don't?" Cory asks.

Before Apple can think of an answer, someone knocks at the door, and both sisters turn toward it.

Conchita comes in with an envelope.

☞ *19*

*A*pple is cold.

Cold as she has never been in the flatland south.

Half waking, she finds herself curled, her hands pressed between her knees; Cory's blankets are thin, inadequate. At home, Apple has goose down comforters, satin blanket bindings, pillows soft as clouds.

Waking up all the way, she sees that the window in the thick adobe wall is barely grey; it must be an hour before dawn. The melting snow that dripped all day froze by nightfall into icicles edging the portal all the way from Apple's window to the front door, which was not locked, although she pleaded with Cory, "Don't you think, given all that's going on—"

"Nothing's going on," Cory said, emphatic.

All that went on, in fact, Apple remembers, squeezing her hands between her knees, was the summons to Washington, its official tone conveying, to Apple, at least, who is used to obeying all summons, that compliance is a foregone conclusion; and another anonymous caller, a man, again, whose young voice Apple was sure she would have recognized if she had answered the telephone, instead of Consuela, who insisted, "Nobody, nobody,"—looking frightened.

After dinner and a fiery lecture on As If—acting as if one had a heart, or a conscience, or a soul, Apple summarized it—Cory said she would not go to Washington, but of course Cory would say that to Apple, as well as to the rest of the household.

Apple believes Cory has already made up her mind to go.

Manuel and the two young women were in on all the excitement, shadowing doorways and passing through rooms where Apple and Cory were not arguing, never that; simply, Apple thinks, disagreeing, although on the surface it would have seemed that she was supporting Cory's decision: Certainly, don't go, there's no reason to, you have nothing to say, you've told me that yourself, nothing but speculation, and such a long trip, and the road down through the pass already a sheet of ice.

As for Tony, he was in and out all afternoon, on one errand or another, glancing at the two women as they sat together or stood together in this room or that, his glance seeming to weave their words together.

He plays some role I don't understand, Apple thinks, stretching her feet further down into the cold sheets. He is what our mother would have called a factor, although Cory will never admit that. And Apple wonders what Tony advised—for certainly, at some point, he did advise—about the summons to Washington.

Then she remembers that Tony opposed everything Roy Cross believed in, and remembers him saying, "No gambling, no nuclear waste storage, that's what the whites say—but we got to have something. Pojoaque putting toll booths on the state road running through the pueblo—four miles. Say they going to make thirty thousand a day."

Apple remembers Luisa saying Pojoaque's too close to Santa Fe—contaminated.

I'm glad I'm not poor people, she thinks, knowing Cory would be shocked by the notion that there is an actual division, tangible as barbed-wire, between those who have and those who have not; but Apple knows she does not mean money or possessions.

Rather, she means a sense of possibilities, or the lack of it. This has always separated her from Cory, who believes in many possibilities, even now. Apple has always been more realistic in her assessment of the future and what it may hold.

Sitting up in the darkness, she realizes that Cory's departure is inevitable and at the same time hears a car starting, down in the parking lot.

The noise seems surreptitious, muffled. Then headlights sweep the room.

She is up and dressing before she has made a conscious decision.

The cold strikes her face as she rushes out her door and down the long hall. It is too early for anyone to be stirring, and there is only one dim light left on in the big room.

Outside the front door, Apple steps into deep snow—more has fallen, since midnight—and crushes her way down to the footbridge and the wooden stairs.

Already the headlights are moving out of the parking lot. It is Cory's Jeep.

Oh my God, she thinks, it's too late, everything's decided, and remembers other times when she gave up at the first indication that a certain turn had already been taken.

Her wedding, for example.

Hold on there, she tells herself, standing alone on the steps, hugging her parka around her; the keen night wind is in her hair, and she can hear the skitter of ice particles blown through the bushes along the acequia. Hold on, don't give up yet.

But there is nothing for me to do, she cries to herself, silently, as on so many other occasions, long since forgotten: when Cory did something, went somewhere, leaving her sister behind.

She rushes up to Mabel's, the house looming darkly above her—not a soul awake.

As she opens the door, she collides, heavily, with a man coming out. She identifies him by his smoky smell.

"She's gone," Apple gasps. "I saw the Jeep—"

"Quick." Tony takes her wrist.

"Where're we going?"

He does not answer, jerking her back across the snow to the bridge and the steps.

At the bottom, he pushes her toward a pick-up parked alongside the fence. He opens the passenger door and shoves her in, like a package and an unwieldy one at that, Apple thinks.

But she cannot continue that line of thought because Tony has jumped into the driver's seat and started the truck, with a quivering, shuddering burst of noise which, Apple feels sure, will wake everyone at Mabel's.

As they pull out, a light flashes on in the house behind them and Apple says, "Somebody heard."

Tony doesn't answer.

She wonders if she has always been surrounded by people whose motives she does not understand. Perhaps Tony understands, hunching down behind the steering wheel, his face hidden by the brim of his broken-crested hat.

Now Apple has nothing to ask, nothing to say as they whirl pass the café Cory frequents, past Primrose's house with the crushed farolitos on the wall, past the corner where traffic usually congests around the stop light. It is blinking; Tony sails through.

"She told me she wasn't going to go, definitely," Apple says, but Tony is silent, his shoulders hunched.

Now they are driving out of town, and Apple suddenly begins to sob.

Tony reaches across the seat after a while and pats her knee, once.

She is so surprised she stops sobbing in mid-gasp. "I'm so worried for Cory," she says. "She's up against more than she can handle."

"Yes," Tony says.

He does not invite her to continue, yet Apple feels there is a possibility he will listen, perhaps even respond.

"I don't really know anything about this situation," she goes on. "But I know enough to guess Cory's getting in deep water. There's been a murder—or at least it looks like a murder—nobody wants to solve; and when nobody wants to solve something, it's better to stay out—at least, that's what I've always thought."

"Yes," Tony says again and Apple tries to draw reassurance from the single word. Tony says it as though it is enough, and she thinks, suddenly, of his wife in the pueblo, nursing the new baby, living from word to word.

"You know my sister well," she hazards, looking out at the long plain that slopes down to the gorge of the Rio Grande, invisible in the thick darkness. "You know she does things for her own reasons. She never has listened to anybody!" Apple cries, appealing to him to agree.

"She listen to me," Tony says grimly, accelerating around the curve. The truck rattles, leaps forward.

"Watch out!" Apple cries as they go into a long skid, slow as a dream.

In her terror, Apple is aware of Tony's fingers playing at the edge of the steering wheel, manipulating it, and she remembers his expertise with horses and tries to distract herself from her panic. The truck slides out of its long skid toward the precipice and, with a weird gracefulness, takes to the straight road again.

"Not so fast, please," Apple gasps, fluttering her hand toward him, in the dark.

He seizes her fingers and lays them firmly on the seat, as though her hand is a bird that must be caught.

And she sees, for the first time, tail lights ahead of them in the darkness and asks, "Is that the Jeep?"

"Looks like," Tony says, accelerating again.

They are racing down the road beyond the big old church whose broad end Apple has glimpsed in the darkness, the big old church, she remembers, trying to distract herself, where Cory told her there's a dark panel which, if stared at long enough, reveals an image of the Virgin. Mother of Sorrows. She is often called that here, even schools carry that name. Apple knows it is that image of womanhood she has always rejected, and feared—the one Cory would embrace. The tears, the wound, the blood—all that wetness.

"I don't want her to be dead by the side of the road," she says, for Tony has taken a skidding turn to the left, following the Jeep's tail lights.

Now they are racing down a smaller road between huddled adobe houses; here and there a yard light casts a pool of florescent blue on the snow. A dog barks, lunging on a chain, and Apple realizes that people are waking up, hard-working people who must rise before dawn.

She knows they will hear the roar of the two vehicles, charging by, and put it down to kids, teenagers, playing with death on the road.

"Is this the way to the airport?" she asks as they plough into hilly darkness, the villages left behind.

"Old way," Tony says. Again he does not seem to understand that she needs reassurance. He is, simply, driving, his attention focused on the red tail lights that disappear into a valley, then appear again on the other side: Cory driving like a fiend, as she always has, always will.

Apple asks him, "If we catch her, what'll you say?"

Tony doesn't answer. Cory's tail lights, five hundred feet ahead, swerve sharply to the right.

Tony curses, brakes. The Jeep is at the edge of a ditch, its front wheels churning as Cory struggles to steer it back onto the road.

Tony lunges the truck onto the shoulder, trying to block her. In a wave of snow and mud, the Jeep pulls back onto the road and speeds ahead.

As it passes within five feet of the pick-up, Apple catches a glimpse of her sister's face, dead-white, set ahead.

"Cory!" she calls, her voice quavering, as she called years ago, a little girl waking at night in her crib.

And her sister came, at times, and at other times did not, and Apple never knew why she came, and why she did not.

"I needed her so much, when we were little," she is babbling to Tony, to fill the silence and the darkness between them. He has pulled out and is following Cory at what seems to Apple a terrific speed. "I need her now, I'm ashamed to admit it, but I do. We never had parents," she goes on, into his uncomprehending silence, his total attention to his driving. "I guess that's why she meant so much to me. She was supposed to mother me, and she didn't, but she was all I had, till I married, and then that separated us—she never liked my husband— and other things as well," she ends, vaguely, and wonders if Tony knows (if it has even occurred to Cory to tell him) what happened with Billy all those years ago.

"Terrible things happened, at least they seemed terrible to me at the time," she continues. "At least I tried to make sure they were terrible, for years; they were my excuse to avoid Cory, to blame her. But really," Apple says, and now she is speaking to herself, "really, I knew all along. There was no betrayal, because I knew. I married Billy, knowing."

"Hold on," Tony says, oblivious to her babbling—why should he care, after all, about the sisters' secrets?—and they skid down a long hill, the Jeep fishtailing ahead of them, past a collection of dark houses. A church sits at the top of a rise.

The Jeep circles the square of snow in front of the church, evading them, nosing toward the road out.

But this time Tony is first. He swings the truck across the road, blocking it; snow is piled in mounds three feet high on either side, and when Cory rams the Jeep into a pile, trying to drive over it, the motor struggles and stalls. The Jeep halts, shuddering, and is still.

In the headlights, Apple sees her sister, getting out, turning, running toward the church. Tony is out already, after her.

Apple climbs out slowly. Suddenly she knows she has nothing to do here, nothing to say, she is simply an irrelevant part of the story, carried along.

Cory is streaking away up the hill toward the church with Tony behind her, a dark figure bending low as he speeds across the snow.

Unbidden, unwelcome, a picture from a children's book of a half-naked savage (as we called them, then, Apple thinks, before we knew how much we needed them) scudding across a hillside after a terrified woman, fleeing in bonnet and shawl, comes back into Apple's imagination.

The next picture she remembers is of a cabin in flames, the woman, a tomahawk in her shoulder, lying across the doorway.

Don't hurt her, she says to herself; don't touch a hair of her head.

And remembers Tony's mixed motives, which she has never thought of before.

Apple thinks he wants to bring it to a head, resolve it, for once and for all: love, and its consequences.

She stands beside the truck and watches, in the gradually brightening light, as the Indian catches her sister on the church doorstep.

Apple sees Cory hammering on the door with both fists as the twin wooden steeples of the old church appear out of the waning darkness.

No one answers. No friendly priest unlocks the door and lets her sister into an unlikely sanctuary.

Instead, Tony has seized her by the shoulders—even at that distance, Apple can feel the fierce strength in his hands—and turns her, abruptly, toward him.

Cory is fighting.

With all her strength—and now Apple knows Cory's strength is limited—she is fighting her way out of the Indian's arms.

Kicking, even.

And Apple, her hands to her mouth, remembers her sister kicking her way free of an encircling teacher (who was trying to help, no doubt) after some playground dispute, kicking, cursing, cuffing until she stood alone in the center of admiring and terrified children and adults—

—panting, at bay, as she is now panting and at bay, fists lifted, a few feet from Tony, who has dropped his hands to his sides.

Apple does not hear what he says to her. She will never know, she realizes, what he said to her, or even feel that she has the right to ask.

Cory steps toward him—one step. It is enough. Tony holds out his hand.

Behind them, a dog barks, and someone turns off a porch light.

It is morning.

⇥ *20*

*T*he time has come, Cory knows.

The time she thought would never come, so slight was her faith, when everything must be sewn together, stitched up—included.

And what do I mean by included? she catechizes herself as she kneels in front of the fire, lighting her cedar smudge.

Everything cannot be defined. Should not be defined. Will be understood, only, in the doing.

On the bed, Tony lies watching her, the big striped blanket pulled over what D.H., bless his heart, would have called his loins.

The early morning sun streams through the window; smoke from Cory's smudge rides the light.

Cory thinks how lucky she has been, how lucky she continues to be to have these presences in her life:

Mabel in her various disguises (including the defeated alcoholic), hovering around her old house as though tethered to it, a kite that can't quite take off (and she must do something about that, Cory knows); all of Mabel's friends, that strangely assorted bunch of Indians, East Coast intellectuals, artists and their fellow travelers—all of them, Cory realizes, returning as the strangers who listen to her lectures.

They are not necessarily easier to bear than blood kin, she thinks, getting up before her knees begin to hurt.

Mabel, for instance, is a sort of harridan, she thinks, calling into question motives I would prefer to leave unexamined; D.H. makes my sexual opening seem minor, inconsequential, because whatever he preached is so much larger, so much more spiritual; and how Taos has abused that word, Cory thinks, made it cheap, and yet it continues to exert the power of the image of the Virgin of Guadalupe at Ranchos church (not the Mother of Sorrows, as Apple insists) who reappears whenever the church is dark and there is a believer present.

Tony is looking at her with his curious slow gaze, not particularly interested in Cory or what she may or may not be doing, but resting his eyes on her as though it is comfortable.

She turns to him, wrapping her robe tightly around her. "The baby doing well?" she asks, taking up an earlier conversation, begun during the night when they lay silently side by side.

"Fine. Yells a lot."

"How many more, Tony?"

He makes a sign with his hand, and turns his head away. This is forbidden territory.

Cory goes to her mirror and begins to brush her long hair and braid it with a red ribbon. She has been needing more red for a while; since Apple came, in fact. The need grew more intense when her sister returned.

"Was Apple scared?" she asks, knowing Tony will understand that she means.

He shakes his head. "Talked all the time, no way to be scared with all that talking," he says with a gruff laugh.

"We're both big talkers." Cory braids her hair close to her head, then fastens the plait with the red ribbon, tied in a big loopy bow.

"You not so much, now," Tony says.

"There's nobody to listen."

Tony is getting out of bed, dragging the blanket with him. His modesty reminds Cory of D.H.'s peculiar fastidiousness. She wonders what the original Tony and D.H. discussed when they went on their horseback rides together; or was Mabel always there, disturbing the current?

"Where're you going?" she asks as Tony steps into his jeans and sits on the edge of the bed to jerk on his boots. His torso, bent to the task, is swaddled in flesh.

"Home," he says.

As he stands up and pulls on his shirt, buttoning it haphazardly, he is looking at Cory with an intent she can't interpret.

"I got to stay there now," he says. "Least 'til everything settles down."

"Of course," Cory says.

"I got to," he repeats.

"I know." She is sharp now, not wanting his repetition, his emphasis. "They need you."

He nods, once. The buttons are fumbled and neglected as he watches Cory, and she knows he has expected, perhaps even wanted, a different reaction: the woman bereft, in tears.

But it will be a relief for both of us, she thinks, to have the freedom of the air again, to come and go, like birds. For she knows Tony has timed his activities, figured out when to visit, when to leave, molding the rest of his life to that framework. As I have, Cory thinks, and it will be a relief to have it over.

Before, it was always a question of attracting and keeping him, at least for short periods of time; all her feelings and efforts were bent to that. But now that he is leaving, she feels the free-flowing current of her love directed fully toward him. She wants nothing, she expects nothing. It is as it should be.

Tony nods, and leaves the room. She hears his boots clump on the stairs and smiles, thinking the new couple from Cleveland will hear him where they lie snuggled in Mabel's big bed.

Hear him, and imagine whatever they need to imagine.

Cory finishes dressing quickly and goes down to the office. Consuela gives her a quick look before offering the grocery list, and Cory knows she's guessed that Tony won't be around anymore, and is expecting—as he did—that her employer will be devastated, although not showing it, perhaps, out of pride.

"I'm fine, Consuela," Cory says.

Abashed, the young woman goes to her desk. To reassure her, Cory sits on the edge of the desk to make her telephone call.

Running Deer answers on the first ring. She imagines him hurrying across the smoky kitchen—Val, his wife, always burns whatever she is cooking—snatching up the telephone with an impatience he tries to control when he's conducting the ceremonies.

"Yes?" Running Deer asks. "What can I do for you?"

"Osiyo!" Cory says.

"You coming up?"

"Yes. I'm bringing my sister."

"She been before?"

"No. I'll tell her what to expect. Who's leading?"

"Me. Val is helping, Unisi can't make it."

"You want me to be Fire Chief?"

"Guess so," he says reluctantly, "unless Ray comes."

There's a definite pecking order among Running Deer's helpers, Cory thinks as she hangs up the telephone. Val is tolerated because she's always there, collecting the gift-way presents, showing the participants the way to the toilet, laying out the food. Ray is a favorite of Running Deer's, a Cherokee medicine man of impeccable credentials. Two other men whose names Cory can't remember are also welcome replacements, serving as Spiritual Leaders, Pipe Carriers and Fire Chiefs when Running Deer and his close group are otherwise engaged. In the outer circle, Cory has taken her place, along with several other women who have attended the rituals regularly and taken some of R.D.'s workshops.

I'll have to explain all this to Apple, Cory thinks, but knows at least she will not have to explain whey they need to go through a ritual, together.

As she hangs up the telephone, Apple comes down the long hall from the Kiva room.

"We'll go up to Running Deer's in about an hour," Cory tells her.

"The sweat lodge?"

"Yes." Cory turns away, not wanting to confront the possibility of her sister's hesitation.

"Listen, Cory," Apple says instead, her hand on her sister's arm. "I thought about something when I was back there trying to get some sleep."

"Yes?" Cory is studying Consuela's shopping list, trying to decide whether anything is needed before dinner.

"If that church where we stopped you—"

"Las Trampas."

"If the priest was there . . ."

"I don't think there is a priest anymore," Cory says.

"Well, but if he was. If he'd opened the door when you knocked and let you in—"

"Would I have stayed there till you and Tony gave up and left, and then gone on to the airport?"

"Yes. That's what I've been wondering."

"I don't know, Little Sister."

Consuela answers the telephone and begins to take down the details of a reservation.

"You must know," Apple says, lowering her voice.

Cory stares at her. In the light that reflects off the snow outside the window, Apple's face looks bleached, the fine lines around her eyes like the hairline cracks in a porcelain cup. "I don't know what I'm going to do until I do it," Cory says.

And then they are laughing, leaning on each others' shoulders until Consuela, hanging up, stares at them in alarm.

The telephone rings again, and Consuela makes a face before handing it to Cory.

Cory is brief and to the point, as she has been each time this stranger has called. She has nothing to say to him and nothing she wants to hear.

As Cory starts toward the dining room, where the guests are assembling for breakfast, Apple stops her. "One more thing—"

"What?"

"I have to tell you something, Cory. I tried to find him." Apple doesn't need to explain what she means; Cory has turned back, with a blazing face. "I tried, but I didn't get anywhere—or at least I thought I didn't."

"You had no right—"

Apple holds up her hand. "There wasn't anything I could do. But the woman I spoke to—"and Apple remembers Festiva Warren's odd hesitation, over the telephone the day before—"she called this place in Salt Lake City, where they have this registry, and I think they've matched you with . . .someone. At least she said the dates and the birthplace were right. Someone who registered there a while back, looking for his mother."

Cory says, "I'll have this number changed. I knew you were up to some mischief"—but her anger is thin, she can't quite make the effort.

"Changing this number is going to cause you a lot of problems."

"Nothing compared to the trouble this craziness of yours would cause me, if I . . ."

She trails off. Apple takes her arm.

"Your guests are waiting," she says quietly.

They compose themselves and go to the dining room, where Cory delivers a short breakfast oration to the assembled guests on the circular nature of giving.

◒⬩◒⬩◒⬩

Apple is moaning, in the darkness.

Cory pats her shoulder.

"I can't breathe," Apple whispers. "I have to go out."

Running Deer is chanting. In the darkness, the celebrants sit silent, invisible, as the fire-baked stones in the center of the circle radiate their intense heat.

"You can't go out," Cory says.

"But I can't breathe!"

"You can't breathe because you're frightened. Lie down on the ground and stretch out with your face at the edge of the tent."

Moaning softly, Apple obeys.

Now Running Deer is offering a fingerful of sage to the hot stones; a dense, sharp smell rises.

The Fire Chief throws a dipper of cold water onto the stones, and Cory raises her hand to shield her face from the scalding steam.

In the darkness, the six people sitting around the edges of the tent are silent; no one except Apple is gasping and moaning. But the others are old hands at this, Cory knows; they understand that there will be five cycles of chanting and prayer, with a moment of fresh air between each cycle when the tent flap is raised. They know that it will all end when they stagger out into the frosty light.

Cory explained this to Apple on the drive up, but she understands, now, that Apple expects the torment to go on forever, like the Hell they imagined as little girls, sitting cross-legged on their twin beds, feeling the pricks of imagined sins.

So much of courage depends on believing whatever it is will end, Cory thinks, whatever hell or torment; believing that there will be a moment when fresh cool air will be let into the simmering unbearable darkness.

Now the pipe is being passed.

Someone is asking prayers for a nephew in jail; a woman's clear voice is calling for a special blessing for her newborn son; a man sobs out something about repentance and changing his ways—the sweat lodge is said to loosen the hold of all kinds of addictions.

Then it is Cory's turn.

She takes the warm clay pipe in her hand and puts the stem in her mouth, inhaling the choking combination of herbs she watched Running Deer tamp into the bowl.

Coughing, spluttering—she is not perfect at this yet and knows she may never be—Cory finally finds enough voice to ask a blessing on her sister "who has endured," she says, realizing she is quoting from the Bible she never thought she knew, "many things."

Next to her, lying in the dirt, Apple groans.

"Take the pipe," Cory insists, pulling her up by the elbow. Apple is streaming with sweat and her elbow nearly slips from her sister's grasp. Finally she is upright, a pungent presence in the darkness. Cory props her up with one arm and pushes the pipe stem into her mouth.

Apple draws on the pipe and goes into a paroxysm of coughing.

"Ask for a blessing," Cory tells her sternly as soon as Apple is quiet.

"For . . . my nephew . . ." Her voice is weak yet determined, each syllable followed by a gasping breath.

"Wado," Running Deer says from the other side of the darkness.

Cory takes the pipe from her sister's trembling fingers and passes it along. It is grasped firmly by the man on her left, who begins a rambling recitation of chronic disasters.

Then the pipe has gone full circle, and Running Deer begins his closing chant.

Apple is on her stomach, stretched out, her mouth pressed to the edge of the tent when the Fire Chief finally raises the flap.

The people sitting or lying around the edges of the tent begin to stir. Fiercely flushed or smoky pale, their clothes clinging, soaked, to their bodies, they crawl out into the light.

Apple is still lying on the dirt.

Cory shakes her shoulder. "It's over, Little Sister."

Running Deer looks back as he is about to crawl out through the opening.

"She's fine," Cory says.

She shakes Apple's shoulder again, feeling bone through the drenched cloth. "Get out in the air. I'll help you."

Finally she begins to lift and drag her sister.

At the entrance, she pushes Apple out and sees her sister stagger to her feet with Running Deer's help. She stands swaying, staring.

"It'll be easier the next time," Cory says, helping her toward the house.

"Are you kidding, the next time—"

"We did what we had to do, to end it."

Apple doesn't answer.

After she has washed and changed into the dry clothes Cory brought (and how Apple stared, alarmed, when Cory told her they would be needed), after Cory has brushed her hair and pinned a bow above Apple's ear, a blue plastic bow, loaned by Val, Apple turns to her sister.

"It is ended," she says.

⟜ *21*

*P*rimrose is kneeling in front of her altar, Mabel's crystal pendant pressed between her palms. She sways a little, keens, her eyes clenched shut, and Apple wonders if under her lids her eyeballs are rolling back in rapture.

Cory reaches over and touches Apple's shoulder, then nods toward the streams of light that illumine the pane of stained-glass hanging in the window. The pane shows a hooded figure, neither male nor female, crossing a flower-strewn field, staff in hand.

Apple looks at her sister.

"The pilgrim," Cory whispers.

Still Apple doesn't grasp the significance, although she is glad to see, beyond the hooded figure, the crest of the sared mountain.

"Let her go," Primrose moans. "Oh, let her go, let her go."

"I have," Cory says in her ordinary voice. "I've given her up."

"Let her go, all the way. Let her rest. Her time here is over," Primrose moans, swaying on her knees.

Apple asks, "Doesn't she want us to do anything?"

"She's satisfied to lie up there on the hill," Primrose says, quickly.

"But I want to get her back with Tony," Cory says. "That's what she said she wanted, in her journal"—and Apple remembers the passage her sister showed her that morning, still visible through a dark-brown water stain: *"Maybe in the end I will be united with him, in spite of everything."*

"She's satisfied," Primrose repeats. "All that is over."

"But I've already started making the arrangements."

"Let them both rest," Primrose says. "They have done their time on earth."

"Both?" Cory asks. "Tony, and Mabel?"

Primrose shakes her head.

"Roy, and Mabel?" Cory asks, wondering how those two disparate souls could ever inhabit the same eternity.

"Roy is tired. Mabel is tired. Let them both go," Primrose intones, and Apple watches the seer's thumbs move over the facets of the big crystal.

"And my Tony?" Cory asks softly.

"You have something of his?" Without opening her eyes, the seer stretches one hand out.

Cory feels in her blue-jean pocket and digs out a wad of tissue paper, which she hands to Primrose. Carefully laying aside the crystal—its usefulness is over, Apple guesses, it can go back to being another of her sister's many decorations—the seer takes the small package and opens it. A dark strand of hair is folded inside.

Primrose places the strand on her alter, in front of the plaster Virgin, the red candle, the seashell collection, the mound of colored stones. "Leave him here," she tells Cory. "He's done all he can."

"All right," Cory says, a little grumpily, her sister thinks. "But what about all the rest of it—the Grandfather trees? When is that going to be resolved?"

"That's just politics," Primrose says, as though no further answer is required. "Place your precious energy elsewhere."

"Just . . . forget about it?"

"Help Roy's family."

"I'm trying to."

"I mean, help them by leaving them alone."

Cory sighs. "All right."

"The wheel has come full circle," Primrose says, getting up from her knees. She snuffs out the candle. Then, turning, she glances at Apple, as though, Apple thinks, she is still surprised to see her there. "And you—go home!"

"I have something still to do here," Apple mutters, offended.

"Let that alone," Primrose says harshly.

"What are you up to now, Little Sister?" Cory asks Apple, smiling. "Not meddling in my life, by any chance?"

"Oh Cory!" Apple says, holding out her left hand, and as she does so, the age spots on the back of her wrist seem to spring to life. "You can't go on this way, never knowing!"

"Never knowing what?" Cory asks, her smile fixed.

Primrose is re-arranging the stones on her alter.

"What happened to your son."

"So you're stirring that pot again," Cory says grimly.

"This is not the place," Primrose says, balancing a last stone, a delicate pink one, on top of the pile.

The sisters do not hear her.

"You can't do this to me," Cory says.

"You mean to live the rest of your life without ever knowing?"

"Yes." Then, summoning herself, she goes on across the current of her irritation, her obvious belief, Apple thinks, that none of this is her sister's business, "I'm not saying it's easy. There're some cold mornings I'd like nothing better than an image of him, to think about, or a letter, a phone call. There are some days when my life here doesn't seem worth living, when it's all an escape, a fraud."

She holds up her hand to stop Apple from interrupting. "But I honor the decision I made all those years ago to live a hard life if a son was going to be the only possible comfort. I thought then it was unfair, and I still think it is—to use another person's life as a justification. a comfort. I know it's different for you!" she tells Apple, who is about to say something. "I'm not saying the way you live your life is wrong—"

"No?" Primrose asks.

In the silence, Apple sees dust motes riding the sunlight that is streaming through the window.

"No," Cory says.

How, Apple thinks, can one word in a certain setting mean so much, settling old scores, putting the world to rights?

And she knows there will be many days, and especially nights, when she will not believe that anything was settled in Primrose's living room, when she will want to go back to the beginning, start the old unresolvable arguments again:

I am different, and you will never be able to love me or accept me because I am different. You scorn my choices because they are so different from yours. Something divides us that is as permanent as our parents' deaths, as solid as their lives.

"Go in peace," Primrose says, holding out her hands in blessing.

Cory drops a check into the blue vase by the door.

Passing through the closet, they part the shifting shapes of Primrose's clothes and smell her obscure, sharp perfume.

Then they are back in the Jeep, speeding along the dirt road to Mabel's house. Cory's front wheel mounts the curb, at the turn, and Apple holds on for dear life. One thing that will never change is the way Cory drives.

"What are you going to do with Mabel's diary?" she asks as Cory slams the Jeep to a halt by the parking lot fence. Manuel has made an attempt to clear away the snow, and the sisters step out onto gravel.

"I haven't decided yet." Cory closes her door and, Apple notices, does not lock it.

"What about giving it to the university so it can be with the rest of her papers?"

"She didn't want it read, that's why she hid it," Cory says. "I wouldn't think of going against her wishes."

Now Apple is hurrying behind her sister, toward the steps. They pass a rental car, resplendent among the mud-spattered pickups and old sedans. "You've gone against her wishes time and time again."

"But not this time." Cory stops at the top of the steps and looks down at her sister. "Maybe I'll have the diary reburied with her—"

"I thought you'd given that up! Primrose told you to leave her in peace."

Cory says brusquely, "I want to give it one more try. I owe Mabel that. She's given me my life. And—" she turns to confront Apple—"don't tell me she wouldn't want to be buried with Tony, because she says in her diary she would."

"She said maybe they'd be reunited," Apple argues.

Cory hurries across the foot bridge.

Following her, Apple notices that the fierce mid-day sun is melting the ice on the acequia; she hears the tinkling sound of water, released under overhanging ledges of ice and snow. It can't be that long, she thinks, until spring, and remembers her garden and wonders if the first crocus are poking through the dense frozen mud.

Consuela is waiting for them just inside the front door. As they stamp the snow off their boots, she is signaling to Cory. "Somebody—"

"Who?" Cory asks, and then Apple sees Billy standing in the doorway to the office.

Consuela retreats.

For a moment, Apple and Cory stand side by side, staring, as

Billy will say later, like two deer caught in headlights.

Then Cory steps forward, holding out her hand.

In the pueblo graveyard, Cory stands, arms crossed, looking at the old wooden crosses stacked haphazardly against the fence.

"How long before they pull them up?" she asks Tony's wife, who is standing at her elbow.

"Maybe twenty years."

Cory turns to look at the woman, who returns her stare evenly. Pabla's face is strained and lined; she looks older than she is, and Cory wonders how she will make it through the next pregnancy. Already, Pabla's ankles are swelling—Cory has seen them, under the edge of her skirt—and she looks exhausted.

What is it, Cory wonders, that keeps women reproducing, time and time again until they wear out and collapse?

She can no longer remember what she felt—if she felt anything at all—that hot summer afternoon twenty-five years ago when she laughed and played like an idiot child with a man whose face she hasn't remembered in more than a decade.

But I was a fool, she thinks, studying the wreak of the old church, slipping sideways into the graveyard hill, and Pabla is a grown woman, and an intelligent one; and Cory remembers the last time she saw Tony, lying on her bed at Mabel's, covered with the big striped blanket.

A woman would do anything for Tony, she thinks, shocking herself. It's no longer a question, with him, of making a rational choice— and realizes she has reached a place in her life where rational choices seem weak and poor, hardly more than excuses for selfishness.

For no good reason I am here with his wife, she thinks, at the old church outsiders are not allowed to visit. Since it was blown up in the seventeenth century by soldiers gunning for Indians during the Pueblo Rebellion, the church has remained unrepaired, off limits, a monument to a desperate success, to the short years of freedom.

"Can we look at the crosses?" she asks Pabla.

"Don't go over the fence. Look from this side."

They walk over to the fence and Cory leans across, trying to decipher the faded writing on the old crosses. But it is impossible; time and weather have done their work.

"Don't the families care?" she asks, and remembers the elaborate Day-of-the-Dead ceremonies in the valley, the sugar skulls, the plastic flowers for all the family graves.

"Have to make room," Pabla says simply, and Cory wonders if the woman has already imagined the day her remains and the remains of everyone she birthed and loved will disappear, unmarked, in the old graveyard, beneath newer graves. Her cross, too, stacked against the ruined church, will be indecipherable, and Tony's cross, and their children's children's.

"But Mabel's Tony was famous. Surely somebody remembers where they buried him."

"Not famous here," Pabla says, and Cory knows she is talking, now, about her husband, measuring the short length of the scandal that caused him to be ousted from the Council.

That won't last either, Cory thinks.

And she remembers the Koshares, those rude clowns, sporting their white-and-black stripes, laughing and gesturing obscenely from the roof of the pueblo during the winter dances.

Everything passes. Everything is meant to pass.

She follows Pabla back to the center of the pueblo. It is an ordinary day; most of the little adobe houses, set one on another, that amaze and delight the tourists, are empty now; there's no smoke from the chimneys, and the only open door leads into the silversmith's shop.

A couple of cars roost forlornly near the drying racks.

"Not too many visitors, these days," Cory says.

"We're thinking about closing the pueblo, next summer."

"Was it that bad?"

"They don't know how to act," Pabla says circumspectly, and Cory imagines the various offenses her fellow outsiders committed, and the circumspect, severe silence that met them.

"Please don't close it," she says, surprising herself.

Pabla looks at her. "Not good for us, all those people. Some of them went wading in the stream."

"They don't understand the significance. You could explain to them—post a sign: Drinking Water."

Pabla smiles. Cory realizes that she is more beautiful when she wears her usual somber, non-committal expression. "Some people don't know how to learn."

"Yes," Cory sighs.

"So there's no chance?" she asks Pabla as they approach the Jeep, parked in the middle of the pueblo's plaza.

The woman shakes her head, and Cory knows she understands that several questions have been asked, and answered.

She crawls into the Jeep. Consuela's shopping list is on the seat and as she backs out of the plaza, Cory is glad she has that to attend to, as well as a visit to the bank; her mortgage payment is overdue, again, she will have to plead with Mr. Gonzalez for a little more time.

The bank wouldn't want to take Mabel's away from me, she thinks as she turns onto the road out of the reservation. Any other owner would make it into condos with Jacuzzis like all the other places in town.

A herd of horses is grazing near the fence, and away across the brown fields, the sacred mountain rises in blue light.

But no one can ever take away what I have found here, Cory thinks, because it belongs to no one.

CORY'S RULES FOR THOSE SEEKING WISDOM

1.You will know you are on the right road when all temporary comforts and satisfactions disappear.

2. Re-interpret your symptoms: Sleeplessness is often the soul's way of trying to get your attention. Use those dark hours as an opportunity for meditation, prayer, or doing a little laundry.

3. Losing your appetite (libido) is another indication of the soul's unease. Instead of stuffing food to try to regain your sense of normalcy, fast for a few days (of course drink plenty of water.) Fasting is one sure way to bring on visions, and visions are likely to show you where things are going wrong.

As to libido, the body has its own wisdom.

4. There is no special or sacred place. Each house, mountain, field, garden, city street is equally blessed. The restless search for sacred space is confusing for the soul, which knows no geographical distinctions. As long as you have a window or even a pane of glass through which the winter sun can shine. . . .

5. Heal your relations, then let them go. Love your lovers, and release them. Instead of bringing more children into the world, love the world that has no space for them.

Do this not in the spirit of sacrifice. Sacrifice embitters and destroys.

Do this to celebrate your time on earth.

6. Breakfast: seven to eight A.M.: scrambled eggs, bacon, burritos, Conchita's famous lead pancakes.

7. Enjoy your stay at Mabel's.

Sallie Bingham's first novel was published shortly after she graduated from Radcliffe, followed by five more novels and three collections of short stories celebrating the lives of women. This latest, *Cory's Feast*, continues to spotlight adventurous women whose challenges and choices illustrate the social changes of the twenty-first century. Her short stories and poetry have been widely published and her plays have been produced both off-Broadway and around the country. She has received fellowships from Yaddo, the MacDowell Colony and the Virginia Center, and is the founder of The Kentucky Foundation for women.

Printed in the United States
89712LV00003B/142-144/A